***What about the ship?* Jaza thought at Y'lira Modan.**
***What about* Titan?**

She hesitated. The black ocean seemed to swell and roll around him. For an illusion created in the pocket of his mind, it certainly felt as if he could drown here.

Modan? he thought at her again. *What about* Titan*?*

"You know," she said, still not wanting to face it herself. "You saw."

The memory accosted him then; he'd seen what had looked like an impossibly vast wall of fire sweeping over the ship, consuming it utterly. He remembered Troi screaming.

"Something's happened! I can't feel them! I can't feel any of them!"

But he still needed to hear Modan say it—needed to anchor his recollections to reality—for her and for him.

What happened to Titan, *Modan?* he thought again, relentless. *What happened to* Titan*?*

STAR TREK
TITAN™

SWORD OF DAMOCLES

GEOFFREY THORNE

Based upon STAR TREK® and
STAR TREK: THE NEXT GENERATION®
created by Gene Roddenberry

POCKET BOOKS
New York London Toronto Sydney Orisha

Pocket Books
A Division of Simon & Schuster, Inc.
1230 Avenue of the Americas
New York, NY 10020

This book is published by Pocket Books, a division of Simon & Schuster, Inc., under exclusive license from CBS Studios Inc.

First Pocket Books paperback edition December 2007

POCKET and colophon are registered trademarks of Simon & Schuster, Inc.

For information about special discounts for bulk purchases, please contact Simon & Schuster Special Sales at 1-800-456-6798 or business@simonandschuster.com.

Cover design by John Vairo Jr.; illustration by Cliff Nielsen; 3D rendering of ship by Ellery Connell

Manufactured in the United States of America

10 9 8 7 6 5 4 3 2 1

ISBN-13: 978-1-4165-2694-0
ISBN-10: 1-4165-2694-3

For Susan, who holds my hand
For Donal, who gave good counsel
For Chris and Barbette, who opened the door

Acknowledgments

This novel could not have been written without the stellar preceding works of Michael A. Martin, Andy Mangels, and Christopher Bennett or the assistance, both literary and moral, of Dayton Ward and Keith R.A. DeCandido.

It would never have come to fruition without the patience and steady hand of editor Marco Palmieri, who must surely need a massive hair transplant to replace the mane he pulled out over my eccentricities.

A special, special thanks to Sean Tourangeau for his beautiful and truly inspiring design for the starship *Titan.* I hope I manage to put a smile on his face as wide as the one he put on mine.

And of course, none of it would have been possible without Mr. Roddenberry and the rest of the crew giving us all such a wonderful and easy birth.

The Great Bird lives.
IDIC.

Historian's Note

This tale is set approximately three months after the events described in *Orion's Hounds*.

Part One

We speak it here, 'neath starlight's sheen,
One truth that all who live must learn.
From first to last and all between
Time is the fire in which we burn.

—El-Aurian proverb

Epilogue

The blaze consumed everything it touched, scorching its way through the air and the foliage like wraithwinds fabled in the prophecies. It slithered between the boulders, devoured the vegetation in monstrous serpentine undulations that left only tracks of dark ash in their wake. What it touched it consumed utterly and it touched everything—everything beyond his haven of stones.

There was thunder out there too, though the sky was essentially clear. Thunder, or something very like. And there were other noises, low and distant rumblings, that made him think of amphitheaters full of chattering crowds.

He wasn't sure the sky should be that particular shade of copper, but then he wasn't really sure of anything just now. Not the lush and sultry vegetation growing in leafy explosions of amethyst beyond the fire, spiraling in great spires toward the amber sky; not the smell of cinnamon that seemed to permeate the air; not the strangely diffuse light from the hot white orb of the local star or the oddly granular texture of the soil beneath him. Nothing was right. Nothing was certain, nothing but the fire.

Volatile gases or some other fuel kept these flames fed, kept them dancing and licking around the trunks and stones.

Watching the display, feeling the feverish heat and tremors, even tasting his own blood on the edges of his tongue, he found himself unable to muster the proper concern. It was as if all that impending doom was bearing down on someone else, someone in a child's night tale, and he was safely elsewhere, free to focus only on the firestorm's hypnotic motions and kaleidoscopic beauty.

His mind sought the memory of the moment of his arrival and was happy to find it missing. Like his identity, the event that had left him here, slowly roasting in the encroaching heat, was nowhere to be seen.

Concussion?

Somehow he managed to assemble enough facts to form a hypothesis; there had been an explosion, one to which he'd been far too close, and which had taken its toll on his memories. He remembered hurtling through the air and the sudden crunching stop.

He had been somewhere else just before that, somewhere small and cool and filled with other people. He was mostly sure of that.

Was it a room? A vehicle of some kind? Who were the people? Where were they?

Half-formed images—*blue or red or gold on black*—snippets of conversation—*I don't believe I've ever seen anything like it, Commander*—something about a woman made of gold—*or maybe that was just the color of her hair?*—even music—*strange trilling melodies, a chorus of flutes*—sparked in his mind and faded again before he could force them to cohere.

Yes, definitely a concussion. You didn't have to be a doctor to know that.

The confusion and the gaps in his awareness were somehow more troubling than the physical pain but not by much. He shifted, hoping to ease at least some of his discomfort, but only succeeded in making it worse.

Something significant had broken inside him, he could feel it, something that throbbed horribly when he didn't move and stabbed at him when he did. A broken rib certainly, perhaps two or three.

Oh, came the wry thought as his lips curled into a grin. *Oh, that's not good.*

He still lay where he'd fallen. Luck had wedged him behind a ring of the oddly conical rocks, his back against something rough and unyielding. He was still close enough to the blaze to see his death coming but far enough away to pretend that the meeting would not happen soon.

Unsettling images bubbled uselessly up again and again from somewhere at the bottom of his mind. He saw the stern visage of an older man whose name did not arrive with him. The face was familiar—gray eyes, deep set, skin like a well-used cloth sack, wrinkles that became chasms that might have been the result of too much smiling or too much time in the desert sun. It was a familiar face, yes, but also still unknown. The stern man was some kind of teacher, he knew that much, someone to trust. The rest was mud.

He shifted, instinctively trying again for a more comfortable position, and instantly regretted it.

There was pain in the lower parts of him as well, he realized, though it was nothing like what was going on in his chest. *Shattered knee? Broken hip?* Though great, the pain was too general for him to isolate to a particular region just yet. He was still too far outside himself, too adrift in his own choppy memory to dredge up any true interest in his damaged state.

Pretty, he thought, enraptured by the sight of the conflagration.

His attention fell away from watching the mercurial plasma dragons writhing and dancing all around in favor of listening to the strange and familiar noises now making soft counterpoint to the din of the blaze.

"What are you doing there, you lazy *batos*?" said a voice he instantly recognized as his mother's. Which was odd because he was sure he remembered her as being quite dead for quite some time.

Or was she? Had she already succumbed to Orkett's disease, bleeding and spasming herself into oblivion, or was that painful trial yet to come? He couldn't sort it and, for the moment, didn't have the energy to try.

"I'm speaking to you, Jem," she said again, though now he wasn't sure if it was really her voice or just the sound of sap, superheated by the fire, popping in the flora around him.

"Rouse yourself, boy," said another voice, male this time and sounding as if the throat from which the words emerged had been scoured with broken glass. "Move now or die."

He knew this voice as well and hated it. Guldejit? Glinforkis? Troknoor? The names flitted like sand flies on the edge of his thoughts, keeping just as completely out of reach as his own name had done. Paradoxically, his hatred for their owners remained, burning nearly as hot as the flames, which, he suspected, had managed somehow to grow closer.

"Get up," said his mother's voice, more insistent this time. "They'll trample us."

A part of his mind told him that this was delirium, that these people and their words were just phantoms, tricks played by his concussed brain. The other part, the larger part for now, was happy to take them at face value. Spectral as they were, they were company. He hated to be alone.

The true believer is never alone. It was a phrase from the prophecies, one he'd not understood until—

Suddenly the circle of stones gave way to another image, another place and time. He was back in the camps, back in the days when his parents hustled him from dwelling to dwelling, from settlement to settlement, apparently without reason but truly to avoid the guns and lashes of the bad people.

Trample him? Yes, they would. There were scores of others now, beside him and his mother, hundreds. They were *borhyas*, ghostly presentments of people he had once known, perhaps still knew, running, fleeing before the onslaught of something massive and deadly.

The bad people. The outsiders.

Their pursuit had transformed friends and relatives, teachers and vedeks and schoolyard nemeses into a herd of frightened cattle. If he lost his footing, if he stopped moving for even a moment, their flight would kill him as surely as the bad people forcing the stampede.

His mother's ghost held out one transparent hand, beckoning. For a moment he looked at her and marveled at the sight of her pale gray eyes in her dark oval face, her thick braids whipping back and forth as she scanned the area around them, her lips that should have been smiling but were pulled now into a grimace. How young she seemed. How long had it been since he'd seen her that way?

"Now," she hissed, terrified, angry. "We have to move right now."

Groaning from the spikes in his chest, in his legs, in his mind, he forced himself up and followed her forward. Behind them the bad people made their presence felt. He couldn't make them out, what with running the other way, but his memory coughed up impressions. Sharp, craggy features, bodies covered in gray metallic uniforms. Each face frozen in a perpetual sneer of disgust for him and those like him.

"Move, Bajoran scum. Move."

Beams of ethereal light whipped out from the guns they held, striking some of the fleeing ghosts, obliterating them, glancing off others but forcing them down to be trampled under the heels of their fellows.

Away, he thought. We have to get away.

As he labored his way upward, over hard and unyielding ground, he felt tongues of heat lapping greedily at his heels, snapping him back to the here and now, if only for a moment. He looked back in time to see the roiling plasma overrun what, seconds before, he had thought a safe haven.

Core disruption? he thought, staring at it disapprovingly. *Deuterium imbalance?* His mind suddenly flooded with familiar concepts and equations. Gerren Kin's first Law of Motion. Obar's rules of gravimetrics. The chemical composition of Argelian mead. The third Song of the Prophets.

He was a little unnerved by the rush until he realized it was just his memory returning. But there was still the disorientation, the sense of being both here and there at once. And there was that strange chorus of noises—like waves breaking on an endless sea of pebbles—echoing in from places close but unseen. He knew that noise—felt he should know it, anyway—and knew, moreover, that it filled him with a sort of dread. There was death in that sound, but it was so hard for him to focus enough to remember why.

What was it forcing his ungainly scramble up the side of this cliff? A fire? No. *No, it's the bad people chasing us now. The explosion hasn't happened yet. I haven't even joined the resistance yet. Haven't split with Father. Right now I'm just a boy.*

Some part of his mind, the adult, the scientist, knew that this trip through his past was a delusion brought on by injuries that almost certainly included a concussion, but it was a small part not yet capable of reasserting dominance. The mass of him accepted what he saw, contradictions and all.

So, now forced to actually climb the suddenly vertical promontory, he scrambled, hand over excruciating hand, up and away from the ghosts of old oppression. His face drawn into a perpetual grimace, he moved toward the outstretched hand of the mother he hadn't seen in a decade and who hadn't been this young in three.

"Hurry," her phantom said. Fearful. Earnest. Desperate. Things she had never been in life. "Hurry or they'll—"

And then she was gone. Not blasted or trampled or pulled away by some as yet unseen attacker, just vanished.

Because she was never here, he thought in another flash of clarity. Just my mind playing tricks.

Increased exertion meant increased blood flow. Increased blood flow to his brain meant lucidity, meant he was coming back to himself. Because this isn't Bajor and I'm not running from the Cardassians. That was long ago, before we won our independence, before the Militia, before Starfleet, before . . .

Before *Titan.*

It was suddenly just there, back in its normal mental cubby, filled with friends and colleagues and—

The shuttle. He'd been piloting one of the heavy-duty shuttles, investigating—something—and something had gone wrong. Had they been attacked?

He and his team were crashing down on—well, that was still fuzzy—whatever this place was—and they had to get out fast. The flashes of black and gold and blue and red had been the uniforms, like his own, of those others in the shuttle.

There was a woman, at least one, with a mane of red-brown hair and eyes that were wide and dark and deep. Her face was there, but the others were still a blur. He remembered her saying something before the transporter effect took him away.

"Something's happened," he remembered her nearly

screaming. *"I can't feel them! I can't feel any of them!"*

His mind was clearer now, almost his own again. The memory still wasn't quite right, but the processes, his ability to make sense of things, was back.

It had been almost a minute since he'd drifted off again into that place that wasn't quite sleep. Back now, still perched on the edge of stone, he surveyed the landscape below.

It was an alien world all right, complete with off-color sky, massive indigo crystal formations and boulders that the elements had carved into weird conical shapes, foliage that was wild and varied, a mosaic of purples and crimsons and whites.

And, of course, there was the fire. The fires.

All around him there were pockets of it, wide sections of the wider expanse that had been somehow set ablaze. Pretty recently, by the look of them.

Were these the result of the plasma storm? The uniform spread and pattern of the burnings made that unlikely. And what about the storm? He had thought it the product of a core breach or some sort of fuel mixture incongruity but now, with his mind clearer, he knew that couldn't be so. Such an accident would have wiped the local landscape clear, made it as smooth as polished glass for multiple kilometers in every direction.

No, whatever had caused the storm and these fires was local. Specific.

Familiar?

Yes. There was a pattern there that sparked again the remembrance of his old life on Bajor. He found it odd that his recollections of those increasingly distant moments would return with such clarity when his more recent memories were so elusive. He had seen these shapes, these patterns before.

Blast craters, he realized. *That's what they are. Somebody's been lobbing incendiaries around.*

He allowed himself a bleak flicker of hope that he'd only stumbled onto a munitions testing range of some sort and not into an ongoing local war. The former might mean the shelling had stopped for the day. The latter meant all bets were off.

It was then that he understood the odd background noises he'd been hearing to be those of a battle. Small arms fire. The shouts of combat factions. The occasional scream.

He needed higher ground to get a sense of where he was. He needed to see what was where, if the battle was coming his way and, most important, if there were any other stragglers from the shuttle crash.

The pain of the climb brought the *borhyas* back. Even as he hauled his protesting body up onto the summit of this giant stone, he returned again to that awful day when the Cardassians had come.

"It's all right, Jem," said his mother as he knelt, gasping from his exertions, at the lip of the precipice. "This will pass. Only the Prophets are forever."

She was talking about the destruction of their homes, of their lives, as the Cardassian boots and ignition-bombs smashed them to bits. He hadn't believed her platitudes then. How could he, with all that death and carnage smoldering below? His friends were scattered or dead. Their homes, their farms, the school, the shrine, all were in charred ruins. Where were her precious Prophets in all that?

He'd lost his faith in that moment, looking at the wreck of the Harka valley and the black-suited Cardassian troops marching implacably through the flaming craters. All because someone had hinted that maybe members of a resistance cell had holed up there.

His belief had dissolved as instantly and completely as the froth on a flagon of Bolian lager and not returned again until—until—

He shook his head, forced himself to focus on the here and now. This wasn't Bajor. This wasn't that time or that place. These fires were something else, something specific to this new location. The beings behind them—not Cardassians but people new and unknown—were still close enough to cause him more trouble than he, in his condition, could handle.

Indeed, the final few meters of the climb had nearly finished him. If he hadn't been bleeding internally before, he certainly was now.

He looked up at the orange-gold sky, his eyes tracking smoke trails until they touched the horizon. He gazed down at the wide expanse of plants and stone below. He noted the pattern of the craters and their fires, noted the expansion of the plasma storm, tried and failed to see its far-off center. He caught motions, quick, violent, and furtive, rustling through the overgrowth. He heard the distant report of weapons fire. Where were his friends in all that? Presuming it had survived the crash, where was the shuttle, their only means of escape?

Where was *Titan*?

A strange chittering noise sounded in the nearby brush, drawing his eyes away from the fires. It suddenly occurred to him that any natives he met in this locale might not be in the mood for a peaceful first contact. It also crossed his mind that a weapon of some sort might be a good thing to have in hand. Just as he was deciding between the broken arm of one of the small purple saplings and a largish hunk of rock, the source of the noise emerged.

It was a hulking thing, about two and a half meters tall, covered in some sort of chitonous exoskeleton, possibly its own body rather than artificial armor. There were four oval protrusions on its head—eyes, most likely. Above them, two slender antennae stretching up and back, wavering slightly in the breeze. There was no visible mouth, and he was somehow glad of that.

Formica mactabilis, he thought. It's a giant bug.

It was also, most definitely, a soldier. You could tell that from the bloody serrated blade it gripped in its lower right hand. It had four in total, the remaining three holding a second machete, something that looked disturbingly like a gun, and another something that might be a grenade.

The creature sported intricate patterns, like tattoos, all over its upper left arm, perhaps denoting rank of some kind.

This entire analysis passed through his mind in the five seconds it took the creature to notice him and raise the ugly little firearm toward him.

"No!" cried a familiar voice from out of nowhere. "Look out!"

The instant the soldier bug fired at him—not a beam

weapon, thank the Prophets—a second creature, not insectoid, leaped out of the brush and smashed into the first. This one was somewhat smaller, and instead of an exoskeleton its body was covered in a number of protective armor plates. Its entire body was like burnished gold instead of the muted green and black favored by its enemy.

What it lacked in size it more than made up for in ferocity. The unexpectedness and sheer brutality of its attack was enough to nearly overwhelm its foe.

The two creatures smashed hard into the gravelly dirt, the gun now spraying its projectiles wildly. Only one of the little pellets managed to graze his right shoulder before the gun was smashed useless. The grenade was knocked free immediately after the pistol, leaving only the two serrated machetes for his golden savior to avoid.

His vision went fuzzy as his injuries, at last, took their rightful toll. Things inside him ripped and tore and, through the haze of pain, all he could make out of the scene before him was a storm of armored arms and legs grappling and pounding at each other.

He groaned, coughing blood as he fell to his knees and then face-first onto the ground as one of the creatures—he had no idea which—beat the head of the other into the rocks a first, second, and final time.

"I can't be dying," he said—or thought he said—as the victorious alien stood, shook itself, and oriented on him again. "This isn't the way I—" The rest was lost in a fit of bloody coughs. His voice wasn't his own anymore anyway. It was rough, phlegmy, as if he'd been beating it against the same stone against which the alien's head had struck.

As a black velvet sheet fell slowly over the world, he became aware of the golden interloper, the victor, coming his way.

With each step forward its body seemed to melt and shift. The thickly muscled arms lost size and definition, becoming smaller and more delicate with each step. The body absorbed its hard armored plating and became a thing of long muscular curves. The long, vicious-looking spines that ran from the bridge of its nose across its head and down its back all shrank and retracted, either being absorbed into the body completely or else softening and drooping until they aped a mass of thick ropey braids. A head of hair? A mouth appeared and a nose and suddenly there was a woman, a golden woman, kneeling down beside him.

Was this reality or just a hallucination created from the cascade of endorphins unleashed by a brain hoping to ease his slide into the dark?

"You're not dying on me, Jaza," said the woman. "I'm counting on you to save us."

Then she was cradling him and he was looking up into her turquoise marble eyes, eyes that seemed always to be smiling. He knew her. He remembered her face and he remembered her name.

"Y'lira?" he rasped, scarcely knowing if all this was just one final delusion before his *pagh* was set free.

"Hush," she said softly, bending closer for what could have been a kiss but wasn't. The tendrils on her head, not hair as he'd supposed, came alive around them, writhing and undulating like serpents. "I have much to do, and there's no time."

As the first of the serpents touched his forehead, the world went mercifully black.

He floated in darkness, drifting in an infinite shadow that rolled over and around him like an ocean of ink. He was aware—of himself, of his name, of his life, of everything that he'd thought lost not long before. He was aware of his body, still distant, still not quite there, being repaired. He was also aware of her.

Y'lira, he thought, somehow knowing speech was both beyond him right now and unnecessary.

"Modan," said her voice from out of the black, chiding. "Y'lira is my crèche designation."

He did know that and more. He knew she was his colleague, his fellow officer. He knew she was from a planet called Selene. He knew she liked to flirt. He knew she had been with him on the ill-fated shuttle. He knew she was repairing him somehow, bringing him back from the Prophets' embrace.

What happened? he thought furiously as he felt his strength returning, his bones and tissue knitting together. *The shuttle? The others?*

"You know what," said her voice. "We crashed. And the others—I—I don't know." It was a lie. She did know. He felt it as much as he felt her need not to admit it.

Something had happened to them, something awful.

Their faces and names came back to him then, and he wished that they hadn't. He wouldn't have felt the loss so acutely had they still been nothing but blurs.

Troi, he thought. *Troi and all the rest.*

"Sshh," she said, a little too forcefully. He knew somehow that she was busy rejoining his shattered ribs, but he felt there was something pushing her emotions too. Something large and dreadful that she didn't want to see just now. Or maybe didn't want him to see.

All the rest.

What about the ship? he thought at her, fearing the answer, knowing it even as his mind formed the question. *What happened to* Titan*?*

She hesitated before responding. The black ocean seemed to swell and roll around him. For an illusion created in the pocket of his mind, it certainly felt as if he could drown here.

Modan? he thought at her again. *What happened to* Titan*?*

"You know," she said, still not wanting to face it herself. "You saw."

The memory accosted him then; he'd seen what had looked like an impossibly vast wall of fire sweeping over the ship, consuming it utterly. He remembered Troi screaming.

"Something's happened! I can't feel them! I can't feel any of them!"

But he still needed to hear Modan say it—needed to anchor his recollections to reality—for her and for him. If they were going to keep this new and obviously hostile place from killing them, they had to face every fact together.

What happened to Titan, *Modan?* he thought again, relentless. *What happened to* Titan*?*

Chapter One

Occultus Ora, Stardate 58358.1

The *Starship Titan* rolled slowly in the dark, dancing between the invisible jetsam, the ethereal flotsam, like some graceful leviathan swimming a terrestrial sea. All around it the other occupants of this region, the inspiration for the ship's lingering ballet, also pitched and spun in apparent counterpoint to the vessel's motion.

Titan's astronomers had dubbed the region Occultus Ora for some reason known only to them. The physicists called the things residing here *exotic matter plasmids* but, lately, those who'd been tasked with ferreting out their secrets had taken to referring to the strange objects simply as *darklings*.

The image came from a myth Dr. Celenthe had heard on its homeworld of Syrath, something about the Catalysts of creation hiding in the dark.

The name fit the new objects well. They were invisible

to every naked eye, irrespective of species, untouchable by all but the most specifically calibrated sensors, intangible by nearly every measure, yet here they were, in the lee of the Gum Nebula, performing their tandem pirouette, bending gravity into knots in complete defiance of their supposed nonexistence.

It was sheer luck that *Titan* had happened upon them at all even with the fantastic array of devices it sported to facilitate its explorations.

A weird but consistent spike in one of the lower EM bands during a routine sensor sweep had drawn the attention of the senior science officer and subsequently that of his captain. Another ship would have missed even that.

"Absolutely, Mr. Jaza," Captain Riker had said, a broad grin cutting a canyon in the dark hair of his beard as he perused the younger man's data. "Let's have a closer look."

Jaza had never worked under a commander with as acute an appreciation for the beauty of the unknown as William Riker, never encountered anyone, scientist or artist, soldier or civilian, who had as pure a love for discovery. There was a free-form quality to the way Riker directed *Titan*'s missions that kept everyone on their toes without giving them all over to chaos. There was always reason guiding Riker's rhyme, even when it wasn't readily apparent.

Over weeks and with much rewriting of code and retasking of systems, the darklings came into sharper and sharper relief. To everyone's delight, they also brought along more mysteries to solve. Days became weeks. A couple of re-tasked systems became a score and soon a good portion of *Titan*'s crew was focused in one way or another on the strange cosmic formation onto which they had luckily stumbled.

They were a strain of so-called dark matter, that was obvious, but, unlike the garden variety of the stuff, the darklings' existence was apparently extremely organized. They were set in a massive ring, evenly distributed and collectively spinning in orbit around a neutron star.

How had this happened? What sustained the effect? What properties set this form of exotic matter outside the normal bestiary? These questions and hundreds more were asked by Jaza and his staff over the weeks *Titan,* now rigged essentially for silent running to avoid any stray homegrown rads cluttering their survey, spent sliding between the massive invisible pips.

It was a good time, the perfect expression of their collective raison d'être.

Which, of course, meant it couldn't last.

The day began badly for him: a fitful sleep full of powerful and unsettling dreams, followed by a return to consciousness that put him in mind of the time he'd escaped drowning.

Caught in a river whose current he had misjudged, he found himself both falling and being swept forward by the pull of something he could neither see nor fight. It had been terrifying then and, even though his father had pulled him out only a few seconds after he'd tumbled from the boat, his time in the water had felt like eternity.

The dream, what he could remember of it, wasn't truly terrifying in that way. There was no risk of death, obviously, and he wasn't drenched or shivering cold. Yet there was the same power in the thing, the same inexorable pull from something invisible and powerful and impossible to touch.

There had been new elements this time, he thought—a flash of vegetation he hadn't noticed in previous bouts, the sound of a female voice screaming his name, something about a crash.

Once a strange and even mystical experience for him, especially the first few times, the dream had mostly become little more than an occasional and occasionally unpleasant puzzle, cut into billions of obscure pieces of which he only had access to portions at a time.

He would solve it one day, he knew. In fact he knew considerably more about the puzzle and its solution than he usually admitted even to himself. But *one day* was not today.

And, of course, the dream was also a kind of promise, one he'd tested over time and found to be true.

He'd been here before and would come again he knew, but each time he returned from the dream, whether he remembered every detail or not, he was forced to take moments to remind himself who he was, where he was and that, so far at least, he was still alive.

One day that would not be true. One day there would be no waking and no reassurances. One day the dream would not be a dream.

But that day was also not today.

It wasn't until after he'd stumbled to the wash basin and splashed cool water on his face (sonic showers would never do for something like this) that he felt almost like himself again. Almost, but not quite. The dream, even the sparse fragments of it that he could usually remember, was always unsettling in a way that he had yet to find words to describe.

Looking in the mirror he studied the details of his face and found them just very slightly alien. The eyes were the right color gray; the ridges across his nose were properly deep and defined; his skin was the same brown and the few flecks of gray that had begun to appear in the black of his hair had not multiplied, and yet there was something unrecognizable about the man staring back at him. It was as if he was looking into the face of some acquaintance, a colleague he might see occasionally in passing or a classmate from long ago. Not quite a stranger but not a face he found entirely familiar.

"You're Najem," he told himself. "You're Jaza Najem."

The computer told him that he was about an hour ahead of his duty shift; his subordinates would wonder why he had shown up so early and perhaps consider it a negative mark against their own abilities. So he decided to dress, get a snack, and take a short walk before heading up.

The galley wasn't quite empty when he arrived. Little clusters of chatting people had gathered at a few of the tables, while others had chosen quiet solitude in the hall's more secluded corners.

"Greetings, Mr. Jaza," said Chordys, the Bolian who ran the place from the closing hours of gamma shift through most of alpha. She was a cheery little thing whose round blue body seemed to be little more than life support for her smile. "You're up early. Getting a jump on the day?"

He managed a smile of his own, nowhere near as bright,

mumbled something that she pretended was coherent as he pointed to the pitcher of protolact on the shelf behind her.

"Upset stomach?" she intuited. He nodded. It was close enough to how he felt though not truly accurate. Upset soul, perhaps? What was the cure for that?

"Dr. Ree usually comes along in the next half an hour or so," said Chordys, going on without him. "He's on the coldblood cycle, you know. Only up during the 'day.' You can probably catch a word with him before his shift begins."

"No," said Jaza, as she reached for the jar of blue liquid. "It's just bad sleep. I'll be fine in a few minutes."

She beamed back at him good-naturedly and handed off the protolact. He drank as he walked, taking swigs between steps and feeling progressively more like himself. He decided to swing by the forward observation area and collect his thoughts there before going up to the pod.

The odd clusters of darklings did obscure most of normal space, making Occultus Ora an almost totally black void, but, sometimes, the light from a nearby star could cut through.

As much as he loved plumbing the secrets of this region—just thinking of it sent a thrill through him—it was nice to see the stars from time to time. It settled his mind to see them out there, perhaps not as eternal as they had seemed to him as a child but permanent enough for all practical purposes. As much as he loved pushing the edges, there was something to be said for that stability, even if it was only an illusion supported by his limited perceptions.

Bajor was out there somewhere, far beyond the range of even *Titan*'s sensors. It was strange how little he actually thought of home these days. There was always so much to see and do that the day-to-day life of Bajor, how his father was, what his children were up to, only floated like buoys on the vast surface of his mind.

Somehow, whenever the dream resurfaced, his mind swam home as fast as it could. It wasn't really homesickness, he had reasons for not spending too much time there, but whenever the dream recurred, there was always that strange hollow ache afterward.

He made a mental note to record a message to his family as soon as this business with Occultus Ora was complete.

Hello to all. Yes, we're all still fine out here. Still alive. Only a few more years to go . . .

The message would take weeks to arrive and be necessarily brief but they expected that from him by now. He'd never been good at verbally expressing the amazing things he'd witnessed in his travels and so had forced himself to become adept at holography. The actual image of a dying pulsar spoke it with far more eloquence than any words he might put around it. Of course, there would be no pictures of Occultus Ora, none that a lay person would find interesting at any rate. Only black, black, black.

Still, on this occasion, he would be forced to try to put it all into words and he would certainly have the time to do it. There was no way to get a signal out now. The darklings' gravity wells and particle discharges made normal communications dicey at best.

He tried to recall a few sonnets to go along with his

descriptions of this place; perhaps a line or two from Erish Elo's *Flames of Darkness* would be apropos.

The observation deck was even more devoid of people than the galley had been. With only two stars visible through the massive plexi wall the only available illumination came from the light strips that ran the length of the ceiling, kept intentionally dimmer than the norm to facilitate tranquility of thought. There was always a somber, contemplative feel to the place and that was precisely what he needed on mornings after the dream's reappearance.

Aside from himself only two other beings, two female ensigns, shared the space. They were both essentially humanoid. One was an Antaran, you could tell by the massive V-shaped cranial ridge dominating her forehead. The other was a member of some species he couldn't readily identify. She was tallish, slender, longer of limb than the average human or Bajoran with a coating on her skin that glinted vaguely metallic in the low light.

Her hair, a thicket of long, ropelike braids, extended to the small of her back, where it was held in a loose bunch by a single regulation blue band.

They nodded professionally at his arrival but, when it was clear he meant to keep to himself, went back to their previous conversation, speaking in intentionally hushed tones so as not to be overheard.

He did his best not to listen, he had no wish to intrude, but the unfortunate acoustics of the place made eavesdropping inevitable.

There was something about a coworker being unreasonable, another about the unreliability of that person's work and the general consensus that, were it not for their commander's personal affection for the buffoon, he would spend the bulk of his on-duty time scrubbing plasma conduits. It soon became clear that the subject of their discussion had been romantically involved with the Antaran and now was very much not.

Jaza smiled.

Titan might be home to the most diverse crew in Starfleet but there was surprisingly little variation when it came to mating rituals. People of every social and biological distinction generally managed to make a hash of love as often as not. He had long since learned the lesson that shipboard relationships were best kept casual and short in duration.

Now this ensign, Loolooa he thought, remembering her name suddenly, was getting the news. She was young. She would likely be *liasing* with someone new in the next few weeks. It was the nature of life on a starship.

The other female said little during their exchange, confining most of her responses to semi-audible murmurs of agreement and support.

He found her fascinating for some reason, despite the fact that her back was too him most of the time. Something about her, the contours of her shape, perhaps, or the way her hair bounced slightly with each of her nods, reminded her of his wife.

She would have hated all this, he thought. *All this quiet, painstaking creeping into the unknown quarters of the galaxy.* Sumari could scarcely conceive of traveling offworld, much less the long-term deep exploration that now defined his life.

"There's too much on Bajor to work out," she would always say. "Too much that needs doing here."

Of course those had been in their days in the resistance, in the time before her death.

It had taken years for the thought of her to come to him as something other than a cold, serrated ache in his chest and years more for him to take any joy in his memories of her, but he had eventually learned to accept the loss of her as another stone on the path he was destined to walk.

"And, anyway," said Ensign Loolooa. "I much prefer your company to his." She ran fingers softly along her companion's cheek, eliciting a sharp exhalation from that quarter.

The other female took Loolooa's hand gently and leaned close enough to her that, at first, Jaza thought they might kiss. He was suddenly self-conscious at the turn of events and, not wishing to intrude on their privacy further, swallowed the last of his protolact and made for the exit.

Only the other female did not kiss Loolooa. Instead, as he passed them on the way to the door, he saw her whispering something to her friend, directly into her aural cavity.

Whatever she said caused Loolooa to draw back sharply and bolt from the room, unmindful of the superior officer occupying the space between her and the exit. She collided with him, even as he moved to get out of her way and sent the two of them sprawling to the floor.

She was up instantly, terribly flustered and full of apologies for which he assured her there was no reason. When she had expressed enough contrition to satisfy her personal sense of decorum, she quickly exited the observation area.

"I'm sorry about that, sir," said the other ensign placidly. "Loo can be excitable."

"So I see," said Jaza.

"She's," the ensign seemed to be searching for the right word. "She requires companionship. I believe her people are not well suited for solitary life."

"I'm guessing yours are?" said Jaza, looking at her fully for the first time. She wasn't wearing a metallic skin tint; her sheen seemed to be the natural look of her flesh. If not for her occasional movement and the size and contours of her eyes, she could have been the sculpture of a humanoid woman cast in copper or gold. *Fascinating.*

"We are suited for many contingencies, sir," she said. "But I am not suited for Loo."

It was the same old story and he didn't press her for more details. In fact he felt a little odd standing there with her, especially as both of them had stopped talking and were just sort of *looking* at each other.

It was impossible to read her expression; her wide turquoise eyes were like glass marbles and, though beautiful in their way, did not have pupils or lids. She didn't blink. He felt naked suddenly, scrutinized, and not a little bit panicked.

"Well," she said.

"Yes," he said.

"I am returning to duty now," she said. "Sir."

"I'm starting my shift as well."

There was another moment of awkward silence before she finally departed. He stood there alone for the next few minutes, his heart beating thunder inside him. He had again that same strange sensation of invisible hands taking hold of him and pulling that he'd felt from the dream—the same sense of being drawn inexorably down.

For a second, he thought of chasing after her and asking if she had in fact intentionally inspired these feelings via some species-specific means. Such exchanges weren't unheard of.

The second passed however and the strange hot/cold pressure in his chest did as well. By the time he reached the turbolift he'd forgotten he'd experienced those feelings at all.

"Begin final phase," said Mr. Jaza from the coordination dais. Had any of his subordinates been capable of tearing themselves from their work to look his way, they would have seen what appeared to be the shadow of a humanoid figure standing in the center of a ring of floating disks of light, the coordination display.

The silhouetting effect was the result of low ambient light settings in effect during this mission. Jaza actually found the perpetual twilight relaxing.

Jaza's position at the base level gave him a clear view of the upper tiers—three segmented decks outfitted with control nodes for the most powerful sensor array Starfleet technology had ever produced.

All around him, hidden beneath the deck and beyond the bulkheads, that array focused itself entirely on piercing the secrets of the surrounding ring of exotic matter.

Ordinarily automated, the *Titan*'s dorsally-mounted sensor pod was configured for temporary manned operation at the discretion of the ship's senior science officer when a less orthodox and more hands-on approach to an investigation was deemed appropriate. On this occasion, the Occultus Ora had pushed Jaza's buttons in all the rights ways.

"Probe three, returning to dock," said a voice from above.

Scattered among the many consoles were other shadows, the members of his research team—Hsuuri, Polan, Fell, Roakn, aMershik, the two Benzites whose names he could never keep straight: Berias and Voris, and the young Cardassian cadet, Dakal.

The other members of the group, Bralik and Pazlar, were cloistered down in the astrometrics lab, analyzing the massive holographic simulations translated from the collated probe data.

Jaza confirmed the arrival on his own display but still asked for a verbal report from Dakal. The young Cardassian had the makings of a good scientist, despite his protestations to the contrary.

"Probe Four, away," said Dakal, somewhat mechanically. "Preparing for sensor sweep, series omega." He was bent over a viewing node in the upper tier of the *Starship Titan*'s dedicated sensor module instead of availing himself of the view from the thick forward viewport that was normally shuttered when the pod was unmanned.

There really wasn't much point in looking out the window. Thanks to the darklings that surrounded them, all he would see that way was endless black. Through his little viewer he could see the real target of his team's investigation.

"Probe Four, accelerating to plus-two ionic," said Ensign Hsuuri in a voice that managed to be equal parts purr and snarl. Only a meter or so away, she too was hunched over an observation node, focused entirely on its readouts, completely ignoring the panorama outside the plexi.

Hsuuri was a Caitian, a feline species from a world Dakal had only read about and in whose existence he hadn't quite believed until he found himself working with actual representatives. There were three others like Hsuuri on *Titan*—another female, Hriss, and two males. All the others occupied positions in Starfleet security. Dakal found the species arresting.

Hriss was covered with fine auburn fur, broken here and there with white speckles about the size of Dakal's thumbprint. She was thick bodied, somewhat imposing—a good quality for someone making a career in security. Hsuuri was smaller, slighter, and curvier, with a coat that looked like an arctic forest set ablaze. The lower part of her face, her throat, and, he presumed, her chest were covered in the snowy white fur. The rest of her was fire. She had a way of flicking her tail from side to side as she stood that was at once playful and somewhat hypnotic.

Hsuuri was Dakal's superior officer, as was nearly everyone on *Titan,* but that didn't mean he couldn't admire her from time to time. There was a lot to appreciate about her, and not all of it had to do with her cultural history. Feline or no, she was a fascinating woman.

They hadn't passed two words to each other that weren't work related, but once omega phase was finished, who could say?

At home there were taboos against too much close fraternization with non-Cardassians. There was also an even stronger proscription against joining the paramilitary organizations of former enemies. He hadn't given a *shtel* about that, had he? So Dakal saw no reason to balk at a chance to interview Hsuuri about their cultural differences over something hot and steamy. Yes, he would ask her to join him for that meal as soon as the work was done.

"Cadet Dakal," said Jaza's voice from below, snapping him out of his reverie. "I asked you for an update."

Back to work, Zurin, he admonished himself. *Mr. Jaza passed over four other candidates to put you on his team. Stop dreaming.* "Probe Four is cresting the inner perimeter now, sir," he said a little hastily. "Telemetric linksys is in the green."

"Activating TOV," said Jaza, reaching for what looked like a large glass bowl impaled here and about with slender metallic rods and connected to the dais by a length of thick cable. It slid down over his forehead and eyes and then, "Counting down from five, four, three, two—"

He was outside, free from the confines of *Titan*'s shell, free from the restrictions imposed by his physical body, out among the darklings. Only the small blinking display in the lower corner of his vision disrupted the illusion that his presence in open space was anything other than simulated.

Using the TOV—telemetric observation VISOR—Jaza saw what the probe saw, its sensor data translated into the visual spectrum with small annotations scrolling by to denote the exact composition of whatever happened to be its target.

It moved as he wished with little more than a flick of his mental will. Though he could never see them naturally, using the probe's "eyes" he found himself floating in the midst of a universe of floating black asteroids of every conceivable shape and size.

He felt a little pang of rue as he moved in on a particularly enticing hunk of darkling matter. They'd had a great time excavating all the data they could from this place, but once the omega sweep was done, *Titan* had to move on.

Later Starfleet might decide to place an outpost here to really plumb the depths of Occultus Ora, but that was years away. If it ever happened.

The only real drawback of deep space exploration was what the humans often referred to as the Faustian bargain. He had no idea about the origin of the phrase, but the practical definition seemed to mean having to press on before you'd done more than scratch the surface of the new.

Ah, well, he thought. Every action has its opposite. At least we were here first. "Lieutenant Pazlar," he said aloud as he moved toward the great black hulk.

"Pazlar here," said a mellifluous voice over the comm.

"Omega series is under way," said Jaza, the pleasure in his own voice audible to anyone in a position to hear. "Prepare to receive telemetry from Probe Four."

"Ready when you are," said Pazlar, as he closed in on his shadowy prey.

"Excellent," Jaza said. "Let's get started."

Bralik shot slowly upward, happy to let her momentum take her where she wanted to go. In this case that meant about thirty vertical feet away from the deck of the stellar cartography lab, up through the strange inky formations, like asteroids and unlike them as well, that floated all around.

The chamber—you couldn't really call something so

enormous a room—was a massive sphere in which star systems, individual cosmic bodies, even the entire galaxy could be displayed, at will, in three dimensions.

Bralik took great pleasure in her visits here, but as a geologist, she normally had little official reason to drop by.

This current project of Jaza's was not only an opportunity to demonstrate her expertise as a rock hound but it also required her to spend lots of time in this lovely, lovely chamber.

Of course the current setup also removed about a quarter of the fun of coming here, leaving only the job itself, the lowered g, and the companionship to entertain her. Bralik enjoyed fun and did her best to wedge it into just about any activity she could manage. Life was too short to do otherwise.

It wasn't a very Ferengi attitude, the seeking of pleasure without profit, but Bralik long ago decided that profit was sometimes in the eye of the beholder.

Most of the crew of the *Starship Titan* found the decreased gravity the mistress of this area enjoyed somewhat discomfiting. Not Bralik.

Years working mining excavations situated on asteroids large and small had made gravity just another variable to her, nothing to get worked up about. Plus, the vibrations her spinning assent sent tingling across her lobes had an erotic quality she found hard to resist.

The remaining quarter of pleasure in this duty was the company of the chamber's only other occupant.

Melora Pazlar, the ship's lead stellar cartographer, was the reason for the area's lowered g. Pazlar's species, the Elaysians, had evolved in environments just like this, though how they'd also managed to maintain their basically humanoid structure was a matter of considerable conjecture. Unlike the squat, utilitarian Ferengi physique, Pazlar's people were almost the living incarnation of delicate grace.

Whatever the truth of her bizarre evolution, Pazlar took to her low-g haven like a slug to the swamp. Seeing her glide effortlessly from one position to the next was, Bralik thought, not unlike watching the flight of a creature from human myth that had once been described to her.

Of course, the only thing about Pazlar that was angelic was her looks. The rest was a combination of prickles and frost, at least at first, but even those qualities could be enjoyable. Once you got past her initial standoffishness—a trait Bralik made it a rule to ignore in any being she encountered—Pazlar was an energetic, even magnetic companion. She'd traveled everywhere, despite being hobbled by gravities that were almost invariably crushing for her delicate frame. Her mind was like a laser drill. She looked after herself and was proof against any display of pity or condescension.

She might look like she was built of *dzura* bones and silk, but Pazlar was solid as osmium ore. Like any raw metal, a little patience was all it took to polish up a gleam.

"Somebody doesn't look happy," said Bralik as she passed between two of the black asteroids to bump lightly against Pazlar's legs.

"I miss my stars," said the younger woman, dutifully helping Bralik orient herself so that their heads faced each other. "I'm sick of all this black."

She meant the current display dominating the entirety

of the chamber. Instead of the normal star field, the two women were surrounded by the computer's best guess at what Jaza's probes and recalibrated sensors had under examination.

It wasn't truly blackness that engulfed them. There were halos of every hue sparking and dying pretty much constantly in all directions. Wherever they appeared, their light created the clear silhouette of something that looked like an asteroid but was very much not. It wasn't the galaxy laid out like diamonds in invisible ether, but it was beautiful in its way.

What the silhouettes were and how they happened to be here, arranged as they were around their invisible star, was the topic of much interest among *Titan*'s science specialists. Even Melora Pazlar had been among them at first. Nearly two weeks of diminishing participation in the actual probing had increased her sense of useless isolation.

"Yeah," said Bralik, peeking over at the other woman's padd. "But buck up, angel. We're nearly done."

"I can't believe I let Jaza talk me into letting him commandeer my entire department for this."

"I wouldn't describe a superior officer ordering you to reset all your equipment to display only exotic matter talking you into something."

"You're right," said Pazlar with another of her rueful but stunning smiles. "But Jaza doesn't come at you that way. He's all enthusiasm and love of pure knowledge. It gets you caught up."

" 'Jaza,' huh?" said Bralik, grinning. "Not 'Najem'?"

"He gets his name back when I get my stars," said Pazlar.

"You're a tough little thing when you want to be, aren't you," said Bralik, showing her own sharp teeth. "Anyway, it sounds more like you're talking about Captain Riker than our Bajoran friend."

"It's sort of the same thing," said Pazlar, watching another halo fire up and die and tapping in the appropriate notations. "By the time I realized what he was doing, my stars were gone and I was stuck with this."

"Forty-eight," said Bralik with a chuckle. Pazlar looked up from her padd but didn't ask the question. Bralik answered anyway. "Rule of Acquisition number forty-eight: The bigger the smile, the sharper the knife."

They were quiet for a time, each watching the halos' erratic discharges and making notes accordingly. Bralik had requested they bring an actual sample aboard for long-term study, but Jaza had deemed the darkling matter too volatile to risk danger to the crew. She'd been forced to make do with the holographic sims. Granted they were amazingly detailed and presented their data in the visual spectrum as much as possible, but you really couldn't ever beat putting your hands on something.

"Huh," said Pazlar absently. "That's odd."

"What is?" said Bralik.

"I'm getting flickers in the boryon range."

"Meaning?" said Bralik.

Pazlar ignored the question and "swam" down to a lower region of the massive display, disappearing briefly behind two enormous clumps of black. When she reappeared, Bralik saw her hovering near several midsized darklings, apparently waiting for something. She watched Pazlar watching as each object's halo lit up in succession.

By the time the third flare had come and gone, Bralik knew what had tweaked Pazlar's interest. So far, without deviation, the darkling halos had been uniformly red or aqua or whatever. This undulating rainbow effect was something new.

"Well?" said Bralik. "What is it?"

"I'm not sure," said Pazlar, her hands now tapping frantically at her padd. Something was obviously wrong. "Pazlar to Jaza."

"Go ahead," came the immediate response.

"Can you change the probe's orientation to grid zed seven and tell me what you see?"

"Executing," said Jaza, clearly puzzled. Then, *"What am I supposed to be—?"*

He stopped speaking abruptly, and Bralik thought she could see why. The strange halos that Pazlar noticed had returned and brought friends. A largish cluster of the rainbow auras flashed briefly around their respective darklings and faded again.

"Caves of fire," said Jaza under his breath. *"Tell me that's not what it looks like."*

"Don't go all Red Alert yet," said Pazlar, her fingers tapping furiously on her padd. "It could be something local, or it could be a glitch in the probe's transfer signal."

"No and no," said Jaza through what sounded to Bralik like clenched teeth. *"Wait a moment."*

"Should we abort?" said Pazlar, after the moment had passed.

"Wait," said Jaza, the stress clearly overtaking him now. Whatever this was, it was something apparently dire. Bralik's own padd was keyed to interpret only the geologi-

cal data—information culled strictly from the molecular examination of the darklings. By contrast, Pazlar and Jaza were focused on subatomica.

"Can you isolate the source of the distortion?" Pazlar asked.

"Working on it . . ."

"It looks like a ripple from some sort of—"

"The distortion's clearly artificial, Melora."

"But there's nothing sentient-made out here." Bralik could tell from her tone that Pazlar was grasping at straws. "Is it possible we missed—"

"You know what this is as well as I do or you wouldn't have contacted me," said Jaza, his anger evident even over the comm. *"That lunatic!"*

Unable to help or even participate, the Ferengi geologist contented herself with floating free, watching and listening as her colleagues worked frantically to solve their cryptic problem.

"Should we abort?"

"We're not aborting," said Jaza.

"But, if all the data are corrupted . . ."

"We don't know that yet."

Time ticked and, though she still couldn't decipher the meat of their conversation, Bralik felt the tension increase with each moment.

Just when she was about to ask again what the problem was, the entire display vanished, leaving the two women floating inside a massive gray sphere whose surface was a lattice of overlapping gold and silver grids.

"*Melora,*" said Jaza's voice, now stripped of any semblance of emotion. *"I'd like you and the rest of the team to go over the collected data and isolate any anomalies similar to what we've just seen. I need a timeline.*"

"We'll salvage what we can," said Pazlar.

A light chime sounded, indicating that Jaza had switched off. Pazlar tapped her padd once, deactivating it.

"What just happened?" said Bralik. "Don't tell me we're dumping three weeks of work over one little glitch."

"Just suspending it for now," Pazlar corrected, a hint of Jaza's pique creeping into her tone as well. "Pending data review."

"So what's the big problem?" asked Bralik, drifting down to join the Elaysian.

"Same problem as always," said Pazlar. "Ra-Havreii."

"*Sometimes the worst thing about a day is living through it,*" her mother used to say. More than once in both her careers Christine Vale had come to know the wisdom of those words.

As she stood in the anteroom waiting for Troi to finish whatever was taking her so long, she wished again that something, perhaps some giant bit of alien war tech still roaming the stars in search of prey, would swoop down on the starship *Titan* and start blasting away. Nothing too fancy or lethal—just a little combat to break up the terrors of the lull.

It wasn't that she enjoyed the potential for carnage created by such circumstances. She had no particular bloodlust to speak of. It was just that, during those times, she knew who she was, knew what to do, how to function fluidly when there was chaos all around. It was just easier than, well, *this.*

"We're out here to explore, Chris," Will Riker said more than once. "Not to fight." His eyes always sparkled a bit when he dropped one of these epigrams, as if he had a cluster of pulsars stored in his skull instead of a brain. She was all for exploration—hell, that was a large part of why she'd joined Starfleet in the first place: to set her eyes and hands on something really new. The trouble was, war got you used to the rush, the constant possibility of attack or death at the hands of an enemy. Exploration, pure exploration, was often very slow and brutally quiet.

It took time to map the contours of an exotic stellar phenomenon or open diplomatic relations with a species that had no understanding of the concept of "I." It took time and concentration and coordinated effort. Coordination takes unity, and unity takes—well, until this duty she thought she knew what unity meant. Life on *Titan* had blown all her notions on that score out the airlock. Lately, when *Titan* was performing its function, she found herself experiencing an increasing sense of dread as she anticipated the next catastrophic problem coming from within rather than without. There were simply too many variables, too many potential trouble spots for her to come up with contingencies for everything. The longer *Titan* went in the quiet, the more anxious she became.

Her nerves had, once again, taken their toll on her hair. When she was too long in stir, she dyed. When she was too long waiting for the second shoe to drop, she cut. Now she was both, so . . .

It's too red, she thought, catching her reflection in the polished surface of the room divider. *It looks like Risan shimmer ink.*

The length was okay. She always enjoyed a severe cut, but, paired with the red in her uniform, well, *too much* was the simplest way to put it. As soon as she had an hour free, she'd go back to some version of blond.

Vale had deliberately avoided visiting the counselors' suites since beginning duty on *Titan*. Not only did she not enjoy people poking around in her psyche, telepathically or otherwise, she simply preferred Deanna Troi in her capacity as the ship's diplomatic officer. There was a clear delineation between their duties then, less potential for boundary crossing.

The command structure was in place for a reason, and those wrinkles that muddied it, say a senior officer being married to the captain, as was the case with Troi and Captain Riker—well, *muddy* was definitely the word for it.

Vale's duties as XO and Troi's in her other capacity as senior counselor created an automatic—and not always comfortable—overlap. Overlap meant confusion. Confusion meant a drop in efficiency, something a ship with a crew as diverse as *Titan*'s could ill afford.

Lives depended, quite literally, on both interspecies and interdepartmental harmony. It was another reason the Sudden Alien Attack scenario was increasingly attractive. Something like that cleared the normal frictions away in favor of duty. Without that Other to offer a binding physical threat? Well.

If nothing else, the friction proved to her what she had long suspected: no matter the planet of origin, people were essentially the same. Too bad it wasn't a guarantee of peaceful coexistence.

A certain amount of chronic discord was inevitable on

long-term space explorations, even among members of the same species. You just couldn't coop up that many people that long in what was essentially a giant metal can and not get some temper spikes. Generally, this sort of thing was self-regulating, only occasionally requiring intercession by counselors—and, once in a while, security.

The carnivores and the herbivores, for example, had managed to ease into something like a polite truce, the former keeping the blood spray at mealtimes to a minimum and the latter respecting the effort enough not to raise a fuss over the occasional stray droplet. Progress.

Some of the other frictions, however, still required a degree of management.

No, you can't remove this bulkhead, Chaka. I'm sorry the accommodations are so cramped. We'll work something out for you.

Yes, Lieutenant Keyexisi, I know Ensign Lavena's quarters are still bleeding heat from yours, but we're only talking about a few decimals of a degree. You can't possibly feel the diff—

He has apologized, Ensign Mecatus. Put him down. You are not entitled to a quart of his lifeblood.

It was like being pecked to death by ducks (another of Mother Vale's maxims). And most irritating of all, perhaps, were the troubles caused by *Titan*'s chief engineer: the mounting tension between him and the ship's senior science officer, the difficulties the engineer's . . . natural hedonism was causing among not a few of the crew's female complement, and, of course, the fact that his air of complete indifference to all of it made Vale's own pressure spike. Routinely pissing off your shipmates might make for a bumpy tour of duty. Adding stress to your XO's day? That could get ugly.

Dr. Xin Ra-Havreii was a genius, yes, but that didn't count for much in stopping someone from punching him in the face. Vale had seen plenty of smart guys pounded senseless by lesser intellects who happened to be in possession of a pool cue. Jaza wasn't quite there yet, but if Ra-Havreii kept pushing him . . .

And so, here she was, waiting to meet with Counselor Troi so they could work out a tandem approach to obviating some of the more persistent issues that had sprung up among the crew.

Only Troi had been off her game too, hadn't she? She and, by extension, her staff were evidently leaving enough cracks in *Titan*'s social cement that crewmen were actually accosting Vale in the corridors to vent their grievances. Being turned into the ship's walking complaint department had definitely breached the perimeter of her personal neutral zone.

What the hell was Troi doing back there? She had to know Vale's to-do list had stretched to the point where it could choke a pig. Troi's own had to be competitively long. They'd agreed to get this out of the way, first thing, so as not to clutter up the day with missing each other and having to waste time—time in which the frictions would only grow—with serial rescheduling.

"First will be best," Troi had said, and Vale had agreed. It was something her mother had instilled in her along with the other little buds of wisdom.

Clear the scrap away early, so it's easier to see what's in front of you.

At this rate, First was in danger of shoving Second to Third and Third to Sixty-Seventh, and that couldn't happen if Vale hoped to remain sane. Of course, another ten minutes cooling her heels in this damnable vestibule might push her over the brink before Troi got the chance.

She'd never enjoyed waiting. Even when she was an officer in the planet Izar's security force the worst part of the job had always been the stakeouts—sitting meters away from some criminal's den on the off chance that they might come or go during the hours you were watching. You watched the clock during those times. You waited, expectant, for something previously unconsidered to occur that would shatter your whole program.

Sometimes it came and you were sort of relieved to have been right—something bad was about to happen. Sometimes it didn't and you were thrilled to be wrong and for things to run as they should. In either case it was the waiting that killed. In joining Starfleet she'd hoped to put that particular torment behind her.

But, here I am again, she thought, taking in the room for the seventy-fifth time. *If there's a hell, you can bet it's a place like this.*

The vestibule was a lot like Troi herself—understated, well put together, professional in appearance but with occasional flourishes. In addition to the walls' muted colors, pale greens and yellows mostly, she'd hung small tapestries from various worlds. A few leafy micro vines were potted here and about, their branches extending across the ceiling in places and subtly undercutting the sense of being indoors. There was a hint of some fragrance in the air as well—traces of some exotic spice? Maybe *cheras* root.

In any case the whole place was obviously set up to put occupants at their ease, which, of course, made Vale edgy. She was just about to loudly remind Troi of their scheduled meeting when the door to the counselor's office sighed open and a large scaly figure emerged.

"Good morning, Commander Vale," said the raptorlike creature genially, the words hissing out of his throat like jets of steam.

"Morning, Dr. Ree," she said.

"Please forgive me for delaying Counselor Troi," said Ree. "I believe she'll be with you in a moment."

"No problem," said Vale. "Not discussing anything that needs my attention, were you?"

Ree's sloping reptilian face cocked to one side and his tongue licked out at her twice.

"Not at all, Commander," he said. "This was strictly a routine visit." His Pahkwa-thanh morphology made the subtleties of Ree's expressions difficult for Vale to read. Sometimes, when he was amused, for instance, his unblinking yellow eyes gave the impression they were tracking prey. Still, she thought she might have detected a mild stiltedness to Ree's words, as if he was perhaps not speaking the precise truth. Or it could have been something totally alien to her human sensibilities and untranslatable.

The doctor complimented her on her choice of hair pigment and then was gone, the claws on his feet scratching softly against the carpet as he passed.

"A little too much red, no?" Troi emerged from the main suite, gesturing for Vale to join her inside.

"No peeking inside my head, Counselor," said Vale jauntily. "We've talked about that."

"None necessary," said Troi with a smile that seemed to Vale a little forced. "Just years of enduring intense fashion criticism at Lwaxana's School for Wayward Betazoids."

Nice try, thought Vale, taking in Troi's demeanor. *But I'm not buying.*

Unlike the doctor, Troi was an easy read. Though she covered it well, the counselor looked, for lack of a better term, like hell. Despite the strictly professional pose and demeanor, there were little hints that, to Vale's eyes at least, added up to something other than happiness lurking behind her mask.

Her eyes were red-rimmed and flat, totally absent their normal inky sparkle. Her mouth was set, stiff, as if to say, *Smile, what smile? I have no idea what a smile is or why I should want to make one*. Her skin, normally a deep olive, was now nearly as pale as Vale's own.

You didn't need police training to see she'd been crying. It wasn't a leap to conclude Ree had given her some unpleasant news.

Routine visit, huh? she thought. *I'll bet.*

Troi gestured for Vale to take the seat opposite hers. "Sorry to keep you waiting."

"No problem," said Vale, easing down into the soft cushion. She had to restrain herself from asking about Ree's house call.

"I'm fine," said Troi, having obviously plucked the feeling out of her mind despite her earlier denials. *Betazoids.* "Dr. Ree's visit was just routine."

Sure it was, thought Vale, and regretted it instantly. Troi had obviously "felt" her skepticism then as well. Vale resolved to redouble her efforts to develop her emotional shields. Jokes aside, she knew Troi better than to think she would invade Vale's privacy, but one of the things that helped to make her so effective as a multispecies therapist was the way her patients' feelings "leaked" out of them, and it wouldn't do for the ship's first officer to be that readable. Despite their time together as crewmates, Vale didn't yet know Troi well enough to keep track of all the subtleties.

The moment passed and Troi was all business again, for which Vale was grateful. This was going to be hard enough on its own.

"So," said Troi. "Shall we get to it?"

"Absolutely," said Vale, punching up the relevant notes on the screen of her padd. "We have a few fires to put out. I think your staff should coordinate with Mr. Keru's once we settle on a game plan."

"That sounds fine," said Troi, her face now little more than a mask of calm. "Why don't we start with the worst and work our way up?"

"The worst. Right," said Vale, scrolling. "There are actually a couple of contenders for the bottom spot."

"Choose one."

"All right," said Vale. "That would be the Ra-Havreii situation."

It took Torvig a few seconds to process the question. It wasn't the wording that confused him or the fact that the question had come from Lieutenant Commander Jaza—though what the science officer was doing this far belowdecks was puzzling.

It wasn't even that he'd been surprised, mid-task, by

the Bajoran's arrival or that said task currently had most of Torvig's body ensconced in the bowels of a ceiling access grid so that only his head and neck were visible from the corridor below. No, what froze Torvig's mental gears was the question itself.

"Well, Ensign," said Jaza, his gray eyes glaring up out of his brown face, his arms folded in a configuration that Torvig had come to understand was meant to express displeasure. "I'm waiting."

"Sir," said Torvig, craning his neck so that he could meet Jaza's eyes. At the Academy a cadet had tried to saddle him with the name Ostrich. Torvig had discouraged it, finding the allusion inexact at best. "Regrets, but I don't understand your meaning."

"It's a simple question, Ensign," said Jaza. "Are you trying to kill me?"

Unlike his own people, the Choblik, who enjoyed precision, humanoids like Commander Jaza often used colorful imagery to convey information rather than simply stating it outright. Other Choblik had mentioned difficulty in processing this idiomatic quirk. Most chalked it up to the fact that, generally, humanoids eschewed the cybernetic enhancement that defined Choblik existence. The more time Torvig spent in the company of humanoids, the more he found himself agreeing with this assessment.

It was sad, he thought, their aversion to biomechanicals. A couple of extra cognition chips or an added posterior appendage could work wonders for a being's outlook.

"I don't believe so, sir," he said eventually, still doubtful that he had a full grasp on his superior's meaning. His long neck ached from holding this position. The servo at the end of his tail was caught on something. "It is certainly not my intention to cause you harm."

"That's odd," said Jaza, apparently meaning the opposite, "because I've just had to pull three of your colleagues out of the ship's guts, each of whom were engaged in hardware upgrades that had been specifically designated as off limits until the end of our current mission."

"We were informed that the mapping operations were essentially complete, sir," said Torvig.

"Informed," Jaza repeated, his eyes narrowing as he leaned closer to Torvig. "Informed by whom?"

"Do I understand you to mean," Jaza asked Ensign Rossini, "that Commander Ra-Havreii himself instructed you to do this?"

"Yes, sir," said Ensign Rossini. He was obviously still a bit shaken by Jaza's sudden appearance in engineering as well as by the pointed questions the science officer had started asking. He still stood where Jaza had found him, one foot on the bottommost rung of an access ladder, the other on the deck. All around them a cluster of Rossini's fellow engineers went about their business tending the great pulsating tower of controlled matter/antimatter reactions: *Titan*'s warp core. Rossini's hyperspanner dangled forgotten in his left hand while his right held tight to one of the upper rungs. "The chief said you'd have wrapped up the mapping by 0600 and we should get on with the upgrades."

Jaza's only response was a slight narrowing of his eyes.

"Did we screw up the mapping, sir?" Rossini asked in real distress. The boss might have no sense of team play, but his staff certainly did. "We would never have started the upgrade if the chief hadn't—"

Jaza held up a hand for silence. Rossini watched as the Bajoran scientist drifted over to a nearby console and tapped in a few commands.

"This is an elective upgrade, isn't it, Ensign?" said Jaza as the data he'd requested appeared on the screen before him. "None of these systems is anywhere near failure, correct?"

"No, sir," said Rossini. "I mean, yes, sir. I mean, you're right, sir. These systems are all performing to spec. But Dr. Ra-Havreii says he wants *Titan* to be the first ship to return to the dock in better shape than she left it, so—"

"Thank you, Ensign," Jaza interrupted. "Can you tell me where I would find Commander Ra-Havreii at this precise moment?"

"Probably in his quarters, sir. Truth is, he's not spending much time down here anymore. Just comes through, makes notes, and tells us . . ."

Rossini trailed off. Jaza was already on his way out of engineering.

"You haven't heard a word I've said, have you?" asked Vale.

Troi made a show of putting away whatever had been occupying her mind. "I've been listening," she said. "Dr. Ra-Havreii has been a concern of mine for some time."

"But you haven't done anything about it," said Vale.

"He hasn't exhibited any truly aberrant behavior," Troi said. "The anecdotes are troubling, yes, but they don't add up to an actual pathology."

"You've been around the man," said Vale. "And you're a telepath. You've got to know something's going on with him."

"I'm an *empath,* Christine," said Troi. "I'm only half-Betazoid. My telepathic abilities are limited." The words came out in what to Vale was a stilted manner, rife with something like bitterness—odd for Troi. She was neither of those things as a rule. "And the accuracy of my empathic abilities varies from species to species. Efrosians are . . . complex."

"The point is," said Vale, "I shouldn't even be involved in this. The fact that I am says somebody's falling down on the job."

"You're blaming me?" said Troi. "Is that what this is about?"

"I'm asking you to do your job," said Vale. "If I have to have an official on-the-record conversation with Ra-Havreii . . ."

"I've been at this a lot longer than you, Christine," said Troi archly. "I think I know how to—"

"You can't play the old veteran card every time, Counselor," said Vale. "*Titan* isn't the *Enterprise*. We're on our own out here, naked. We don't get to swap Ra-Havreii out for a better model."

"You're in no position to lecture me, Commander," Troi snapped.

Suddenly all Vale could think about was the argument she'd had with her mother after announcing her intention to join Starfleet.

There have been Vales in Izar's Peace Office for generations. You're spitting on your heritage!

There were ugly words and uglier feelings between them then, all tangled up in the dance of mother and child and all of which had been resolved to remain unresolved years ago. Why would she think of that now?

The moment passed.

Vale blinked, unsure how things had spiraled this far so fast. "That's where you're mistaken, Counselor. As first officer, it's my duty to make sure the ship runs smoothly. When something impedes that, I have to take steps. This is step one."

For a moment it seemed that Troi was about to respond with something caustic. It was now clear to Vale that she was worked up about something other than their conversation. The counselor sat, composing herself by degrees, breathing deeply. When she was done, when her mask of serenity had reassembled, she stood, indicating that, for her at least, this meeting was over.

"I think we understand each other, Commander," she said. "I'll have a proposal for remedying the Ra-Havreii problem by the end of the day."

"And the other situation?" Vale asked, rising to her feet.

"That's not your concern."

Vale hated what she was about to say, but it was too important to the well-being of the ship and its crew to leave unsaid. "I've noticed the captain's been a little slow off the mark lately as well." In fact, Riker had been stiff as a board for the last two weeks, and he also had consistently deflected Vale's concerned inquiries. "Is something going on between you two that I can—?"

"As I said," Troi interrupted, "whatever is or isn't between me and Will is our concern, not yours. Now if you'll excuse me, I have duties to attend to."

But it is my concern, Deanna, thought Vale, as the doors to the counselor's suite whispered closed behind her. *And I can see I'm going to have to move on to Plan B.*

She waited until she was around the bend in the corridor before tapping her combadge. "Vale to Counselor Huilan."

Chapter Two

The Federation archive at Memory Alpha described the Bajoran people, sometimes called the Bajora, as *"one of the very few humanoid species that have managed to achieve balance between scientific progress and their organizing spiritual lifeview. Bajorans account for this harmonious integration of faith and reason by citing these lines from the Eighth Song of the Prophets:*

" 'One hand holds the stone, the other the spark. To make fire they must come together.' "

Jaza wasn't precisely sure why that particular line kept running through his mind as he pounded on Xin Ra-Havreii's door, but he found himself identifying with the stone.

Jaza considered himself a fairly even-tempered person, never quick to judgment or anger. He and *Titan*'s chief engineer had discussed the delicacy of the mapping endeavor at length almost a month ago. *Titan*'s ultrasensitive sensor nets had been painstakingly recalibrated to detect and probe this uniquely configured dark matter system.

Titan's sensors were state-of-the-art. Even in their base configuration they were orders of magnitude more sophisticated than anything outside the equipment sported by the very newest stationary observation arrays.

In their current setup, specific to *Titan*'s charting of the darkling phenomenon, even the slightest spike in ambient radiation could completely obviate all their readings, forcing them to start again.

Ra-Havreii had, it seemed at the time, been in total agreement with the need for his people to do absolutely nothing that could upset the balance of software and hardware that Jaza and his team had taken days to create. "I know you wanted to upgrade several systems," he had said. "But if you can hold off until we're done, it would be much appreciated."

He remembered the conversation perfectly. He had expected it to be contentious, as Ra-Havreii had lately seemed increasingly self-absorbed, ignoring anything that fell outside his own specific area of expertise and showing little concern for the work of departments other than his own. Jaza assumed this was due to Ra-Havreii's having spent the bulk of his Starfleet career not in the field but in R&D labs, which, traditionally, took a more feudal approach to interdepartmental diplomacy.

More than once in recent months, Jaza and his people had been forced to scrap or suspend ongoing experiments because some of Ra-Havreii's staff were tinkering with systems their superior had deemed in need of attention.

The episodes put considerable strain on their professional relationship.

In this case, however, Jaza's fears proved unfounded. His meeting with *Titan*'s chief engineer had been cordial, almost jovial. Ra-Havreii had played him a selection of strange Efrosian music—all chimes and strings—even offered him a glass of Andorian ale, which Jaza had politely declined.

"Have to stay sharp," he'd told the engineer. "It's not every day one finds concentric belts of exotic matter asteroids in orbit around a neutron star," he had said. "We may never see anything like this again in our lifetimes."

Ra-Havreii nodded in all the right places and stroked his mustache wistfully while making little affirmative noises in his throat at each of Jaza's requests. When they were done, Jaza had gone off to his work on the sensor nets in the sure knowledge that he and the engineer were on the same page.

But Ra-Havreii had instead reverted to type. More than reverted—this disruption of Jaza's work was tantamount to the engineer's throwing down a gauntlet. Weeks of recalibration, of code writing, of direct probing and observation could have been wiped clean because of an impatient chief engineer. It would be several hours before Jaza would know if the current sensor maps had to be scrapped. Pazlar, Dakal, and the others were poring over the data, looking for signs of corruption. Before they delivered their verdict, it was very possible that the brilliant and famous Dr. Xin Ra-Havreii's next entry into the record books would read, *First Efrosian in history to be strangled by a Bajoran.*

"I know you're in there, Commander," Jaza said. "Now open up or, by the Prophets, I'll have the transporter chief beam me in." After the engineer had seen fit to ignore the door chime, Jaza had resorted to pounding on the door.

"You're wasting your time," said a soft feminine voice passing behind him. The words were accompanied by the rush of displaced air tinged with the barest hint of something like hyacinth. He turned to see who had spoken and was treated to the rear view of a familiar humanoid female in black Starfleet exercise uni, jogging toward the other end of the corridor. Without looking back, she added, "He's with Ensign Evesh right now."

Then she disappeared around the far corner, her long golden braids bouncing in time with her easy gait. Jaza stood there for a moment, feeling the same strange tightness in his chest as before, the same chill in his skin. And for a moment, his thoughts of confronting the Efrosian engineer completely vanished.

By the time Jaza arrived at Ensign Evesh's quarters, Ra-Havreii had gone from there as well. The ensign, a muscular little Tellarite, was just heading off to her duty shift. Jaza noticed that the thick hair that formed a sort of mane around her head was still a bit damp, as if she'd just come from a shower.

"He left ten minutes ago, sir," she said with more than a trace of ruefulness. "Apparently, he isn't one to linger."

It seemed, in addition to his other eccentricities, Ra-Havreii made a habit of removing his combadge whenever he felt like it, effectively defeating the computer's ability to easily track him. The man could be anywhere on the ship at this point, and Jaza, his frustration having finally squelched his anger, accepted defeat.

He sighed, leaning heavily against the corridor wall, and considered just exactly how he was going to convince the captain that *Titan* would need another month to properly map Occultus Ora.

"It's not particle bleed," said Hsuuri, her syrupy voice now rife with concern. Her ears and whiskers twitched nervously. "Not random field distortion."

The lights were up to full in the sensor pod, and the team had gathered around the various collation nodes to sift through their mountains of raw data.

"Of course it's not random distortion," said Klace Polan, a little too aggressively to Dakal's mind. The Catullan ensign had a habit of starting conversations with an attack of some sort. "The core has been on dampers for weeks now."

There were murmurs of agreement from the others, each of whom was deeply focused on some particular facet of the results of their scans.

"I'm sure Commander Jaza will be triple pleased to hear what it is not," said aMershik, tentacles from his upper cluster dancing across several consoles at once as his segmented eyes pored over multiple data streams. His combadge made him sound as if he were speaking through a mouthful of suet, but his tone was unmistakably sarcastic, as usual. Thymerae were like that—always looking for the gloom in a bright sky. *"But it would be agreeable if he could be told what it* is *as well."*

"About half of the gravimetric readings check out so

far," said Fell, a bit too brightly. It was clear she didn't want aMershik's dour demeanor to infect the others. "The initial baseline scans look sound."

"How many times must this one inform you, Peya Fell," said aMershik. *"Optimism without facts is—"*

" 'Wasted intellect,' " said the others in chorus. Berias let out a good-natured chuckle, his gray skin darkening with pleasure.

After a month working so closely, all of Jaza's team were well used to the Fell and aMershik Traveling Festival of Sarcasm. Deltans and Thymerae were polar opposites as far as species ethos went. Rumor had it these two had been rankling each other since their first Academy days.

Dakal, his participation neither requested nor required for this sensitive work, sat on a chair under the lowermost tier, listening to the others grouse.

He wasn't fooled by their banter. They were as nervous about the outcome of their investigations as he. That much work, that much time wasted due to the irresponsibility of a single engineer—it was hard for Dakal's mind to fathom.

On Cardassia people like Dr. Ra-Havreii—iconoclasts, individualists—used to disappear after their first public misstep. Where they went or what happened to them there was a mystery that failed to interest most of the citizenry. It was enough that the irritant was gone with minimal disruption to the flow of normal life. Those ways were done, certainly, but one couldn't dismiss the level of efficiency achieved by the old state.

"Hey, Dakal," said Roakn, his great dark drum of a head peering down from the upper tier. "Quit moping and make yourself useful."

"How can I assist you, Lieutenant?" said the young cadet, instantly snapping to.

"You're Cardassian, right?"

"Yes, sir," said Dakal with practiced regulation decorum. He'd gotten used to nonhumanoids having difficulty distinguishing him from a Vulcan or a Trill. From their point of view a humanoid was a humanoid was a humanoid, at least when it came to appearance.

"Cardassians are good at pattern recognition, right?" Roakn's people had never had any direct dealings with Dakal's, but that didn't mean some of the more popular stereotypes hadn't trickled down.

The Cardassian government had proven itself adept at code-making and clandestine operations so, *obviously,* to Roakn at least, that meant every individual Cardassian had the gift. Lovely.

"I wouldn't say it's an actual genetic trait, sir," said Dakal, being careful not to imply his superior was expressing a racial slur. "More of a cultural—"

"Whatever," boomed Roakn, waving Dakal's remarks aside as if they were a swarm of gnats. "Take a look at the time-lapse record of the visual EM translations. And play back at triple speed or you'll be at it another month."

"What am I looking for, sir?" said Dakal.

"Anything anomalous, Cadet," said the wide stony face. "Just like the rest of us."

Were Roakn not a lieutenant, Dakal would have argued that the visual translations were, at best, approximations of what the sensors were actually seeing. The lapsed-time recording, in particular, was almost completely useless for providing anything forensically meaningful.

Dakal might have pointed these things out and he might have gone further to say that, as a member of a species that was little more than a collection of animated boulders, Roakn ought to be a bit more reluctant to assign work based on racial stereotype.

Besides, Dakal knew what was truly at work here. The reason he'd been assigned the useless duty was to impress upon the young Cardassian how insufficient his skills were to the team effort. *Cadet Dunsel,* some of his younger crewmates called him. It was Starfleet slang, a term Dakal had been forced to look up the first time he heard it.

"Dunsel: a part that serves no useful purpose," the linguistic database had informed him. Roakn had changed Dakal to Dunsel as some sort of joke. How amusing.

Two minutes into the playback Dakal knew he'd had enough. At triple speed the halos seemed to explode across his screen like a sort of natural fireworks display. Except there was only one sort of explosion and they never lasted longer than a second or two. "Dull" simply didn't come close to describing it. If triple speed was desirable to detect a pattern in the playback, septuple or octuple would be more so.

Above him the chatter continued between the officers. Unable to give attention to the actual words, his peripheral awareness still managed to detect the tone of conversation as it swung from guarded optimism to total defeat and back again.

". . . wasted time," said someone, probably Hsuuri.

". . . damned engineers," said one of the Benzites.

". . . nothing but gears for brains." That was aMershik for sure. He was well into yet another of his dissertations on the futility of optimism when something on Dakal's display leaped out at him.

A weird shimmering distortion had appeared in the darkling halos, faintly at first, but with steadily increasing effect.

"Hope is an illusion," aMershik droned on above him.

Slowing the playback to its normal rate of progression caused the variances to disappear. Whatever they were, they inspired only minute incremental changes in the scans. They were nothing the sensors, even *Titan*'s sensors, would detect in the moment, but they stood out sharply when viewed at hyperspeed as he had done.

This effect wasn't new then and, therefore, probably not the result of the engineers' tinkering.

Accelerating the playback again to septuple speed brought out the pattern, now growing even more distinct as the time stamp progressed.

He'd started on day one of their examinations and was now up to the dawn of day five. The distortion pattern vanished for several hours, only to reappear at roughly the same time as when it had made its debut. It vanished again at approximately the same interval and subsequently reappeared.

"Hope in one digit cluster," said aMershik. *"Excrete in the other. Observe which fills first."*

aMershik's pronouncements were consistent if nothing else, but Dakal now had his own little maxim in mind, a Cardassian one.

Pull the thread and watch the curtain unravel.

The fireworks sped by, now very clearly examples of the same pattern of distortion discovered by Melora Pazlar.

They vanished and reappeared at the same regular intervals but, sometime around the middle of day twenty, they became more severe, randomly shifting the colors of the halos from one end of the spectrum to the other.

It was certainly unusual, but was it significant? If there was a hidden meaning to the pattern of the distortions, Dakal couldn't see it.

"What have you got there, Cadet?" said Jaza, suddenly standing beside him. Dakal had been so enraptured by the fiery halos he hadn't heard the senior officer reenter the pod. From the sound of aMershik's tedious monotone and Fell's occasional pithy retorts, none of the others had either.

"I'm not sure I know, sir," said Dakal a bit more slowly than he would have liked. "It looks like some kind of quantum distortion, but it's so diffuse—" He meant to slide into an explanation of the chore Roakn had set him, but Jaza was already nudging him aside.

"Quick playback. Quantum distortion translated to the visual. Got it," said Jaza absently, his hands whipping across the console so fast they were almost a blur. "Did you cross-link this with Pazlar's boryon scans?"

"I didn't think to," said Dakal. "I only just discovered this."

Jaza disappeared into himself for a few seconds as he processed what he saw, made changes and additions to the software he employed to dissect the data. When he looked up again he seemed like his normal self, as if this new mystery had somehow inoculated him against the fallout from the destruction of the original search. "Jaza to stellar cartography."

"Pazlar here. Go ahead."

"I'm linking you with the sensor pod's documentary files of our mapping venture, Melora," Jaza said. "Tell me what you see."

There was a short silence as Pazlar's systems aligned themselves with Jaza's, accepting and incorporating the new data. Then, simply, *"Wow."*

"Notions?"

"Sped up like this, it looks like EM spill from a faulty sensor beacon," said Pazlar. *"That could explain the boryon issue and the uniformity of the intervals, but it doesn't account for the fluctuations in the distortion itself."*

"Or why it's spread out over weeks," he finished for her.

"But it definitely looks like a kind of signal-to-noise effect," she said.

It was obvious to Dakal that Commander Jaza was a good five steps ahead of Lieutenant Pazlar on that score. He was already shutting down most of the more esoteric sensor modifications in favor of those that specifically related to the boryon emissions and midrange quantum fluctuations.

"Lieutenant Roakn!" said Jaza suddenly, loud enough to announce his presence to the whole room.

"Sir!" boomed Roakn's voice from above. Instantly he was peering over the edge of the upper tier, looking down at Jaza and Dakal. The rest of the team's chatter was suddenly absent, as if the others' voices had been blown into the vacuum beyond *Titan*'s hull. "You're back."

"Yes," said Jaza. "And I'd like to ask you why I found Cadet Dakal down here, running playback of the EM record instead of up there with the rest of the team." Roakn's hide roughed with embarrassment as he opened his mouth to reply, but Jaza cut him off. "Never mind. We'll talk about it later. Right now, I need a probe reset to track quantum rippling."

"Sir?"

"Yesterday, Mr. Roakn," said Jaza, now splitting his attention between the viewer and the various control consoles around him. "I need it done yesterday."

"Aye, sir," said Roakn. The upper tier actually vibrated beneath his feet as he thundered off to do as he'd been told.

Forgotten again, Dakal contented himself with watching the senior officer work. Jaza's fingers danced, systems deactivated or rerouted or realigned, causing the attendant displays to darken or spark, depending. All with a speed and precision Dakal would have never guessed the older man capable of achieving.

On Cardassia he had once seen a broadcast of a performance of the virtuoso Winim Teekat. Teekat was the acknowledged master of the *kynsleve,* an instrument of hundreds of filaments strung tight in a sickle of *thera* bone.

When plucked by the maestro's nimble fingers, it made the most haunting melodies. Watching his digits skip across the various control consoles, Dakal was sure that Jaza would be a natural for the *kynsleve*.

"Bridge to sensor pod," said a brisk voice.

"Jaza here. Go ahead, Mr. Tuvok," said Jaza, still working away.

"It seems that you are, once again, reorienting ship's main sensors into a new and fairly esoteric configuration."

"Yes," said Jaza, distracted by a set of unexpected symbols that had appeared on a nearby display. "I was just about to inform you."

"In future, Commander," said Tuvok. *"Please apprise me of such modifications before implementation rather than during or after."*

"Special circumstances," said Jaza. "We're tracking a signal, possibly sentient in origin."

"Then it would be logical to incorporate Titan*'s communication grid into your recalibration, would it not?"*

"That was next on the list," said Jaza.

"Proceed, Mr. Jaza," said Tuvok. *"I will adjust the communication system to fit your needs."*

"Probe five prepped and in the tube, sir," said Roakn from somewhere unseen. "Launching."

The others on the upper tier, intent on their original tasks, quietly buzzed among themselves. Dakal listened to them passing data, comparing hypotheses—if the distortions were the result of a signal of some sort, could their effect be scrubbed from the original darkling scans, thus salvaging their month of work?

Even aMershik, all four of his digit clusters gesticulating wildly, now seemed filled with uncharacteristic optimism. He and Pell, their habitual enmity forgotten, were running a tandem simulation to describe the parameters of the distortion. Hsuuri and the rest were engaged in similar activities.

Attack the new mystery, Dakal thought, watching them all approvingly. *But save the old if you can.* Something to remember.

What he didn't understand was why they were all

so frantic about it. Whatever the effect was, it had been progressing for weeks. Indeed the distortion had grown stronger over that time, allowing the latest effect to be seen by Pazlar in real time. Why now all this haste to ferret its secrets?

He returned from his musing to find Jaza staring at him with the queerest expression on his face.

"Back with us, Cadet?" he said. Dakal nodded. "Good, because I need you to run the probe for me."

"Sir?"

"Everyone here is checked out on the TOV rig, but the others all have their hands full," said Jaza, half pulling the stunned cadet toward the central dais. The various control stalks rose silently from the floor around him as the central ring lit up. "Except Roakn. Anyway, his head's too big for the VISOR."

"Yes, sir, but, I mean, wouldn't you prefer—"

"You're elected, Cadet," said Jaza, grinning now. And, in that grin, Dakal saw what he was up to.

"Sir," he said. "I appreciate this, but I am not the appropriate person for this duty. I don't even know exactly what all this talk about quantum rippling means. Why do you think it's some kind of signal?"

Jaza spoke quickly as he adjusted the control harness and the TOV for Dakal's slightly smaller dimensions. "There are two ways to get around relativity when it comes to communications, Dakal," he said. "One is subspace, which every world in the Federation uses to keep in contact with the others. The other is quantum broadcasting, which Starfleet uses for long-range emergency beacons and in limited fashion with sensor probes."

If the TOV was too small for Roakn's giant Brikar body, it was a bit loose on Dakal's slender frame. The helmet in particular seemed to sit precariously on his head, threatening to fall off and shatter against the deck with his every slightest movement.

"There are only two sources of quantum rippling in nature," Jaza went on, pulling the straps of the harness tight. When he was done Dakal looked as if he'd been transformed into some sort of enormous marionette, his cut strings sagging onto the circular platform. "Wormholes and pulsars. Both create a regular ripple or distortion in the quanta. They never, ever, shift or increase. So, either our distortion is caused by some sentient-made device, or . . ."

Jaza let the sentence dangle until Dakal realized he was meant to pick it up. "Or it's something we've never seen before," he said.

"Exactly," said Jaza. That made sense to Dakal, but it was clear his presence in the TOV gear still did not. "I don't believe in dunsels, Cadet. Never have. Never will. Now get to work."

On *Titan*'s bridge, two men pretended. Captain William Riker pretended not to be pacing back and forth, and Commander Tuvok, his chief security and tactical officer, pretended not to notice.

Tuvok hadn't served with the captain long, but he'd made tentative assessments about his personality that, thus far, had been borne out.

After witnessing his behavior in multiple mission scenarios ranging from military to exploratory, Tuvok had found Captain Riker to be courageous, decisive, and intelligent (for a human), with an exceptionally flexible and improvisational mind.

Despite his large size and proficiency at hand-to-hand combat, Riker was at his core a thoughtful being, serene in his sense of self, confident in bearing, and jovial in disposition. He was not one to pace. Yet, at Tuvok's count, the captain had crossed, recrossed, and crossed again the bridge's deck twenty-three times since coming on duty that morning.

Riker did a passable job of concealing this activity from the rest of the bridge crew—pretending to peer over the helmsman's shoulder ("A little tighter on those arcs, Aili. Impulse engines need a firm hand.") or to move in on the main viewer for a closer look at the screen ("Amazing. There's an entire stellar system sitting right there, and it's completely invisible to the eye.").

None of it fooled Tuvok for an instant. Something was occupying a good deal of the captain's attention, and it had nothing to do with their current mapping mission or its recent odd permutation.

"You seem irritated, Mr. Tuvok," said Riker, moving in beside him at tactical control. "Mr. Jaza's hijinks getting to you?"

"Not at all, sir," said Tuvok, projecting the appearance of complete focus on the task before him. "Even if irritation were not an emotion of which I am incapable, sudden modifications to established mission parameters are, as humans say, the nature of the beast."

"Modified probe approaching target coordinates," said Cadet Dakal's voice.

"Acknowledged," said Tuvok, his brow knit ever so

slightly as he methodically recalibrated one system after another. "Patching universal translator into probe control."

"Thank you," said Jaza's voice. *"Probe will be in position in five seconds. Three seconds. One."*

The countdown finished and nothing much happened. *Titan* continued forward in its gentle ellipse, Ensign Lavena deftly navigating the ship between the invisible and intangible darklings.

Riker drifted away from tactical, taking a position at the vacant science officer's station, where he could watch the proceedings without a filter.

Displayed before him was the telemetry from Jaza's modified probe, now set to scan for and isolate the incredibly diffuse signal the team in the sensor pod had discovered.

Riker hadn't had a chance to try out the TOV harness yet, but watching the probe's lifelike dips and spins as Dakal adjusted its positioning, he made a promise to add himself to the pilot roster the next time the probes were needed. Captain's prerogative.

Could have used that distraction now, he thought, running one hand slowly through his beard. This thing between him and Deanna had grown to elephantine proportions in only a few weeks. Their schedules had kept them mostly apart lately, but when they were together, things were increasingly frosty between them.

He would press—*Deanna, you know I'm right about this*—and she would evade or dig in—*Dammit, Will, let it go*—and little by little, their ability to talk had dwindled almost to nil.

After years of nearly complete openness about every subject or emotion, the growing chasm between them might actually do what all the maniacal conquerors, apocalyptic phenomena, and interstellar warfare had been unable to accomplish.

The worst thing was that they both knew his attempts to press her were ultimately benign. The manifestation was unpleasant, friction making, but he just couldn't seem to stop.

"Signal acquired," said Dakal's voice. He sounded almost giddy. *"Uploading to pod."*

"Scan under way," said Jaza. *"Hold steady, Cadet. You're bobbling."*

Hundreds of lines of coded data began to dash across Riker's monitor. At first it was all hash—random symbols denoting as yet unknown information—but once the UT really sank its teeth in, the chaos began to resolve.

One by one, the symbols transformed into those he could understand. Two recognizable symbols became three, became ten, became an entire line of deciphered code, all of which Riker began to find unsettlingly familiar.

"Tuvok?" said Riker. "Are you seeing what I'm seeing?"

"I am aware of the situation, sir," said the Vulcan. "As, I suspect, is Mr. Jaza."

"Transcoding now," said Jaza's voice, but his tone was as grim as the Vulcan's.

A few seconds later, with nearly seventy percent of the signal acquired, they were all thinking the same thing.

"That's the best we're getting, Captain," Jaza reported. *"There's too much distortion to sift out the rest."*

"Run what we have," said Riker, moving quickly from the science station to the captain's chair. "Let's see this thing."

"The visual component is too corrupted for reliable translation," said Tuvok mechanically.

"Give me what you've got, Mr. Tuvok."

"Reconstructing audio."

A hush fell over the bridge as everyone waited to hear what some of them—those who'd paid attention in communication class at the Academy—had begun to dread.

> "*********** *TITAN* ************* SENTIENTS ******* RECEIVE *************** DANGEROUS ********* EXPANDING ********** ******** ATTACK ********* HOSTILE ACTION ******** SPECIES ****** UNKNOWN ****************** *********************"

The alert sounded near the end of Vale's meeting with Counselor Huilan. She'd chosen to conceal the fact that it was a meeting by having the little psychologist accompany her as she walked the ship's corridors, ostensibly on her way to the mess hall. If anyone asked, they were grabbing a quick snack before going on duty.

Involving Huilan in her Plan B was not the course she would have taken had she not felt compelled, but of course that's what Plan B's always were—the less desirable alternative of first resort.

Huilan had been reluctant to accept portions of the duty she was assigning, but when she spelled out the full picture, most of his misgivings vanished.

"You're mistaken about one thing," he said in his growling chirp of a voice. "There's no way I could be concealed inside a satchel or carried anywhere by most members of the crew. I'm small, Commander, but exceedingly dense."

Vale had actually smiled at that. Huilan was a S'ti'ach. To human observers, his people resembled small, blue, four-armed bears.

On most Class-M worlds, such creatures were relatively unremarkable. S'ti'ach, by contrast, was a hyper g planet and, while its flora and fauna were compact by Federation norms, their molecular structures were another matter entirely.

Though Huilan's head barely reached Vale's knees, his mass exceeded hers by a factor of four or five times. He'd be more likely to lift her than the converse. Hell, he could probably toss her from one side of the cabin to the other without much effort.

"So, what do you suggest?" she said. "There's no way either of them is going to sit down with you and bare their souls."

"Yes," said Huilan thoughtfully. "Counselor Troi has been fairly blinkered about this matter."

It would have been stupid for Vale not to expect that Huilan had pegged some of the same symptoms in Troi and the captain as she. He was a professional, and he worked as closely with Troi as Vale did with Will Riker.

She was both gratified and disappointed to know that her misgivings weren't the result of generic XO paranoia. Something was happening with Riker and Troi, something unpleasant that neither of them would divulge.

Vale and Huilan found themselves at the galley, suddenly assaulted by the clamor from within. The shift change meal was one of the noisiest, and this was no exception.

"I'm not asking you to spy on anyone," she said, fighting to be heard over the cacophony of chattering voices. "I just want you to get a look at them together, make an evaluation, and submit your recommendations to me."

"I don't know, Commander," said Huilan, clearly still somewhat dubious about the whole thing. "Clandestine therapies are extremely problematic. As is diagnosis without a close interaction with the patient."

Vale was about to counter with some Pakled axiom about using the tools one had, but before she could, the alert sounded.

"All decks, go to Yellow Alert," said Tuvok's voice. *"This is not a drill."*

As the mass exodus from the galley got under way, Vale's combadge chirped. Riker's voice summoned her to the bridge.

"On my way, Captain," she said, heading out.

"It's one of ours. You're sure?"

"The signal was fragmented, but it had a Starfleet signature, Chris," said Riker as she slid into the first officer's chair beside him. "And whoever they were, they called *Titan* by name."

"So, we're already under way," she said as the dwindling black mass of Occultus Ora was reabsorbed into the larger pattern of streaming stars on the main viewer. "Any idea which ship it is?"

"Not yet," said Riker. "Aside from the fact that the

signal itself is almost completely shredded, the gravity distortions in Occultus Ora prevented us from getting a directional lock."

"Clearing darkling system now, Captain," said helmsman Lavena.

"Thank you, Ensign," said Riker, then, turning to his tactical officer, "Tuvok?"

"The signal seems to have originated somewhere in or near the region of FSR-B2157, also called the Elysia Incendae system," said Tuvok as the data came through. "A moment, Captain. Mr. Jaza and I are—" Tuvok stopped speaking and moved from tactical to the science station. "There is still some interference preventing us from pinpointing or communicating with the sender."

"What's causing it?"

"That is unknown at this time, Captain," the Vulcan said coolly. Vale envied him his composure. Her own pulse was already beating more quickly than she liked, and she hadn't even heard the distress signal herself.

"Ensign Lavena," Riker said, "what's our ETA to the Elysia Incendae system?"

"Twenty-seven hours at warp six, sir," said Lavena.

"Set course and engage."

"Aye, sir," Lavena said as her sheathed fingers danced over her navigation console.

"You think it's *Charon,* don't you?" said Vale, leaning in for a private whisper with her captain.

"She's closest," was the grim response. "But it could be any of them."

Vale's mind flashed immediately to the rest of the fleet. Including *Titan,* Starfleet had four identical *Luna*-class vessels exploring the reaches of the Beta Quadrant. The ships were spread across the region like microscopic pearls on an infinite ebony beach.

The nearest of them, the *U.S.S. Charon,* was many parsecs away the last time her mission updates were transmitted.

That was weeks ago, thought Vale. By now *Charon* should be somewhere deep inside the Ring Nebula, not loitering around these parts.

"What do we know about the Elysia Incendae system, Mr. Jaza?" Riker called out.

"The cursory survey on record lists FSR-B2157 as a G1 star orbited by five planets, one of which is located in the habitable zone for Class-M life. However, the presence of such life has never been confirmed."

"The words *sentient* and *species* were both in the transmission," Riker said.

"True, sir," Jaza acknowledged. *"But we cannot know with any certainty in what context they were being used."*

Riker turned to Vale. "Is Drakmondo or Fortis captaining *Charon*?" said Riker.

"Captain Bellatora Fortis," said Vale, punching up their sister vessel's personnel files on her chair display. "Born on New Riyadh. Graduated the Academy three years ahead of me. Got her pips after the Second Battle of Chin'toka."

"Battlefield promotion," said Riker, frowning slightly. Vale understood. She remembered Fortis now: Tall, pale, and slender to the point of being reedy, she was no one you'd would expect to enter, much less survive, a fight. But when a Breen attack had taken the life of her captain and first officer on the *U.S.S. Sparrowhawk,* it was Bellatora Fortis who'd kept the nearly crippled ship in the fight. And it was Fortis who brought her home. Her reputation was that of a good soldier but not one possessed of the most flexible mind. The necessities of the war had put a lot of people in the captain's chair without giving them the chance to truly develop space legs as explorers. Vale hoped *Charon* hadn't stumbled into something too complex for her captain's linear sensibilities to navigate.

"Give me warp seven, Ensign," Riker said.

"Warp seven, aye."

"Nice color, by the way," Riker said quietly, and Vale suddenly realized he was speaking to her again. "Brings out the red in your uniform."

"Very funny," she said, not the least bit amused by the joke, but grateful to see some glimmer of the old Riker emerge. He was quiet after that. The entire bridge was. The stars, transformed to pinprick strokes of white by the ship's warp field, streamed past *Titan*'s main viewer as silent as the void that held them.

Vale had wanted some external force to arrive and snap them back into cohesion. Now she'd got it, and it stuck going down.

What was it her mother always said?

"Be mindful of wishing, Christine. You might get what you ask for instead of what you want."

Chapter Three

The pulse hit *Titan* ten hours into her journey, slapping the vessel out of warp the way a Klingon fist knocks teeth out of an enemy's mouth.

The tidal forces created by *Titan*'s return to what should have been normal space shorted out systems, disrupting everything utterly, washing over and through the ship as if its amazing catalogue of defenses were nonexistent.

Before the gravity reasserted, a fair number of the crew were slammed into bulkheads or ceilings by their own pent-up inertia. The most durable or agile of them were unfazed, snapping into duty posture even before the Red Alert klaxons directed them to their stations.

The more fragile crew members—the primates, the smaller reptiloids, the relatively spindly Dr. Celenthe—took the brunt. Ensign Torvig spent a harrowing fifteen minutes forcing his cybernetic enhancements back to heel after nearly all of his primary control subroutines had been wiped by the pulse.

Contrary to appearances, the pulse hadn't come out of nowhere. Both Tuvok and Jaza managed to belt out timely but ultimately fruitless exclamations of warning in the second or two before the ship was overcome.

They had been studying the pattern of the distortions that led them here, seeking its point of origin, but while there was evidence of some sort of massive quantum disturbance throughout this region, there was as yet no sign of its cause. The interference itself defied analysis.

Just as they were calling Ra-Havreii to get his input on the problem—perhaps it lay not with the phenomenon but with *Titan*'s sensor nets—the pulse hit.

When the emergency lights came on and the shouting died to sporadic spikes in the post-disaster pall, there was a single question in the minds of *Titan*'s crew.

"What the hell was that?" Riker asked, picking himself up off the deck as the emergency lights came on. "Status report!" He watched as Vale climbed back into her seat and immediately began to pull information from her console.

"Secondary systems are still initializing, Captain," Vale said, the crimson light casting her in harsh black shadows.

"Helm control is wobbly," said Lavena, after righting herself. "Warp engines are offline."

"The hull is intact," Tuvok said, as other systems came online. "No breaches reported. Minor torque striation on the port nacelle strut."

"The effect seems also to have subsided," said Jaza, who had returned to the bridge only in the last hour. "It's still present, but preliminary scans show local conditions are approaching normal."

"What hit us, Mr. Jaza?" Riker asked.

"Energy pulse of some kind, but readings are still imprecise. Analysis under way."

Riker acknowledged this with a curt nod and listened intently as the voices of his crew flooded in over the comms.

This is not good, Vale thought. The ship was running exclusively on emergency power; if its condition was the result of an attack, *Titan* was ill-equipped to repel or even to run from a second volley.

"Tactical status, Mr. Tuvok," she said.

"Phasers are down," said the Vulcan. "Photon and quantum torpedoes are online, but targeting systems are unresponsive. Shields are currently at half strength."

A figure moved to stand next to Riker. Vale looked up and saw Troi standing beside the captain. Vale hadn't even noticed her arrival. She caught Deanna's softly delivered report in her husband's ear: "A quarter of the crew is in a near panic."

Again Riker nodded, and Vale was grateful to see that whatever was going on between them, they both knew when to set it aside. Troi took her station to the left of the center seat, and immediately began coordinating with Keru the support/rescue efforts of their respective staffs.

"Bridge to sickbay. Status report."

"Ree here. Sickbay systems are operating at less than peak, but while a great many injuries are presenting, they are thus far all relatively minor . . ."

While Riker took Dr. Ree's report, Vale left her seat and crossed the deck to sciences. "Could this be what happened to the other ship?" she whispered to Jaza.

"I wish I could say," Jaza said without looking up, his voice tinged with frustration. "So far none of these readings make sense. I'm going to need more time to find the answers, Commander."

"We need to know what we're dealing with, fast," Vale stressed. "We're sitting ducks out here, Najem."

He glanced at her and flashed a small smile. "Then you need to stop distracting me, Chris."

". . . We'll continue to keep you apprised, Captain."

"Thank you, Doctor. Riker out," the captain said, then followed with, "Bridge to engineering."

"Ra-Havreii here," said the Efrosian's voice, his normally melodius tones now rife with tension. *"This isn't a good time, Captain, but I'll have something for you in a few minutes. Engineering out."*

Riker looked at Vale, almost too surprised to speak. "Did he just dismiss me?"

Vale's expression hardened. "I'm on it," she said, glancing at Troi as she marched toward the turbolift. "Counselor, you're with me."

Main engineering was a hotbed of activity when the two bridge officers arrived. Tool-laden techs scurried everywhere, scrambled up and down gangways, bellowed commands and confirmations back and forth over the noise of other shouts. Some of the activity was due to the ongoing state of emergency, certainly, but there was something else at work, something she couldn't isolate.

The pulse didn't cause all this, she thought, surveying the scene of chaos. *These people are stripping the place down to the chips.* Unable to spot Ra-Havreii in the bedlam, Vale snagged a passing engineer and asked where his department head had got to.

"Not present in this moment, Commander," said Ensign Urgar, a big ursinoid who seemed more concerned with the cycle inverter he had resting on one massive shoulder than in talking to his XO. "Engine master has come and gone."

"He was just here," said Vale, her temperature spiking higher than the considerable ambient heat. "And what's he got you people doing? It looks like a full overhaul."

"The engine master tells and it is for us to do," said the big engineer. "Though Urgar's mind is full of questions. This grinding eats too many moments. Why not patch first and then upgrade when all is well, yes?"

Why not indeed? What the hell was Ra-Havreii doing? This was a damned Red Alert. *Titan* was a big metal bucket rolling in the dark right now—slow, stupid, defenseless. This was no time for anybody's eccentricities.

Then Troi's hand was on her arm, tugging her gently away from the scene.

"I'll deal with Ra-Havreii," she said softly, having obviously zeroed in on the inspiration for Vale's current emotional turmoil. "Can you get this place under control?"

Vale nodded curtly. Troi was back in the lift an instant later, her mission set. Vale took a breath, turned back to the theater of pandemonium.

"Attention," she said, shouting to be heard over the cacophony of voices. After her third try and smacking a spanner against the bulkhead, they stopped and looked her way. "All hands are to belay every order that doesn't include getting this ship back online ASAP. If it's patchable, patch it. No unnecessary swaps, no upgrades that aren't one hundred percent required. Understood?"

It was. From their faces she could tell that some of them were even relieved to be given an order they could comprehend. Ra-Havreii was definitely off the map this time.

"We'll need a separate team in each of the nacelle conduits," said Xin Ra-Havreii to a very tense-looking Ensign Rossini. The latter was doing his best to keep pace with the Efrosian's longer strides while simultaneously entering the senior officer's orders into his padd. "There won't be time to replace the flow couplings once the core is back online."

He would have gone on—there was a lot more to do, more than anyone knew—but he found himself struck speechless by the dark cloud hovering near his quarters.

"That will be all for now, Ensign," he said, dismissing the grateful Rossini without a glance. "Well, Counselor Troi, to what do I owe the pleasure?"

"This isn't a social call, Doctor," said Troi in a glacial tone. "Your conduct has become too erratic to ignore."

"Ah," said Ra-Havreii, managing what Troi supposed was meant to be a wry grin. "If we're going to talk about me, might I suggest we do it inside my quarters?"

"We're in the middle of a Red Alert, Commander—" Troi began.

"Precisely," said the engineer as the doors to his quarters parted. "Let's talk inside."

He was across the threshold before she could respond, and while his tone was upbeat, there was another emotion comet-trailing off him that raised her concerns even higher. Seeing little alternative, she followed him in.

Ra-Havreii's quarters were more Spartan than Troi expected. Contained in the three small rooms with their regulation-issue off-white walls were a regulation couch, regulation desk and chair, regulation dining table, and in the much-discussed Ra-Havreii sleeping area, a simple standard-issue bed.

Titan had been out of the dock for months. Ra-Havreii had been aboard nearly all that time, and yet he had not moved in. There was not one personal modification to his regulation personal space.

Under the strictest conditions even a Vulcan could be expected to display an IDIC symbol or construct a meditation shrine. Xin Ra-Havreii, *Titan*'s most notorious hedonist, had nothing. That, coupled with the thick aura—what was that, guilt? melancholy?—that emanated from him, made the hackles on Troi's neck stand at attention.

"*Luna 80102,* Second Model in D Minor," said Ra-Havreii as he dropped into the chair. Immediately the room was filled with the sounds of a string sextet playing what sounded like a combination of Terran music—classical Japanese—and a Romulan lute chorus. For several moments Troi was fascinated in spite of herself. The melody was quite lovely, the interplay of sounds both delicate and somehow powerful, but a couple of discordant notes snapped her back to reality.

Ra-Havreii hushed her first two attempts to engage him, seeming lost in the complex interplay of sounds.

"Hm?" he said at last, coming back from wherever he'd been. "Did you say something, Counselor?"

"You can't continue this way, Xin," said Troi. "You're using your job to exorcise your personal demons."

"I am?"

"I saw what was going on in engineering," said Troi. "You were supposed to be getting *Titan* running properly again as quickly as possible. Instead, you had your people performing what looked to me like a complete overhaul."

"And by this you gleaned I was somehow working out feelings I've been sublimating about my past mistakes." He paused to listen to a particularly complex refrain before going on. "Is that it?"

"Close enough," she said.

"Let's assume you're right," he said. "Isn't it best to let the patient cure himself whenever possible?"

"Sadly," she said, "that's not always how it works."

"I'm the engineer," he said as the music swelled around them. "Shouldn't I be telling you how things work?"

There was another discordant note. Ra-Havreii cocked his head to one side, listening, as the note became a progression of jumbled sounds quite unlike the rest of the admittedly unusual piece.

"Don't joke," she said, ignoring the noise.

"Just a moment, Counselor," said Ra-Havreii, clearly annoyed by her interruption. "Stop, resume playback at the beginning of the last phrase."

The music returned, its lilting melody permeating the room for a few seconds until the dischord reappeared. Again Ra-Havreii's aspect hovered somewhere between aggravation and curiosity, and Troi was at a loss to find the line between them.

Something was burning inside the engineer; that was obvious. She could feel his turmoil almost as acutely as she did her own, though, as usual, she couldn't pinpoint the exact source. If this odd musical interlude was an attempt to soothe himself, it didn't seem to be working.

"I'd thought you'd agreed we would discuss any recurrence in your feelings about the *Luna* incident," said Troi eventually.

"What do you mean by that, Counselor?" he asked.

"You said the title of this piece was *Luna,* didn't you?" she said. "And I know how serious threats to *Titan* sometimes cause you to relive certain aspects of the *Luna* disaster."

"Yes, well," said Ra-Havreii, still seemingly a bit distracted. "I'm sure I will always carry some baggage from that . . . event."

"Don't you think it might be helpful to work on putting that baggage away?"

"There's away, Madame Troi," said Ra-Havreii as the music resumed its normal pleasant strains, "and there's *away*. In either case, I assure you, I have myself, my baggage, and my demons well in hand."

Why do they always lie? thought Troi. *They have to know that I'll know.*

She could sense, despite his serene exterior, that he was hanging on to his composure by his fingernails. If anything, listening to this music seemed somehow to make matters worse.

"There's no need to put up a front with me, Xin," said

Troi, trying to navigate another way into the Efrosian's psyche. "You know I can feel when you're—"

"Stop," he said, rising. It was only when the music evaporated without returning that Troi realized he hadn't meant her.

She watched as he gathered up his padd, tapped in some commands, and rose to go. Red emergency lighting spilled in from the corridor beyond, casting the engineer's sinuous frame into a stark black silhouette.

"Are you coming, Counselor?"

"Commander Vale has engineering under control, Xin," she said. "I think we should get to the bottom of what's happening with you."

"What's happening, Madame Troi," said Ra-Havreii, "is that I've just discovered precisely what knocked *Titan* out of warp and is currently running roughshod over her systems. I would like to inform the captain of my findings, as I'm sure he'd consider them to be of great interest. However, if you believe the ship and crew would be better served by my sitting here with you and discussing my feelings, I will be happy to oblige."

Aside from Dr. Ree, who tended to be chipper even under the most trying circumstances, and thus eager as ever for small talk, the forward observation lounge on deck one was silent as a crypt. Vale studied the room's occupants with interest as they awaited the captain's arrival.

Troi sat to the left of the table's head, directly opposite Vale. She seemed deeply focused on the activity of her hands, which were folded in front of her on the tabletop. No eye contact. No comment. No innocuous conversation.

Whenever not focused on a task, it seemed, she withdrew into herself, storm cloud waiting to burst.

Beside her sat Tuvok, still tapping some last-minute input into his padd, his placid exterior betraying nothing of his inner workings. Next came Jaza, standing before the viewports, his back to the room, his hands folded behind him in apparent repose as he gazed out at the surrounding void.

At the foot of the table was Ree, cheerful Ree, burbling on about how the remarkable Dr. Bralik had missed her calling by going into geology.

"She has a bedside manner most physicians would eviscerate their own offspring to possess," he said. "She hasn't left Pazlar's side since she arrived in sickbay."

"She's not underfoot?" said Vale.

"Far from it," said Ree. "In addition to her own work, she has managed to be quite helpful as some of my staff were injured in the pulse. An exceptional creature."

"Where is Captain Riker?" said Ra-Havreii. He too aped the appearance of someone in repose. His eyes were closed, his long fingers forming a pyramid in front of his face. Framed by his mane of silver-white hair, his face was grimly set. Xin Ra-Havreii the libertine was gone. This was Dr. Ra-Havreii, one of the Federation's most apt pupils in the study of warp physics.

"The captain will be here when he's ready to begin the meeting, Commander," Vale said in a warning tone. The Efrosian nodded his head slightly and was quiet again.

She might have felt better about that small victory over the engineer, but the hairs standing at attention on her forearms told Vale they were about to be treated to another of Will Riker's patented improvisations. Wonderful. Under these circumstances, that should go over about as well as a tribble at a Klingon wedding.

"The Prophets have deemed patience one of the five necessary aspects, Xin," said Jaza, his back still to the room.

"Considering their relationship to Bajor, Mr. Jaza," said the engineer, "that is small wonder."

"Why would you say that?" asked Jaza.

"It seems reasonable to assume, when one party is sufficiently superior to another, the former must exert inordinate amounts of patience if only to maintain sanity."

"The Prophets teach that there are no such things as superior and inferior," said Jaza. "Only those minds that open and those that don't."

"Yes," said Ra-Havreii. "That sounds exactly like something the superior would tell the inf—"

"All right, that's about enough from both of you," said Vale, her own patience having reached its limit.

"Your pardon, Commander," Jaza said.

"My apologies," said Ra-Havreii.

The silence was almost worse than the verbal sparring. It made the tension more palpable, if that were possible. *Too thick for a thin blade,* as her mother might have said. Much of the tension seemed to orbit Ra-Havreii, and after her recent duty in engineering, Vale could understand why. The man was infuriating. Genius could only deflect so much.

Vale wondered how she looked to them. Did any of her own disquiet show on her face? Was her anxiety over the slow, top-down dissolution of Will Riker's grand experiment as obvious and powerful as it felt? She hoped not.

"All right," Riker said as the doors parted and he strode into the room. He'd been on his feet for more than a day, coordinating departments, pitching in with repairs, ensuring that his ship and his crew were as secure as possible under the circumstances. You'd never know it to look at him. Best poker face in two quadrants. "Let's get to it."

There were two women with him—the taller one was a gold-skinned Selenean ensign. Her name was Eera Maren or Arda Oden—something like that. Vale had a vague recollection that she was in communications or a related department. The shorter female was an Antaran, thick boned and sullen eyed for some reason. She looked sturdy enough. Both ensigns wore service yellow. Why Riker felt their presence was necessary was a mystery.

She caught Jaza looking at the Selenean with the queerest expression on his face. He seemed to be trying to work something out. The ensign only smiled back at him politely as he took his seat.

"I trust you've had time to peruse my report," said Ra-Havreii, coming out of his faux trance.

"*Titan* was hit by some kind of massive energetic pulse," said Riker, taking his place at the head of the table. The ensigns, without available seats, were content to hover by the door.

"A massive warp pulse, to be precise, Captain," said Ra-Havreii.

Jaza gave a derisive snort.

"You have a problem with Dr. Ra-Havreii's findings, Mr. Jaza?" said Riker. There was ice in his voice that Jaza failed to notice. Even the captain was on the jagged edge of something and in no mood for squabbling.

"No, sir," said the science officer, his tone betraying that his true meaning was the reverse. "But it's a fairly large leap to classify all this as the result of a warp pulse—a warp pulse intense enough to disrupt *Titan*'s systems, no less—without any sign of the ship that created it."

"It needn't have come from a ship," said Ra-Havreii.

"Unless there's a secret trinary pulsar around here that no one has seen," said Jaza. "It had to be someone's version of a ship."

"Perhaps the ship was cloaked," offered Ree.

"No," said Jaza, frowning. "Local conditions would disrupt a cloak just as they have all of *Titan*'s energetic systems."

"In fact, there are a number of devices that could generate such a pulse," Ra-Havreii said. "I've invented some of them myself."

"There's no ship," said Jaza. "There's no pulsar. There is nothing detectable out there that could have caused this. With *Titan*'s enhanced sensors, that means there's nothing out there."

"Yet *Titan* was definitely hit by a warp pulse," said Ra-Havreii. "What is your explanation?"

"Still collating," said Jaza, clearly unhappy about the admission.

"A warp pulse is consistent with my findings as well," said Tuvok. "Though it fails to account for the remaining distortion of quantum synchronicity in the region."

"Exactly," Jaza said. "A warp pulse doesn't cause that sort of distortion and certainly nothing as sustained as what we're experiencing."

"Did you notice the Cochrane valences are in flux?" said the engineer.

"Of course we did, Ra-Havreii," snapped Jaza. "We're not idiots."

"Quantum synchronicity? Cochrane valences?" said Vale, attempting to keep the lid on. "We're not all scientists here, people. Keep it simple."

"In lay terms, it means the subatomic particles in this region have had their properties scrambled," said Jaza. "It's like sucking the O_2 away from a fire. The reactions that power the warp core, those that allow us to create and sustain a warp bubble around *Titan,* can't progress."

"What about impulse power?"

"We have enough to keep the lights on but little else," said Ra-Havreii.

"Becalmed," said Riker thoughtfully. Then, when he noticed the confusion on the faces of the others, he added, "It's how ancient Terran sailors described a ship being unable to catch the wind."

"It is an apt analogy, Captain," said Tuvok. "*Titan* cannot move until we counteract the ongoing effect."

"It will be difficult to do that if we're hit by another pulse," said Ra-Havreii.

"You think that's likely?" said Riker.

"Though I've never heard of an occurrence on this scale, quantum disruptions are common with primitive warp devices, Captain," said Ra-Havreii. "Whoever is using such low-end technology almost certainly has no idea of its grander effect. Thus they have no reason to stop."

"I don't understand why you're so sure that the pulse was caused by sentients," said Troi. "I'm not sensing anything in this area outside of *Titan*'s crew."

"If you'll allow us, ma'am," said a low voice from behind them. "I think we can answer that."

Everyone's head turned toward the two ensigns who had been standing nearby, apparently awaiting the opportunity to speak.

"For those of you who are unfamiliar with them," Riker said, "these are Ensigns Loolooa Tareshini and Y'lira Modan. It seems, while all of us were trying to keep the ship in one piece, the ensigns found our culprits."

"Well," said Modan, stepping forward, her partner now obviously a little too nervous to go on. "We found their footprints at least." Her thick braids shifted ever so slightly as her gaze swiveled between the faces of her superiors.

"Footprints?" said Ree. "What does that mean?"

"We're cryptolinguists," said Tareshini, chiming in again. "Whenever *Titan* encounters anything that could be classified as a signal of sentient origin, all relevant data is automatically cross-linked with our work stations."

"Signal of sentient origin," Jaza repeated. "By that I take it you mean something other than the Starfleet signal we were investigating."

"No, sir," said Tareshini nervously. "I mean, yes, sir. But there's more. A lot more."

"The Starfleet signal was affected by the same distortion that we understand corrupted your mapping of Occultus Ora," said Modan. Jaza looked about to interject something but instead leaned back in his seat, letting the younger woman go on. "You were so occupied trying to salvage the damage caused by the quantum ripples, you didn't give the ripples themselves more than a cursory look. We did."

"What prompted you to look at all?" said Ra-Havreii.

"Candidly, sir, we didn't know what we were seeing," said Tareshini. "The computer kept informing us of a pattern being present, but it took us all this time to isolate it. And, of course, the pulse didn't help."

"And what is that pattern, Ensign?" said Tuvok. He had left off his note taking and had fixed Tareshini with that penetrating stare for which his people were famous.

"Each of the quantum ripples contains signal information," said Tareshini. "This information corresponds to the same sort of signal bleed we'd detect from broadcasts coming off a planetary civilization with class K technological development or better."

"But the quantum rippling is just an aftereffect," said Jaza. "Like waves in a pond after a stone drops in."

"Nonetheless, sir," said the Antarean ensign, clearly excited. "I found what has to be months, perhaps years, of broadcast signal bleed—informational communications, some sort of dramatic entertainment, sports contests—all compressed and recompressed so many times they initially came across as static."

"How is that possible?" said Jaza.

"We don't know, sir," said Modan. "Our métier is linguistics, code-breaking, not physics."

"This certainly adds weight to the theory that the pulse was created by sentients," said Riker. "If we can find these people, we might be able to convince them to stop whatever it is they're doing that's causing this."

"At least until we make repairs and locate *Charon,*" said Vale. "I'd settle for that."

It was clear from the electric silence that descended

upon the party that more than a few of those present agreed with the XO, though Troi cautioned against too much optimism. There were still a great many unknowns to account for, any one of which could pull the rug out from under them.

"After all, we have no idea as yet who these people are," she said. "Or how they may respond to an alien first contact."

"Well," said the captain. "Let's hope for the best and plan for the worst."

"In other words," said Vale, forcing her face into a plastic grin, "standard operating procedure."

"Well put, Number One," said Riker.

For a moment, the frictions that had been burning the life out of the room regressed to a simple simmer.

Captain Riker, grateful for the momentary sea change, sailed forward, tasking his people with providing him with as many options as they could in as short a time as possible.

The cryptolinguists' information had to be catalogued and translated. The mystery civilization had to be found, understood, and contacted.

Titan was almost completely dead in space, and though she seemed to have ridden out the worst of the pulse effect, it was clear she wasn't going anywhere. There were hours of hard work ahead on that score, if not days.

Their duties set, the officers fairly scrambled to get to work, leaving Vale alone.

"That was enlightening," said a scratchy, high-pitched voice, apparently from nowhere. "And this was a much better plan than hiding me in a satchel."

"You heard all of it then," said Vale.

"With ears this size?" said Huilan, climbing out from where he'd concealed himself beneath the table. "Most definitely."

"And?"

"And," said the little S'ti'ach, scrambling up into what had been Troi's chair. "I think you're right about them all." Vale knew it was only an illusion created by the natural structure of his face, but Huilan's perpetual smile softened her mood somewhat.

"So, I'm right that the command staff is on the verge of a complete meltdown," said Vale. "Great."

"But the pigment in your hair smells lovely," said Huilan. "Take comfort in that."

Hours crept along like weeks as the crew split their time between repairing as much of *Titan* as they could and ferreting out the location of the mystery aliens deemed responsible for their predicament.

The warp core gave the engineers fits, refusing to initialize despite their most creative efforts. *Titan*'s sensor nets, ironically the most durable of the state-of-the-art systems, were back online, their operators trying furiously to penetrate the soup of exotic particles that held the ship in the subatomic equivalent of a tar pit.

As more of the mystery signals were tagged and deciphered, Troi spent increasing time shuttling between Tuvok and Jaza's coordinated effort to pinpoint the broadcast source and Ensign Modan's station in the linguistics lab.

If nothing else, Vale was grateful that their predicament had forced Troi squarely into her role as diplomatic officer, leaving Counselors Huilan and Pral glasch Haaj to manage the emotional well-being of the crew.

Ra-Havreii remained a problem, but no longer a serious one. Once Riker had spelled out in no uncertain terms precisely how little leeway the engineer had when it came to upgrading versus repairing, the chief engineer had beat a polite but clear retreat back to his quarters.

Under normal circumstances Vale would have forced him back onto the floor with the rest of his people. Yet, somehow, in spite of his self-imposed mini-exile, Ra-Havreii managed to stay on top of the repair schedule, disseminating the necessary orders and recommendations via the comms. Department heads—particularly chief engineers—were afforded a degree of latitude in how they ran things in their corners of a starship. The Efrosian's tendency to ruffle feathers notwithstanding, Vale had to concede that he was getting the job done.

The impulse engines, while still unable to shift *Titan* more than a few thousand kilometers in any direction, managed to remain a point or two above the red zone.

Good enough, she thought, leaning back in her chair for a quick look around the bridge. Ensign Lavena, having wrestled first with her helm control console and then with the overloaded chipset meant to facilitate that control, seemed finally content with her lot. She and Ensign Revtem Prin Oorteshk, the beta shift navigator, were occupying themselves with increasingly esoteric theories as to how they might shift the ship's position should drive capability never return.

Vale enjoyed Oorteshk whenever it was present. It gave off an agreeable odor of mint when it was pleased, which was, apparently, most of the time. It spoke by vibrating the reedy protuberances around its oral cavity, giving its words a breathy, almost childlike tone and lilt.

"Controlled plasma eruption from one of the nacelles," said Oorteshk. "Big enough blast, we spin out of this swamp too quick, I think."

"And spin and spin," said Lavena with a snort that created a flow of small bubbles behind her hydration suit's faceplate. "No directional control. No friction to slow us down or stop us."

"Sure, we stop," said Oorteshk. "We explode second nacelle, force counterinertial reaction. Too easy."

"So your solution is to blow both the nacelles and leave us adrift in some other equally unmapped part of the Beta Quadrant?"

"Contact other starships, wait for pickup," said Oorteshk. "Spend interim swimming with Lavena."

"I'm not sure your epidermis could take the salt content in my pool, Oort," said Lavena.

"For Aili Lavena, many dangers could be risked."

Vale smiled. For a sexless being, Oorteshk was a hell of a flirt.

The captain was pretty well locked into a triangular tennis match, between working with Tuvok and Jaza on the sensor modifications, Ra-Havreii with power distribution, and Vale's own seven billion crew-related tasks. His hands were full, and from what she could tell, he was happy to have them so. And with Troi equally engaged by the crisis, whatever was going on between them had been sidelined for the time being, as well it should be. But Vale's concerns remained, and not just for the sake of the ship, but for these two people she considered her friends.

"The captain's and Deanna's solution to their problem seems correct," Huilan volunteered in their most recent clandestine turbolift chat.

"They're too busy to be working on it," said Vale. "I'm not sure that actually solves anything."

"Their scents are less mingled, true. But both their rates of respiration are within the norm."

"So, they're breathing okay."

"They seem to require distance from one another, Commander. *Titan*'s current predicament provides that."

"How much distance can they get?" said Vale. "This isn't that big a ship."

"We'll have to watch and see what develops between them."

Excellent. More waiting for the other boot to kick.

"And Dr. Ra-Havreii," said Vale wondering just how long she could extend her current round of "spot checks" before the captain began looking for her. "What's the prognosis there?"

For once Huilan's perpetual smile seemed to fade a bit. His ears drooped ever so slightly and he let out a sigh that Vale thought was about two sizes too big for his body.

"S'ti'ach have a game," he said. "Volition. We all play. We mix fast-breeding bacteria to see which will out-evolve the others. Many new forms are created and die in the span of a few minutes."

"Sounds interesting," said Vale, and thought, *not to mention morally questionable.* "What's it got to do with Ra-Havreii?"

"The winner of the game is the one with the most complex surviving bacteria," said Huilan. "Observing our chief engineer was like watching the championship match of Volition."

"If one more person tells me he's *complex*—"

"Then let me say simply that I begin to see why Deanna kept his therapy for herself."

"I notice he's still dictating things from his quarters," Vale said.

"Which seems also to suit both his staff and the ship," said Huilan. "Obviously isolation is not a permanent solution, but for now, at least, his eccentricity seems to be serving the repair effort rather than hindering it."

"So," Vale said, resigning herself to Huilan's hands-off approach. "We just tread water with Ra-Havreii."

"For now, yes."

"And we just trust that Will and Deanna can solve whatever's going on between them on their own?"

"In my experience with primates, that way is often best."

" 'Primates?' " said Vale, not sure if she and all the other humans on *Titan* weren't being insulted.

"With mates of any sort," said Huilan.

Chapter Four

REPORT OF PRELIMARY ANALYSIS AND EXTRAPOLATION
prepared by COMMANDER DEANNA TROI
(CDO, *U.S.S. TITAN*)

SUBJECT:
PLANET ORISHA
(STARFLEET DESIGNATION: Elysia Incendae II)

CLASS: M (variant)

Captain, as requested, after collating 35% of the data culled from the alien signal bleed, we believe we have enough information to provide a foundation for any action you may decide to take vis à vis First Contact. Be advised that this is only a preliminary assessment and that subsequent data retrieval may necessitate reformulation of any plan based upon these findings.

FINDINGS:

A) Planetary Characteristics

Elysia Incendae II is a Class-M planet with a variant oxygen-nitrogen atmosphere with a gravity of 5.1 on the Federation standard scale of measurement and orbiting Elysia Incendae (Class-G stellar body) at one hundred forty-two point six million kilometers.

Though it has no moons, it is likely that the two larger gas giants orbiting at the mid and outermost regions of the system serve to protect their smaller sibling from meteor strikes, allowing for life to thrive there over the last several billion years.

Elysia Incendae II is a lush world, composed of four contiguous landmasses and an H_20 ocean that covers three-fifths of the planet's surface. The atmosphere is rich with ambient water, the landmasses are thick with vegetation and teeming with a multitude of different forms of animal and insect life, many of which are, at this juncture, outside Starfleet's bestiary.

The dominant Orishan form is an insectoid species (see Xindi, Nasat, Lactran) who refer to themselves as the Children of Erykon.

B) Sociopolitical Development

Thus far we have been able to determine that the Orishan society is a modified theocracy, broken in three or more distinct castes and organized around worship of their deity, Erykon.

All Orishan communications, including entertainment and governmental transmissions, are oriented around the Orishans' perception of the wishes of their deity.

We cannot be sure how much is simply local custom and

how much is truth, but the snippets of Orishan history we have been able to retrieve thus far seem to indicate at least two and perhaps as many as six civilization-ending cataclysms over the last thousand years.

While we have no means as yet of determining the veracity of these beliefs, it is clear that the Orishans have organized much of their social and religious discourse around discussing and analyzing the significance of each of these events.

C) Technology

Current Orishan technology is approximately that of 23rd-century Earth or 15th-century Bajor, including etheric communications and multiple variant technologies used to manipulate energy fields, but where the cited Federation cultures always displayed a strong bent toward exploration and expansion, the Orishans are decidedly insular in their outlook.

There are indications that the Orishans may have been extremely violent in times past. Several discussions of ancient conflicts permeate the available data distillations, and for a society this stable and homogenous, there simply isn't the necessary spark to create large conflicts.

D) Physical Structure

At this point in our observations we have determined that the average Orishan (see holographic representation) stands roughly two meters tall and has six extremities—two legs and four upper arms, two on either side of its body. Like other insectoids, they seem possessed of a durable exoskeleton and sensory organs that include a set of antennae set on their heads above their four faceted eyes.

It is possible that this species has specialized representatives—hunters, workers, breeders, etc., each with variant characteristics—but at this time we have seen no evidence of this.

E) Addenda
They seem wholly uninterested in the universe at large or even in the local bodies and idiosyncrasies of their own system. All their attention seems focused on maintaining perfect piety in the eyes of their deity or, in this case, the Eye.

The Eye of Erykon is the dominant symbol of this culture, and while we are not yet sure of its full significance, it is clear that the Orishans believe the Eye to be a physical manifestation of some sort, capable of inflicting apocalyptic damage upon their civilization should some aspect be found wanting.

They have no artificial communication devices in orbit and seem to have organized themselves into hive-like cities of various sizes. There is no indication that they have developed any vehicle or technology capable of reaching much less traveling in space. They are simply not interested in anything outside their religious construct of the universe.

RECOMMENDATIONS:
The Orishans, stated, are not truly xenophobic, only intensely insular. Their single driving ethos seems so far to be worship of Erykon and fear of this so-called Eye.

Under normal circumstances I would advise we bypass this planet or, at most, leave a clandestine observation team behind according to the "duck blind" scenario, to get a better idea of how well they will handle a true First Contact situation.

Of course, these are not normal circumstances, so the expected recommendations do not apply. We will have to improvise something.

Filed on Stardate 58443.7 by Commander Deanna Troi, Diplomatic Officer, *U.S.S. TITAN*

DISTRIBUTION: Capt. W.T. Riker; Cmdr. C.J. Vale; Cmdr. Tuvok; Cmdr. S.Y.E. Ree, Cmdr. Jaza N.; Lt. Cmdr. R. Keru, Cmdr. X. Ra-Havreii, inclusive.

"Wait a minute," said Vale, looking up from the padd in disbelief. "You're saying these people are in the process of developing warp technology, but they don't plan to use it for space travel?"

"That seems to be the case," said Troi. "They're extremely insular, and while they are aware of the larger universe and the possibility of alien intelligence, they have no interest in exploration."

It was obvious that no one in the room was happy with this news, least of all Captain Riker. His eyes had taken on a hooded, steely quality, the one he generally reserved for facing down opponents in contests of resolve.

Troi didn't need her telepathy or her telempathy to know what he was thinking. Starfleet's Prime Directive was in danger of dropping down on their plans with the force of an archaic firewall.

Will? she touched his mind tentatively, nervous after their long weeks on opposite sides of the chasm.

He blocked her, as had become his custom, keeping her probing mind out of even the shallows of his, just as completely as he had on every other recent occasion.

It was as if he'd shut his mental door, boarded it up, and painted DO NOT ENTER in large garish letters across its face.

Behind that door, as the briefing continued, Riker's mind flickered like lightning between the regulations, searching for any loophole or exception, anything that would allow them to save their lives without risking the Orishans' natural development.

"Are we absolutely certain of these findings?" he asked at length.

"Thus far the data seem to indicate a uniform cultural viewpoint, sir," said Tuvok. "They are not truly xenophobic so much as intensely pious and self-focused."

"Granted, we've only deciphered about a tenth of what's been culled from their transmissions, Captain," said Troi.

"I'm still bothered by the fact that there was so much signal compression," said Jaza. "There's some missing piece here that I don't understand."

"We can ask the Orishans about it, maybe," said Modan. "Once we contact them."

The rest of the news, including the revelations about the Orishans, was pretty bleak.

Science and engineering had done what they could to get *Titan* moving again, which, as it turned out, wasn't much.

Power held steady at just above forty percent, allowing the crew to resume a version of normalcy, but *Titan* was still becalmed, as Riker had put it.

The quantum distortion that surrounded them continued to prevent the shields from achieving full strength and the phasers from initializing. It also prevented any motion beyond the herky-jerky one hundred meter lurches that so distressed Ensign Lavena and currently kept Xin Ra-Havreii cloistered away in his quarters.

When he'd reconvened his staff, Riker had hoped to be presented with more than just a few more scraps of cultural data. There was something about the Orishans that made him nervous, though he couldn't yet say why.

Cultural myopia wasn't unusual, even in known space. In fact, out-and-out xenophobia was common. The Organians, the Melkotians, even the Daledians had all taken the protection of their privacy to what seemed to many to be insane extremes. But these sorts of cultures, when they developed warp tech, either exploited it for limited space travel or, as with the Organians, had no use for it at all.

Beings from a culture that avoided the sky but wielded a technology with that much destructive potential had to be handled with extreme delicacy if they were handled at all.

"Why would one develop warp technology if not to move between worlds?" asked Dr. Ree.

"Power," said Jaza. "A stable warp reactor generates a considerable amount of energy. A single rudimentary device could power an entire planetary culture for centuries."

"Wow," said Vale. "Why haven't I ever heard of anyone using warp generators that way?"

"It's too dangerous," said Jaza. "Creating a warp field inside a planet's atmosphere and having it destabilize could have catastrophic effects, and perhaps not confined to the planet."

"That's if things go wrong," said Ra-Havreii. "If they continue using their device without trouble, *Titan* will be trapped here indefinitely."

Indefinitely. It might as well mean infinitely. The same conditions that prevented *Titan* from regaining power, from sparking the warp core, from using nearly any of its energy-based systems were the same ones that prevented them from scanning the area for their missing sister ship or contacting it even if they should succeed in finding it.

"I have the beginnings of a notion about the warp core, Captain," said Ra-Havreii thoughtfully, after the silence stretched too far. "And another about, perhaps, using the shuttles to tow us free of the affected area."

"The problem with that idea," Jaza said, "is that the second the shuttles launch, they'll be subjected to the distortion effect. They'll be just as becalmed as we are."

"Can we contact the Orishans by subspace?" said Vale. "Just let them know there's somebody up here who needs them to hold off their experiments for a while?"

"Not at the present time, Commander," said Tuvok. "The distortion effect, though somewhat weaker around the planet Orisha, is also in a more pronounced state of flux. While their signals seem capable of bleeding into open space, *Titan* lacks both the technology and the power to punch through the flux from the outside."

"Even if we are able to figure some way of contacting them," said Jaza. "It may not be as simple as just asking them to please stop."

"Are you concerned about the potential Prime Directive violation, Commander?" asked Tuvok.

Jaza frowned. "Aren't you?"

"I admit this situation does present some unique permutations," said the Vulcan judiciously.

"Pardon me," said Ree, his great reptilian head cocked slightly to the side. "I don't believe I understand. How do these circumstances invoke the Prime Directive? Starfleet is prohibited from contacting civilizations before they have independently developed warp technology, yes?"

"That is correct, Doctor," said Tuvok.

"But our current predicament is due to these Orishans having done precisely that."

"Not exactly," said Troi, eliciting a look of mild confusion from Vale. What the hell was she talking about? It was clear from her expression that she too was uncomfortable with the way the conversation had turned. "The Orishans have warp technology, or a version of it, but they do not engage in space travel, so we may not be permitted to—"

"Wait," said Vale, switching from Troi to Riker. She knew her incredulity was plastered across her face like Hybarian wall art and she didn't care. "Are you saying, even though we know what's causing this and who's responsible, we aren't going to ask them to stop?"

No one spoke. No one moved. All their eyes were on the captain, waiting for the only response that actually mattered.

"You're all dismissed," he said at last. "Chris, Counselor, you stay."

"You can't be serious," said Vale. "You can't honestly be considering not contacting the Orishans."

"I think she's right, Will," said Troi softly. It wasn't the most solid declaration of support one might hope for. Vale wasn't sure how happy she was to have the counselor on her side. The trouble between her and her husband couldn't possibly help his mood, which was darkening by the second. "I think we have to find some way to—"

"John Gill," he said, cutting her off. By this time he had positioned himself by the plexi window wall and was gazing out into the black.

"Don't give me that," said Troi, moving closer. "There's no similarity." She kept her distance though. Something about Riker's posture screamed *back off.*

"Leonard McCoy," he said, turning to face her.

"Will . . ."

"Benjamin Sisko," he said and rattled off several more names in quick succession. "James Kirk, Mark Jameson, Rudolph Ransom, Joshua Grant."

Vale recognized some of the names of course—Sisko and Kirk were immediately ID'd—but the others gave her trouble. Troi obviously knew them all. With each one, she seemed to withdraw further into her original mask of emotional distance. He was striking at her with the names, obviously, but how?

Riker spat out more names—Tracey, Pike, April, Calhoun, B'Liit. Still more captains? What did they have in common? What did any of them have to do with *Titan*'s current distress?

"Jean-Luc Picard," said Troi, as if coming to the end of some lengthy and fantastically constructed legal argument. To Vale her demeanor was like that of an Izarian judge that had slammed her gavel down on the marble top of the bench.

Riker stiffened, almost as though he'd been told to snap to attention.

"No, dammit," he said, slamming one big fist down on the conference table, making Vale's padd dance. "No."

He left the two women standing there, silent in the wake of his anger. When Vale had deemed an appropriate amount of time had passed, she asked what the hell that had been about.

"All of those people have violated the Prime Directive, Christine," said Troi. Her voice was low, full of some powerful emotion. Anger? Disgust? It was too complex for Vale to decipher. "Almost all of their violations brought irreversible change, sometimes complete destruction to an entire culture. Will doesn't want to be added to the list."

"But," said Vale. "I thought—I mean, he's never been happy with the PD."

"He's fine with the spirit of the directive," said Troi, clearly in agreement with her husband on this matter. "It's the letter he doesn't like. How can we judge the worthiness of a culture simply by the level of their technological development? There are many things that constitute civilization and maturity. Why is technology the Federation's only arbiter?"

Vale didn't have an answer. Warp tech was so potentially volatile—even more than she'd first imagined, thanks to her attendance at the Jaza and Ra-Havreii Show—that it seemed to her the perfect yardstick by which to measure a new culture.

If a civilization could handle it without blowing itself up, it followed that they were mature enough to be invited into the larger universe, the one teeming with beings totally unlike themselves.

If they weren't mature enough? Ka-boom; they wiped themselves out with escalating warfare or planetary environmental degradation, cleaning the slate and giving some other species its shot in the sun.

It had always seemed so cut and dried to her, a perfect expression of everything the Federation stood for. Now, with *Titan* in its current state, breaching the PD might be their only way to freedom.

Not so easy now, eh? said her mother's voice from the past. *Not quite the grand adventure you thought.*

"There are three hundred and fifty sentients on *Titan,* Deanna," said Vale quietly. "There are children here. Babies."

Another indecipherable expression, possibly some esoteric mixture of surprise and sorrow, flickered across Troi's face and was gone.

"He knows that, Commander," she said. "He knows." The doors shushed open, Troi passed through, and Vale was alone with her thoughts.

Males. Can't live with them. Can't rip out their throats and eat them for supper.

Ensign Hriss had thought that so many times during her days at the Academy and her subsequent duty aboard the *U.S.S. Voorhees*. Tonight was no different.

She'd bristled when Keru had assigned her this duty. In the middle of a Red Alert, pandemonium and shattered tech all over and he sticks her down here in the guts looking after ships that can't fly and would have nowhere to go if they could. Was he expecting crazed crew members to steal one of these tubs and scramble off into the black?

It would be a hell of a trick, considering the current state of affairs.

Nevertheless, "It's not all blood and sex, Hriss," Keru had told her. "Sometimes you get to sit."

So she sat in the shadows of the huge empty hangar, the minutes crawling over her fur like blood mites.

The hangar's high vaulted ceiling, the many deck protrusions, the hulking shapes of the new heavy-duty shuttles all combined to remind her of the great cavern on Cait and the gatherings of the various prides that she had attended there in her youth.

Even then she had never been content to sit with the other cubs through the interminable boasting speeches of the elder males.

Females do all the work, she had thought to herself more than once. *Why am I even listening to this nonsense?*

Males. They had their uses, certainly, some of them quite pleasant, but, once they fell to chattering, it could be hours before anything meaningful got done. And it seemed so regardless of the species.

Aside from Mr. Tuvok, who managed to adopt an appropriately stoic demeanor, even the males who outranked her could all stand a good grab by the scruff and a shake. Even Keru. What was he thinking sticking her down here when he could have saddled that cold fish Pava with the job? Andorians were good at standing around waiting. It was practically their religion.

Humanoid. Felinoid. Reptiloid. It didn't matter. Wherever you went, a male was a male was a male.

Hriss was a hunter, and while the art certainly employed stillness and quiet from time to time, it was only the quick bloody action of the culmination that brought sparkle to her eyes.

She amused herself by varying the path she took on her circuit of the hangar deck. Instead of simply walking the length and breadth of the place in the same clockwork fashion, Hriss devised a complex patrol pattern that involved climbing the nearly frictionless walls up to the shadowy heights and leaping from shuttle roof to shuttle roof as silently as possible.

She had just landed atop the massive, larger-than-normal heavy-duty shuttle *Ellington* and was eyeing the *Marsalis* as the site of her next perch when Mr. Jaza entered the hangar. He was followed in short order by Chief Engineer Ra-Havreii, who was obviously well into a snit.

"I'm telling you," said the Bajoran scientist sharply, turning on the engineer. "It can't work."

"It can," said Ra-Havreii. "When I was with the Skunkworks, we—"

"I don't need to hear another dissertation about your great past, Commander," said Jaza, cutting him off. "Everyone has a past."

"True," said the Efrosian. "But mine mostly involves research and discovery rather than, say, blowing up random Cardassians to make some arcane political point."

Hriss had never worked with Bajorans before coming aboard *Titan* and really not much since. Thus far the best she could tell about them was that they didn't smell as much like prey as other humanoids, which was a blessing. It was so hard sometimes not to just tear one of the furless apes open and eat, especially after pulling a double shift without a meal break.

Mr. Jaza was broad across the chest and long of limb like a Caitian male, and the hue of his flesh matched some of their coats. He was obviously intelligent. Starfleet valued that over blood skills for reasons Hriss sometimes still didn't quite grasp. You couldn't rise high in the sciences without a laser-sharp mind.

Hsuuri worked with Jaza closely and claimed to actually admire the man. Hsuuri was an odd one. She also seemed to have "admiration" for that skinny Cardassian creature, Dakal, having expressed clear appreciation about the changes in his scent whenever they were close. In fact, much to Hriss's distaste, she seemed to entertain the notion of exploring his obvious affection for her in depth.

Blech! Humans were one thing. Despite smelling like a good meal, some of them could be occasionally compelling. But Cardassians, with all those ridges and the constant odor of day-old *preth*? Never. She'd sooner bed down with Dr. Ree. Luckily she had Rriarr to keep her warm. Caitian males might be boastful and lazy, but they had their pleasant qualities as well.

Hriss was gratified that, thus far, neither of the senior officers had marked her presence; even the engineer's Efrosian ears weren't good enough for that. Though protocol required her to make her presence known to them, something in their postures told her it might be best to let them think they were alone for the time being.

"Is that what the problem is?" said Mr. Jaza, squaring off before the taller man. "That I was in the resistance?"

The engineer snorted. "Let's just say, while you were tossing bombs and dodging plasma bolts, I was reshaping warp theory."

"Meaning?"

"Meaning," said Ra-Havreii, "in matters of anything related to warp cores, warp propulsion, warp bubbles, warp theory, or warp technology, you would be wise to defer."

"*Titan* can't sustain a stable warp field, Doctor," said Mr. Jaza. "No amount of deference is going to change that."

"And what was it you said earlier about minds opening and closing, Mr. Jaza?"

Jaza's eyes narrowed.

"You're a specialist," the science officer said finally. "Specifically adapted to one set of tasks." He moved past Ra-Havreii, their shoulders brushing hard against each other briefly before he dropped into a crouch beside the *Ellington*. "But warp physics doesn't bypass quantum physics in every case." He gestured at the visible nacelle that ran the length of the shuttle's hull. "As long as the shuttle is inside the hangar bay, protected by *Titan*'s hull, it is possible we could form a stable warp field around it," he said. "But, the second it goes outside, the same randomization of quantum properties that's causing *Titan*'s problems will take effect. Even if you account for momentum and inertia—"

The science officer stopped speaking abruptly. His eyes were wide and his mouth frozen open in mid-sentence so that he reminded Hriss of a *shetr* calf she'd once stunned and then eaten. The look on his face was so suddenly comical that she was forced to stifle a chuckle.

Mr. Jaza stood and, ignoring Ra-Havreii completely, began to walk slowly around the edge of the *Ellington*.

Above him, hidden by shadows on the roof of the *Mar-*

salis, Hriss was struck again by how similar Mr. Jaza was to one of the males from back home.

He's stalking something, she thought. *He's definitely on the hunt.*

As the science officer walked, Ra-Havreii continued to lecture him about the vagaries of warp fields and how, with just a little creativity, he was sure they'd be able to light up the heavy-duty shuttles and use them to tow *Titan* to safety.

"No. We won't," said Jaza, rounding the far corner of the *Ellington,* returning briefly to his original spot beside the engineer. "But it doesn't matter. I've got a better idea."

"Please don't take offense, Mr. Jaza," said the Efrosian. "But I sincerely doubt that."

"I'm sorry," said Vale, silently praying she'd misheard or misunderstood. "You want us to *what*?"

Jaza repeated himself, outlining the hows and whys and the benefits and drawbacks of his notion and watched as his XO blanched at the thought.

"That's insane," she said finally.

"Maybe," he said. "But it should work for something the size, mass, and particularly the shape of a shuttle."

In clear desperation Vale looked to Xin Ra-Havreii, hoping that, at the very least, the friction he'd developed with Jaza might inspire him to throw a spanner into the works. No such luck. The engineer only stood by, stroking the edges of his mustache, humming that blasted tune, apparently lost in thought. Wonderful.

"You'll destroy the hangar," she said. "At least."

"I don't think so," said Jaza. "If we do this right, we'll just ding it up a bit. We're only talking about a microsecond or two. Barely enough time to perceive, much less do serious damage."

"I don't know, Najem." She was more than dubious. This was one of those insane schemes that would probably work but, if it didn't, could make their current situation astronomically worse. Not to mention killing several indispensable members of her crew.

"It'll work, Chris," said Jaza softly, noting her distress and placing a big gentle hand on her arm. The grip was firm, familiar, almost reassuring. "Just take it to the captain and let him decide."

"He wants to *what*?" said Will Riker from behind his desk at the far side of the ready room. He'd been cloistered away in there for the last couple of hours wrestling with his conscience, and it showed.

The captain's eyes had taken on that stony distant quality that Vale had learned to recognize and dislike. His jaw was clenched, set in a way that somehow made his features, normally puckish and engaging, into something that seemed carved from granite. Captains needed this quality of dispassionate calculation if they hoped to make the tough decisions, but she hated to see it evidenced so strongly in Will.

She also noted, for the first time, the stark contrast between the offices of Counselor Troi and her husband's ready room. While Troi's domain was rife with personal touches meant to put visitors at ease, Riker's was as impersonal as a room could be.

There was the desk with its computer access node. There was a standard-issue chair, high-backed, sitting behind the desk with her captain in it. There was one relief sculpture, also of standard issue, of the Federation insignia on the wall behind the chair.

That was it. It was as if Riker had set this place to remind himself that, once within it, he had no other role beyond that of ship's captain.

"Jaza wants to use the Picard Maneuver to get a heavy-duty shuttle into beaming distance from Orisha," she said. There was something about Jaza's plan that short-circuited the processes of a rational brain on the first couple of hearings. "Then the idea is to use maneuvering thrusters to land the shuttle there."

"And he wants to initiate while the shuttle is still in the hangar?" said Riker. Vale nodded.

"We lock the place down, erect some energy dampers to block most of the damage to the equipment, open the hangar doors, and let 'er rip," she said. "By the time the distortion out there destroys the warp bubble, they'll be light-minutes away. After that they can use thrusters to make planetfall."

"Bumpy ride," said Riker, mulling.

"It'll definitely be that," she said.

"And it's potentially a one-way trip if they can't make contact with the Orishans," he said. "If they don't, they'll be months away from *Titan* at sublight speeds."

"And there's still Ra-Havreii's hypothesis that the pulses could continue," she said. "Things could get much worse."

"Things could get much worse," he said to himself. "Well, that's always true, isn't it?"

She could tell something was ticking over in his brain but, as his expression still hadn't returned to normal, she wasn't eager to hear the result.

"Jaza knows the risks, but he thinks they're negligible compared to the alternative," she said.

"And Ra-Havreii?"

"He's unhappy about it, I think," she said. "But he signed off too."

"What do *you* think, Chris?"

There it was: recommendation time. For an awful moment she had the sense of all the members of *Titan*'s crew somehow looking in on her, listening intently, and judging how she answered.

Risk, maybe sacrifice, the lives of a few to save many. Was that always to be the equation?

"I think we don't have enough options to be picky," she said finally, pushing the faces and doubts away. Her own mind had followed his into that hard granite place. She hoped it didn't show. "I think we have to try it. Presuming you've made a decision about contacting the Orishans."

"Yes," he said, rising. "I have."

Once the order was given, things went fast. It was a relief for all concerned to finally be doing something to put an end to the disease rather than just temporarily patching a few symptoms.

The dampers went up all over the shuttlebay, their featureless ebony surfaces transforming it into a massive silver-black grid.

The *Ellington* was scoured from top to bottom by Ra-

Havreii's engineers, who replaced any circuit or chip that showed the slightest defect or wear.

The mission specialists were vetted and chosen—Vale as field commander, Ranul Keru as her second, Xin Ra-Havreii, who, in his capacity as warp specialist extraordinaire, insisted on joining the team, and of course Jaza. The wild card was Y'lira Modan, whose presence both Troi and Jaza deemed necessary but whose inexperience made Vale nervous. Modan was a bookworm and hadn't pulled more than the obligatory field time necessary to fulfill grade requirements. Weak link.

"I'll need her to help with any translation issues," Troi had told her. "The universal translator can't handle everything."

It was obvious early on that Troi assumed she was to be part of the team, which led to a minor dustup between her and the captain. He wanted her on *Titan;* something about her being needed more there than leading the away mission—something that, frankly, seemed a bit thin to Vale—but Troi would have none of it.

"I'm the diplomatic officer, Will," Troi reminded Riker. "We have no clear idea what we'll find there or how receptive the Orishans will be to our arrival. There is no one else as qualified to navigate potential trouble than me, and you know it."

The captain wasn't happy about it and grew visibly less so when his XO sided with his wife.

"You said it yourself," said Vale. "We have to do this right. We may only get one shot."

She *was* right. *They* were right, and the captain, realizing it, conceded the point.

"We're ready, sir," said Olivia Bolaji, emerging from the *Ellington* still wearing the same aura of unhappiness that she had during the entire exercise. "But I still think it's a mistake not to have an experienced pilot at the helm."

"I am an experienced pilot," said Jaza, coming down from the open hatchway behind her. "But, in this case, the computer will be doing the driving."

"I'd just be happier if I was with you, sir," said Bolaji. "Instead of just dropping in navigation algorithms for the autopilot."

"We'll be fine," said Jaza, grinning as if he knew something she didn't.

Y'lira Modan strapped herself into one of the two remaining jump seats, then waited while Ranul Keru checked her work. Despite the slight tremor in her voice, her face was a mask of calm. In fact, Modan herself still resembled nothing so much as an animated metal sculpture. If not for the occasional blink and the blue-on-black uniform, like all Seleneans, Modan looked as if she'd been hammered out of gold.

"You're good to go, Ensign," said Keru, dropping down into his own seat and buckling in.

"Wonderful," said Modan, her slender fingers fidgeting with her equipment bag. "The next time I get an inspiration, will one of you remind me to tell my department head instead of the captain?"

"Learn to love the chain of command," said Keru with a twinkle.

"I thought your people were pragmatists, Modan," said Jaza jauntily from the forward part of the cabin. It was his fourth time checking over the flight plan and computer commands. "That sounds an awful lot like worry."

"Different crèches cultivate different traits, Najem," said Modan, her voice firm again. "The Y'lira crèche was bred for curiosity, analysis, and flexibility of thought. I guess that means I can worry."

"Najem," huh? thought Vale. *Didn't realize things had got that far with them.* She had finished securing her own gear and safety harness and was accounting for the weapons and isolation suits with Keru.

While, in theory, this was a simple diplomatic mission, in her experience, going in with intel as spotty as what they currently had on the Orishans could lead to some potentially fatal misunderstandings.

In addition to the obligatory analysis and translation gear, she'd packed the team a brace of phasers, doubled up on the holographic isolation suits "just in case" and added a second quantum beacon on the off chance that the first might be somehow fatally compromised. Indeed, Keru himself was part of Vale's own emergency kit; the big Trill was one of the best close-quarters fighters on the ship. She wasn't sure she actually expected trouble from the Orishans, but if they brought some, having Keru along to help shut it down was more comforting than all those phasers.

"Anyway," said Keru, checking off the final inventory item and looking up. He gave Modan a warm smile from behind his thick mustache. "A little worry is healthy. Lets the universe know you have respect for it."

"Just remember your job and follow orders, Ensign," said Vale. "You'll be fine."

"We'll all be fine," said Jaza, dropping into the jump seat beside Modan's. Despite the danger of what they were about to attempt and the larger consequences should any part of the attempt fail, the Bajoran scientist seemed almost happy. "I have no doubt about it."

"More wisdom from your Prophets, Mr. Jaza?" said Ra-Havreii. He'd been mostly silent as they waited for the final systems check to conclude, only humming occasionally to himself some breezy Efrosian tune.

"Well, yes, as a matter of fact," said Jaza, clicking the final buckle into place and checking over his own field kit. Ra-Havreii snorted derisively. Jaza ignored him. "But, in this case, we don't have to look to the Prophets for guidance."

"What then?" said Modan.

"Simple," said Jaza. "Dr. Ra-Havreii is here with us. He wouldn't have set foot inside this thing if he wasn't certain he'd be coming back."

Everyone laughed at that, even the engineer, though it was anybody's guess whether or not any of the apparent relief of tension was authentic.

Troi would know, thought Vale absently as her gaze strayed from the members of her team to the view of the hangar beyond the forward canopy. The entire hangar was shrouded in light-absorbing black, the variously configured energy dampers that would, theoretically, keep the shuttle's warp field from destroying the place.

Here and there engineers in EVA gear scurried back and forth, securing couplings and quadruple-checking relevant systems. They seemed so small in comparison to all that black. Even the massive hangar doors, normally open to space, were currently closed, the force field that usually protected the deck from the hard vacuum having been rendered as inoperable as the rest of *Titan*'s energy shields.

As she took in the enormity of what they were about to attempt, it was difficult not to feel some nervousness about this whole thing. Jaza's plan was like a clock with a million working parts, the failure of any one of which would spell catastrophe.

She just wished they could get on with it. The longer they sat, the more time frayed nerves would have to fail altogether. Keru and Jaza were rock steady, of course, but she was less confident about Modan and Ra-Havreii. Living and working among even *Titan*'s diverse crew was one thing. The shared ethos of all present went a long way to smoothing otherwise rough edges and apparent inconsistencies. Putting their feet, unannounced, on alien dirt was another matter entirely. Still, between herself and the other veterans, there shouldn't be too much trouble from the rookies.

Just as Vale was wondering what the hell was keeping Troi, she appeared, followed closely by the captain. Both looked grim and said little beyond that conversation made necessary by their duties and positions.

Well. At least they'd get the breathing space that Dr. Huilan had claimed was necessary. *Take purchase where you find it,* as her mother used to say.

She could see they had been at it again, whatever it was, and it, whatever it was, had taken its toll on both of them. To the casual observer there was no trace of their secret conflict, but to Vale, the signs had become abundantly clear.

The tension in the captain's jaw, the steely focus of his eyes, the counselor's mask of placidity painting a false veneer over the emotions roiling beneath. Once again, as Troi took her place in the last empty jump seat, Vale felt a wave of melancholy wash over her, dredging up thoughts of battles she'd had with her mother over everything from what to wear to her induction ceremony for the Izar peace office to her choice to leave the family business for a life in the black.

It wasn't as intense as the storm that had taken her in the counselor's suite, but it was certainly noticeable. At least it was to Vale. The others seemed totally unaware of anything beyond their conversation about the mission and their chances of completing it.

"So. We know how this works," said Riker, his big frame forced to stoop in order to hang there in the open hatchway. He looked like a bear trying to squeeze into a foxhole. "The big doors open, the atmosphere vents, and then the countdown begins. Ten seconds later the shuttle will accelerate to warp two for just under three nanoseconds. About a minute after that you'll be in striking distance of Orisha and, hopefully, close enough to beam through the distortion."

"That's provided we make it out of the shuttlebay," said Modan, but only to herself.

"Yes, Ensign," said Ra-Havreii, having heard her. "Provided that. You see, a warp bubble—"

"No speech here, folks," said Riker, cutting the engineer off before he could build up a head of steam. "You all know your jobs. You know what's at stake. Get it done and get back here as soon as you can." His personal good-bye to his wife was something in the eyes. There was always something crackling between them that way, and now, despite their obvious troubles, it bound them still. What was the Betazoid word they used to describe that connection? *Imzadi?*

As he backed out of the hatch, Riker's eyes conveyed to Vale her own silent communication. *Bring them back, Chris.* It might not have been the same sort of empathic contact he enjoyed with Troi, but Vale got the message.

Then he was gone, and there was nothing left but the sounds of the hatch sealing shut behind him and the evenly modulated tones of the computer beginning its launch prep.

"Shuttlecraft Ellington *ready for launch,"* said the artificial female voice. *"All personnel please clear the flight deck."*

The EVA suits scrambled for the nearest exits, and soon the hangar was empty. For a few moments nothing stirred in the black and silver expanse, but then, almost imperceptibly at first, the enormous doors at the far end began to separate.

Vale was a little surprised to see the twinkles and black of normal space peeking in through the widening aperture. From all the trouble caused by these pulses and their aftereffect, she'd expected something more dramatic.

"Shuttlebay doors open," said the computer. *"Force shield protections offline. Atmosphere venting. Twenty-four seconds to shuttle launch. Twenty-two."*

As if anyone needed to be told. The outgassing was like a raging torrent outside the *Ellington,* the noise and violence of the air flow eliciting a nervous hiss from Y'lira

Modan and a few words of comfort in her ear from Troi.

"This is the worst part, Ensign," she said in what Vale guessed was the voice she usually reserved for agitated patients. "In a few seconds it'll all be over."

"I'm not sure that's the best choice of words, Commander," said Modan, but she smiled. Keru and Jaza both managed chuckles before they were given another update, this time from the *Ellington* itself.

"*Initializing warp core,*" said the second voice, in tones identical to that of *Titan*'s own. "*Safety protocols LII through QI, disabled. Modified flight control program initiating. Away team, secure for warp three in six seconds. Five seconds. Four seconds. Three seconds. Two seconds. One—*"

The final syllables were lost in the shattering of reality all around the little vessel. While the shuttle itself only shuddered a bit, for a portion of a moment that was nearly too brief to perceive, the shuttlebay around it and the field of stars outside fused into a single kaleidoscopic whole.

It was nothing like going to warp under normal circumstances. There was no streaming of stars, no sense of nondirectional acceleration. There was, for some of the team, only the momentary feeling of having neither weight nor mass, but it too was gone almost too quickly for their minds to process.

There was the fraction of a blinding flash, an instant of the warp drive whining under the strain of initialization and then, as abruptly as it had come, the moment was gone and so was the shuttlebay.

• • •

It took a second for Vale to realize the odd, high-pitched keening sound was coming from one of her teammates rather than the ship's warning system.

When the *Ellington* slammed back into normal space, it did so almost as violently as *Titan* had when it entered the Elysia Incendae system. Though pretty much everything was secured, including the team, several items—a loose padd, an unaccounted-for bag of clothing, and what looked like a forgotten sonic screwdriver—bounced around the shuttle like ball bearings fired into a zero-g omnasium.

The keening came from Y'lira Modan: some form of scream or other expression of distress, Vale surmised. She was the rookie here, and the surprise of reentry had shaken her spindly resolve. One of the flying objects had smacked into her golden metallic face.

Before Vale could do it herself, Jaza reached out a hand to Modan, quietly comforting her, reminding her that she and the rest of them were still alive, things were proceeding as they should.

"Take a breath, Modan," he said softly, watching as she pulled herself together. She glanced around at the rest of the team, all sitting stoic in the face of the jolt. Even Ra-Havreii seemed totally unflapped. "See? We're okay."

"*Warning,*" said the computer. "*Warp core offline. Artificial gravity and inertial dampers fatally compromised.*"

"We expected that," said Jaza, noting Modan's renewed distress. It was odd seeing someone who looked like a gold statue bend and twist like ordinary flesh. He made a mental note to study up on Selenean physiology when they got back to *Titan*.

"*Artificial gravity and inertial dampers online,*" said

the computer just as the team were feeling their stomachs again. *"Firing breaking thrusters."*

As the gravity took hold, Modan relaxed by degrees until she was apparently her old self again. With the exception of Ra-Havreii, who continued to softly hum away, the team sat in silence for the few moments it took the deceleration sequences to play out.

When the computer announced that they would drift for a few minutes before repositioning for their approach to Orisha, Jaza was unbuckled and up almost instantly. It was as if he were a sprinter and had been waiting for the sound of the starter pistol.

"Jaza," said Vale. "What the hell?"

"Come up and see," he said, disappearing from view as he slid down into the forward pilot's cradle.

Shooting Keru a quizzical look and getting the expected shrug in response, Vale unbuckled quickly and joined Jaza, dropping down beside him in the navigator's cradle. Unlike the smaller-type 1's, the *Ellington* was built for short-distance system hops. In a pinch it could function like a very small runabout. Vale had hoped for a more peaceful situation in which to shake the shuttles down, but she knew she could play only those cards she'd been dealt.

She looked over at the brown-skinned Bajoran in the pilot's seat, watching his hands tapping commands into the computer.

He's taking readings, she thought. *How optimistic can someone be? We've got a thirty-seventy chance of pulling this off, at best, and he's got to know it.*

Yet, despite the danger and the ongoing potential for complete ruin, Jaza was excited. You didn't have to know him well to see it. His eyes had that familiar wide intensity; just above the ridges of his nose his brow was furrowed ever so slightly; his mouth was just on the verge of a smile. More than excited, he was actually happy.

"I love this," he said quietly. When she raised an eyebrow, he pointed. "Take a look."

Ahead of them, beyond the plexi observation window, a smallish vermillion and white orb hung against the black: the planet Orisha.

"We've been in space for centuries, you know," he said, looking out at it. It did seem to Vale like a large and beautiful gemstone now that she could see it up close. Pretty. "Bajorans made it all the way to Cardassia Prime in ships as small as sailboats."

"Amazing," she said, crediting the words as the product of local folklore. She didn't know much about Bajor's history, but that seemed far-fetched.

"But I never got offworld until after the occupation was over," he said. "Now, every time I get the chance to see a new planet this way, hanging in the dark, glowing like one of the Orbs, I take it. Makes me feel closer to the Prophets somehow."

Behind them in the cabin the others had fallen into conversation related to what would be expected of them once the shuttle touched down. Troi and Keru switched off taking Modan through quick refreshers on emergency med protocols, diplomatic procedures during First Contacts and what not to do if being chased by a pack of angry twelve-meter-long crustaceans. Vale knew they were doing it mostly to keep the ensign calm and it seemed to be working.

Ra-Havreii, damn him, continued to hum that irritating tune.

It wasn't that the song itself was unpleasant—quite the contrary, in fact. The melody hovered somewhere between a human symphony and the musical language of primitives on Liuvani Prime. The engineer's low tenor wasn't objectionable. It was just the relentlessness of the thing. Whenever he wasn't engaged in necessary conversation, within minutes Ra-Havreii was back to his tune, playing with it in his mouth the way a kitten might with a ball of string. It was maddening.

She was just about to tell him to belay the noise when Jaza said, "Ra-Havreii, I need you."

His tone snapped her gaze away from the slowly rotating planet far ahead and back to him. He wasn't smiling, and his brow was now deeply creased with concern. Deep vertical furrows were leading to the horizontal ones on his nose.

"What is it?" she said. He muttered something, obviously believing he'd responded aloud, but he was too concerned with the sensor controls to correct himself. "Jaza?"

Ra-Havreii, no longer playing with his tune, suddenly occupied the space between the two flight cradles. He looked down at the HUDs, out through the forward plexi and then back at the readouts. He face was a mirror for Jaza's.

"Any idea?" said Jaza.

"None," said the engineer.

"But you can see it," said Jaza.

"See what?" said Vale, squinting into the black. As far

as she could tell, there was nothing there but the orb of the planet and the star-filled inky carpet behind.

"Only vaguely," said Ra-Havreii, pensive. "An afterimage? A reflection of some sort?"

"I see it clearly," said Jaza. "It's neither."

"What is it?" said Vale, still completely failing to notice anything unusual.

"Some kind of energy mass, Chris," said Jaza, his fingers tapping new commands into the sensors as he spoke. "Vaguely spherical, very large, about . . . fifteen degrees behind the planet, moving in the same solar orbital path."

"Why can't I see it?" she said.

Jaza shrugged and said, "IDIC." She understood. Humanoids all shared a great many surface characteristics, but despite the visual similarities, Trill were not human, who were not Bajoran, who were not Betazoid or Selenean or Efrosian. All were similar but not truly identical. Obviously, in this case, Bajoran and Efrosian vision encompassed a slightly wider spectrum than the others on board.

By now Troi, Modan, and Keru had moved in behind Ra-Havreii, all squinting to see for themselves and failing. Most of the ship's sensors failed to see the thing as well, which was a little disconcerting.

Only those set to look for minute boryon distortions could detect anything at all, and that only barely. The mass was a very large ghost.

"I think we ought to fire a probe into it," said Jaza at last.

"Is that wise?" said Modan. "Perhaps it is some sort of defensive device."

"You wouldn't say that if you could see it, Modan," said Jaza. "It's huge. Slightly bigger than Orisha, in fact. And it's between us and the planet."

"Any chance we can sidestep it?" said Keru.

Jaza shook his head. "Our course is preset and the sensors only evade what they can see. We're going to pass through it, whatever it is." Jaza looked to Vale as if to say, "What's it going to be, Chris?" For her part, Vale glanced back at Troi, whose features betrayed some tension but not overt concern, not yet. In any case, until some actual diplomacy got going, Vale was running this show.

"Launch a probe," she said at last. "If we're going through, I'd like a little warning about what to expect."

Jaza's fingers danced for a few seconds. They all heard the noise of the torpedo launcher and then watched the tiny silver probe zip toward the unseen mass.

"There's some distortion in the signal," said Jaza, muttering over the display as the sensor data came back. "But it's not detecting anything un—"

Before he could finish the sentence, several things happened at once, ensuring that it would never be completed. The probe crossed over the arbitrary point he'd set as the strange formation's event horizon and vanished from his screens.

A strange shimmering halo of energy, quite visible to all of them now, coalesced around the invisible thing, giving it definition of sorts for those who couldn't see it before. Static, loud and grating, ripped out at the team via the *Ellington*'s comm system, followed immediately by a voice.

"Interlopers! You have dared to approach the [un-

translatable] *Eye! You will be punished for your* [*possible meaning: blasphemy*]*!"* This was followed by more of the harsh static—the UT's unsuccessful attempt to decipher a large portion of the alien language—and then a very ominous silence.

"Orishans," said Modan very softly after a moment.

"I'm guessing," said Vale. So much for them not having space travel. If they survived this, they wouldn't have to worry about violating the Prime Directive. "Mr. Jaza, we're aborting the preset flight program. We don't want to piss anyone off more than they are."

"Already on it," he said, his eyes steely as they tracked his hands dancing on the control panel.

"Keru, try and raise these people," said Vale, not even looking to see how quickly the big Trill had dropped into the communication station to do as ordered. "I'd like to talk to them before—"

"Before," said Ra-Havreii, "they blast us to cinders from their enormous spaceship."

"Spines of the Mother," said Modan in a tiny voice as she absorbed the sight.

There was a lot to take in. This time they all saw it very clearly; a massive cruiser of some sort, roughly twice *Titan*'s size, was in the process of shimmering into view before them. Despite its odd coloring—heavy scarlet streaks along the lower struts against a silvery material that could have passed for something woven—it was as deadly-looking as anything Vale had ever seen.

Its appearance was very much like that of a gigantic mechanical animal of some sort—a scorpion maybe, with tails above and below—and, as they watched it bear down on the *Ellington*'s position, it was clear the new vessel had none of *Titan*'s problems maneuvering in this region. That did not bode well if they meant to get aggressive.

"From their *formerly cloaked* enormous spaceship," said the engineer. "How in the world were they able to pull that off?"

"You can ask them about it later, Commander," said Vale, trying along with Keru to get some weapons up or partial shields at least. It was useless, of course. They had left from *Titan* essentially naked and defenseless, and so they remained.

She asked Troi if she was getting any kind of empathic hits off their new friends.

Troi shook her head. "No, Commander. I feel something from them," she said. "It may be anger and it may be something like curiosity, but there are other emotions there that don't correspond to anything I know. They feel we are not only alien but in some way sullying their space."

"You are [*possible meaning: unclean*]*!"* said the harsh alien voice over more static. *"You will be* [*possible meaning: purged*]*!"*

"I don't like the sound of that," said Keru. "And I can't raise them."

"Looks like they'd rather talk than listen," said Jaza.

"Get us out of here, Najem," said Vale, tense. "Easy, if you can, but back us off now." Jaza grunted something and continued to work with the controls at a fiendish pace. She understood his difficulty. They had modified so much of the shuttle's works to facilitate even simple motion in this area that they'd sacrificed a good portion of direct control. It had been one of the riskier aspects of this mission, but deemed acceptable when weighed against the alternative. Now the risk might kill them. The computer was not making the switch back to manual an easy thing.

"Almost," he said.

"*Titan* can see them," said Troi suddenly. "I can feel the crew's attention on this."

"Hell," said Vale, picturing the Red Alert status that had to be under way on their home vessel. "*I* can feel their attention on this. Look at that monster."

"They're powering some sort of weapon, Commander," said Keru. "Readings are distorted, but—"

"But?"

Keru looked at her. "But this isn't something we want to be hit by."

She saw it then. The alien vessel's upper "tail" was bent close to its "head" now, and in the space between, a blue-white ball of energy was building in intensity. There was no mistaking its intent.

"Interesting," said Ra-Havreii as Jaza worked his console. "That appears to be a warp field. They've weaponized it somehow. Clever."

"Clever like a knife in the throat," muttered Vale. She nudged Jaza, who nodded without looking up. Almost there. "Right. Everybody strap in. Whether they mean to or not, they're giving us a chance to get out of here, and we're taking it."

Jaza swore as the others flung themselves back into their seats. There was a staccato chorus of buckles rebuckling and what sounded like a prayer from Modan. The alien weapon glowed white and large outside their little shuttle.

"Jaza . . ." said Vale.

"Ten seconds," he said through his teeth.

"I don't think we have—"

"Got it!" he said, triumphant, and, just as the alien weapon erupted, "Firing starboard thrusters!"

The *Ellington* lurched violently to port as the beam of coalesced warp energy ripped through its previous position.

"Yeah, that's not good," said Vale. "Not nearly fast enough. We have to get moving."

"They're charging the weapon again," said Keru from his post. "Whatever you're going to do, Mr. Jaza . . ."

"Ra-Havreii!" said Jaza, his eyes fixed on the new ball of energy building on the alien vessel. "Assume I know nothing and tell me why we can't sustain a warp bubble here. Specifically."

"We can, in a ship this size, in theory," said the engineer. "But it would be unstable, porous. The safety protocols would de-initialize the drive to prevent our being shredded by the tidal—"

"So we can use the drive," said Jaza, already out of the cradle and heading back to the rear of the shuttle.

"Only if you want to kill us," said Ra-Havreii.

"Nobody's dying," said Jaza, suddenly rising from his chair and heading aft.

"Jaza!" said Vale, her own gaze zeroed on the alien weapon. "What are you doing?"

He didn't answer. For a moment all Vale could hear was the rush of blood in her ears. They might dodge this thing once more, maybe twice if they were lucky but maneuvering thrusters just weren't going to cut it against plasma weapons.

"Jaza!" she called out to him. "What the hell are you up to?"

"Chris," his voice rose up muffled from the aft engine compartment. "When that thing fires I want you to go to warp."

"But I thought we don't want to go to warp," said Modan. "Because of the dying."

"Commander Vale, I strongly recommend not listening to anything Mr. Jaza says from this point forward," said Ra-Havreii. "An unstable warp field will create catastrophic effects for us."

"Find another plan, Mr. Jaza," said Vale.

"No time," came the response. "We'll make it, Chris. Trust me. Just be ready to activate the drive when I say."

Vale's mind flashed to Troi, who hadn't participated much in their discussion. Indeed, she had been silent throughout the encounter, attempting instead to reach out to Will Riker on *Titan* and somehow convey their situation. With the comms down she was the best link between them and home. Her telepathy might be substandard under normal conditions, but in situations like this, stress, coupled with the bridge she shared with him, could sometimes overcome that limitation.

Will, she sent her thought to him. *Will, are you there?*

Deanna? Yes. She had made contact. It was tenuous, but it was there.

She tried to project—*we're under attack—help/escape.*

There was the barest hint of exchange, the thought equivalent of a garbled coded message, from which she could be sure he got nothing useful, not even the feeling of love she projected. She could feel him, of course. She could feel all of *Titan*'s crew. But he couldn't feel her. Not now.

Almost worse was the fact that, in its current state, *Titan* was almost completely unable to defend itself or to run if it came to that. All they could do was watch as the Orishans, or whoever these people were, destroyed the *Ellington*.

"Chris," said Jaza's voice. "Get ready!"

The Orishan vessel clearly meant to fire another shot. The nimbus of destructive energy in what Vale's mind had already begun to call its warp cannon continued to grow. It was odd. While a part of her watched the weapon power up with a certain amount of dread, another part was intrigued. The charge time between firings clearly showed that, aggressive as they were, these people had never been in anything like a real battle. On equal footing, the lag between volleys was a fatal abyss.

Good.

Titan, with its still-viable complement of torpedoes, might not be totally helpless against this thing that was now so obviously not a warship. The *Ellington,* on the other hand, was on borrowed time. Eventually the alien weapon, slow as it was, would find its target.

"The weapon is near maximum charge, Commander," said Keru. "They're definitely going for another shot."

"Jaza!" she said, hoping the fear that had crept under

her door didn't show too much in her voice. "Tell me something!"

"I've disabled the safeties, Chris," he yelled. "When they fire the weapon, punch it."

"I reiterate," said Ra-Havreii. "This is an extraordinarily bad plan. The shuttle will be torn to—"

"I heard you the first time," snapped Vale. The great blue-white ball of writhing energy had grown to its original proportion. "Everybody, brace."

"Christine," said Troi, in a voice Vale had not heard before but recognized as possessing the same steel that had often characterized her mother. "Be sure."

She wasn't, not about any of it, but it was too late. The Orishan cannon fired and time slowed to a crawl. Adrenaline surged through her body, and it seemed that she was outside herself watching as the lethal tongue of space-distorting energy roared out at them, watching as her hands danced across the manual control console, activating the drive.

It came alive at precisely the instant the beam hit the shuttle, and whether it was the cause of the violent upheaval they suffered or the reason they survived it, she wasn't sure. The ship was rocked horribly, lurching in a new direction with every tick of the clock. Systems all over the *Ellington* went insane, sparking, spewing their guts into the main cabin. Alarms sounded. Some random bit of sudden debris narrowly missed Vale's head as she was jerked out of its path by the ship's distress. Modan screamed again but Vale forgave her. The others rode the tumult in grim silence, obviously as terrified as the young ensign and, just as obviously, having the experience or sufficient grit to keep their fear at bay.

Then, just as suddenly as it had washed over them, the storm of violent energies was gone. Despite its pummeling, the *Ellington* hung where it had in space, listing a bit, to be certain, but still very much intact.

Far ahead the Orishan vessel continued to loom but, for now, took no further aggressive action.

Weren't expecting that, were you? thought Vale. *Well, take as long as you like to chew it.*

Ra-Havreii was the first to speak. "I can't believe that worked," he said. "We should all be dead."

Vale had the feeling that he was more right than anyone wanted to admit, but she wasn't about to look too deeply into the throat of this particular equine.

"Well done, Mr. Jaza," said Vale. There was no response. "Jaza, report." Still he said nothing, and she began to fear the worst. It suddenly occurred to her that there were no safety nets in the shuttle's power room, no place to safely ride out the sort of pelting they'd just had. There was nothing down there but hard metal.

"Modan," said Vale, sliding instantly to damage assessment and control. They weren't nearly out of the rough yet, and she would need him. "Get aft and see what's happened to Mr. Jaza."

"Aye, sir," said Modan after the briefest hesitation. She was unbuckled and sliding down the ladder in an instant. Good. She might not be dead weight after all. Keru was already back at his station, running diagnostics to see what, if anything, they still had to work with. The report was not the best. Emergency systems were all that was keeping them from the vacuum, and several of them had dipped to critical in the time it took him to check their status. At best they had been given a small reprieve. Still, the failure of their weapon seemed to have given the Orishans pause.

Let's see if we can extend that feeling, she thought, staring at the ominous, vaguely insectile ship.

"Counselor?" said Vale, not taking her eye off the alien vessel. "Anything from the Orishans?" Troi shook her head. "Dr. Ra-Havreii, can you tell me anything? Why are we still here?"

The Efrosian seemed frozen in contemplation, his deep-set eyes far away, staring past Troi and Keru and Vale to the space that was visible through the forward viewport.

"Two warp fields," he said at last. "I should have thought of it. The dissonance between the weapon's warp frequency and that of this ship acted as a shield."

"I thought it might work," said Jaza, returning to the cockpit with Modan following close behind. He looked a little the worse for wear—there was a field patch over his left temple where Modan had bandaged what was obviously a wicked gash—but otherwise he was all right.

"You *thought* it would work?" said Vale in mock irritation.

"Yes," said Jaza, wincing as Modan helped him into the pilot's cradle.

"If we survive this, Commander," said Vale. "You're going on report."

"Of course," said Jaza with a smile.

"Commander," said Keru in a tone Vale was sure she didn't like. "Probe telemetry indicates a massive energy flux in the area of Mr. Jaza's ghost field."

"Let me see that," said Ra-Havreii, nearly pouncing on the sensor controls. Jaza too made an effort to shift position for a look at the incoming data, but some hidden injury only allowed him to wince.

"This is bad," said Ra-Havreii. "There is something inside the field, Commander. Something with mass and gravity. The readings are garbled. It's as if there's something there and yet—"

Again their conversation was shattered by the sound of alien static and that same grating, stilted speech of the Orishan representative.

"You have been [*possible meaning: judged*]*,"* the creature said. *"Now you will face the* [*possible meaning: wrath*] *of Erykon's Eye."*

"Now what?" said Modan.

As if in response, the Orishan vessel broke off, shimmering back to invisibility even as it receded into the distance. Just as it vanished completely, "Uh-oh," said Keru. Before anyone could ask what he meant, the *Ellington* was rocked by a massive shockwave. Everything and everyone that wasn't strapped down was flung against the port bulkhead.

Only Counselor Troi, still seated, still trying desperately to make contact with *Titan,* remained more or less undisturbed.

"Everyone strap in!" bellowed Vale, as if there was any need for the order. The others were already scrambling to the jump seats. "What the hell was—"

Again the ship was battered by a massive jolt, even more violent than the first. This time everything was rocked forward, as if a giant fist had taken hold of the ship and was dragging it into a new position.

Will! Troi sent with as much force as she could put behind the thoughts. *Something's happening here. We're in trouble! Real troubl—*

Outside the forward viewport, Jaza's so-called ghost field was a ghost no longer. A massive spiraling, undulating chaos of light and motion the size of a planet was suddenly writhing there in the space ahead and, despite their efforts to break away, was pulling them inexorably in.

Worse, if worse was possible, the shimmering globe began to spit energy, great arching tongues of something unknown and deadly, kilometers wide and thousands long, in random directions. The *Ellington* was being pulled into that maelstrom, and there was nothing they could do about it.

Vale bellowed commands, and Keru and Jaza moved to obey—any evasive measure, any shielding trick, anything to keep them from being drawn in. Nothing worked. Soon all they could see outside was the sea of boiling energies sucking them down.

"Set for collision!" yelled Vale over the noise of sparking machinery and computer warnings about energetic discharges.

Just as they were sucked down, the entire mass erupted at once, spewing its energies wide in a tsunami of force that had to be witnessed to be believed.

Waves of the weird multicolored energy leaped out in every direction, consuming or obscuring every scrap of normal space that had previously been visible.

Troi's mind screamed out to her husband. *Will! Get out*

of there! Get away! Now! She could feel him there, feel his distress as if it were her own as the great wave of energy swept toward *Titan* like an ocean of fire. They couldn't move. There was nowhere to run and no way to do it if there were. *"Will! Imzadi!"*

But it was useless. She could feel him, barely, but he couldn't feel her, neither her panic nor her love, except as ephemeral echoes of what they should be.

Then even that spindly connection was suddenly gone, ripped away along with the sight of the stars and blackness of normal space. The wave of wild energy ripped outward, swallowing the tiny shuttle utterly, obliterating its connection with the space around it. She was alone for the first time in years, perhaps ever, absolutely alone.

"No!" she screamed.

"Deanna!" yelled Vale, fighting alongside Jaza to get some sort of manual control of the shuttle's motion. It was useless. "Are you hurt?!"

"It's *Titan,*" said Troi. "It's gone!"

"Gone?" said Modan, nakedly terrified. "What does she mean, it's gone?"

"I can't feel them anymore!" said Troi in obvious distress. "I can't feel any of them!"

Whatever empathic contact she had with her husband, whatever ebb and flow had normally passed between her and the three-hundred-plus members of *Titan*'s crew was gone, severed as soon as they were caught in the field eruption. Vale had no idea what such a severing might mean, but she was sure it couldn't be good.

"Planetary impact imminent," said the computer over the din. *"Implementing automatic safety protocols."*

Planetary impact? thought Vale. *What the hell? Orisha is hundreds of thousands of kilometers from here.*

"There's something in the field, Chris," said Jaza as if reading her mind. "I don't know how it's possible, but it's solid and it's coming up fast."

Those that could watched in astonished horror as the effects of the energy wave gave way to the simple clouds of the upper atmosphere of some unknown world. There were landmasses down there, a vast sparkling ocean of something both white and blue, and the sort of vegetation one generally only saw in nightmares. This world was like an enormous jungle, stretching from horizon to horizon in all directions. Mountainous leafy plants of impossible proportions, huge towering spires of turquoise or red that stood in clusters surrounded by hills and other plants that they dwarfed the way Izarian cityscapes dominated her homeworld.

This was a wild planet, *terra incognita,* completely untouched by anything recognizable as civilization, and they were about to crash into its heart. The pressure of reentry, without the normal shielding to protect them, pressed relentlessly against them all. Vale knew she was a moment from a blackout.

She saw something then on her periphery that drew her eye. A great black mass had appeared in the swirling chaos of energies around the planet, with a shape that was chillingly familiar.

She watched in horror as the shape, very obviously that of *Titan* now, was buffeted and ultimately torn to bits by the rampaging waves of energy. It went screaming down toward the surface in great burning chunks.

"Impact imminent," said the computer as her mind rebelled against the sight her eyes forced it to process. *"Implementing emergency protocol priority alpha."*

The transporter nimbus enveloped the members of her team, spiriting them to the ground where, in theory, they would have a better chance of survival than with the shuttle's impact.

Vale had no time to grieve for her friends or to ponder whether their chances would be better naked on this unknown and likely hostile planet, but as the transporter beam took her and she slipped into unconsciousness, her last thought was, *"At least I don't have to hear Ra-Havreii's damned humming anymore."*

Chapter Five

The memories of the previous days came back to him in a rush, and with them the sort of shattering despair that only a supreme act of will could force to recede.

Titan. Dead with all hands. The whole crew. The rest of the away team scattered, maybe dead as well, and him and Modan trapped in the middle of some massive local conflict.

Jaza had seen bad days in his time, horrendous ones, in fact, but nothing to compare with this. He had lost friends before, fighting the Cardassians, during his previous Starfleet assignment as science officer on the *U.S.S. al-Arif,* even a few on *Titan,* but he had never lost so many so quickly.

Modan had dragged him away from the scene of her killing of the alien soldier, concealing him under a canopy of the massive leaves that made up so much of the local flora. She was off somewhere, making sure the soldier's body would not be discovered by its fellows.

The change in her was remarkable and went far beyond the cosmetic. In shifting into what he could only guess was some sort of naturally evolved hunting or fighting mode, her body now sported, in addition to the new dermal plating, an assortment of spines running the length of her back from the base of her skull to the bottom of her spine. Her "quills" she called them.

She had adopted an almost hunched posture that forced her face forward and down in the way he had noticed in many lower forms of predator on several worlds. She still looked like a golden sculpture, but now, instead of some sort of idealized version of a humanoid female, Modan looked like something out of one of the fables he used to read his children when he wanted to give them a healthy scare.

He couldn't let himself think of them now.

It was one thing to take these long missions of exploration away from home and family and something else to think that he might never see them again. No.

He froze the images his mind had tried to form and forced them back into the dark recesses. Plenty of time for that sort of grief later.

"There's something wrong with the sky," he thought, looking up at it. It wasn't the color—a kind of copper and gold—or the complete absence of clouds or that the shape of the sun was somehow refracted into an oval by this planet's atmosphere. There was just something *wrong* with it as far as he was concerned, and something familiar too, though he couldn't exactly say what that something was.

"Can you move?" asked Modan, suddenly beside him. It was odd hearing her mellifluous voice coming from that spiny animalistic face, but it helped reassure him that, despite appearances, she was still herself. "The battle is moving this way."

He still hurt all over, especially where his ribs were obviously broken, but he knew from experience what skirting the edge of a pitched firefight could do. He could move and told her so.

As she helped him to his feet, he realized the sounds of battle—familiar shouts, explosions, and weapons fire—had shifted toward what he had arbitrarily named east.

"Where are we going?" he said. He had no clear idea how long he'd been in his delirium, but from the thin appearance of new hair on his jaws and chin, he presumed at least a day had passed since the computer had beamed them here.

"The shuttle," she said.

"It's intact?"

She nodded, one of her head quills stabbing lightly into his cheek. "Mostly. I fixed what I could. You can do the rest."

"Why didn't we go there straightaway?" he said, marveling at her confidence in his abilities. He wasn't an engineer, after all.

"The way was blocked by the Orishan fighters," she said, helping him navigate what looked like a small forest of enormous lavender palm fronds that grew straight up from the soil. "They're all over this area, Najem."

"Orishans?" he said, surprised. "What makes you think these are Orishans?" The last he knew, they were crashing down on someplace entirely new that was a good half million kilometers from Orisha.

"Didn't you ever look at the visual signals we harvested?" she said, slashing at the snakelike vines with the serrated edge of her forearm. Jaza realized he hadn't. He had been so busy getting the shuttle ready for the trip, he hadn't actually gone back to look at the visuals that Modan and the rest had sifted out of the signal chaff. "Well, these are them. I don't know where this war came from. This is supposed to be a rigidly stable society. They don't even have nation states."

As if to punctuate their confused state, a series of large explosions sounded somewhere behind them, close enough to shake the ground and the nearby foliage. *They might not have nations,* thought Jaza. *But they've certainly got the conflict part down.*

For a moment he was again transported back to those awful bloody days on Bajor when he spent every waking moment figuring and implementing ways to kill as many Cardassians as he could as efficiently as possible. Those days were long gone, thank the Prophets, but the memories were sometimes as fresh and immediate as the thought of his mother's smile.

"Maybe this is a colony," he said, stumbling over a small but hidden cluster of stones. "We thought they didn't have space travel and we were wrong. What else could we have missed?"

"It seems as though we missed a lot," said Modan, helping him stay upright. "But these are definitely Orishans. How they got here, wherever we are, I can't say."

"A broken colony of some kind," he mused aloud. "That

would explain some of this. The Federation has had a few of them. They're often conflict engines."

She stopped abruptly, motioning for him to be quiet and still. He nodded, resting his weight against the base of a massive vine that was as thick as one of the smaller sequoias he'd seen on his first visit to Earth four years ago, shortly after he'd transitioned from the Bajoran Militia to Starfleet. Huge as the vines were, they were all still relatively close to the ground, never rising higher than ten or fifteen meters. One day he envisioned there would be towering versions of these things, stretching high into the sky.

Modan disappeared briefly into the brush, only to return looking as agitated as her golden armored skin would allow.

She motioned for him to stay absolutely mum and still, as if he had enough energy to do more than nod. As they huddled there in the crook of the great vine, something moved past them in the jungle beyond.

Though he couldn't see it directly for all the leaves and vines, he did catch a glimpse of what looked like one massive segmented eye and maybe a set of feathery scales running along the creature's side. It was enormous, whatever it was, and he was happy Modan had chosen to give it a wide berth. The jungle seemed to hold its breath as the thing went by; the sound of insects and the larger creatures that fed on them died to a whisper until the monster had passed.

After what felt like a collective exhalation, Modan said very softly, "It's a predator. I saw it kill one of the big avians yesterday. I'm sorry, but we will have to go the long way around."

"It's okay, Modan," said Jaza. "I can make it."

She looked at him then; her large blue-green eyes seemed filled with sadness and, despite her changed appearance, served, as did her voice, to remind him that she was still the same young woman he'd been flirting with for the last few days on *Titan*.

"No," she said sadly. "It's not okay and I am sorry for what you'll have to see. Come."

So he followed her lead as they trudged in silence through the lush and occasionally hostile alien jungle. He asked her at one interval about her fierce metamorphosis, and she said that once the Seleneans had all looked as she did now but that, since joining the Federation, they had taken to breeding crèche siblings to mirror as best they could the dominant races of the UFP. Rather than an effort to blend in with those societies—the golden metallic skin prevented this in any case—it was an attempt on behalf of the Pod Mothers to put their new neighbors at ease.

However, the Mothers did not want their children to be defenseless in the wider galaxy and so allowed the primary DNA, that which accounted for this more durable and lethal form, to remain. In cases of imminent physical attack, a Selenean would revert to her feral aspect until the danger had passed.

"It's not as if we keep our nature secret, Najem," she said as they fought their way through yet another hyperdense thicket of ten-meter leaves and six-meter blades of ochre grass. "All this is in the Starfleet medical database."

"Good thing your minds don't go feral along with your

bodies," he remarked, thinking how dire his current situation might be had that been the case. "I wouldn't want to have to fight you like this."

"The Mothers are wise," said Modan in the sort of reverent tone that Jaza had only heard in the voices of Bajoran vedeks when talking of the Prophets. "And, no, you wouldn't want to fight me."

"Which is your natural form?" he asked her, wondering if he could manage to shove this vision far enough away to remain attracted to her. The banter was only a cover in any case, something to keep his mind off the fates of his friends both on the away team and *Titan*. Plenty of time for the worst news later.

"Both forms are mine," she said. "I am as I am."

She had pulled farther ahead of him while ascending another of the steep little hills and now disappeared completely behind a particularly thick clump of the giant fronds dominating the summit.

"Modan, wait," he said, wincing at the strain on his battered skeleton. "Let me catch up."

She said something that was eaten by the noise of animals chattering in the brush all around. The smell was different here somehow; the normal all-pervasive musk of decaying organic matter and flowers in heat had given way to something unpleasantly acrid and metallic.

Smoke.

Something had burned here recently and might still be burning. With all the explosions from the incendiaries being employed by the Orishans in their battle, it stood to reason that there would be many burnt or burning areas to navigate.

This sort of destruction was also, unhappily, familiar to him. As he climbed the last few meters, the smell of soot and metal triggered yet another memory from his days fighting on Bajor.

He was running through the streets of Ilvia, desperately pushing his way between bodies in the flood of his people going in the opposite direction. The bomb he'd set had gone off hours too early. A problem with the timer? A faulty circuit? He never found out but, just at that moment, didn't much care. The cause wasn't a priority.

His father was in there, tending to patients in a makeshift clinic only a hundred meters from the ordnance storage facility that had been his target.

He had hinted, obliquely of course, that it might be best, for that day at least, not to see patients or to see them elsewhere, but his father either didn't or wouldn't understand the soft warning.

"Someone in this family has to do the Prophets' will, Najem," Jaza Chakrys had told him.

It was a familiar refrain and produced a familiar effect. The two of them had spent the next few minutes screaming at each other. *What have the Prophets ever done for us, Father? If you have to ask, then you've strayed too far from your path, Najem. I don't stray from my path, Father, I reject it*— But by then his father had had enough and had left him there alone, seething in the dusty street.

Had the bomb gone off as programmed, his father and the patients would all have been long gone, back to their homes and hovels, far away from the town center. But it hadn't and they hadn't and he had to find his father.

"Jaza Chakrys," he called out to anyone in the stampede of people. "Has anyone seen Jaza Chakrys?"

It was no use. The plume of ugly smoke spewing up behind them from the ordnance depot coupled with the noise of the Cardassian civil alert system—*Culprits and their families will be found and punished!*—had transformed these people into a herd of fleeing beasts.

He'd fought his way through them, almost literally in a few instances, until he managed to break through only a few meters from the empty shrine that his father used as his hospital.

He remembered being thrilled that the temple's front façade, a long stone wall with a large stone ring with a sculpture of an Orb at the crown, was only scorched a bit, its windows only shattered by the force of the nearby explosion.

He'd burst in, kicking the remains of the destroyed front door away and screaming for his father to show himself if he was present. Jaza Chakrys was not there. No one was. Aside from Najem, the shrine was empty. Under its new covering of shattered wood and glass there was hardly a sign that anyone had been there at all. He had allowed himself to think that maybe his father had actually listened to him for once.

It was then that he had heard that strange sound, like wind chimes in chorus, and his head had begun to ache.

"Najem," said Modan, gently shifting him from the place where he'd fallen unconscious. "Are you all right? Can you continue?"

"Fine for now," he said. "Sorry about that."

"No," she said softly, an incongruous gentleness from something that looked so fierce. "I'm sorry. For you."

She helped him rise again and this time let him lean on her as they made their way back to the top of the hill. She shoved the leaves away or cut them with her talons as they pushed through and then, as they emerged in the open again, he saw the reason for her sadness.

"Caves of fire," he said, incredulous.

There before them, lying in a billion smoldering pieces at the end of the deep gash its impact had cut in the terrain, was a starship. Or what was left of one anyway.

Though nearly none of the bits were intact enough to identify, the ones that were told the story. There was one of the nacelles, sticking up out of the dirt, still glowing faintly. There was the long sloping arc of a saucer disk, oddly pristine among the charred and burning wreck, the remains of the saucer section. The wreckage was spread over kilometers, the groove it had dug even longer.

There were bodies in there as well. Hundreds of broken sentients peppered the destroyed machine's carcass, each bent or shredded or contorted horribly and all of them burnt to charcoal by what had obviously been a hideous explosion. It wasn't hard to ferret the source of the conflagration. The ship's warp core, still dangerously intact despite its scorched and battered state, continued to belch plasma and to radiate so much energy that he could feel the warmth from where he stood tens of meters away.

"That's not good," he said after a time.

"No," she said. "I'm worried about it too. If it blows . . ."

He nodded. These words, the simple clinical assessment, were the best he had right now.

Titan. This was *Titan*.

He had lost friends before, fighting the Cardassians, on away missions for Starfleet, even a few since joining this most recent crew. But he had never lost so many so quickly and never ever in this horrible way.

Bralik. Ree. Melora. Dakal. All of them. Dead. Dead. Dead. And, of course, he had survived it. His blessing from the Prophets had protected him again, though, just now, it felt a little bit more like a curse.

He fell silent again as the enormity of it all went through him.

Modan let him stare at the scene for another full minute before urging him on.

They came upon the shuttle as the sun dipped low behind them and, had he not known exactly what to look for, he would have missed it, which was the point.

The providence that had protected him and Modan thus far had also left the *Ellington*'s stealth field projector mercifully intact. It too had smacked into the surface of this unknown world but had found a better resting place than *Titan*.

The slight ripple in the air, like a breeze drifting along an invisible curtain between what looked like a closely clustered stand of the viney trees and a massive crystal formation, was the only sign that the shuttle was present at all.

It wasn't a cloak really, as it only bent visible light around the ship and couldn't block even cursory sensor scans, but for missions like this one was meant to be, where secret observation of the new culture was part of the brief, the stealth field was ideal.

As long as it lasted, they would be safe from premature discovery here.

"Come on," she said, helping him over the natural ditch that ran between them and it.

Modan had done a good job getting the primary systems back online, though her success was due less to her engineering skills than to the fact that the bulk of the damage was cosmetic. The shuttle's guts had exploded all over the interior, making it look well past ready for the scrap heap, but very little of it had sustained any truly catastrophic damage.

The systems that had been most compromised were those that had shorted during the first hit from the Orishan warp cannon.

By simply swapping a few isolinear chips from less important components to those they needed, and reattaching or sealing a few wires here and there, he was able to get the *Ellington* back up to nearly eighty percent of full functionality. The remaining problem, now that the ship was actually running, was to get it flying again.

Not being an engineer, it would take him hours, perhaps days, to figure out precisely what was wrong with the propulsion system and then determine if that thing could be fixed.

As she lowered him into the rehabilitation bed and he felt the beams of healing energy course through his body, he told her how to use the computer to fix their location so that they would have some idea at least of where they were.

"I will, Najem," she said as the sedation beams sent him into the dark. "And maybe I can find a spare uniform now that some of this junk as been cleared away."

"Uniform," he asked as he drifted off. "What . . . ?"

"Mine got shredded when I transformed," she said, moving out of his field of vision. He could hear her rummaging. "Why did you think I didn't shift back? I'm naked."

His dreams were dark flitty things, full of ugly portents, which he was pleased not to retain once he came back to himself. The pain in his abdomen was little more than an ache by then. His skull no longer throbbed, and she had cleaned the blood off his face. He felt like himself.

"Modan?"

"Here, Najem," she said, and she was. Clad in the white and gray undermesh of an EVA suit, she looked like the old Y'lira Modan, and he was glad. "You look much better now."

"I feel better," he said and even his voice had more strength in it than before.

He tried to sit up, but the rush of blood to his brain made him dizzy.

"Wait," she said soothingly. "Try again in a moment."

"That's a good plan, I think," he said and relaxed again. He might be healed, but it was wise to let his body realize it before he forced it to do too much.

He tried again more slowly, and was rewarded with a smile from his golden companion. It was hard to picture her the other way now, and he was glad of that as well.

"All right," he said, swiveling his legs off the recovery table and facing her. "Did you fix our location?"

"I'm sorry," she said. "I must have done something wrong."

He got up under his own steam this time and made his way to the science station, still lit up from Modan's recent use. She hadn't made any mistakes. The sensors were online and had fixed points for the local sun, using it as a central reference from which to generate star maps and, from them, generate a location mark relative to the Federation. Travel through the strange vortex could have deposited them anywhere.

"What in the—?" he said, checking and rechecking the sensor data.

"Yes," she said. "According to this, the stars are in the wrong places. It must be a malfunction, yes?"

"No," he said as the realization of what had happened washed over him. "No, it's not a malfunction."

"But this says we are on Orisha, Najem," she said. "This can't be Orisha. There are no cities, no high-level technology. These warriors are killing each other with crude projectile weapons and fuel bombs."

"It's not a malfunction, Modan."

"And the stars?" Her confusion was quickly devolving into the fear she'd displayed during their bumpy flight. How odd to see her so fierce in combat and yet cowed by these more abstract concepts. "It has all the stars in the wrong positions. Fractionally so, but still."

"They're not in the wrong positions," he said. "I think—I think *we* are."

His fingers tapped in a few frantic commands and requests, asking the computer to verify his deepening apprehension.

"Verification," said the computer. *"Analysis is confirmed."*

He sat there for a moment, letting the words sink in. He hadn't really needed the computer to verify the charts and extrapolations. Just looking at the data had told him all he needed to know.

He sat there, feeling his limbs, still weak despite their healing, sensing Modan's increasing agitation. He wondered if her Pod Mothers had designed her this way or if it was something unaccounted for. Then a thought came to him that made him smile first and then laugh.

"Najem," she said, visibly shaken by his outburst. "Are you well?"

"Fine, Modan," he said when the last fit was done. "I'm just laughing at the joke the Prophets have played on me. On us, I suppose."

"The Prophets?" she said. "The beings your people revere as gods? What have they to do with this?"

"They made me a promise a long time ago," he said, swiveling to face her. "And this is how they keep it."

"Najem, I don't understand you."

"This is Orisha, Modan," he said. "This is the planet Orisha. That energy mass we discovered was obviously some kind of temporal aperture."

"We have traveled through time?" she said slowly, feeling the weight of it and its truth as well.

"Looks that way, yes."

"No," she said, aghast. "Oh, no."

"Yes," he said. "We should have died. We should have smacked into this place and burned like *Titan,* like our friends, but because of the promise the Prophets made to me, we're here, alive, a thousand years in the past."

"And this makes you laugh?"

"Of course," he said. "Because, no matter what else happens, we absolutely have to get off this planet, as soon as we can, and we have absolutely no way to do it."

Her golden head tilted slightly to one side as she tried to determine if he was not still a little delirious from his injuries.

Chapter Six

Orisha, Stardate 58449.1

It took Vale almost twenty minutes to disentangle herself from the vines, much of which time was also spent making sure she didn't free herself too soon. Sudden release would have sent her plummeting twenty meters to the jungle floor.

Seen from above, the place had looked lush, bubbling with ambient moisture that rose off the violet flora in thick rolling clouds, but also somewhat peaceful. Now, in the thick of it, her body nearly immobilized by the spiderweb of sticky grasping vines, she was forced to revise that opinion. Everything moved here. Everything was not only alive but actively so. The vines, some as thick as a human arm, twined themselves in their multitudes around larger growths that, to her surprise, were themselves nothing more than enormous stalks. The thinner tangles that held her seemed to resist her exertions to get free, inspiring a few moments of panic. But with effort and patience, she managed to loose herself from their grip.

Pulling herself onto the lip of one of the thicker vines, she took a look around. The jungle stretched in all directions without a sign of a break anywhere. She could see stalks in the distance that rose up to a canopy higher than the tallest buildings on Izar.

There were scores of insects, birds, reptiles, and at least one creature that looked like a hodgepodge of several mammals crossed with a cactus. It stopped a few meters away to stare at her out of bulbous milky-white eyes.

"Vale to Troi," she said, tapping her combadge. No answer. She tried again with Keru and then with the rest of the team with the same result. Either her badge was damaged or something was interfering with the signal.

Or she was alone.

She knew the longer she stayed at this height, the worse her chances for avoiding a deadly fall. But going down also meant losing any hope of keeping her bearings; little daylight penetrated to the ground, and she knew, without instrumentation of some kind, that it would be brutally hard to navigate a way out of this on foot, much less to find the others. They should have all materialized in the same vicinity. Emergency transports were meant to put the entire team and their supplies on the surface of a target world without damage. Clearly something had gone wrong.

"I can't feel them! I can't feel any of them!" The memory of the panic in Troi's voice went through her again like an icy knife. She shoved the feeling away and considered her prospects.

The drop to the jungle floor was not sheer. In fact, were

she simply to let herself fall, she could be assured of having every bone in her body shattered and her flesh torn by the innumerable serrated brambles, vines and leaves she would hit as she fell.

The way across the top of the canopy was far more treacherous. She might make a go of leaping and swinging from stalk to stalk, but eventually a vine would snap in her hands or her feet would slip on a mossy bough and down she would fall.

Every scenario eventually put her on the ground, and in mostly unpleasant ways. So, after deciding which way was east and fixing it in her mind, down she went. Better to get there on her own terms.

It was dark on the forest floor, the entire area suffused with that same gloomy twilight that seemed to permeate places like Ferenginar and Berengaria VII. It was cooler on the bottom as well. She lost her jacket fending off the attack of some large multilegged lizard and now felt its absence acutely.

Mites and other unknown creatures flitted and skittered in the hidden reaches, and there was a sort of deep moaning sound—animal or artificial, she didn't know—that rumbled through the area periodically. For all of that, Vale was alone.

East, she reminded herself. There was no reason to go that way specifically. She just felt better walking—all right, trudging—through lichen and forest muck toward the light, even if the source was hidden behind the seemingly endless stretch of purple jungle.

It didn't make sense. Once her body got used to navigating the wild but fairly predictable contours of the jungle floor, her mind was free to drift without impeding her progress.

Somehow, she knew, this was Orisha. There had been a range of mountains in one of the visual signals they'd managed to decipher that was identical to the one she'd seen from the canopy.

The strange energy mass hadn't contained a new world but had served as some kind of shunt, bridging the hundreds of millions of kilometers to the planet in an instant. But what explained such a phenomenon? Was it natural or artificial? How had it formed?

In a way that was good news. They had made it to shore more quickly than they had anticipated, but what they found there did not match the data they'd collected.

Orisha was, at least in part, an industrial society. She had watched the snippets of visual data Troi and Modan had culled from the bizarrely warped signal bleeds. Granted there was no real pattern to any of it; they had been watching three to five seconds snipped from moments isolated from what could have been hundreds of years of signal bleed. It was a sure bet that they'd missed a lot; certainly they had missed all the subtleties that must be present in a society this large.

There were still things they had thought they knew for certain, and yet, now that she was here, none of them had been borne out.

Where were the cities? She had seen something that resembled one in one of the snippets. It had been a gathering, Troi supposed a religious gathering, of a few thousand Orishans in some sort of open arena, with a night sky and something like skyscrapers clearly visible in the background. Granted the Orishan architecture—a strange admixture of familiar constructions, the same woven metal she'd seen on the watchdog vessel, and massive blue crystals carved into useful shapes—was foreign to her, but some commonalities always arose no matter how alien the species.

So, where were the cities? Where were the roads connecting the cities? Where were the signs that the Orishans had mined, farmed, or otherwise domesticated the natural resources of their world?

Nowhere, apparently. This was as close to a pristine ecosystem as she had ever seen, and that couldn't be if the Orishans had developed any version of high technology.

Invisible cities. Warp energy for something other than space travel. Space travel for something other than expansion or exploration. Weapons powerful enough to wreak havoc on alien vessels, but which had clearly been designed without an inkling that the enemy might wish to protect itself or fire back.

It was a puzzle all right, something Vale didn't like normally. She was a fan of solutions, but in this context the puzzle kept her mind off the eventual concerns of her belly and the very strange thing she'd seen just before she'd blacked out.

"I can't feel any of them!" Troi had said, meaning the emotions of *Titan*'s crew. They all just vanished from her perceptions, switched off like three hundred fifty lights. There was only one thing that could have caused that, as far as Vale was concerned. One thing and one thing only. In view of the large black shape she'd seen being torn to bits in the energy storm, she had a very solid suspicion that her feeling was correct.

• • •

Something was tracking her.

She'd been trudging for about four hours by her reckoning without sight or word of the others when she noticed her shadow.

There wasn't anything she could put her fingers on exactly, beyond the gradual absence of animal noise in the surrounding jungle, but years as a peace officer had taught her to trust her instincts when her hackles rose even the slightest bit. Right now they were at full attention.

Something was watching her and moving with her, a few meters beyond the densely clustered vines and leaves. Of course there would be predators in a place like this. Of course some of them would be big enough to give her trouble, especially considering the new scents her simian-descended body had introduced to this place and the amount of noise she made as she went. She could only hope she was too alien to be recognized as prey.

Heartbeat slow, she told herself, remembering her survival training. *Pace regular, body relaxed and calm.*

In a normal jungle, even one that was exceedingly lush, there would be bamboo shoots or tree branches or even stones she might use as weapons, but this was Orisha. The vines and leaves were either too spindly or too thick or too supple to allow her to make anything more dangerous than a length of rope, and the crystal formations, while certainly durable enough to cause damage, were also too solid to break or even damage with her bare hands.

She was just thinking about maybe trying for some higher ground at least when the thing attacked. It was so fast she barely had time to react. It whipped out at her from her left side, barely disturbing the flora. In the glimpse she caught of it as she spun out of its path she saw something long and thick like a constricting snake but with thousands of tiny legs running in two rows along its belly.

She hit the ground hard as it passed and looked up to find it had disappeared into the thick foliage the way a shark disappears into an ocean.

There was a tear in her undershirt but not in her flesh, thankfully.

The thing ripped out at her again, just as she was getting to her feet, this time giving her no time to dodge.

She managed to get her hands up as it smacked into her, catching its head between them even as it bore her to the ground.

It was a monster, all right, its skin a shifty scaly texture that modulated its color to match the plants around it.

Its face, if you could call it a face, was a nightmare, little more than a gaping hole filled with multiple rows of tiny fishhook teeth. Its breath stank like a hundred corpses left too long under a hot sun, sweet and musky and full of blood.

As it lunged at her, its throat let out an ugly gurgling sound as if it, rather than she, were being constricted to death.

She could feel its million legs clawing at her as its serpentine body tried to wrap itself around hers.

"No!" she said through her teeth, forcing the hideous maw away from her face. "I'm . . . not . . . your . . . dinner!"

Of course it ignored her. If there was a brain in there at all, it was just complex enough to tell the thing to eat and eat often.

She tried to shift her weight, to get some leverage against

it, but its lower coils already held her legs fast. The tiny legs had encircled her torso by then and were in the process of squeezing off her air. She had minutes, maybe seconds, to think of something, but with that slaughterhouse of a mouth bearing down on her, she had no attention to spare.

Her lungs burned as they struggled against the increasing pressure. Her heart raced. This thing was going to kill her, right here in the sopping decay of the alien jungle, and then it would eat her or drink her blood or whatever it did to survive.

The giant maw forced her hands back and back again until it was in kissing distance of her face. She felt the crushing tightness around her stomach and chest forcing her breath out in short ragged gasps.

She told herself to fight, but her arms were numb and there was music and her mother scolding her about something and why did her head hurt so much?

Then there was a sound she recognized, a humming noise that brought with it a flash of incandescent light. Suddenly the monster was gone.

Standing nearby, with a phaser in his hand, was a big man in a mud-spattered Starfleet uniform. His thick mustache did nothing to hide the look of profound relief on his face.

"Keru!" she rasped at him as she struggled to stand again. "Took you long enough."

"Sorry, Commander," he said, moving to help her. "I'll try to be quicker next time."

Keru's report was better than expected, considering. He and the others, Troi and Ra-Havreii, had materialized close to each other along with many of the survival supplies they would need.

While Troi and Ra-Havreii tried to get their malfunctioning equipment working, Keru had concerned himself with searching the jungle for Vale, Jaza, and Modan. There was no sign of the latter two as yet.

"Something's interfering with the combadges," said Keru as he let Vale walk on her own the final few meters to their camp. "Dr. Ra-Havreii is working on the problem. I located as much of our gear as I could. Some of it is still missing. I was actually looking for it when I found you."

"Lucky me," she said.

"Me too," he said, managing a grin.

Vale was glad of Keru in that moment. He was a rock, as unshakable as they came, and without his support, she wasn't sure she would be able to continue, in light of their larger dilemma.

"We can't be sure what happened, Christine," said Troi once Vale had gotten some field rations in her and injected herself with a broad-spectrum inoculant.

The counselor looked surprisingly unfazed by the current circumstances, which somehow irritated Vale. She was alert, relatively free of mud and other detritus and working, as best she could, to assist the engineer with his repair of the communications pack.

Ra-Havreii, by contrast, seemed little more than a robot, working away in silence on whatever task was set him and looking none of his companions in the face or speaking. His body was there, but as was increasingly the case with him, the Efrosian's mind was far, far away. This time Vale didn't begrudge him that. She wished she could escape too.

"I'm sure, Deanna," she said. "I know what I saw."

"And I know what I felt," said the other woman. "But the *Enterprise*—"

"We're not on the *Enterprise* anymore, Counselor," said Vale, suddenly angry and wanting to hit something, many times, as hard as she could. "*Our* ship is dead. Everyone on it is dead. I saw it happen. I don't know how it got so close so fast, but I know what I saw. So, please, shut up about the *Enterprise* and let me try to figure out how we're getting out of this mess."

"I know what you're feeling, Chris," said Deanna evenly. "I feel some of it too. But my own experience tells me to wait until we have real solid proof of whatever happened to *Titan*. You may not like to hear it now, but Will and I have been in this place before and survived. I'm not declaring him dead or any of them dead, until I see it."

"You're in denial," said Vale.

"You're not qualified to make that assessment, Commander," said Troi. Then she went back to work with Ra-Havreii without another word.

They had limited resources and fewer options, so Vale's eventual plan was about as basic as they came: Find the shuttle. Find Jaza and Modan, alive if possible. To that end, armed with phasers and the four now working combadges, they had set off in opposite directions, each describing a circular search pattern that would eventually bring them back to the camp, hopefully with the shuttle's location and with their two missing companions in tow.

Troi was left to work with Ra-Havreii, and it was all uphill. He wouldn't speak, or, if he did, it was only to ask for some tool or to correct her clumsy attempts to follow his repair instructions. Beyond that, the engineer had folded up inside himself and, she knew, was currently building a very solid door to lock himself behind.

She understood it. His response, while somewhat unhealthy, was neither unnatural nor unexpected. He had helped to design *Titan,* after all, as he had all the *Luna*-class vessels.

He'd already presided over the destruction of one such ship and now had suffered through a second. Troi would have been surprised, considering his mental state even before their current troubles, if he wasn't somewhat withdrawn now. The problem was, if they were to survive, he would need to process this and get through it sooner rather than later. Much sooner.

She could feel his emotions boiling inside him like an infinite sea of lava beneath his apparent calm. It was too much energy to bottle, and if he couldn't let some out now, the eventual blow would be as catastrophic to him as what had happened to the *Luna*.

"Xin," she began again. "This was not your fault. You know that."

"Yes, of course, Counselor," he said eventually and obviously lying. "This was just an unfortunate result of dangerous explorations."

"Yes, Xin," she said. "We don't even know that *Titan* was destroyed."

"Commander Vale seems fairly certain," he said.

"Chris is under a lot of pressure," said Troi. "It helps her to think the worst has already happened."

"A prudent response," he said, reaching for the isolinear filaments.

"Not really," she said. "Only a natural one. Pessimism is a waste of intellect."

He worked away in silence, apparently puzzled at the tricorder's stubborn resistance to his ministrations. None of the energy-manipulating devices had worked properly at first. Something about the transport or the nature of this planet had scrambled them. Watching him work on the thing, methodically resetting commands or repairing damaged filaments, gave Troi a deeper understanding of how his mind worked.

He was an entirely compartmental being, having simple but solid walls drawn between his emotions and his intellect in a way that reminded her of Vulcans but that was infinitely more complex. Vulcans shoved all their emotions behind the same wall, denying them access to the surface of their being. Ra-Havreii didn't have a single wall but a maze. He certainly felt things and showed it, but only what and when he wished. She wondered if all Efrosians were this way or if it was a particular quirk of the engineer's.

"One of my colleagues on the *Luna* project felt that way," he said eventually, frowning over the exposed guts of the tricorders in his lap. "Dr. Tourangeau felt that our work was in the nature of a competition, with us setting ourselves against the limitations imposed by nature and finding ways around them. 'Sometimes you get the *sehlat*,' he would say. 'Sometimes it gets you.'"

"It's a good way to see life, Xin," she said.

"I pushed myself to follow his example," said the engineer. "I completely redesigned the drive systems of the

Luna class, you know. I changed the mixture rates, streamlined the force-field networks. It was like making art rather than building machinery."

"I'm afraid I don't know much about engineering," she said, smiling. "But I know your work is considered to be cutting edge."

"Yes," he said. "We were always seeking that edge. Living on it as long as we could."

"They say that's where the best discoveries are found."

"Mmh," he said. "It is also the place where Dr. Tourangeau and several hundred others were caught in the matter inversion event that was born of my 'artwork.'"

Seeing the questioning look on her face, he explained the horrible consequence of matter inversion and how its single positive attribute was a quick death for those caught in the center of the effect.

The maiming and mutilation of bodies unlucky enough to be at the periphery, like those of his friend Tourangeau and so many others, was something he never let himself forget anymore.

"I promised I would never lose another ship," he said at last. "And I would never kill another person or harm another friend. And yet here we all are."

She could feel him folded inside himself, like layer upon layer of steel. His pain was deeper and, strangely, more rational than she had ever thought, and in the face of it, she wondered if any amount of quiet conversation could ever lessen his burden.

"I am sorry, Xin," was all she could muster. She knew it wasn't enough, that perhaps nothing could be. Worse, his certainty that he had somehow failed to prevent the death of another ship and her crew sent a sliver of ice through her own soul.

Seeing that she wouldn't press him further, Ra-Havreii closed the tricorder's access panel and switched it on. The green lights lit and the familiar chime sounded, signaling that he had got it working correctly again. To look at him, one would think he had just performed this miracle in the comfort of some workshop on *Titan* or at Starfleet Headquarters.

He smiled at her, a surprisingly warm smile, stood and moved off to test the tricorder's basic functions.

Keru burst out of the jungle as if a horde of Borg drones were on his heels.

"We're going," he said, and immediately set to packing up the campsite.

He wasn't panicked exactly. Troi could tell the big Trill had more control of himself than to allow panic, but he was nervous and in a hurry.

"What's happened, Ranul?" she asked, moving to help him gather up their meager store of equipment and supplies.

"The commander stepped on something," he said, closing up the first pack and tossing it to her. He looked around, noticed the engineer was not present, and asked about it.

"He got a tricorder working again," she said, finishing the second pack. "He's still testing it."

Keru swore. Seeing that Troi had the packing in hand, he dived into the area of the jungle where she indicated Ra-Havreii had gone. He and Vale had the only working combadges as yet, and she could hear his voice relaying the situation to her for a few moments before the sound was eaten by the jungle. Almost immediately she heard, from the opposite side of the little clearing, the muffled sound of phaser fire.

She finished the fourth pack and was about to round up the stray bits of equipment when Vale appeared. She was winded and sweating, and she held her phaser very much at the ready.

"No sign of the others," she said, catching her breath. She cast a glance around the small campsite and frowned.

"Keru and Xin aren't back yet," said Troi. She tossed the younger woman her finished pack, watching as she quickly slid her arms through the loops. "What's happening?"

"Stepped into a nest of some very angry bugs," she said, gathering up the other hand weapons and handing one to Troi. "I think the phaser scared the first few hundred, but the others are massing behind them."

Troi nodded, slipping on her own pack and gathering up the other two.

"Vale to Keru. We're leaving in one," said Vale. "I don't care what Ra-Havreii's into. Stun him if you have to, but get back here now."

"Already on it," said Keru, emerging from the sea of vines with a very unhappy Ra-Havreii in tow.

"Glad you could join us, Doctor," said Vale, grabbing one of the packs away from Troi and throwing it at the Efrosian. "The counselor tells me you've got that thing working again?"

"Yes, Commander," he said.

"Think you can find the shuttle?"

"I was just telling Keru that I could when he—" The engineer was interrupted by a sound like a thousand turbines spinning in unison.

"Bugs?" said Troi. Vale nodded.

"Let's go, people," she said, as if anyone present needed to be told.

The swarm stayed with them for two kilometers, right up to the moment they found a wide creek of clear running water and, despite Ra-Havreii's protest, plunged in.

Their scents sufficiently masked, the team watched from under the water as the horde of alien insects swept over them. It took only seconds for the swarm to pass—an army of things like crimson locusts the size of small dogs screaming through the brush with blood in mind.

"Good enough," said Vale as the others joined her on the surface of the water, each filling their burning lungs with air. She looked at the engineer expectantly.

"Yes," he said, bringing the tricorder up. "I have a fix on the warp core. Shall we?"

It was odd following Ra-Havreii anywhere. He kept up a good pace, but he didn't bother to tell them when he turned left or right or took a sudden detour through what appeared to be a solid bank of tightly interwoven vines.

"Have you wondered why there are no signs of technology?" said Troi. "Even the tricorder hasn't found anything."

"As long as it finds the shuttle," said Keru.

"Fixed position another kilometer ahead," said Ra-Havreii. "The pulse is steady and strong."

"Heh," said Keru, huffing a bit through his mustache. "You sound like a doctor."

U.S.S. TITAN NCC-80102

LUNA-CLASS LONG-RANGE EXPLORER

LATERAL VIEW (STARBOARD)

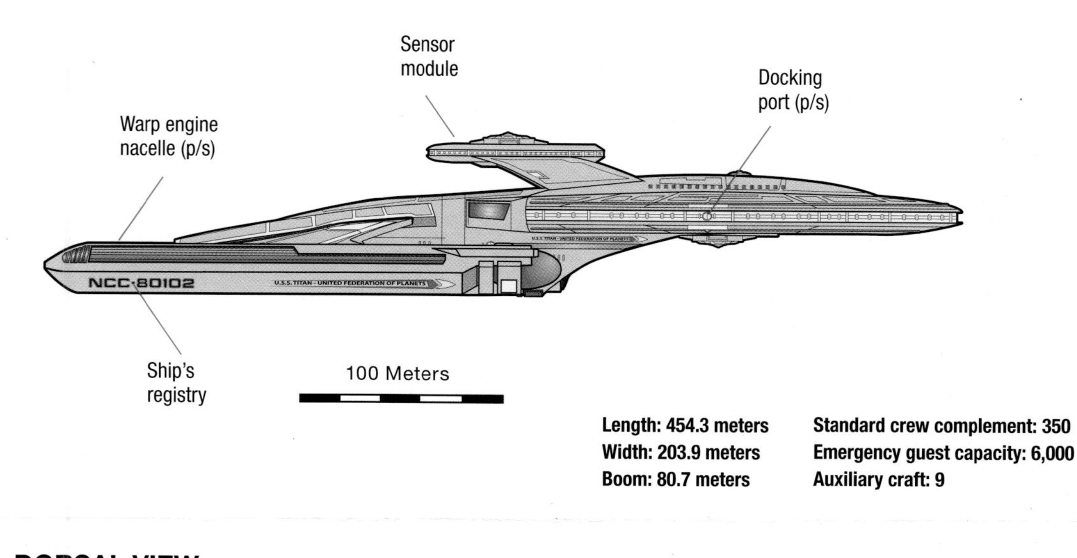

Length: 454.3 meters
Width: 203.9 meters
Boom: 80.7 meters

Standard crew complement: 350
Emergency guest capacity: 6,000
Auxiliary craft: 9

DORSAL VIEW

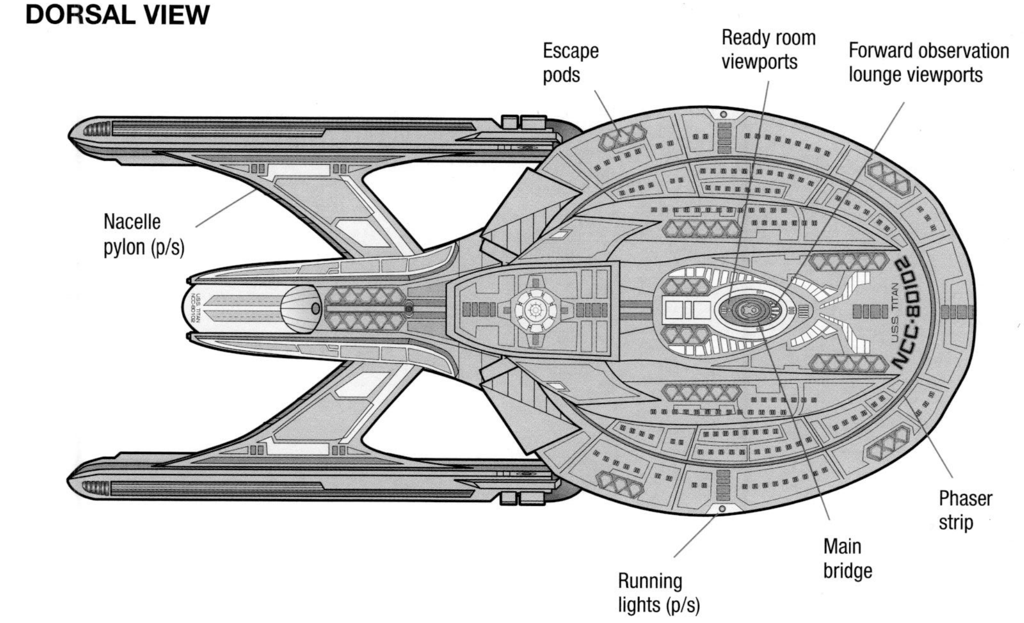

VENTRAL VIEW

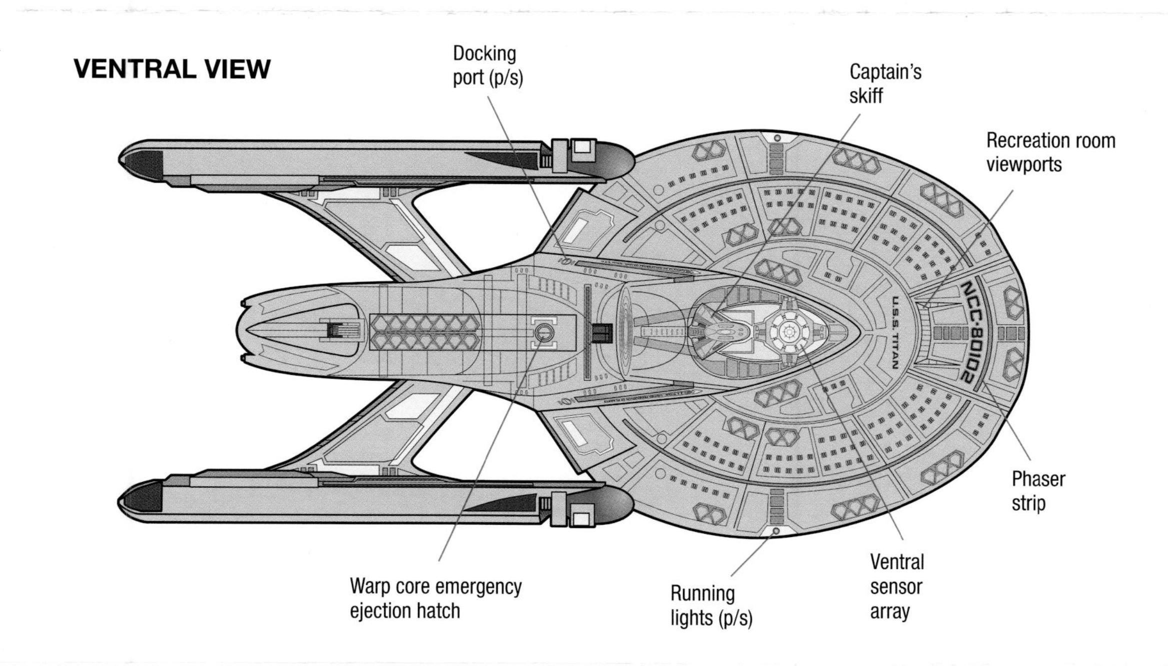

FORE/AFT VIEW

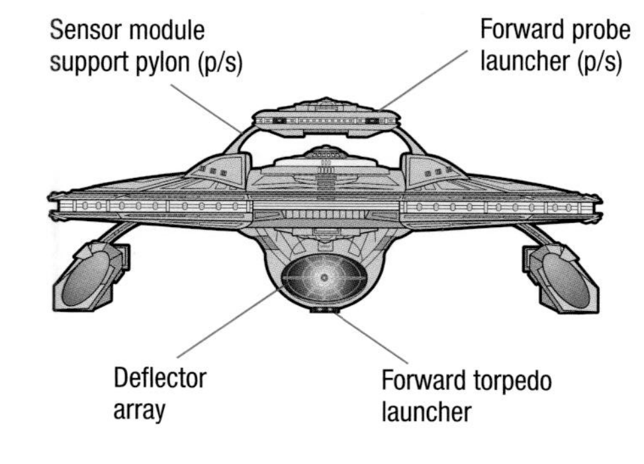

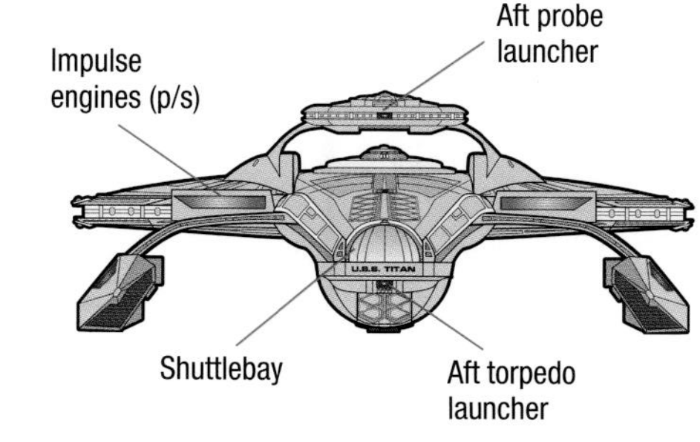

***Luna*-class fleet:**

***Amalthea* NCC-80108**
***Callisto* NCC-80109**
***Charon* NCC-80111**
***Europa* NCC-80104**
***Galatea* NCC-80112**
***Ganymede* NCC-80107**
***Io* NCC-80105**
***Luna* NX-80101**
***Oberon* NCC-80103**
***Rhea* NCC-80110**
***Titan* NCC-80102**
***Triton* NCC-80106**

Designed by Sean Tourangeau

"I am a doctor," said Ra-Havreii. "A steady, regular pulse means the shuttle is more or less intact. Actually these readings show—"

Troi sensed a sudden spike in his emotions, a sort of surge that was equal parts confusion and elation. "Xin?"

Without responding, the engineer took off at a dead run, plunging into the dense foliage ahead as if it wasn't full of things that could easily kill him.

"Dammit," said Keru and went off after him as if fired from the same cannon.

"I thought he was under control," snapped Vale, following.

Troi didn't respond. She couldn't. She had caught the tiniest flash of what had appeared in Ra-Havreii's mind. It was an image that both thrilled her and chilled her to her marrow. She knew why he had bolted, and she felt the same. She actually passed Vale, scrambling after the lanky engineer and his burly pursuer over the treacherous vermillion terrain.

Vale would have liked to grumble, but she had the others to keep safe. She held the rear position and kept her phaser ready. Whatever it was that had sparked the engineer had set him running toward it, so it was safe to assume something positive lay at the end of their little sprint.

The tiniest vines, rough spiny things with occasional barbs, clutched and scratched at her exposed flesh as she passed between. She kept sight of Troi, only a few steps ahead as she too tore through the jungle, and was impressed by how easily the counselor was able to adapt to their circumstances. It might be irritating to have her reference her longer time in the field and noteworthy adventures, but if the benefit of all that experience resulted in someone who could take all this in stride, Vale accepted it as a welcome blessing.

There was a rise ahead, composed of what looked like the exposed sinews of some impossibly giant animal stacked on each other several meters high. Troi scrambled to the summit and disappeared between the massive cluster of leaves that grew there.

Good climber too, thought Vale. *She never missed her footing once—*

Suddenly her mind, her whole being, was flooded with, well, grief was too small a word to describe it. For an instant she felt, all at once, the loss of every friend, the perpetual absence of her father, the pain of every misspoken word or ugly unreasonable thought she'd ever had. It lasted only a second, maybe two, but it hit her hard enough to make her gasp and fall to her knees.

Titan.

It wasn't the shuttle that Ra-Havreii had found after all but the great starship that had been their home for more than half a year. It was no one's home now. Even the local wildlife kept well clear of this hideous place.

Titan, what was left of her, lay in hundreds, perhaps thousands of broken twisted bits at the end of a trench that was easily three kilometers long. The pieces were charred black, melted and twisted by the heat of planetfall. What she had seen had been true. *Titan* was dead.

Despite her harsh words, she had been swayed by Troi's unshaken faith that even this horrible turn could have been avoided or corrected. The scene before them had shattered

Troi's resolve into jagged shreds, and each of those had sliced through Vale.

Dead. All of them. Dead.

Troi said nothing, only stood gazing down at it with tears streaming down her face. She had bottled the excess emotion that had hit Vale just before, but you didn't need to be hit with an empathic broadcast to know she must be dying inside.

"Deanna," she said, placing a hand on her shoulder. "I'm sorry."

Troi nodded, a tiny thing, almost imperceptible, but she still had no words. This moment was completely outside anything she had ever experienced or conceived. Even in her darkest moments there had always been a last-minute reprieve or some miraculous rescue to put things right.

What could ever do that here?

Keru was like stone. This was, Vale guessed, the face he'd shown when news of the death of his beloved Sean Hawk had reached him. She hoped never in her life to see this face again.

Ra-Havreii drifted past her and, before Vale could protest, scrambled down the hill of vines, apparently to get an even closer view of the carnage.

"Keru," she said, her voice sounding hollow and strange. "Better get after him."

"Right," said the big man after a moment. "Right. On it, Commander." And then he was off after the engineer.

The two women stood there silently, hating the sight before them and unable to turn away.

"We were arguing," said Troi at last. "Will and me."

"Deanna . . ."

"We wanted a baby, but there were complications," she went on, almost as if Vale wasn't present at all. It was as though the words themselves had to come out, had to be spoken, regardless of how they fell. "There were DNA incompatibilities. Dr. Ree was treating us both. It was invasive, lengthy."

"It sounds like a barrel of fun," said Vale. "I'm sorry. I didn't know."

"It was fine," said Troi. "We wanted the baby more than anything, but the more procedures we underwent, the more Will and I fought."

Troi went on, the words flooding out of her, telling of their battles behind closed doors, about Will's desire to keep Deanna and the baby they were working so hard to create safe.

He began shifting her duty schedule, recommending she hand off more and more work to her staff. She would have none of it, of course, and so they fought.

Was this how he meant to treat her once their child was born, like a delicate, breakable thing? There was no safety to be had in any kind of life and no guarantees about any of it.

On some very basic level she knew that he understood and even agreed, but, perhaps due to the nature of *Titan*'s first few missions, some other part of him could not keep the fear of harm coming to her at bay. His mind began to fill with scenarios in which she or their child or both would be somehow killed or stranded or otherwise harmed by the simple facts of life on a deep-exploration ship.

Never mind that there were already children on *Titan* and certainly more to come. Never mind that there had been families on *Enterprise*, going about the business of living, happily, if not always easily. His feelings weren't rational. This was some animal thing, a vestigial aspect of his primate ancestry maybe, and its grip on him only continued to grow.

So, they fought and fought and dug that awful chasm between themselves that nothing had ever managed to create before.

Their last words together had been cold, businesslike. He didn't want her on this team and she didn't want to hear another word about her not going.

She had planned to patch things up on their return from Orisha. She had planned to concede, to accept anything rather than have this rift between them. She had planned many things, not the least of which was their baby. All of it was dust now, charcoal black dust, flaking off *Titan*'s bones.

"Keru to Vale," his voice cut a welcome hole in her reverie. *"Dr. Ra-Havreii has something down here you need to see."*

"What now?" she said.

"I don't know what he's talking about, but he seems pretty happy," said Keru, obviously perplexed. *"It's something to do with the warp core."*

"On our way," said Vale.

It was worse being there. The blackened remains of *Titan,* hideous enough from a distance, were like a giant's charnel pit from within. Vale was grateful that the descent that had burned *Titan* had also cauterized the flesh of the crew. There was no stink of death here, at least, only the towering ebony monument to their loss and the absolute, relentless stillness.

While the jungle teemed with plant and animal life of nearly every description, this area was as tranquil as the graveyard it was.

The two women moved within the black maze of *Titan*'s remains in absolute silence, neither daring to break the quiet or disturb each other's thoughts.

This lasted all of two minutes before the sound of phaser fire cut through the peace.

Troi and Vale broke into a dead run, bringing their own weapons up almost in unison. Far ahead of them, tens of meters away, they could see shapes, Keru's and several others scuffling. Keru's phaser fired again, slicing a bright narrow slash in the air.

Whatever they were smashed him to the ground and ran off into the place where the jungle crept closest to the crash site.

They had almost reached Keru, already back on his feet, before they realized the large black pillar towering over him was *Titan*'s warp core and that it was somehow still glowing with power.

"Orishans!" said Keru as he dashed into the jungle after the unseen attackers. "They took Ra-Havreii!"

His phaser had time to fire once more before Troi and Vale plunged in after him.

Chapter Seven

Orisha, No Stardate

Jaza had a plan, but Modan didn't like it. They needed to get the shuttle's flight capability back and get off the planet sooner rather than later. The longer they stayed on Orisha, the more damage they might do to its natural timeline. They could only hope that Modan had not killed the Orishan soldier who had attacked Jaza or, if she had, that he would have died anyway as a result of the conflict raging around them.

The plan was simple enough in itself. *Titan*'s unstable warp core had to be neutralized. The shuttle's flux regulator had been burned out by the energy discharge, but at least two of its counterparts in *Titan*'s warp core were still active and could be adapted.

The problem was that, though he had the necessary expertise to neutralize the core, the rad levels around the crash site were too high for him to get close. Modan's Selenean physiology would allow her to survive the effects long enough to get the job done, but she was not an engineer.

"It's okay," he told her. "I'll talk you through it, and then we will take this shuttle somewhere else where there are no sentients to corrupt with our presence."

"This will work?" she said again, still dubious about the role he had set for her.

"It will," he assured her. The isolation suit, one of two left when the others had vanished (along with a good portion of their emergency supplies) was set in rest mode, but it was working. She would be essentially imperceptible in the visible spectrum and well into the infra and the ultra as well.

"I'm not sure I have the skill set to do my part," she said. "I'm just a code breaker, Najem."

"Modan," he said, a strange intensity in his voice that she had not heard before now. "The Prophets have put us together here for just this purpose."

"The Prophets."

"Yes," he said.

"The beings who exist in Bajor's stable wormhole."

"Yes, Modan," he said. "Yes."

"I don't understand," she said. "You believe your Prophets are controlling your actions, your life?"

"I believe," he said, "that the Prophets guide my steps and shape my fate. Or, in this case, ours."

"That's perverse," said Modan. "Selene doesn't have deities. We know the universe is a mechanism."

"It's that," Jaza acknowledged with a smile. "That simply isn't *all* it is."

"We are rational beings, Najem," she said. "You are

a scientist. You cannot seriously believe what you say."

"I can," he said. "I do."

"I cannot process how this can be."

He smiled. It was the first real smile he'd managed during this ordeal, and she was strangely glad of it.

"I was like you," he said. "I was worse. But a mind that rejects new data, even if the data contradicts what the mind thinks it knows, is not functioning at peak."

"And you have received this data?"

"Oh, yes," he said.

She stared at him then, the turquoise orbs of her eyes seeming to bore straight through his being. He could only remember being scrutinized that closely once before in his life.

"The Mother has made me to think, as you say, at peak," she said at last. "Present your data. If I agree with its rationality, I'll obey your orders. If not, we must find an alternate plan."

"I am the senior officer here, Ensign," he said, not unkindly.

"There is no Starfleet now, Najem." She wasn't making an argument, she was stating a fact. Starfleet and any authority over her it granted him were a thousand years in the future. "There is no Federation. I can't risk my life for an irrational notion."

"Modan," he said. "We've already wasted enough time. You don't need to believe as I believe to get this done."

She sat. She stared. She said nothing, and somewhere not far off, the dangerous substances inside *Titan*'s warp core continued their unregulated ebb and flow.

"All right," he said. "All right, listen."

• • •

The shrine was an old one, the kind that was usually built near the founding days of a settlement. It harkened back to those times before Bajor had developed space travel.

The hands of the founders of Ilvia had surely excavated the stones, seeded and cultivated the garden. Some local artisan had surely carved the image of a Tear that dominated the façade.

It was exactly the sort of place the Cardassians usually destroyed under some pretext or another in their bid to separate the Bajoran people from their backward spiritual past.

Somehow this one had survived, even doing duty as a makeshift hospital where Jaza Chakrys tended to those deemed undesirable or unacceptable by their Cardassian occupiers.

He stood there, thanking the Prophets that his father wasn't present after all and that at least one of the charges he had set, the one at the secondary target near the data processing station, had failed to blow.

Then it did.

He felt the explosion before he heard it and, in fact, never actually heard it at all. The shock wave flung him forward like a rag doll, smashing him against the broken stone courtyard of what once had been the first interior garden,

He felt he should have lapsed into unconsciousness—that was normal for this sort of bone-crushing injury—but instead, he heard the chimes.

"Hello, love," said a voice that was enough like Sumari's to send a hot electric thrill rippling through his body.

"Hello, Jem," said another familiar female voice.

"Mother?" he said, knowing it couldn't possibly be, and yet longing to believe it anyway.

He rose and found that the shrine around him had transformed. There was no damage now, not from the bomb or anything else.

A strange preternatural glow suffused every visible space and, within that halo, people. There was his wife, Sumari, alive again. There was his mother alive as well. There was his first teacher, Donal Leez, still sporting that perfectly trimmed goatee and the sparkling bright eyes. Leez was also long dead, of the same Orkett's epidemic that had taken his mother, and yet, here he was. Here they were.

"You're confused," said his mother.

"You're broken, Najem," said Leez. "Shattered into splinters."

"What is this?" he said, forcing himself to his feet. His body felt just as insubstantial as everything else around him yet this was no dream. He was alert, lucid, thinking as clearly as he ever had in his life. And there was the pain in his neck and spine where he somehow knew he'd taken shrapnel though there seemed to be no wounds.

"Pain is a ghost," said Sumari. "Only the Prophets are forever."

Even here, even in this weird dream that was not a dream, Sumari would invoke those laissez faire deities who did nothing but watch and wait in their damned Celestial Temple.

Suddenly he was filled with a rage that he had never felt before. It was like fire inside him, hollowing, cleansing, ripping the chaff from his mind and leaving behind the only thing that mattered: the question.

"Why don't they help us, Su," he said, his body literally vibrating with anger. "We've worshipped them for thousands of years. We've done everything to honor them and they still let the Cardassians come! They let them come and kill us and torture us and destroy what we've built."

"You can't solve everything with a hammer, Najem," said his mother. "You can't answer violence with more violence."

"They haven't left us anything else," he said, whirling on her. Years of anger over everything, the occupation, his mother's death, his estrangement from his father, the loss of so many friends, all of it fairly erupted out of him, spewing his hot wrath on these ghosts or whatever they were. "They won't help us. They won't stop the spoonheads. People pray and pray and they do nothing."

"There is a purpose to everything, Jem," said Leez. "You have to trust the Prophets."

"You can't keep saying that, over and over," said Jaza. "Don't you understand; it doesn't mean anything. We pray to them. They do nothing. We still die. All we do is die."

"The Prophets are outside life and death, Jem," said his mother softly. "You have to try to see things the way they do."

"How can I?" he said and suddenly became aware of the tears that had been pouring out of him the whole time. "I'm just a man."

He was just a man, just one little soul, doing what it could, anything it could, to free his people from oppression. Fighting, dying, killing, whittling away bits of himself every day when, with a wave, they could end all this.

How did they dare do nothing? How did they dare to call themselves gods?

Suddenly he was elsewhere, somehow transported to a new locale with a foreign landscape and an unknown sun in the unfamiliar sky. Or was it the sun? He could see something that looked like what he understood to be a sun setting near the distant horizon. This other object, this weirdly glowing and oscillating orb hanging in the sky above him, was something completely new.

Eight turquoise crystals grew in the moist dark soil, clustered by chance or design into the shape of an Orb of the Prophets, and behind him something made by sentient hands, a vehicle or a structure, loomed, casting a long dark shadow. There was a charge in the air as if there had been a recent lightning strike or maybe a ground quake.

"What is this place?" he said, more to himself than to the others who had somehow followed him here.

"The end," said Leez, bending to inspect the stones. "And the beginning."

"I don't understand," he said as he took in the sight of the alien landscape, imprinting it on his mind.

"That's the smartest thing you've ever said," said Sumari, smiling her beautiful wicked smile. How he missed her even after all this time.

"But what is this place?" he said. "Why do you show it to me?"

"The end," she said. "It's the end for you, Najem."

"The end?" he said, trying to follow. "You mean—you mean this is where I die?"

"Only at the end can you see as the Prophets see, Najem," said Leez. "Only then will you know."

"A hallucination," said Modan when he had finished.

"No," he said. "A vision."

"You were injured," she said. "The explosion."

"Yes, I considered that," he said. "When I woke up the shrine was in bits around me. I wasn't scratched. I wasn't even concussed. The Prophets protected me."

"This is irrational, Najem," she said thoughtfully. "Many survivors of disaster tell such stories. Have your Prophets protected them all?"

He laughed. "Maybe," he said. "I don't know. But I know what they did for me."

"And this *vision* you saw," she said. The word twisted in her mouth, but he let it go. "You know its meaning?"

"Yes," he said. "I know my death, Modan. Until I'm in that place and in that moment, nothing can kill me. That's why I survived the bomb and the occupation and everything we've been through. Until that moment, nothing can touch me."

She protested again, citing simple coincidence and the need in primates like himself to see patterns in everything even when no such pattern was present.

"Modan," he said. "How many coincidences will convince you of the pattern? Don't you find it the least bit odd that we have been sent back to this moment and place with precisely the right skills between us to prevent *Titan*'s warp core from blowing a continent-sized hole in Orisha? This defies coincidence, Modan. There are hands at work here, and they're not ours."

Modan was silent. She had heard everything he had to say, but it was not clear she understood. Around their hidden shuttle, the Orishans continued to bomb and shoot each other with zeal.

Whatever fuel had sparked this fighting, there was no sign of its running dry in the near future. Yet he knew that, as a result of this conflict or something that came after, the Orishans not only put aside their differences but became peaceful enough and unified enough to build a stable, aesthetic culture on a par with many in the Federation. They had to be allowed their chance to survive this dark moment in their history.

"All right," said Modan at last. "I do not share your conclusion, but your reasoning is sound. I will do as you say."

Things went more smoothly than he had anticipated. Despite the confidence he'd shown Modan, the Prophets' protection was not always as clear-cut as he'd led her to believe. He still carried deep and painful ambivalence about his wife Sumari's death from a disruptor blast that could have been meant for him.

He had never known for sure at which of them the Cardassian gunner had been aiming, but the possibility that her life had been sacrificed to protect his had tormented him for years. He'd put their children in his father's care after that rather than risk their lives as he had their mother's.

Indeed it was with Sumari's death that he knew he must eventually leave Bajor. So, first the Militia and then, when the opportunity came, Starfleet, adventure, and discovery and so many friends.

He didn't want Modan to be another sacrifice to the Prophets' will, but there was no other way.

"Almost there," came her whispered words over the comlink. "Only a few more meters."

The Orishan war zone had expanded in their direction while he had related the story of his epiphany, so she was obliged, even with her holographic invisibility, to skirt the farthest edge of the battle rather than take a direct route to the core.

"Acknowledged," he said as he kept one eye on the sensor scans of the battle. *Titan* hadn't yet been discovered by the Orishans; there was too much blasting going on in the region for even that awful crash to have been noticed by more than a few. The readings of the warp core, if they could be trusted, were stable enough. If they held, Modan would easily shut the thing down, lift out the flux regulators, and return. They could be off the planet inside two hours.

"Done," she said softly. There had been a tense moment when the primkeys had jammed instead of opening the manual shutdown plates, but he had talked her through the use of the link glove to get them open. After that it was a simple matter to perform a manual shutdown.

Jaza talked her through it, step-by-step, and she did precisely as she was told.

The entire process took ten minutes. After another ten, she was a good way toward pulling the first of the flux regulators free of its housing. As she worked in silence, he continued to scan periodically for signs that the deuterium suspension was still becoming solid or that the antimatter was not securely held by the thickening plasma.

Eventually the entire core would cool and go essentially dormant. Nothing short of a solar flare at close proximity might restart it. Such a flare would also wipe all life from Orisha, so the subsequent matter/antimatter explosion would be redundant.

"Najem," she said, almost too softly for him to hear. *"There's a problem."*

"What is it?"

"I think my suit is failing," she said. *"I'm becoming visible."*

Jaza swore. It was so obvious he should never have missed it. The rad levels around the core were high enough to kill a humanoid in short order, so it wasn't unlikely they would play hob with an energetic system as delicate as the stealth field.

"You have the flux regulator?" he said, trying to keep the tension out of his voice.

"One," she said. *"But not the backup."*

"Good enough," he told her. "Get back here, now."

"Najem," she said in a voice so small he was surprised the badge was able to broadcast it. *"Two Orishan soldiers have entered the crash site."*

He had a vague image of her position in his head. To get at the manual step-down controls she would have had to climb to the top of the core, some ten meters above the ground. If she was still there, the Orishans might walk beneath without ever looking up.

"Be still," he said. "Let them pass."

There was silence for longer than he liked, enough time for him to mouth a silent prayer that the boon the Prophets had provided him might extend to Modan for just a bit longer.

The clock ticked in his mind. The *Ellington*'s sensors and defensive systems hummed dispassionately around him. If he didn't look out the forward viewport, if he ignored the aches that remained from his recently healed injuries, he might be back in *Titan*'s shuttlebay running an odd but simple survival scenario.

Of course he saw very well the giant vermillion fronds draping over the front of the vessel and caught tiny glimpses of the copper-colored sky through the breaks between. This wasn't *Titan. Titan* was dead.

The clock ticked. Jaza waited and meditated. A full three minutes passed and he found himself eyeing the remaining isolation suit and the phasers. He didn't know what the stun setting might do against the Orishans' dense chitinous exoskeletons, but he knew the kill setting could not be employed under any circumstance.

If he was forced into a choice between saving her life and killing one of these beings, he knew what it would have to be. He prayed that it wouldn't come to letting Modan die to preserve the timeline. The Orishans, of course, were under no such proscriptions.

"They've gone," she whispered suddenly.

"Good," he said. "Come back."

"Not yet," she said. *"I think I can get the backup unit."*

"Modan," he said, suddenly more nervous for her than when she had been silent. "Come back now. Right now."

"You sent me for both units, Najem," she said. *"What if this one fails?"*

"Ensign Modan," he said. "I am ordering you to come back now. Now."

"One moment," she said. *"It will take only a few more seconds to—"*

She never finished. At that moment the sensors all went haywire and the ship begin to scream multiple alarms simultaneously.

"Warning," it said. *"Unquantifiable energetic field effect in proximity. Take evasive action. Gravitic conditions in flux."*

"Computer," he yelled over the din. "Record all sensor data for analysis."

"Acknowledged," said the voice.

There was the sound of thunder overhead, as if two impossibly massive hands had been clapped together, sending ripples of concussive force in all directions. All around him the ground began to shake violently.

The shuttle continued its attempt to smash him into the bulkheads, but he held fast. As the data came through he began at last to understand what had happened. He wasn't sure of the *how*, and the *why* was completely obscure, but he felt he now knew *what*.

Time, he thought. *Of course.*

The revelation distracted him enough that he relaxed his grip on the control console. The shuttle lurched violently, hurling him to the floor. He groaned from the impact and immediately thought of Modan.

"Jaza to Modan!" he yelled. "Ensign Modan! Report!"

Maybe she tried. There was the awful grating sound of

static with what could have been her voice underneath. Or maybe he imagined it in the chaos.

The quake stopped abruptly, and for a moment, the entire world, within the shuttle and without, was unnaturally still and silent. It was, he thought, as if the entire universe had held its breath for fear that the release would inspire another of the violent temblors.

It never came. Jaza let himself relax by degrees, pulling himself back into the pilot's cradle. He watched as the shuttle's systems recalibrated themselves and performed the analyses he'd ordered.

"Modan," he said. "Are you all right?"

"Najem?" she said after a terrible moment. Her voice was distressingly weak and her speech was slurred. *"I fell. Hit my head."*

He tried not to picture her lying there in the wreck of the starship, perhaps with a broken appendage, perhaps with something worse, unable to move or—

Her scream cut through the cabin like a laser through a sheet of silk. She had obviously meant to continue talking, leaving their channel open, and now, because of that, he could hear her grunting and perhaps growling as if in the midst of some struggle.

"The soldiers," she managed to say before the link died. *"They've come—"*

It was obvious what had happened and just as clear what he had to do. He snatched up the remaining isolation suit, a phaser, and a tricorder by which to track her comm signal.

I'm coming, Modan, he thought. *Just hang on.*

He slid down the ladder from the crew cabin into the

hold and grabbed a second phaser as he made for the rear access hatch.

The shuttle's stealth field was still intact, thank the Prophets, still making it look like an innocuous bit of jungle. All he had to do was get to her, free her, and get back here. Then they could go and maybe, just maybe, send their friends in the future a beacon that could stop all this from happening.

He wouldn't even need luck. This was something from the old days, the dark days, the time of blood and retribution. He would come at them invisibly, blast them away from her, and make the dash before they knew what hit them.

It wasn't even a plan, just the application of lessons learned and perfected years before when his world was black and white and all his enemies were obvious and uniformly without *pagh.*

It would be quick and easy and—

Just as he crossed the threshold, the ground rippled with another quake. He was smashed down again, this time into the more yielding dirt and crystal of Orisha's soil. He landed on his back and found himself staring up at something his mind could only barely comprehend.

The sky was on fire. Lateral columns of flame and force leaped and danced there from horizon to horizon, obscuring even the sight of the planet's sun. The ground rumbled and churned beneath him like a living thing. He saw something like lightning bolts rip down from the heavens, boiling the landscape wherever they struck and, at the center of it all, like an eye gazing down on the destruction, was an undulating sphere of forces and energy that could only be what the Orishans had called the Eye.

Jaza Najem had another name for it, now that it had shown itself, and it was neither godlike nor demonic.

Tesseract, he realized, and then, as the effect subsided, *and something else.*

As suddenly as it had appeared, the apparition was gone and the world was quiet again.

That's what's wrong with the sky, he thought. *It's flooded with enough highly energized chronometric particles to affect the visible spectrum.* That didn't explain the massive tidal forces ripping across Orisha when the "eye" opened. It didn't even explain how the damned thing existed at all outside a laboratory, but it explained enough, perhaps just enough to salvage this disaster. First, though, there was Modan to rescue.

When he was sure there would be no further upheavals he gathered up the weapons, activated his isolation suit, and stopped dead, frozen in place by the scene before him.

There was the flat orange disk of the Orishan sun, dipping low in the sparkling copper sky, a sky that had seemed both familiar and strange the first time he'd seen it.

There was the shimmering afterimage of the massive tesseract that trailed behind the planet mostly unseen. There in the dirt, unearthed by the rumbling ground, were nine of the ubiquitous blue crystals clustered either by chance or design into a pattern that recalled a Tear of the Prophets.

The air was ozone and ice around him, but he knew the cold was not from anything so mundane as a change in the local weather.

This was his vision. This was the place and time of his death.

Chapter Eight

ORISHA, STARDATE 58449.5

It was difficult tracking Keru through the chaos of giant vines and towering violet stalks. The pace Ra-Havreii's abductors set was ferocious, eating up meters the way a horde of locusts devours a field of grain.

Despite his size and the trillion natural obstructions offered by the unfamiliar and hostile landscape, the big Trill tore through the jungle as if it were an open, level field.

Once the women lost sight of him completely and were forced to rely on Troi's empathic abilities to stay on his trail. Troi could feel Keru's grief, so similar to her own, burning white hot somewhere ahead of them. He masked it well, but there was fire raging under that calm, efficient exterior. If he did catch the ones who'd taken Ra-Havreii, she wasn't sure if he or they would survive the encounter.

Though Troi was too intent on maintaining her fix on

Keru's emotional aura to notice much else, Christine Vale continued to marvel at the woman's ability to bear up.

The death of her husband had obviously stripped her of every shred of hope she had once possessed, and yet here she was, doing her duty, doing her utmost to save the engineer.

I'd be catatonic if I was in her skin, thought Vale. *Catatonic or worse.*

Troi faltered suddenly, uttering a short ragged cry as she stumbled forward to the ground. Vale was with her in an instant, supporting her, keeping her on her feet.

"You okay?" she said.

"Feedback," she said. "It's Keru. He's unconscious."

"But alive," said Vale. She couldn't take any more deaths today, and certainly not Keru's. "He's still alive?"

Troi nodded. "There are two of them there, Christine," she said. "Just over the next rise."

"Only two?"

"I can sense them," she said, rising. "They're the same type of beings we encountered in space. I assume they're Orishans." Troi winced. "Their emotions are so alien," she continued. "They're getting easier to sort, but I think they're waiting."

"For?"

"Us," said Troi.

"Their mistake," said Vale.

Ch'ika'tik was unhappy. It was bad enough being out here in the open lattice with the midday sky peaking through the vault of vines above, but to have to approach the Shattered Place? To get there and to find these *creatures* wandering among the ebony Spires, creatures that were both as bizarre and as hideous as something from a hibernation fantasy?

And the weapons these creatures had. The funny noises they made when they fired was a weak herald to the destruction of the wave they produced. The first one they had taken had been no trouble, but the second, the one who tracked them, caught them and attacked, that one was deadly.

Ch'ika'tik was not taken out of the Dreaming caste, but she knew an ill omen when she saw it. This omen was as ill as they came.

It was soft like a *tk'sit,* though nearly hairless and with too few arms. It made noises like a *tk'sol* though neither as loud nor as deep. It had no armor, no spikes, no venom, no acid. The ugly little monster didn't even have wings for escaping. For all that, it had taken three of her sisters to bring the creature down without killing it.

A'yujae'Tak had been quite clear about that.

"Find it," she had said about the one who had dared to direct a wave at Erykon's Tear. "Find it and bring it to me alive."

As caste Maters went, A'yujae'Tak could be somewhat eccentric at times. She had come from the Dreamers and sometimes, when a thing should be clear as sparkle stone—killing anyone or anything that entered the Shattered Place, for instance—A'yujae'Tak would often find ways to make things foggy.

Still, she was the Mater and her will was Ch'ika'tik's law, as it was for all the others in the caste. Though she was just a soldier, just a scout, she knew this latest eccentricity of the Mater would prove to be trouble.

She could still taste Tk'ok'iik's pain as the alien wave had smashed into her, instantly stealing her consciousness. The Children of Erykon had nothing like this wave weapon.

The second creature had been so much trouble that Chk'lok'tok had told her and Kk'tik to wait behind and break the final two before returning to the Spire.

"These may be killed, yes?" said Kk'tik.

"No," Chk'lok'tok had told them and added a command chemical to her scent for emphasis. "Only break them and bring them to the Spire. And any of their wave devices as well. A'yujae'Tak desires them."

Kk'tik had been taken out of the Weaver caste and had difficulty with too much complexity. She was a done-or-not-done sort of drone. Still, she offered no protest, only mixed a hint of disappointment into her chemical aura.

Now, waiting for the second set of ugly creatures to make their appearance, Kk'tik's scent was full of questions.

"Patience," said Ch'ika'tik. "They will come to us or we will go to them. Then we break them and go home."

As if on cue, one of the creatures climbed up over the ridge of vines and stood there, its upper appendages extended above what Ch'ika'tik was fairly sure was its head. It was different again from the first two examples of whatever they were, smaller than both and with more of a mane than the second one though less than the first.

"I [surrender/reveal myself] to you," it said. It spoke strangely, with no real chemical mixture under the words for clarity or emphasis. In fact, its scent was unpleasantly static. Another mark against these things. The creature seemed to wish to go on speaking, but Kk'tik had her wave lance up and trained on its face.

"Be still, ugly thing," she said, and flooded her scent with a locking chemical. Whether command scents would work on these creatures remained to be seen, so Ch'ika'tik hung back, keeping her own lance targeted on the newcomer while Kk'tik took a closer look.

Ch'ika'tik's scent advised caution, but it was clear that Kk'tik was secure in their superiority over this thing. Unlike the last one, this creature seemed fairly docile. There might not be a need to break it before returning to the Spire.

"It has no wave devices," she said, still looking the creature over. "It smells . . ."

"I can smell it, you stupid slug," said Ch'ika'tik. "Just break it and let's go."

"Wasn't there another one of them?" said Kk'tik.

"Yes," said Ch'ika'tik. "Go get it and bring it back here. I will watch this one."

Kk'tik's scent aura contracted until it was nearly imperceptible. As Ch'ika'tik took her position next to the new creature, she leaped up over the rise to capture the other. She didn't have the sharpest mandibles when it came to planning, but when it came to following orders, she was perfect.

Ch'ika'tik took a better look at the alien while she waited. Not enough eyes (if that's what they were). No armor that she could see to protect that soft, mushy flesh. No scent variation. And its face continued to twist in that odd and unsettling manner.

"Stop doing that, creature," she said after a moment of watching it.

"What?" it said.

"That thing you do with your face," she said. "The twisting. Showing your ugly teeth."

"It's called [facial contortion/expression of pleasure]," it said.

"Well, stop it."

But the creature didn't stop and suddenly all Ch'ika'tik could think of was how awful, how terrifying it was to be outside, under the sky with the Eye looking down in displeasure at everything below. It could see her, she realized. It could see her and, in seeing, know that she had hoarded nutrient jelly that had been meant for the larvae, that she had made sport with one of the breeder males when she should have been guarding the Spire.

The Spire! It would know about the Spire and their plans and then—and then—

The merest thought of the Eye's wrath over her and her people's misdeeds sent Ch'ika'tik into a paroxysm born entirely of fear. She fell to the ground before the ugly creature, taking no comfort that it had at last stopped twisting its face that way. All she could think of was the Eye, the Eye, the Eye and its awful righteous anger if it ever found the Spire.

She pulled her carapace close around herself, folding up into the same sort of ball she'd made during the first days of her martial training when the bigger pupae had scared her so. All she could think then was, *Hide! Hide! Protect!* Now, in the face of this new terror, it was all she could think again.

As her conscious mind began to shut down, she heard the ugly creature say, "All right, Christine. Go!"

Then there was that funny sound that had accompanied the use of the alien's wave weapon only somehow louder and less amusing.

Then there was nothing. For the time being at least, Ch'ika'tik's mind had gone away.

"Wow," said Vale as she slid down the rise and saw the enormous and formerly fairly intimidating soldier curled up in something very much like a fetal ball. "What did you do to it?"

"Exactly what you asked," said Troi.

Vale held up the two phasers. Neither of them had wanted to kill these creatures unless it was warranted. Vale guessed that two phasers set on maximum stun might take them down without killing them, and she was right.

Deanna's part was harder, requiring her to use her empathic abilities in a way she normally didn't or even couldn't.

"I wish you'd told me before that I was shunting my emotions into you when I got stressed," said Troi. "It's a possible side effect of the fertility treatments I'm undergoing with Dr. Ree."

"Sorry," said Vale. "At first I didn't know exactly what was happening, and then I didn't want to pry."

"We're family, Chris," said Troi in a tone that pierced Vale to her core. "Whatever else happens, you should know that."

"Thanks," said Vale, hoping she wasn't actually blushing. "It's a hell of a trick, but it looks like it worked too well."

"How so?"

"Look at this thing," said Vale. The Orishan was almost literally folded up into itself, having gone into some version of shock from the emotional overload. "It's not going to be able to tell us where they took the others."

"It doesn't need to," said Troi. "I might not be able to read minds as well as a full Betazoid, but when one is screaming at me, I can certainly hear it."

"The Orishan told you the location?"

"Some place called the Spire," said Troi. "It's not far from here, but I don't think we would have found it on our own."

"Why not?"

"You'll see," said Troi. "Come on."

Troi was right, they would never have found it on their own. Yes, it was massive, effortlessly towering over the jungle as well as its nearest neighbor. Yes, now that they were close, the tricorder could easily pick out the strange energy emanations pouring off the thing at intervals. But they would never have found the Spire on their own.

The stalks that rose up out of the chaos of vines were many times the size of the biggest redwood on Earth, their uppermost reaches not only standing well above the jungle canopy but seeming to disappear into the clouds above.

They were like the beanstalks in the old nursery story but without leaves or angry giants living in castles at the summit. This one, the Spire, had a few unique additions to separate it from its fellows.

"The metal looks woven," said Vale softly. "Like the watchdog ship."

"The tricorder says it's some kind of resin," she muttered, still trying to make sense of the readings.

The Spire was important to the Orishans. After their terrible deity this might be the most important thing on the planet, but she still had no idea why.

They had taken pains to camouflage the Spire, somehow making the technological additions to the stalk's structure mimic as closely as possible the foliage around it. The woven metal Vale spoke of seemed to rise up out of the earth, winding around and through the great stalk, conforming to its color and contours, until she lost sight of it in the upper distance. There were openings dotting the thing all around that could be windows or lights or exhaust chimneys or even missile tubes, but each sported a sort of hood of artificial fronds, clearly technological from below but, at least on those she could see, from above the hoods were indistinguishable from the surrounding flora.

She wondered if all their structures were made this way and if that might not be the reason for the absence of the obvious industrial footprint Orishan civilization had to have left on its planet.

Looking down on the Spire, indeed, looking at it from any angle that wasn't directly below, there was no way to make a distinction between it and the hundreds of thousands of other stalks jutting up from the sea of vines that covered most of the world.

"Sneaky buggers," said Vale. "What are they hiding it from?"

"God," said Troi. "I think they're hiding from their god."

It was easy getting into the Spire. There were several apertures at the base of the stalk, one so large they could have flown the shuttle in had they been able to find it.

There were no sentries, not on the ground level at least, and no warning system that they could detect. Inside, the place was alternately a maze of wide corridors and a series of large domed chambers into and out of which the corridors led. All of them were empty. Their good fortune made Vale nervous, but Troi thought she understood it a little.

"They don't have crime here," she said softly. "They don't have wars. They don't even have any of the social chaos that we take for granted even on the most advanced worlds in the Federation."

"Hive mind?" asked Vale. The interior of the Spire, with its thousands of hexagonal facets and openings within the facets, did remind her very much of a wasp's nest or possibly an impossibly large ant colony.

"Possibly," said Troi, fretting with the tricorders. "The known sentient insectile species do tend toward order and rigid social structures as a rule. There's something more going on here. One moment."

There was indeed more to the Spire than met the eye. Though at the base level it seemed to be empty and its technological aspects were only hidden if looking down from the sky, the entire inner structure supported a network of force fields of some sort. The place almost hummed with the energy of these fields, though the tricorders could make no sense of their composition or purpose. It made scanning for Keru and Ra-Havreii very difficult.

"Faith," said Troi as they entered the third of the giant

domed rooms. "Their faith in this Eye, their fear of it, it's shaped their whole society."

"What society?" said Vale. "I watched the same footage you did. Those signals had to bleed off from somewhere. There should be cities here. There should be farms and, from the size of that space vessel, there should be a pretty large shipyard somewhere. There's nothing out there but open jungle."

"I don't know," said Troi, frustrated with the device she held. She handed the tricorder to Vale to see if she could get something useful out of it. The lattice of force fields continued to confound her scans. "I think there's something obvious here and we're missing it."

As Vale adjusted the settings on the tricorder, Troi ran her fingers lightly along the nearest curved wall. It was not metal and it was not like any plant life she'd ever touched, even here on Orisha. It was a strange mixture of both.

They fear their god, but they revere it just the same, she thought. *They don't care about exploration, but they built a giant space vessel. They built this tower, hid it, and then left it empty. Where did they go? Where could they have taken—*

"Deanna," said Vale, her tense whisper breaking in on her thoughts. "I think I know where the Orishans are."

Turning away from the wall, Troi was about to ask Vale where when she also knew. They were impossible to miss after all.

On the far side of their chamber several of the hexagonal facets had opened and from them a swarm of Orishan warriors, each with its own glowing lance, flooded in. In seconds there were fifty of the creatures there, training their weapons on the two women.

"I don't suppose you can do that fear trick on all of them," said Vale. Troi shook her head. "No. Of course not."

After the fight—there was no way they could be taken without one—Vale struggled to remain conscious as she and Troi were carried off in different directions by their insectoid captors.

As she drifted in and out of consciousness, she tried to get a sense of what was happening.

She was being carried. The bug held her close in two of its four arms, pressed tight to its abdomen, as it scrambled along what looked like an access tunnel of some sort. The dimensions were only slightly bigger than those of her captor, forcing it and its fellows to run single file.

She could hear them all chattering, skittering along the hard smooth surface—*chikkachikkachikkachikka*—and was happy when the darkness pulled her down away from the sound.

She woke again, briefly, now slung like a sack over the soldier's shoulder. It might have been the same one that had carried her down (she felt it was down somehow) or it might not. They really did all look almost exactly the same.

This time she got a flash of a huge empty space, a high vaulted ceiling made of the same ceramic that entwined the Spire. Purple and black Orishans crawled everywhere along its surface, climbing in and out of more hexagonal openings, some carrying bundles of some sort, some stopping briefly to chatter at one of their fellows. Some were bigger than the others. Some had wings, clear and veiny, that reminded her of dragonflies.

I'm underground, she realized, still fighting the losing battle to remain conscious. *That's where the cities are. They built down to get away from the sky.* Then the darkness took her again.

The first thing she thought when she woke was, *Deanna! Where have they taken Deanna!?*

The second thing she thought was, *Why am I still alive?*

"Do not fight, creature," said a voice that reminded her of a handful of nails being scraped across a sheet of metal. "Stand, but do not fight."

With difficulty she pushed herself off her belly, up to her knees, and then finally to her feet.

She was not prepared for what she saw. This creature towered over the other Orishans by a good two meters. It was a darker shade of the ubiquitous violet that seemed to be the theme on Orisha. It had the same extra arms and the same armored exoskeleton, but there were bright markings on this one and, in places, protrusions that looked like small bulbous inverted bowls. Its face was more angular than the rounded ones of the soldiers, and both sets of its eyes blazed yellow instead of white.

"I am A'yujae'Tak," it said. "I am the Mater of the [possible meaning: guardian] caste. What are you?"

On every visible surface, Orishans scuttled between giant viewing screens depicting at least two of the Spire's siblings—one rising from the center of a lake and the other was near what looked like a volcano.

Notations of some sort appeared and vanished at regular intervals beside each image. Elsewhere in the chamber technicians manipulated what were so obviously power control systems, she almost laughed. The technology was alien, certainly, partly ceramic, partly organic, and partly utilizing the unknown force fields for various purposes.

Vale could actually see some of the fields flash briefly into the visual spectrum, shift color, and then vanish again.

Still, as alien as all of it was, she had been in rooms like this regularly for most of her adult life.

This was the power control center, the same as the engineering deck on any starship. The giant Orishan version of a warp reactor protruding from the distant ceiling was the final giveaway. The oscillating blue-white plasma flowing from two sources into a single pulsating reactor core was also familiar.

What the hell were these people doing?

When she didn't respond right away, one of the soldiers that flanked A'yujae'Tak prodded Vale's ribs with its lance.

"Speak when spoken to, creature," it said. "Obey the Mater."

She gave her name, her rank, and the name of her vessel. She tried to answer the flurry of obvious questions that followed as best she could, but she was never certain that the Orishans grasped all of it. There was some aspect of their communication that the universal translator couldn't grip.

"You are from above?" said A'yujae'Tak at last. "From another of Erykon's creations?"

"In a way," said Vale. It was obvious this creature believed that the universe and everything in it had been created by its god. "We travel from creation to creation, seeking understanding."

"Travel, how?" said A'yujae'Tak. "My seekers found you in the Shattered Place using this device to direct waves at Erykon's Mirror."

The device was obviously Ra-Havreii's tricorder, but Erykon's Mirror? Did she mean the warp reactor? These creatures had moved fast, naming both the crash site and the wreckage and folding them into their mythology in only a few days.

That didn't stack up in Vale's mind somehow, but she couldn't say why. "We were only examining it," she said.

"How did you come there?" said the Mater. "The Shattered Place is [possible meaning: taboo] except to those the Mater allows."

Vale was thinking that maybe telling her about the battle with the watchdog ship wasn't the best idea when it struck her that A'yujae'Tak should have already known about that. She should at least have known about the watchdog's destruction. Why didn't she? Why didn't she already know about the shuttle crash and about her own people being obliterated along with *Titan*?

"It's complicated," she said finally.

"You have wave devices that we do not know," said A'yujae'Tak, holding up the tricorder in one talon and the phasers in two of her others. "Weapons that do not kill."

"We are peaceful explorers," said Vale. "We try our best not to kill anything if we can avoid it."

This seemed to please A'yujae'Tak. Vale wasn't sure how she knew that, only that an air of approval seemed to radiate briefly from the alien and wash over her. Maybe it was something pheromonal.

"What do you know of the Eye?" said A'yujae'Tak

after a little. When Vale didn't answer right away, she took another sharp nudge to the sternum.

"Answer, creature," said the soldier. "Do as told."

"Less than you, I think," said Vale. They were in dangerous territory, she felt, wandering close to the religious construct that informed this whole society.

She missed Troi's presence even more acutely then. Vale was no diplomat, and this genial conversation could become lethal in seconds if she didn't handle it exactly right.

"We know so little," said A'yujae'Tak almost wistfully. "We try to please Erykon, to let the Eye sleep, but so many times we have failed and it has [possible meaning: destroyed] us."

"You seem to be doing fine now," said Vale.

"Since the time of the [possible meaning: Oracle], yes," said A'yujae'Tak. "We have grown and we have hidden ourselves. The Eye sleeps and all is well."

A'yujae'Tak sailed into a rambling account of Orishan history, describing how, at intervals, the Eye had opened, looked down on whatever the Orishans had built and, not liking the view, had destroyed it utterly. According to her the Eye had split the earth, burned the sky, and generally wreaked apocalyptic havoc on the poor Orishans below. After each apocalypse the survivors would rebuild, believing themselves to have learned from the recent punishment how to modify themselves to suit their god's desire.

Only, nothing worked. It sometimes took a hundred years, sometimes four or five, but, no matter what sort of society the Orishans created, when the Eye looked down upon it, that society was doomed.

The cycle continued for millennia until—and this was fuzzy to Vale—some sort of supernatural presence appeared and spoke to one of A'yujae'Tak's ancestors. This Oracle guided the birth of current Orishan society, giving them the concepts of castes—Dreamers who did the planning, Hunters who did the fighting, Weavers who did the building, and the Guardians whose job it was to protect the world and its people.

When, after a century of guidance, their Oracle fell silent, it was the Guardians who had led the Orishan people underground, where they could continue to live and thrive without fear of displeasing the Eye.

"The others go about their lives," she said. "They breed and weave. They toil and build. But we must protect them."

"It seems you've done well with that too," said Vale.

"The [Oracle] has not spoken in many cycles, Commanderchristinevale," said A'yujae'Tak. "So much time without word to say if we have pleased Erykon. We have done so much. We have come too far this time to have it all destroyed."

In that moment Vale thought she understood. These beings weren't hostile or malevolent. They were terrified. Whatever the Eye really was, whatever the truth of her religious stories really was, one thing was clear. Something had happened to Orisha, over and over, to the point that the entire civilization was little more than a whipped dog, fearing even the hint of its master's displeasure. Having been on the wrong side of terror more than once in her life, she knew very well the lengths to which someone might go to find peace of mind.

They had been on their own, in a permanent state of

fear for centuries, without even this Oracle of theirs to help them. They were smart, inventive, and increasingly skilled at hiding themselves from the thing they feared most.

"We must protect Orisha," said A'yujae'Tak. "We must never suffer that way again. Erykon must see this. You come from above. You were in the Shattered Place. Do you know Erykon's will, Commanderchristinevale?"

They were all staring at her. Every Orishan in the room, from the Mater down to the lowliest drone, had focused all their attention on Vale and whatever tiny hope she might give. They had lived with the fear of their imminent destruction for so long, so constantly, that it now permeated everything they did, everything they thought. What could she possibly tell them that could take that away?

"I don't know Erykon's will," she said. "I'm sorry."

"Do you know Erykon's nature?" said A'yujae'Tak. "Is Erykon [possible meaning: God]? Or merely some [possible meaning: mundane] celestial phenomenon?"

"I—" *Easy, Chris,* she told herself. *These people are desperate and terrified. You don't want to shake their paradigm more than you have to.* "I can't answer that."

Something like regret rippled through the entire company, and Vale was sure she had disappointed them all in some fundamental, even primal way.

"All right, Commanderchristinevale," said the Mater. "Then perhaps we can learn the true nature of Erykon together."

A'yujae'Tak made a clicking noise in her thorax, and several of the smaller Orishans began frantically inputting codes into their various stations. The great central viewing monitor rippled, losing the image it had been displaying of one of the other Spires in favor of, well, Vale wasn't exactly sure what it was she was looking at.

There was a sort of undulating rainbow effect rolling across the screen, peppered all over with tiny black dots that seemed fixed in their positions.

It took her only a second to realize she was looking at deep space via means developed by these beings. The black dots were clearly stars and, she guessed, the rainbow effect must correspond to the weird energy patterns in this system.

Presently the image shifted again and other shapes became visible, ones that Vale found distressingly familiar. The first was a massive swirling orb of chaos. Was that Erykon? She couldn't get a sense of its size without a reference point when that reference point presented itself in the form of a heavy-class Starfleet shuttle dropping out of warp distressingly close to the thing.

All the blood rushed out of her face when she realized what she was seeing, what had obviously happened. *That's us,* she thought. *Before we fired the probe.*

It occurred to her also that there had to be something up there watching all this and relaying the signal back to the Spire, and she realized that she was watching her own actions of two days ago from the point of view of the watchdog vessel.

They weren't watchdogs at all, she thought. *They were exploring, just like us. Only their motivations were different.*

"There is a larger [possible meaning: intruder] corrupting the local waves out beyond the other of Erykon's creations," said the Mater, and Vale was sure she heard a bit of malice creeping into the tone. "Do you have [possible meaning: knowledge] of this thing?"

There it was. She could admit knowledge of *Titan,* of the mission, of the shuttle's attempt to land on Orisha and get them to stop their warp experiments. She could beg the Mater not to allow the events she knew had already occurred to progress as they had before, thereby creating a paradox that should save her friends. Or she could follow the rules, protect the temporal line and let them and probably herself, Troi, Keru, and Ra-Havreii die.

This was where Will Riker had been only days before, and now she understood the horrible price noninterference could exact on any officer, much less a captain.

Screw it, she thought. *They can court-martial me when we get home.*

The information poured out of her so fast she was sure the translator in her badge could never keep pace. She told them, as quickly as she could, of the events that had led *Titan* here, what *Titan* was, who it represented, and how there really was no need for anyone to fire anything at anybody much less the warp cannon on the nose of the Orishan ship.

"You are [possible meaning: brain injured]," said A'yujae'Tak once Vale was done.

"No," said Vale, suddenly desperate and struggling futilely against the grip of the soldier who now held her. The watchdog vessel had already fired on the shuttle once and missed. It was now gearing up for its second shot. "It's the truth. If you just let them alone—"

But it was already too late.

Vale watched, fascinated in spite of herself, as the warp cannon fired. The space around the bolt rippled very much like the waves the Orishans described. At the last instant another ripple appeared around the shuttle—Jaza's unstable warp bubble. The bolt hit the bubble and after sending more ripples out through the waves of multicolored energy, seemed at last to grow still.

Vale was the only one who knew it was just a momentary breather before the storm, and sure enough, even as the Orishans were puzzling over how the shuttle had twice survived their greatest weapon, a small spark of light appeared in the center of the thing they called the Eye.

Vale, knowing what to expect, saw it first, but soon, one by one, all the Orishans present took notice. They all watched in obvious horror as the spark grew to encompass the entire swirling orb and then erupted.

"They have awoken Erykon," said A'yujae'Tak, aghast. "The Eye is open! Deploy the Veil. Now! Before we are lost!"

It took Vale a confused moment to realize "the veil" did not refer to her, but something else entirely. Whatever it was, they were clearly desperate to have it activate. Everywhere workers scurried to obey their Mater. Buttons were pressed, commands were entered by trembling talons. Machinery, in the walls, in the floor, and for meters above began to hum and vibrate. Suddenly some force, some kind of invisible energy, rolled through the chamber, rattling Vale's teeth as it went into the walls and up, up, up to the apex of the Spire.

There was a flash of incandescent white that, for a moment, obliterated all sight. When it was gone, so was the image on the giant viewer. There was nothing to see there but a solid field of white.

"Something is wrong," said A'yujae'Tak. "This did not happen bef—"

Everyone present was suddenly slammed to the ground as the earth above and around the chamber did its best to rip itself to bits. The noise was thunderous, impossible. It lasted long enough that Vale actually thought this might be the planet shaking itself apart, but as quickly as the quake had begun, it vanished.

She barely felt the claws of the soldiers hefting her back to her feet, barely noted the Mater ordering someone to give her a visual shot of the world outside.

"The sky," said A'yujae'Tak. "Let me see the sky!"

There was another flurry of workers running to obey, and then, slowly, the field of solid white on the main viewer gave way to an image of the sky above the Spire.

Vale knew it wasn't possible, that what she saw there was only the visual display of massive cosmic forces banging against each other, but it looked like fire. It looked exactly as if the sky over Orisha was burning.

Vale lay on the floor where they had dropped her, unmindful of the bruises and cuts she'd sustained on the way down from the control chamber.

She couldn't hate them or weep or feel anything really beyond the wide black chasm opening up inside her and sucking her down and down and down.

This was twice now that *Titan* had died in front of her, but unlike the first time, this last destruction had been her fault. She had been too thick or too clumsy or not enough something to make the Orishans see in time what they were about to do.

They were all dead, again, and as soon as the quakes had subsided, the Mater had assured her that she and the rest of her companions would join them.

"You will feed our larvae," she had promised Vale.

Yes, she thought. *I'm sure we will.*

So she lay there, waiting for it, feeling the occasional rumble in the walls and listening to—

Somebody was humming.

"Hello, Commander," said Xin Ra-Havreii from some dark corner of the little cell. "When you are ready to hear it, I believe I have some news."

He went on humming after that and she went on listening, this time without the critical ear she'd given him previously. None of that mattered now. His eccentricities were trivial things, as were most of the frictions that had plagued them before.

The melody was actually quite pretty, she realized, as was his voice, which was not deep, but full and somehow sensual. She'd heard him humming it so often in the last few days but had been too irritated by the fact of it to ask him what it was. She did so now.

"It is an aural schematic of a *Luna*-class starship, Commander," he said. "*Titan,* specifically. I've been deconstructing and reconstructing it for days."

She recalled how his people on Efros Delta had been required to develop a predominantly oral tradition as they weathered the rigors of their world's ice age. An entirely oral means of storing data necessitated an entirely aural means of deciphering it.

She laughed then, bitterly. All the time she'd thought he was becoming less and less sane, becoming more and more intractably eccentric, he had, in fact, been carrying the entire schematic of the starship *Titan* around with him in the form of this tune.

Her laughter became hysterical at that, wrenching out of her in long shuddering jags that could just have easily been sobs. When she was done she looked over at him, sitting on the floor with his legs folded just so.

"So what's your news?" she said.

"I was confused at first," he said. "When I examined the ship's wreckage, there was so much missing, so much that was destroyed, that I could feel the ghosts of the *Luna* reaching out for me. This is not an exaggeration, Commander. I'm sure Counselor Troi has kept you somewhat abreast of my . . . situation."

"It's come up," said Vale.

"And rightly so," he said. "Though I doubt it will again."

"Probably not," said Vale, thinking of the hungry larvae.

"I have aural schematics of all of the *Luna*-class vessels committed to memory," he said. "Though they all leave drydock essentially the same, very soon their music changes as they experience different events."

"All right," she said, picturing the starships swimming through the void, singing to one another like whales.

"I have them all in my mind," he said. "And specifically I have the music of their warp cores committed to memory."

"The news, Ra-Havreii," she said, happy to feel something as mundane as irritation with his wandering conversation.

"I listened to the warp core at the crash site, Commander," said the engineer. "And I can tell you that, beyond any doubt whatsoever, while that is certainly a crashed *Luna*-class Starfleet vessel spread over the ground out there, it is, just as unequivocally, not the *Starship Titan*."

Part Two

Then Soon Now Once
Once Then Soon Now
Now Once Then Soon
Soon Now Once Then

—Tholian Axiom, First Iteration

Chapter Nine

There was a split second—just long enough for everyone who was watching to realize what was coming—and then the wave hit.

Titan screamed as the surge of energy washed over it and through it as well. Metal twisted, software spiraled chaotically, and every member of her crew scrambled to protect whatever they could from the onslaught, mostly to little avail.

The effect went through them all like a wave, inspiring everything from nausea and disorientation in some to catatonic neural shutdown in more than a few.

Every device or system that dealt with or utilized energy fields as a matter of course buckled or shut down or exploded.

Engineers blanched as the warp core bubbled and

seized, riffling though the color spectrum until the plasma inside was nearly translucent.

Rossini barked orders at his subordinates, including for someone to heft the stricken Ensign Torvig up from where he'd fallen on the deck and get him to sickbay ASAP. As it had before, the pulse had hit Torvig as hard as it had any of *Titan*'s mechanical systems—perhaps harder, as his mind certainly knew what was happening to his body. *Titan,* at least, couldn't feel pain or terror.

As he tried not to focus on the frail body of his friend twitching and writhing on the floor, his cybernetic appendages flailing wildly, Rossini couldn't help but think that Torvig's condition mirrored that of *Titan*.

All around him there was pandemonium as those few who hadn't been slammed into bulkheads or pitched over high railings ran to get their machines back under their control.

Ten people trying to do the work of forty, he thought. *Good luck.*

He didn't feel he was ready for this, despite having survived *Titan*'s other harrowing adventures, but with the chief engineer off-ship and Baars having been knocked unconscious when he'd fallen from one of the upper tiers, he didn't have time to let his insecurities reign. It was him or no one. He'd always hoped his time as chief engineer would follow years of climbing up through the ranks, after which he'd get assigned to some small research vessel where he could learn by doing and not have to worry too much about being killed.

His greatest fear had always been of being given too much responsibility before he was confident he could handle it, and now here he was, living the nightmare. Although he might not be living it long if *Titan*'s warp core kept behaving as it was.

His eyes stayed focused on the core as he prayed for it to return to its normal blue-white oscillation. If it settled in the next few seconds, thirty at most, they might have a chance of not being killed. If it didn't settle, well, best not to think too much about that.

"Secure for manual core ejection," he bellowed to the room. "On my mark!"

Bodies leaped to do as they'd been ordered. With her still-working arm Kanenya waved down from the uppermost tier that she was set. Someone had grabbed up poor Torvig and was in the process of hauling him away when the Choblik's rear appendage whipped out, latched onto the doorframe, and held fast.

"No!" he said. "No, I can help. With the core."

"You've got twenty seconds," said Rossini.

"Tuvok!" shouted Will Riker, pulling himself back into the captain's chair. Like everyone else on the bridge, he'd been hurled to the floor as the massive wave of energy hit. "Status!"

Somehow the Vulcan managed to maintain poise even in this circumstance, though the message he related in his calm baritone was less than reassuring.

"Shields are buckling and down to thirty-one percent," he said. "Failure is imminent. Artificial gravity and basic life support have failed on decks eight and thirteen. *Titan*'s warp core is cycling toward inversion."

Riker heard the casualty reports flooding in from everywhere. Dr. Ree obviously had his work cut out for him. There were people with shattered extremities and cracked skulls; at least a couple of the telepaths were incoherent. None of the children had been hurt, thank God. Only scared out of their minds. Riker knew how they felt.

"Computer," he said. "Initiate warp core ejection protocol. Authorization: Riker-Beta-One-Zero-Two."

"Unable to comply. Ejection system offline," said the computer. The ship lurched again, violently, and he had the horrible notion in his mind of *Titan* rolling end over end in the darkness until the core finally killed them all.

"Captain," said Lavena, struggling to keep not only her seat but also what little control she had of the helm. "I'm getting massive torque readings on the port nacelle strut."

"How bad?" he said.

"Bad, sir," she replied. "Too much more of this and it will definitely splinter."

"Bridge to engineering," he said and was quickly answered by a very tense-sounding Ensign Rossini. "Where is Baars?"

"Down, sir," said Rossini. *"Along with about twenty of the shift."*

My God, he sounds young, thought Riker. *And scared to death.* "I need you to perform a manual core ejection, Ensign."

"Yes, sir," said Rossini, obviously unhappy about it. *"But there's just one thing."*

"Now, son," said Riker. "No time for any alternate plans."

"But, sir, I think," came Rossini's voice, a little stronger maybe, a bit more firm. *"I think we fixed the problem."*

Riker was about to ask the young engineer what the

hell he was talking about when, all of a sudden, the lights stopped flickering, Lavena gasped as her helm control returned, and Riker could feel his stomach properly seated inside him, which signified that the artificial gravity was no longer a problem.

"Well done, Ensign," said Riker, sweeping his gaze around the bridge to take in the damage.

It seemed minimal. Tuvok was at his station, hip-deep in incoming data. Lavena grumbled over her helm but in a way that seemed less frantic and doubtful than it had in the previous minutes. Bohn and Kesi were back at navigation and science, respectively, and while the ship continued to lurch in the throes of the alien energy storm, it did so with considerably less violence. They were all right for the moment. *Titan* was all right.

"Tuvok," he said, dreading the response. He had felt Deanna's flash of panicked warning just before the wave had exploded at them apparently from nowhere. He had felt the sudden and absolute absence of her presence in his mind. He had felt it like an icy spear ripping through him, and now he felt the ache of the wound. "What about the shuttle?"

"Sensors are unreliable, sir," said the Vulcan, clearly having difficulty. "I am attempting to recalibrate."

"Aili," said the captain. He couldn't think about them now. He couldn't think about her. "What's the status on the port strut?"

"Nominal for now, sir," she said, obvious relief in her voice. He could see the same expression on her face even through the distortion of the water in her drysuit. "But I don't recommend any more shakes like that last one."

"No promises," said Riker. "Good work, Rossini."

"It wasn't really me, sir," he said. *"It was Torvig."*

At first sight, main engineering looked as it had for the last few days: battered and patched as if it was under perpetual repair, which, of course, it was.

Access plates hung off the walls; cables and chipsets hung from the openings as if some impossibly gigantic octopus had been trapped behind the paneling.

The engineers themselves looked only slightly better than their domain. The humans were bruised, bleary-eyed, and spotted with the lubricants that had belched free during the recent unpleasantness. Riker wasn't sure what the normal state of some of the nonhumans was, but if drooping antennae and orange-ringed eyes were any indication, they had been pulled through the same wringer.

Worse than the sight of the engineers, worse than the ongoing pitch and roll of the ship as it continued to be battered by the forces outside, was the vision of Ensign Torvig splayed out on the floor beneath the main control console mumbling to himself as if in a trance.

Riker had always found the ensign to be more sturdy than his appearance might imply. The Choblik's seeming delicacy had always been offset by the many cybernetic enhancements he bore. Now it was those very mechanical bits that drew attention to just how frail and helpless Torvig was without them.

Data cables ran from the control console to exposed nodes on every one of Torvig's cybernetic parts. Some were translucent, pulsing with light at intervals in time with the convulsions of the ensign's body.

"What is he doing?" asked the captain at last.

"He's talking to the computer, sir," said Rossini.

"Is he," said Riker, stopping as another shudder ran through the ensign's body. "Is he all right?"

As if in response, all the overhead lights blinked once, briefly but distinctly.

"That means 'yes,' sir," said Rossini, looking a bit sheepish. "Until he's done, that's the only way he can respond."

It seemed, after Torvig had been laid low by the effects of the initial pulse, his backup processors had kicked into high gear, rewriting the codes that allowed his body to interface with its cybernetic parts.

It had never occurred to the little engineer that those same codes could be used to help *Titan* reestablish communications between its own systems. It hadn't until the second destructive wave had washed over them and sent him plummeting to the floor.

"It is sound," said Tuvok, looking up from his analysis of Torvig's code modifications. "Ship's systems are returning to normal."

"Shields?" asked Riker, happy to have even the smallest amount of good news. "Weapons?"

Tuvok shook his head slowly. "No, sir," he said. "The same local conditions are still in effect. However—I believe, after seeing Mr. Torvig's solution, that there may be a way to modify the shields as well."

"But not the phasers?" Riker hated to harp on the same subject, but the phasers were more reliable than either form of torpedo. If there was martial trouble, they could swing outcomes in *Titan*'s favor.

"No, sir," said Tuvok. "That is currently beyond my abilities."

Riker quickly calculated the number of torpedoes, quantum and photon, in the ship's armory. He then began bringing to the front of his mind all the battle scenarios involving phaserless combat between starships.

Though it had been closer to the source of this destructive wave, there was no guarantee that the alien vessel that had been menacing the shuttle had not also survived.

Another thought of the shuttle brought with it those of its fate, and of Deanna's as well. They'd survived a lot together, enough for him to cling to the hope that they might yet come through this, but then he'd never been so completely severed from contact with her before. There had never been that yawning emptiness inside him that was shaped like her.

"Sir," said Tuvok. "Are you well?"

"Fine," said Riker, resuming his poker face. He doubted he fooled Tuvok's telepathic sensibilities, but he didn't have the luxury of showing the junior officers how deeply her loss affected him. He told Tuvok to take who he needed and get the shields up ASAP.

"Yes, Captain," said the Vulcan, and turned to go.

"Incoming vessel," said Kesi's voice over the comm. *"Captain and tactical officer to the bridge."*

The alien ship had survived after all. The sensors still had a hard time keeping a fix on it, but now that it was close enough, they could use the midrange viewers to get a look.

No one present was happy with the sight. Whether

intentionally by its makers or simply as a result of an unfortunate esthetic, the vessel resembled, at least to Riker, some sort of bizarre mixture of a predator insect and the head of a trident.

They had registered the thing discharging a massive amount of energy when it had first appeared, and everyone had assumed it to be a weapon. They couldn't be sure, with the sensors malfunctioning, but the power of the device, whatever it was, dwarfed their own phasers.

This in itself wouldn't necessarily have given Riker much pause—he'd smacked down enemies possessed of superior weaponry before. But those had mostly been in stand-up fights where he or his allies had been in possession of the full range of offensive and defensive accessories.

Now, with *Titan* wobbling in the marsh of bizarre energies, made even worse by the recent eruption, with her shields failing and her weapons mostly offline or untrustworthy, he knew this would be anything but a stand-up fight.

"That seems unfair," said Bohn, watching the alien ship glide easily and ominously toward them through the soup. "How are they getting away with that?"

"I am endeavoring to ascertain the answer to that exact question," said Tuvok.

"Are those warp nacelles?" said Riker.

"Something similar, sir," said Tuvok. "Scanning is difficult with so much distortion, but it seems they are somehow compensating for local conditions with some sort of external field buffers."

"Can we do the same?" said Riker.

"I think not," said Tuvok, pensive. "Though there is a large margin of error, current scans indicate the approaching vessel to be out of phase with normal space."

Under normal circumstances this news would have soured Riker's mood. Years before he had been indirectly associated with a former C.O.'s ambition to create a cloak that could make a ship into a virtual ghost, able to pass through matter and energy without damage. Such a vessel would be the perfect weapon, capable of horrible destruction and at the same time totally immune to counterattack.

The results of Starfleet's abortive work had been both disastrous and tragic, leaving several officers dead and those in charge of the project with years' worth of guilt over their actions.

All the Alpha Quadrant's major powers had since tried to make the cloak work. Thus far none had succeeded, for which Riker was always grateful. He'd had a bellyful of war over the last decade, and the conflict ensuing from the successful development of the phased cloak was something he didn't want to entertain.

There was one upshot that, in spite of everything, brought a very slight smile to Captain Riker's face.

"Mr. Tuvok," he said. "Arm the first volley of quantum torpedoes and have them ready to fire on my order." Plasma weapons and energy beams might not be effective here, but Riker had yet to see any energetic system, phased or unphased, that a few well-placed torpedoes couldn't disrupt.

Maybe this fight, if it came to that, might be more stand-up than he had supposed. He hoped it would surprise the hell out of the aliens as well, should that be their intention.

He was about to tell Tuvok to hail them and get this ball rolling when *Titan* suddenly ceased its pitch and roll, resuming the normal, relatively upright position that her crew enjoyed. The shields were back up.

Riker couldn't hear it, but he was sure there was some version of cheering rippling through the decks below. Good news always travels fast.

"Shields at eighty-three percent and holding," said the Vulcan without any display of triumph.

"Well done, Mr. Tuvok," said Riker. "If you can get *Titan* some of our new friends' maneuverability or the warp core back into the green zone, I may have to promote you."

"Unnecessary, sir," said Tuvok, bending to whatever new set of problems had flashed across his screens. "I have Mr. Jaza's sensor pod team working on the problem now."

That made sense. Jaza's people had the most direct experience with the strange phenomena present in this region. They would have the best chance at turning the new data into something they could use.

"Good," said Riker, never taking his eyes off the new ship. It had taken a position almost directly in front of *Titan* and now hung there, perhaps waiting for some indication from Riker of his ship's intentions.

Well, thought the captain, taking in the sight. *That's not provocative.*

He told Tuvok to hail the aliens. "This is Captain William T. Riker of the Federation *Starship Titan,*" he said when the Vulcan looked up. "We have entered your space peacefully, seeking some missing comrades of ours and—"

And you killed my wife, he wanted to say. He was suddenly so angry at the thought of her death in this useless situation that he almost wished the aliens would fire on them and give him an excuse to vent.

His words were cut short by a burst of static as *Titan*'s universal translator, fighting both the effects of the distortion outside the ship and the vagaries of the alien language, attempted to do its job.

"You dare to call yourselves peaceful!" said a low, grating voice that was full of clicks and humming. *"You dare to approach Erykon's Eye!"*

"There's much here that we don't understand," said Riker. "Our mission here is only to—"

Again his words were cut short by a burst of angry static as the UT tried and failed to translate the alien's angry words. It wasn't really necessary. Everyone present got the gist.

"*Orisha is gone,* [possible meaning: soulless] *creatures!*" said the alien captain, enraged to the point of incoherence. *"It has been destroyed by the* [possible meaning: wrath/judgment] *of the Eye! You awakened the* [possible meaning: Holy] *Eye! You invited Erykon's* [possible meaning: destruction/anger]*!"*

"We meant no insult to you or your people," said Riker, silently motioning for Tuvok to provide him with a visual component to the signal. "We are only—"

"You will be punished," said the alien voice. *"I am A'churak'zen, first among Erykon's children, and it is my joy to purge you from creation!"*

Communication was abruptly severed before Tuvok could provide a visual, but Riker didn't need one now. The alien captain had confirmed her connection to Orisha, and he had a basic idea of what to expect. He pictured a small army of four-armed insectoids, each seething with fury over the death of their world and holding *Titan* and her crew to blame.

Oddly enough, he knew precisely how they felt.

"They are charging some weapon, Captain," said Tuvok. "The readings are different from the ones we took earlier."

When they fired on the away team, Riker finished the thought. *When they killed Deanna.* "Set to fire quantum torpedoes, full spread, on my mark," he said. If these bastards wanted to bang heads instead of figuring a way to power down and maybe find a solution to all this, for once, just this once, he was happy to oblige.

"That is not advisable, sir," said Tuvok. "The vessel's proximity to *Titan* is—"

Before either of them could utter another word, the Orishan weapon fired. This time it was not the immensely destructive power beam that erupted from the alien ship but a massive lattice of interlocking energy fields.

It looks like a net, thought Riker, just before it hit.

Titan shuddered violently as the new weapon overtook them, but it did not suffer the same jolting that it had during its recent difficulties. The shields, for the moment, held the weapon at bay.

"Tuvok?"

"Tractor beam," the Vulcan reported. "Similar to our own but more powerful by several orders of magnitude, and it is contracting. Our shields are holding it back at this time, but I believe its purpose is to crush us."

"Can they do it?" said the captain.

"Eventually, yes," said Tuvok. "Shield strength has already fallen by four percent."

"So we're on the clock," said Riker.

"Captain?"

"Time, Mr. Tuvok," said Riker. "We're fighting time. Either we get free of that thing and give the Orishans a reason to back off or they crush *Titan* and us like an egg."

Tuvok considered the analogy for a moment before responding. "Yes, sir," he said eventually. "That is essentially correct."

"Sensor pod to bridge," boomed Lieutenant Roakn's gravelly voice.

"Go ahead, pod," said Riker.

"If you can spare us one second, Captain," said Raokn. *"We think we may have something for you."*

Riker didn't spend much time in the sensor pod. After seeing it for the first time when he'd taken his initial inspection tour of *Titan,* he hadn't been up again until they'd begun to map Occultus Ora. Then he'd only stayed long enough to get Mr. Jaza's report, have a few words with his team, and then head back to the business of running *Titan* and trying to get his wife to see sense.

The pod was darker than he remembered, running with emergency lighting to conserve precious power. All he could see of the upper tier was the grid work, and that only barely.

Jaza's people—Roakn, the two Benzites, the Deltan

woman Fell, the Caitian female Hsuuri, the acerbic Thymerae, and Jaza's pet project, Dakal—all stood there, expectant, weary, waiting for Riker's command.

"Well," he said, not too gruffly. "Let's have it."

For some reason all of them looked at Cadet Dakal, which was odd considering he had the least experience of the lot. Jaza had taken a shine to the kid, pulling him out of his rotation in systems analysis for duty with this crew.

"He thinks he's an operations specialist," the science officer had written more than once. *"But he's got a mind that's made for science."*

Dakal looked as surprised as anyone that the rest of the team expected him to deliver their news, but he sucked it up, put on his best expression of Cardassian detachment, and began to speak, only stammering once at the outset.

"Space-time, sir," said the cadet. "Everything the Orishan technology has done has in some way manipulated space-time similarly to the way we use warp fields to travel."

"Similarly," said Riker. "But not the same way."

"No, sir," said Dakal. "At least, not in every case. We'd need to get a look at their technology to see how they're doing it, but we now know that the instability in this area is the result of multiple folds in the local space-time. Even their weapons are not warping space so much as aggressively folding it. I have to admit that I didn't know the difference before, but it's significant."

Riker knew the difference. Warp fields created bubbles, relatively small ones, around a given vessel, allowing it to mildly bend physical laws in order to bypass relativistic speed limits. His mind flashed to his Academy days and a lecture hall where a very stern professor had stripped a hard-boiled egg of its shell, squeezed it into a plastic tube that was slightly too small, and then applied suction at both ends.

The analogy wasn't exact, of course: the demo had been to show the fragility of any object traveling within a warp field. The technology was so ubiquitous that most sentients forgot very quickly exactly how dangerous it actually was to circumvent physical laws in that way. The image of that egg exploded all over the interior of the tube never left Riker's mind for long, and with Dakal's little lecture, it resurfaced.

Space folds, by contrast, needed no such visual analogies. Their name told the story quite literally. Usually by means of massive manipulation of gravimetric fields, space-time could be folded in on itself in order to bring two usually distant points close together. But the technology to make even simple short-distance folds was so dangerous that most civilizations abandoned it in favor of warp fields early on. Those that didn't tended to destroy themselves when their folds destabilized their suns or knocked their planets out of their normal orbits.

"Someone has folded a lot of space-time here, sir," said Dakal. "Too much for anything like safety, and something has caused the knot they made to unravel."

"This is all well and good," said Riker, trying not to seem too harsh with them. They had obviously been attacking this problem nonstop since the first quantum ripples had been discovered. "But how does that help us now?"

"Well," said Dakal. "We think, now that we know the

exact nature of the effects in question, as well as the nature of the Orishan weapons, we may have a solution."

"A partial solution," said Hsuuri softly. Dakal nodded.

"You can get us moving again?" said Riker.

"Maybe not that, sir," said Roakn, stepping in to make sure they didn't give the captain more hope than was warranted. "Local conditions and the ship's own geometry still make the warp core too unstable to generate a viable bubble around *Titan*."

"But," said Peya Fell, "we think we can stabilize things enough to get the shields up to full and keep them there. And we can give *Titan* her phasers again."

"What's the catch?" said Riker.

"The catch, sir?" said Dakal, looking to the others for assistance.

"There's always something, Cadet," said the captain. "A downside to the plan. Some tiny flaw that makes the course of action we're contemplating less than appealing."

"Time, sir," said Dakal at last. "It will take us another three hours, minimum, to complete the necessary modifications."

"Riker to bridge," said the captain. When Tuvok responded, he asked the Vulcan how long the shields could withstand the pressure from the Orishan grapple before collapsing.

"If all local conditions remain constant," said Tuvok's voice evenly. *"Approximately two hours and thirty-six minutes."*

Titan lurched violently, forcing all present to grab the nearest stationary object or be knocked to the floor.

"The Orishan vessel has increased the pressure, Captain," said Tuvok again. *"We now have two hours and seventeen point six minutes."*

Riker's eyes fell on the TOV apparatus clustered dark and unused in its designated alcove. He smiled.

"All right, people," he said. "Why don't we see if we can make local conditions a little less constant."

Chapter Ten

The second quake was worse than the first, and the third and fourth were worse still. Vale and Ra-Havreii sat, listening in silence to the mounting chaos around them.

They could hear the Orishans chittering and calling to each other in terror and desperation. There was so much happening so quickly that their translators could only lift out the odd word here and there among the screams.

The end! Erykon! Fire! No! No! Please! and on and on.

As the foundations of the Spire trembled and shook, Vale allowed herself a grudging admiration for these creatures. They had built downward, deep into the ground, in an attempt to hide their civilization from the wrath of their god, and so far, their structures had withstood the worst their angry deity could dish out.

Still, that didn't mean Vale wanted herself and the

others to be there when and if the walls did come tumbling down.

Had this been a normal cell, with solid doors and pick-able locks, she might have had them free already. She had a knack for that sort of thing left over from her peace officer days. The trouble was, there were no locks. Like most of Orishan technology, the cells were a combination of organic material, that metallic resin that seemed to make up ninety percent of their constructions, and the ubiquitous energy fields that had already caused her people so much grief.

Without tools or even a tricorder to generate a disruptive field, they were stuck here in the bowels of a world that was shaking itself to death.

She looked over at Ra-Havreii who, despite their current predicament, seemed somehow more relaxed than she had ever seen him. It was as if he'd been carrying an invisible weight around all this time that was suddenly removed.

He had his combadge off and was fiddling with its guts, trying perhaps to boost its signal enough to contact Keru or Troi. The Orishans, ignorant of their function, had left both Vale and Ra-Havreii with their badges. If Keru had gotten out somehow, or Troi for that matter, the field around Vale and Ra-Havreii might still prevent them making contact.

"How's it coming, Doctor?" she said.

"Well enough," he said, still fiddling away. "This is delicate work to be doing in the middle of an earthquake with only a bit of wire for a tool."

"I feel your pain, Commander," she said, bracing herself

to ride out the current temblor. "But I'd like to feel it on the surface with Troi and Keru, if we can manage that."

He said something—something pithy, she was sure—but just at that moment, the quaking grew so severe that she was smashed to the floor despite her efforts to hold on.

Then, just as abruptly, the shaking stopped. She pulled herself up again, casting around to see if maybe that last jolt had ripped an opening in the wall that they might climb through. She would even have settled for the damned force field losing power as its unseen generator was crushed under tons of dirt and crystal. No such luck.

The fields and the walls and the ceiling and the floor were all as intact and functional as when she'd been tossed in.

"Dammit," she said, angry at her complete impotence in the face of this catastrophe. "Dammit, dammit, dammit."

"Wait, Commander," he said.

"Wait? Wait for what?"

"Just listen," he said.

She was about to ask him what there was to hear when she heard it.

Silence.

Absolute, all-pervasive silence had descended on their little prison and, apparently, the universe beyond. There were no screams, no sounds of shredding or exploding machinery, so abject Orishan pleas for Erykon's nonexistent mercy. There was nothing, nothing at all.

Ra-Havreii smiled and extended his hand. "May I have your combadge, please?" he said.

She gave it to him and watched, fascinated, as he held

them both up against the wall containing both the exit and the energy field blocking it.

A low-pitched whine began to emanate from the badges. She felt it in her bones as much as she heard it, a persistent and, frankly, discomfiting vibration that made her teeth ache.

There was a flash, a brief rainbow halo around the two badges, that was followed by what appeared to be a liquid ripple running through the wall. When the rippling stopped, so did the ache in her teeth. The noise was gone.

Ra-Havreii handed her badge back to her and pressed his palm against the exit door, which slid instantly and easily to one side.

"Pressure sensitive," he said.

The field was down. The door was open. They could, with a little luck, locate the others and get the hell out of here before the quakes resumed. She had no plan beyond that yet, but just now, she didn't need one. Let them find Troi and Keru first. Let them all get to the surface. Then they could search for the shuttle and maybe get off this rock.

"Well done, Commander," she said, replacing the badge on her tunic. She also was beginning to feel a bit more like herself again. Even with Ra-Havreii's findings about the crashed starship, they had no real evidence that *Titan* had not still been destroyed in the conflagration, but she had what she needed: hope. "Very well done."

"I believe, Commander Vale," said the Efrosian, moving past her into the corridor beyond, "this is the appropriate juncture in our relationship for you to start calling me Xin."

• • •

The Orishan holding cells were really just storage containers as it turned out, the place where the larval jelly was mixed and warehoused until it could be processed and consumed.

There was no crime on Orisha, after all, and therefore, no need for jails. Vale had been unsettled by the idea of being broken down into base chemicals to supply meals for the Mater's young. Now, seeing the jelly itself flooding out from behind each cell door Ra-Havreii opened, and moreover, seeing the remaining bits of animal and insect carcass still breaking down inside—well, unsettling just didn't cover it.

She hurried the engineer to the last few doors and hoped, whatever else Erykon's wrath might have done, that it had allowed their friends to survive.

They found Keru first, essentially unharmed but for the bruise on his head and itching for some one-on-one time with the bug who had hit him. Vale was happier to see the big Trill than she could have imagined. She actually felt a bit naked when he wasn't present to cover her six. He took the news about *Titan*'s possible survival fairly well.

"I knew it," he said, slapping the Efrosian's back. "I *knew* she wouldn't go down without a fight."

"Yes, Lieutenant," said Ra-Havreii, gasping. "But my scapulae might not be so sturdy."

They found Troi almost instantly, and though she had not been physically damaged either, she had, nonetheless, been hurt. When the door on her cell slid away, she never moved from the corner of the room into which she had presumably crawled. She only sat there, hugging her knees and staring straight ahead, her enormous ebony eyes seeing nothing.

She didn't respond to their entry, and at first Vale feared the worst.

"What's wrong with her?" said Keru.

It was the fertility treatments she had undergone, Vale realized in a flash. The same side effect that had made it possible for the little Betazoid to project emotions intensely enough to incapacitate a passerby had also left her more open to the emotions of those around her.

Vale and the others had sat through the Orishan cataclysm, listened to the terror in their screams, the horror in every cry for mercy as the apocalypse they had feared for generations finally rained down.

Troi had not only heard all that, she had felt it as well. Vale could only imagine what damage all that terror flowing in and out of her mind might do. Catatonia might be the least of it. But even now she knew that the true reason for Troi's state was a private matter between her and her husband, so Vale answered Keru's question with a simple, "I don't know."

"Let me talk to her," said Ra-Havreii softly.

There was no time to argue with the engineer or to express their surprise at his stepping up in this way. Either Troi would come back from wherever it was she had gone inside and walk out of here, or she wouldn't and Keru would carry her.

The engineer bent close to Troi, cradling her in an oddly fatherly gesture, and began to speak into her ear so softly that Vale couldn't make out any of what he said.

She heard the words *Riker* and *alive* and she might have heard the phrase *Rhea or Oberon,* but she couldn't be sure of either. Regardless, after a few seconds of listening, Troi's posture relaxed into his arms, the life returned to her eyes, and she looked up at Vale.

"We have to get out of here," she said at last.

The damage was worse than any of them had imagined. The bodies of Orishans, large and small, some with wings, some with sluglike protuberances instead of lower legs, lay crushed and broken all around them.

As they made their way upward from the food storage bins, the extent of the destruction only widened. The few glimpses any of them had had of the subterranean civilization had shown it to be a masterwork of smooth honeycombed arches, massive open causeways spanning from one side of a great cavern to the other, lights and sounds and technologies both strange and intriguing even to their practiced eyes.

Now all there was to see was death.

There was smoke everywhere, belching up in huge exhalations through the cavernous cracks in the floors. Great shards of the blue crystals, some as large as the missing shuttle, had broken through the walls, in some places exposing new fissures that reached all the way up to the surface.

"We're almost half a kilometer down," said Ra-Havreii, staring up into one of the enormous tunnels.

"Look at the sky," said Keru, though he needn't have bothered.

It wasn't fire, but it did a damned good imitation. Gigantic undulating tongues of it crossed and crisscrossed the sky like some sort of enormous net. Bolts of something like lightning ripped down at the surface, their impacts unseen but their resulting destruction obvious to all.

And behind it all the strange undulating orb of Erykon's Eye showing soft and green through the intervening veil of fire.

If this was the author of the cycle of destruction that had plagued Orisha, it was small wonder that their fear of its attention had driven them to such lengths. To have that hanging over you all the time? Believing it could see every thought, every action, and would punish any misstep with the fires of heaven?

Vale couldn't bring herself to hate the Orishans anymore or even muster anger. All she had left was a growing sympathy for an entire civilization that had been so abused, and not a little awe at the sight above her.

"Is that what you and Jaza saw before?" Troi asked, breaking off to look at Ra-Havreii, at anything, really, other than that terrible beautiful sky.

"Not exactly," said Ra-Havreii, puzzlement seeming to win out over all his other concerns. "It seems the destructive field is between the planet and the Eye rather than being projected by it."

"We have to stop this," said Vale quietly. "Whatever else we do, we have to shut this down."

It was slow going making their way back to the Spire's control chamber, with the party having to shift the corpses of dead soldiers from their path or navigate around a sudden chasm that was filled with exposed cables writhing like serpents and spewing lethal energies in random directions. Vale's memory of the trip down and the near uniformity of the details in the structure itself made for many wrong turns and dead ends.

Finally they won through to find the place as empty of living Orishans as everywhere else but crowded nonetheless with their bodies.

The chamber was more or less intact, perhaps having been built with the intention of surviving this sort of cataclysm, with all of its machinery humming and buzzing away.

The visual displays showed the Spire's counterparts, now clearly arranged all over the planet, if the multitude of dots blinking on the holographic map were any indication. Whatever this thing had been built to perform was still very much under way.

Ra-Havreii wanted a close look at the console, finding much of the technology familiar somehow despite the alien pictograms dotting the instrument panels and flickering on and off on every screen.

"Go ahead," said Vale.

As he approached the unattended control console, Ra-Havreii literally stumbled over the tricorders the soldiers had stripped from his hands, still working.

As the others shifted the bodies and searched for signs of any survivors, Ra-Havreii scanned and examined the alien device.

"You said they called this the Veil?" he asked at last.

"Yes," grunted Vale as she helped Keru move another body from where it had fallen. She, Troi, and Keru moved nearly all of the Orishans into several rows where they could at least rest in apparent repose rather than in the contorted positions in which they'd been found.

Vale knew it was a useless gesture in some respects. Nothing they had seen had indicated the Orishans cared one way or another about the bodies of the dead.

Burials are for the living, her mother would say. She understood it now in a way she hadn't before. Her mother had been in her mind a lot lately, she realized. Now she wondered why.

"You notice anything?" Keru asked as he hefted his side of the last dead Orishan. He kept his voice low so the others wouldn't hear. "About the bodies, I mean."

"You mean that they haven't been crushed or burned or whatever like the ones farther down?" said Vale. Keru nodded, dropping the arm he had been using to pull the last soldier into position. "Yes. I noticed."

"Suicide," said Troi, coming up behind them. Keru actually blushed when he realized she'd heard their exchange. "Mass ritual suicide."

Vale understood. The Orishans had failed. They had failed to protect their people. They had failed to appease their god. Rather than face Erykon's awful judgment, they had taken the verdict into their own talons. Was it some final act of defiance on their part or simply acquiescence to what they perceived to be their fate?

In either case, as she had sat confined in her little cell, Troi had felt each and every death, felt the terror and bleak acceptance of their deity's will. That more than anything had immobilized her mind. Fear was one thing after all—eventually it could be processed and put away—but the absence of hope? That was worse than dying.

They stood there for a moment, taking in the sight of all the dead Orishans. There was rumbling in the distance that none of them mistook for thunder. Only Ra-Havreii, occupied as he was with the alien machinery, seemed unaffected by the atmosphere of mass death that still hung over the place.

"Commander," he said, looking up from his work. There was something in his eyes none of the others had seen in their time with him. It was a sort of sparkle, as if a giant fire was raging in his skull that could only be seen through the tiniest of keyholes. "I think I may know what—"

Something large and dark and possessed of an extra set of arms dropped, chittering and screeching, from the darkness above them. It hit Ra-Havreii hard, knocking the wind out of him, its weight and momentum smashing him first into the control console and then to the floor.

"You!" said A'yujae'Tak, turning on the others even as she lifted Ra-Havreii's limp form in one massive talon. "You have brought this upon us! The Eye slept until you desecrated this creation!"

Before the others could move or speak, she launched the engineer's body at them like a missile. The Mater herself was close behind. Even as Ra-Havreii crashed into Troi and sent her flying, Keru had stepped in to grapple with the enraged alien.

"We're not responsible for this," said Vale, scrambling to see if their phasers had also been left behind with the tricorders. "Your people took their own lives!"

A'yujae'Tak screamed a clicking chattering response that the translator simply could not decode. Not that Vale needed the help. The Orishan leader's actions told the story quite effectively.

She was more massive than the biggest of her soldiers, standing a full meter over Keru, whose burly form seemed almost childlike before hers. Somehow, so far at least, it didn't seem to matter. She flailed at him, attempting to claw him or tear at him with her talons or shred his flesh with the serrated ridges on the backs of her arms and legs. Nothing seemed to touch Keru, who danced under every swing, swerved away from every lethal blow as if he were playing mag ball with his friends.

Of course he wasn't playing mag ball, and he let her know it in short order.

"Commander," he said, narrowly avoiding decapitation as he ducked under and between two of A'yujae'Tak's flailing arms and sweeping her legs with one of his. "I could do with a lot less talk here and a lot more shooting."

He managed to land several blows on the Mater's abdomen as she fought to keep her balance, but because she was covered in a super-dense exoskeleton and he was just flesh and bone, the punches did him more damage than they did her. Keru's knuckles were already a bloody mess.

"You will die for what you have brought down on us!" said the enraged Mater, slashing at him, this time missing his throat by millimeters.

He was good; those Ligonian battle forms he'd been practicing had worked wonders on his already formidable skill at hand-to-hand. Still, eventually he would slip or dodge a second too slowly and she would connect. It was only a matter of time before A'yujae'Tak landed a blow, and all of hers were killing strikes.

As Vale cast around for something she could use to at least stun the hysterical alien, she caught sight of Troi helping Ra-Havreii back to his feet.

Tougher than he looks, she thought, getting back to the weapon search and finally maybe spotting the grip of one of the phasers poking out from beneath a fallen bit of crystal.

"Any time now, Commander," said Keru, clearly beginning to struggle to keep the pace. A'yujae'Tak seemed under no such difficulty.

Vale dived across the several dead Orishans that lay between her and the weapon. She landed near it, slid the rest of the way, palmed it, armed it, swung around, and fired just as A'yujae'Tak finally landed a bone-crunching blow to Keru's chest.

Keru groaned and fell away even as the phaser beam struck the Mater squarely in the face. A'yujae'Tak made another untranslatable chittering noise and staggered back a few paces, but she did not fall.

Damn, thought Vale, getting to her feet and keeping A'yujae'Tak square in her sights. She adjusted the weapon to its highest setting and took careful aim.

"Don't make me kill you," she said.

"You have murdered my world!" bellowed the enraged insectoid, and lunged for Vale. "My entire world!"

Vale fired again, again catching A'yujae'Tak square in the face with the phaser's now-lethal beam. Only it wasn't lethal. The beam's impact hurt A'yujae'Tak, that was clear, but it didn't put her down and certainly didn't kill her.

"Kill you," said A'yujae'Tak. She looked a little wobbly on her feet, despite her firm tone, so Vale shot her again.

A'yujae'Tak fell first to one knee and then to both before dropping forward to use her upper arms for support.

This time there were no more threats, only hums and clicks that, even without translation, seemed to indicate that A'yujae'Tak had been pacified.

Vale edged toward Keru, who groaned in pain as he struggled to rise. It was clear she'd broken a couple of his ribs and perhaps even cracked his sternum.

Nearby, Troi continued to support Ra-Havreii, who, while in better shape than Keru, was not quite as hardy as Vale had at first thought. His tunic was torn across the chest where A'yujae'Tak had slashed him, and there was blood in his hair from a gash Vale hadn't seen before. Troi was attempting to clear some of it off his face with her sleeve.

"You are a [possible meaning: pestilence]," said A'yujae'Tak. "You have murdered us."

Looking around her at the destruction and death, at her missing, probably dead teammates, listening to the sounds of thunder and catastrophe outside, which were not nearly as distant as they had been, Vale had to wonder if there was some truth to the Mater's accusation. How many of these events would not have occurred if *Titan* had not come to this place?

She was still wondering a few moments later when the world around her began to sparkle and she was transported away.

The next sight she saw was so welcome that she at first thought she might be hallucinating. As the shimmer of transport dwindled and the world became solid around her again, she easily recognized the contours of the *Ellington*'s hold.

She could see through the nearby porthole that the little ship was high above the planet, just meters shy of the energy field that had set the sky on fire.

She rapped hard on the nearest bulkhead, assuring herself of its solidity. This wasn't a dream or a hallucination. It was real. The shuttle had survived and, in doing so, confirmed that Jaza and Modan must be intact as well.

She cast around happily, checking on the other returnees. There was Keru, wheezing a bit from his injuries as Troi helped him into the medical cradle. There was A'yujae'Tak, still groggy from all the phaser hits, still fighting to get back to her feet and still failing. Ra-Havreii was not with them.

"Computer," said Vale. "Erect a level-two containment field around alien intruder."

"Acknowledged," said the familiar female voice.

A thin sheet of impenetrable energy rose up around the corner where the Orishan Mater still continued her struggle to remain conscious, to continue the fight.

"Locate and contact Commander Ra-Havreii," said Vale.

"Commander Ra-Havreii is aboard this vessel."

The shuttle lurched a bit, causing A'yujae'Tak to stumble backward and to drop the little strip of cloth she had been clutching in her lower left talon. It was a piece of Ra-Havreii's uniform, torn off no doubt during her ambush of the engineer.

When she heard a small clattering noise as the strip impacted with the deck, Vale looked and saw that Ra-

Havreii's combadge had come off in the Orishan's fist as well.

Emergency auto-retrievals targeted badges, not life signs. The engineer was still on the planet, still in the Spire's control center where they'd left him.

Vale hollered up to flight control for Jaza to get a bio-lock on Ra-Havreii and get him out of there. When neither Jaza nor Ra-Havreii appeared, she yelled up again.

"Jaza! What's the problem?" she said. "Mr. Jaza, report!" Again there was no answer.

"What do you mean, he didn't make it?" said Vale when Modan had climbed down from the upper deck to inform her of Jaza's status. "Are you saying he's dead?"

"Yes, Commander," she said, and none of them, not even Troi, could read the emotion under the words. It was something new, perhaps unique to her experience. "For quite some time now, I expect."

There was also something odd about Modan's behavior. The pattern of her speech was different, chaotic in a way. It was as if she was randomly shifting between two completely separate idiomatic patterns without realizing it.

"What do you mean, Ensign?" said Troi, sensing Vale's confusion and fury and needing to give her time to get it under control. "How did he die?"

"I don't know," said Modan. "I wasn't there."

"You weren't there?" said Vale, her anger winning out over her grief for the moment. She grabbed Modan by the shoulders and slammed the younger woman against the bulkhead. "You left him somewhere and you don't know if he's dead?"

Modan's body seemed to shift suddenly in Vale's grip. Her face elongated, her shoulders grew what looked like armored plates, and her long ropelike braids began to writhe as if they were alive.

"Christine!" said Troi, putting a hand on her in an attempt to calm her. Vale shrugged her off.

"He is dead," said Modan. "He's certainly dead. I didn't have to see it. I know." She was, just as obviously as Vale, in great anguish over Jaza's loss. Her placid metallic features made a better mask than Vale's fleshy ones, but Jaza had left a hole inside Modan as well. Vale was too caught up in her own anger and grief to know it, but to Troi it was clear.

"Can you tell us what you mean, Ensign?" she said.

"There's no time, Deanna," said Modan. *Deanna?* "I'll have to show you."

"Show us what?" Vale asked, not relaxing her grip despite the fine golden spines that had begun to grow through Modan's uniform to puncture Vale's flesh.

In response two of the tentacles on Modan's head whipped out at Troi and Vale, attaching themselves to the women's temples.

"This," said Modan, as Vale found the strength draining out of her arms and the world around her going dark. "I have to show you this."

Chapter Eleven

Black.

The world was black and formless, made of something liquid that rolled over and beneath them like an ocean of molasses. They could hear voices, their own and each other's certainly, but also in the distance, that of a man, a father they suddenly knew, talking to his young son.

"The Prophets express their will through us, Jem," said the man. They could suddenly see him—deep brown flesh on a big, thick-limbed body, with kindly gray eyes, standing just outside a battered building of wood and clay. Their home? "They show us what they wish but do not tell us always how to get there. Our life is to learn their will and follow it as best we can. Do you understand?"

"Yes, Father," said the other. They could suddenly see him too. Not older than ten years, not quite grown into his own large bones, yet he was a near-perfect copy of his father in miniature. "I think so."

It's him, thought Vale. *It's Najem as a boy.*

She had never seen him this way, so innocent and small. She had never even pictured him as a child. As something pulled her awareness from the scene, she was sure she would have difficulty picturing him any other way from then on.

"We have to hit them back," said another voice, this time female and intense. "Every day. We have to let them know they bit off more than they can ever chew by coming here."

A smallish, almost elfin woman who looked as if she'd been carved out of sandalwood appeared, naked but for the sheet that covered her and half of a young, equally nude man who was also somehow Jaza.

Vale felt her body flush as she thought of her time with him and the things he'd taught her about the placement of Bajoran ridges. Despite their evolution into close friends, this too was an image of him she would never let go.

"They own the planet, Sumari," he said, his voice low and very slightly slurred. He seemed a little drunk. "They can do anything they want."

The woman, Sumari, rolled over onto his stomach and gazed at him. "You hate them," she said. "I know you do. For what they let happen to your mother. For what they've done to all of us. For the way they spit on the Prophets."

"I don't give a damn about the Prophets," he said. His face had turned to stone. "And they don't give a damn about me."

"You're wrong, Najem," she said. "It's the Cardassians

who've done this to you as well. They've stolen your faith." She pushed herself closer to him, her hands moving over his chest slowly. "I want to give you that back. You're going to need it for our children."

He sat up sharply, inadvertently knocking her off the bed that was too small for two, and making her smile and laugh.

"Children?" he said. "You're not—"

"Oh," she said, climbing back up. "I think I am."

"But we've only . . ." he stammered as she smiled and continued to kiss him. "I mean, we've barely—"

"Your father's a doctor," she said, laughing. "You should know once is enough."

Again Vale felt herself being pulled away and was grateful. This wasn't for her to see somehow, and she knew it. And, really, she didn't want to see. This was a private moment, something of Jaza's alone. It felt wrong that anyone should know of it.

There were other images then, other scenes—Najem and his father screaming at each other during his mother's funeral; Sumari dying in his arms, the victim of a Cardassian disruptor blast that he still felt had been meant for him; the sniper who had killed her dying in his hands only moments later; the birth of his children, Esola for his mother and Kren for her father—but all of these moments rushed past in a blur. Something—Modan, she realized—was forcing her away.

What was all that? she thought.

Apocrypha, came the reply from Modan. *Extra bits that weren't intended for me but spilled over anyway. Ignore them.*

They lingered on the vision Jaza had seen—or believed

he'd seen—which Vale found odd and mystical and somewhat disconcerting. She was happy when it went away.

Here, said Modan's voice in her mind. *Here is what you need to see.*

What's wrong with the sky? thought Vale, looking up at it and seeing for the first time the chaotically oscillating Eye of Erykon. She had gotten glimpses of it during its eruptions, mostly the odd flash or strange multicolored ripple. These were all her human physiology had let her observe. Jaza's Bajoran genes allowed him a better view, and she was seeing that view now.

He stood there, motionless, frozen in fear by the realization that he had stepped into the scene from his vision. Ever since his meeting with the Prophets he had wondered about the moment, sometimes dreading it, sometimes wishing it would come so that he could finally understand its meaning. Now it was here, and all he felt was the brutal cold of his own imminent mortality.

He couldn't move. He couldn't think or, if he thought, it was only the one sentiment playing over and over and over in his mind.

I'm going to die. Here. Today. In moments or in hours, I'm going to die.

He couldn't move. He didn't want to do anything that would either disturb the vision or, worse perhaps, bring it to its predicted end.

Thoughts of his friends and his loves and his many adventures now flooded his mind like a storm. His entire life was suddenly laid before him. Every valley, every peak, every blemish, every virtue, everything rushed through him in its totality, and he was left breathless.

There was fear with all of it too, unexpected, unplanned for, and inescapable for all that. Now that his moment was finally here, he feared that he might try to avoid his fate, proving that he loved his life just a little bit more than he loved the Prophets.

It wasn't true. It hadn't been true since he'd regained his faith. But the fear, the terrible fear of oblivion ravaged him all the same.

And he still couldn't make himself move. He was held in the grip of this moment and it wouldn't let him go.

Then, as they always do, the moment passed.

The moment passed and he didn't die. It was followed by another in which he did not die. Another moment passed and another and, defying his expectations, through each of them he still continued not to die.

The fear didn't leave him then, but its effects began to drain away, allowing his rational mind to reassert.

What was it he had been taught as a child?

The Prophets reveal but they do not direct. We have to do the work ourselves.

That was all well and good, he thought, but his work, his life was a thousand years in the future. There was nothing to do here but get off this planet before he and Modan did anything irreversible to the timeline.

He suddenly remembered Modan. She had to be saved and both of them had to get away from here as soon as possible. If he died somewhere between this moment and that or in some moment yet to come, that must be part of the Prophets' plan for him and he could only accept it as he had accepted their boon in the shrine so many years ago.

He still wore the isolation suit. He still had his phasers, and as long as Modan still wore her badge, he could use the shuttle's sensors to pinpoint her location. A few well-placed shots should scatter these primitives and he would have her away before they could regroup and follow. Easy.

If he could manage it, no matter what else happened, he might be able to keep her from giving up her life for the Prophets' vision, as had so many of his friends before.

The two soldiers were of different factions, each sporting intricate but differently hued tattoos that had been scrawled all over the sides of their carapaces and each bearing a selection of similarly lethal hand weapons.

Finding Modan, someone so outside their sensibilities that the words they used to describe her could not yet be translated, had caused them to put aside their differences for the moment while they tried to figure her out.

"You are a fool," said the one with the green and gold tattooing. "It is obviously a [meaning unknown] sent from Erykon to [possible meaning: test] us."

"You dare to claim to know the will of the Maker of the Eye?" said the one with the red and white. "You dare to speak the Maker's name aloud?!"

"See its odd appearance?" said the first soldier, her glassy black eyes twinkling in the evening light like a helix of precious stones. "It is not a creature of this creation. It is from Erykon. There is no other explanation."

"You are the fool, Tik'ik," said the other soldier. "Your mind is broken if you think this is anything more than some [possible meaning: birth mutated] animal. How else could you have broken it and brought it to me?"

"It was in the Shattered Place."

"We were in the Shattered Place," said Kakkakit. "Are we sent by the Maker?"

"I was sent by my Mater to murder the sisters in your blasphemous clan in quantity," said Tik'ik. "But you agree that this creature is more important."

Kakkakit made a few skeptical clicks with her inner mandibles and began to circle Modan's prone form, prodding her occasionally with a weapon that resembled a long walking stick with some kind of crystal formation at the top.

Modan twitched away from the contact and moaned. From his vantage point a couple of meters away Jaza could see that she'd been caught in mid-transition between her humanoid and feral forms. She was still mostly humanoid, but there were spines breaching her suit.

"I have a solution," said Kakkakit at last. "We can eat it."

"Your brain is broken."

"Tell me, Tik'ik," said the other. "Are you hungry?"

"Soldiers are always hungry," she said. "If you had a soul you would know this."

"I am as hungry as you," said Kakkakit, leaning over Modan. "My soul tells me there is food here."

"If you touch it," said Tik'ik, leveling her own nearly identical weapon at Kakkakit, "I will kill you here and now. To harm one of Erykon's things is to beg the Eye to open again."

"The Eye has opened," said Kakkakit. "We know it is because of your blasphemies. It is our slaughter of your hideous clan and all of the others that has caused it to close again. When the last of you is dead, the Eye will sleep."

"Your disgusting clan and all your sisters will be larvae

food before the Daystar rises again," said Tik'ik. "That will please Erykon. This creature is a gift to us for carrying out your destruction."

"Don't be foolish," said Kakkakit. "Think: If we can eat it, then we know it is just some animal. If it is something sent by the Maker to test us, as you say, or if it is some gift, the Maker will not let us eat it."

Tik'ik thought about it, chewing the idea as if it were a small and succulent mammal. "All right," she said at last. "We will try your plan."

Each soldier had a long-handled serrated blade strapped to her back that they now withdrew from their respective sheaths.

Taking positions at either end of Modan's body, they raised the blades, which resembled machetes. Before they could bring them down again, twin beams of destructive energy lanced out at them from what seemed to the soldiers like empty air. The machetes dissolved to nothing in their talons, and both soldiers were thrown to the ground.

They were up again in a flash, this time with guns in hand, firing small metal projectiles in the direction of the beams' origin. Plants shredded, crystals exploded in every direction while the soldiers continued their lethal barrage.

Tik'ik was empty first, the nose of her weapon so hot that smoke wafted up from the hole in a lazy undulation. She leaped over to the place she and Kakkakit had just destroyed, hoping to find a body in the broken turf or a blood trail at least.

There was nothing.

"What was it?" said Kakkakit. "Is it dead?"

There was nothing.

"You see?" Tik'ik said thoughtfully. "It is Erykon's will that this creature must not be harmed."

"This is some trick of your clan's, I think," said Kakkakit, slowly and quietly replacing her gun's empty packet of projectiles with a fresh one. "I will kill you and this creature and eat both your—"

She never finished. Tik'ik's clan blade, the small one she kept hidden in the broken part of her carapace, had pierced Kakkakit through the thorax, spewing her juice on the ground and sending the rest of her to Erykon.

When Tik'ik had retrieved her blade and assured herself that Kakkakit was dead by eating one of her eyes, she stood and said, "I know you are here. I can taste your aura." When there was no response she continued. "I know this creature belongs to Erykon. I have protected it from harm. It is my wish to know if Erykon desires further service from me."

Jaza regarded the creature from the protection of the isolation suit. He had only narrowly escaped death by diving clear when the warriors had opened fire.

It had been instinct that told him to leap, an animal's need to continue living, but now that he had done it, now that he had heard the request of this lethally pious creature, he wondered. Why had he not just stood there and allowed their bullets to shred him along with the landscape? Would that not have fulfilled the Prophets' vision?

The only answer was that he had to protect Modan, to get her back to the shuttle alive, to make their escape.

But there was now the problem of Tik'ik.

She stood there, all innocence despite her skill with murder, waiting for any word from her god as to what she must do next. She reminded him of himself, he realized, and in a fashion that was less than flattering.

She was a puppet, unable to act in any way beyond what she deemed to be the wishes of Erykon. She was empty of motive, of desire, of anything but the automatic need to follow. Was that truly piety, or had she simply made herself an organic automaton, no more awake to the universe than a screwdriver or a calculator?

The Prophets do not want us as their toys, his father had told him as a child. *They want us to fulfill our lives, to expand our minds and knowledge as far as they can go.*

All right, he thought as realization washed over him. *I think I understand.*

"Pick it up," he said, and watched the little shiver that ran through the startled soldier. Tik'ik did as she was told, hefting Modan's body with surprising grace up into the cradle of her four arms.

"Follow," he said, and she did. Apparently the isolation suit's scent-masking properties needed work.

Modan woke about a minute into her stay on the shuttle's medical table. The lacerations and breaks she'd sustained fending off the two soldiers were uglier than Jaza's had been but also less severe. She healed fast under normal conditions and even faster under the restorative beams.

She rose to her elbows to see what he was up to and found him bent over the computer and the sensor controls. Sensing her motion, he turned to her and held his finger to his lips.

She rolled quietly onto her feet and joined him at the console. He was inputting massive amounts of code into several systems. Some she understood to be navigational algorithms, but the rest were incomprehensible, even to her cryptographer's eyes. She could tell the math was incredibly complex, but that was all.

Motioning again for her to stay still and silent, he reactivated the stealth harness, disappearing from her sight. Presently the rear access hatch opened and closed again.

Modan activated the exterior monitor and saw, to her surprise, one of her attackers standing just outside, engaged in conversation with the empty air. Jaza was talking to the creature.

Presently the Orishan soldier prostrated itself briefly and then disappeared into the jungle.

The rear access hatch opened again, and when it was closed and secure, Jaza reappeared. He had the queerest expression on his face, and she wasn't sure it was one she liked.

"Najem," she said.

"Najem," he repeated slowly, as if tasting it for the first time. "Yes. Please say that. I think I'd like to hear someone say my name for a little longer."

She watched as he began selecting items from various storage lockers—the class-two medical kit, the remaining stealth harnesses, two phasers with replacement power packs, the poison analyzer, and various other survival equipment that was designed for extended stays in hostile locales.

"Najem," she said. "What are you doing?"

"I'm sending you back, Y'lira," he said. Then, turning

on her with that same unsettling expression, "And I'm staying."

She stared at him, uncomprehending, as her mind failed to process what he had said.

"You will have to explain that," she said eventually.

In response he leaned past her, activating the astrometrics station. A schematic of a rotating, undulating globe appeared on the monitor.

"That's the Eye," he said. "At least, it's the part of it that exists here. I mapped it while you were healing. With a little bit of luck, you can use the sub-x-11 vertex there to slide back to our era."

"I can?"

"Yes, Ensign," he said. "I'd say it will put you within a few days of *Titan*'s arrival. Hopefully a few days before rather than after."

"I'm sorry," said Modan, staring at the construct on the screen. "What?"

"And you have to go fairly soon, I think," he said, making a minor adjustment to the figures on the screen. "I'm not sure how stable that thing is."

"I failed to return with the flux regulators, Najem," she said. "I don't think the shuttle is going anywhere."

"Not a problem," he said, plugging a tricorder into the download cradle. All *Titan*'s accumulated data about Orishan history and culture began to transfer itself into the smaller device.

The proximity alarm pinged, automatically activating the external viewers. The Orishan soldier was back, carrying both of the flux regulators that Modan had dropped during her attack. She watched as the creature set the components down on the turf outside the shuttle. It knelt again in that same abbreviated way and then disappeared once more between the leaves and vines.

The sounds of the battle outside had diminished somewhat, but periodically, a fuel bomb exploding or the report of projectile weapons firing could be heard.

"I wish she'd stop doing that," said Jaza, removing the tricorder from the cradle and shoving it into the pack he was building. "This hierarchical clan system is going to be a problem."

"Commander—"

"Najem," he said.

"Najem," she repeated, fighting to stay calm. "Please tell me what's happened."

"I've told you," he said.

"You haven't," she replied. "Nothing you've said has made me consider leaving you here in this planet's past."

"If I tell you I finally understand the vision the Prophets showed me, will you accept my decision?"

"I'm sorry, no," she said. "That is irrational."

"All right," he said, sitting down beside her. "Rationally, then."

In soft reasonable tones he explained his thinking to her, how *Titan* might yet be saved from destruction and their fellows on the away team as well.

He talked about coincidence and the need to prevent paradox. Someone had to take the information about the tesseract's exact contours back to their own time. Those contours couldn't be mapped in their era by the tesseract's very nature.

Lastly, but most important, someone had to stay here

to ensure that the Orishans continued to develop as their history required.

"That person has to be me," he said. "You don't have the necessary background in the sciences to handle any trouble that might arise from *Titan*'s wreckage. Stabilizing the warp core was primary, but there are all sorts of tech and chemicals that might show up to plague these people. I have to be here for that."

"But that creature," said Modan. "It was kneeling. To you. Does it believe you are a god?"

He laughed. "She thinks I represent their god," he said. "Like an Oracle."

"Or a Prophet?"

"I doubt I'll be quite so cryptic." He smiled. "But I'll disabuse her of that notion in time."

She digested it. Most of it made a certain kind of sense, except for the bit where he stayed behind.

"Won't you pollute the timeline if you stay?" she said. "Isn't that why we both have to go?"

"It's already polluted," he said. "The crashed starship alone has already done catastrophic damage. I have to stay and make sure the society gets as close to its proper track as possible."

"Starfleet will never condone this," she said.

"This is bigger than Starfleet."

"Then send the shuttle back on autopilot," she said after some consideration. "I will stay also." He shook his head. "I can be of help to you."

"No, Modan," he said. "Autopilot won't work if there's any trouble on the other end. This takes a living mind, and luckily, we have one to spare."

She was silent for a time, still weighing arguments, still searching for the one that would compel him to leave with her or force him to let her stay.

"Najem," she said slowly. "These beings, the Orishans, they are nothing like you, nothing at all."

"That's true."

"How can you imprison yourself here, with them, forever?"

He smiled that familiar smile, the one that lit up his face when he was on the verge of some new and exciting discovery.

"Because I can help them," he said.

"You will be alone," she said, feeling the despair over his choice that he wouldn't, perhaps couldn't. "All alone."

"It's my fate," he said, taking her shoulders in his strong gentle hands. "I thought the vision meant I would die, but maybe it wasn't meant to be a literal death, Modan. Everything that was Jaza Najem is dead in our time. It has been for hundreds of years. Here I'll be something new. An ending and a beginning."

They spent an hour fitting *Titan*'s flux regulators to the shuttle's much smaller warp core, and then it was time to go. Modan had not been gifted with tear ducts, so her parting from him, while emotional for both, was a parched affair.

He had found a place in *Titan*'s wreckage where he could build a comfortable and mostly hidden shelter. The Orishans had already begun to refer to it as the Shattered Place because of its obviously destroyed nature and the random arcs of electricity that continued, from time to time, to erupt from a few of the components. Most of them gave the area wide latitude, a tendency he meant to cultivate.

They stood on the ground just inside the shuttle's stealth field, saying the final good-bye. She couldn't really comprehend his decision. Too much of it was based upon an esoteric understanding of reality that she had not been designed to process.

She told him that this experience was significant enough for her to share it with the other Seleneans at the next confluence and even with her Pod Mother. Perhaps future Y'liras would be capable of understanding faith in the way that he did.

"You understand it well enough, I think," he said. Then he told her the final reason for her being the one who had to go back. She was a failsafe. "I need you to link with me the way you did before."

"Why?"

"In case the computers fail or get scrambled in transit," he said. "The information in my head can still be passed on through you."

She saw the wisdom in that and came close to him, letting him hold her as he would a lover as her linking spines undulated around her head.

"What I take I can't keep long," she said. "A day or two at most."

"Let's hope it won't be needed at all," he said. Her spines attached to his skin and her mind burrowed into his, lifting out those bits he wanted her to take as well as a few more that couldn't be avoided.

Sometime during the exchange he asked her for the last kiss he would ever have.

She gave it to him.

• • •

Modan couldn't see the tesseract as Jaza could, not even with the memory of its image temporarily stored inside her, but she felt it when the shuttle crossed its event horizon.

Reality seemed to flicker and bend around the *Ellington* as it navigated the unseen contours of the immense four-dimensional object. There was no real sense of acceleration or of time passing, only the initial jolt, the bizarre light show, and then suddenly she was back in normal space in low orbit over Orisha.

The computer lit up immediately with the locator signals of three of the combadges of the missing away teammates, and she was elated. She wondered at the missing member of the team, whether he or she had been lost or if the absent signal was only the result of a damaged combadge.

She didn't wonder long. As soon as the ship detected their signals, the emergency protocols initialized and beamed them all back to the hold.

Vale, Troi, Keru, and the largest Orishan she had seen yet materialized before her within seconds of her emerging from the tesseract.

Chapter Twelve

The three of them came away from the link as if hit with a mild electric shock. The entire exchange took only a second or two but Vale gasped and stumbled back from Modan when the latter released her linking spines.

"You just left him there!" said Vale, after regaining some composure. "Alone!"

"It was his wish, Commander," said Modan.

"We'll discuss this later, Ensign," said Vale archly. She was only barely containing her anger over Jaza's loss. She knew it wasn't rational or professional but she couldn't help it. She also knew that this wasn't the time. "Right now you need to get down to the planet and do what you can to help Commander Ra-Havreii."

"Yes, ma'am," said Modan. "Right away."

• • •

Ra-Havreii was back at work on the alien system when the three women materialized. Keru had been lucid enough to be left awake in the shuttle's healing bed with his phaser trained on the still-subdued A'yujae'Tak. He was unhappy about being left behind, but someone had to ensure that the big insectoid stay out of trouble.

"Status, Doctor," said Vale when the transport effect faded. She was immediately rocked into a nearby wall by another of the ground tremors. This one was at least as violent as the first.

"I'm having difficulty," he said as another jolt forced him to leave off his ministrations in favor of holding on for dear life. "I believe I know what this Veil device is, but I'm having trouble with the Orishan symbols and idioms."

"Modan," said Troi. "See if you can help him translate."

The golden woman half slid, half jumped her way to join the engineer by the control console. Once there she began to translate any Orishan symbol that she could.

Much to Ra-Havreii's surprise, she also began to help him manipulate the controls themselves, many of which had to be activated four or eight at a time.

"I must say," he said, during the lull in their activities that was forced on them by yet another temblor. "Your knowledge of esoteric computer systems is impressive. Especially for a linguist."

"It's not me, Ra-Havreii," she said, getting back to work as soon as the shaking subsided enough. "It's Jaza."

"Is it now?" he said, falling back in beside her. "You will have to explain to me how that is possible, Ensign. Provided any of us survive this."

"What the hell is that thing?" said Vale, still very much

smarting from the loss of Jaza and having nothing to do but stand and watch the others work.

"A tremendously dangerous piece of technology," said Ra-Havreii, not bothering to turn. His and Modan's hands moved in a quartet of blurs over the console. "I doubt they have any idea what they're playing with."

"Do you?" said Vale.

"I—" another violent tremor shook the entire structure, forcing the Efrosian into an unnatural stammer. "I believe it's a massive fold device. A network of them actually."

"So you're, what," said Vale, also struggling for balance, "shutting it down?"

"No, ma'am," said Modan through clenched teeth. The current quake was not only failing to dwindle in severity but was actually growing worse. Huge chunks of the Spire's upper floors began to crack and fall, forcing Troi and Vale to dive for cover more than once. "We're stabilizing the network."

"Stabilizing it?" said Troi, shouting to be heard over the din. "Shouldn't you be shutting it down?"

"No," yelled Ra-Havreii. Then, all at once, the shaking and the noise both stopped. "Not unless we want to crack this planet into much smaller bits."

Vale took a moment to enjoy the quiet and the unshaking ground. She fancied she could hear a very low, very steady hum emanating from the walls around her. As they were not dead and the planet seemed to be intact, she felt it reasonable to assume that, for the moment, things were in fact stable.

"All right," she said. "Slowly. What is that thing, exactly, and why can't you just turn it off?"

Chapter Thirteen

"What do you call this again, sir?" said Dakal, more nervous now that he was actually strapped into the TOV than he had been when Roakn had suggested him and not Pel or Hsuuri for the duty.

"Riffing, Cadet," said the captain, standing over the Benzites as they made the final adjustment to the probe. Merlik nodded to his counterpart, who gave Riker the thumbs-up. They were ready. "It's simple."

I'm glad it is to someone, thought Dakal. *Because it makes no* nazzing *sense to me.* It was strange enough having the captain in the sensor pod for more than the time of a quick inspection, but to have him not only here but actually rolling up his sleeves to pitch in with the work? Well, it was unsettling.

"Our enemy is only a few hundred kilometers away,"

said Riker as the Benzites slid the probe into the dock. "They're safe in a vessel that is not only protected from the conditions that are hitting *Titan* by being partially out of phase but which is actually able to use those conditions to their benefit."

"Probe is in the dock and set, sir," said the Benzites nearly in unison as they stepped away from the closing aperture.

"We know that they use both space folds and a version of warp technology," said the captain in a tone somewhere between that of an Academy lecturer and someone passing along private information to a close friend. "We know that they use force and plasma fields in unusual ways."

"TOV is active," said the computer. *"Cadet Zurin Dakal is operating."*

"Our phasers, on maximum setting, could probably disrupt their ability to use a good deal of their energy manipulating technology, but the conditions here won't let us initialize," said Riker, now beside Dakal again. The pinpoint lights in the TOV's translucent helmet created a bright halo around his head, giving Dakal an almost cherubic aspect. "What's the solution?"

"Quantum torpedo, sir?" said Roakn smartly.

"Good thought, Lieutenant," said the captain. "But, no. The alien ship is too close to *Titan*. A torpedo detonation would hurt us as well."

"What, then, sir?" Hsuuri asked.

"The Orishans use energy fields the way we use metal and computer code," said Riker. "When Dakal puts that probe in the center of the same space as the out-of-phase ship and tells it to project its quantum broadcast signal back to *Titan,* what do you think will happen to all their interlocking fields?"

"Disruption," said Peya Fell as the realization hit her.

"Well done, Ensign Fell," said Riker. "And correct."

"Sir," said Dakal, then waited for Riker to turn his way. "You appear to know all these systems and you're checked out on the TOV."

"The captain has to have a working knowledge of as much of the equipment on his ship as he can," said Riker. "Are you trying to ask something, Cadet?"

"Only that it seems as though it should be you in the TOV harness for this," said Dakal. "Rather than me."

Riker was about to tell the young cadet that they all had their duties and that his rarely included joyrides when, before he could respond, Tuvok's voice broke in over the comm system and made the point for him.

"Captain Riker, report to the bridge immediately," he said.

"What is it, Tuvok?" said Riker already on the move. "Have our Orishan friends changed the game?"

"It's Charon, *sir."*

"You found her?" said Riker as the turbolift doors closed on his view of the sensor pod.

"No, sir," said Tuvok. *"She found us."*

"This is Bellatora Fortis, captain of the U.S.S. Charon,*"* said the woman on the screen. She was precisely as Riker remembered, with perhaps a little more meat on her and a little more edge to her demeanor. *"We are in distress and requesting immediate aid from any vessel in the vicinity."*

Behind her Riker could see a slice of a ship's bridge, identical to his own. *Charon*'s tactical officer, an Orion by the green tint of his skin, was barking at two ensigns who then scurried off to follow his orders.

Their computer had filtered the bulk of the alarm klaxons out of the message and drastically dampened the rest, but Riker knew a Yellow Alert when he saw one.

"Answer her," said Riker.

"We have been trying, Captain," said Tuvok. The distortion in this region . . ."

"Is the Orishan vessel aware of them?"

"No, sir," said the Vulcan. "They seem entirely focused on destroying *Titan*."

"Catastrophic shield failure in one hour, fifty-five minutes," said the computer. Though they weren't ignoring it exactly, the computer voice counting off the time until their demise in five-minute intervals had quickly become little more than background noise.

"What's *Charon*'s location?" said Riker.

"Local conditions prevent our getting an exact fix," said Tuvok. "However, she appears to be in close proximity to the space once occupied by the planet Orisha."

Suddenly, as they watched, the image of *Charon*'s bridge flickered spasmodically, cycling through the color spectrum and spitting out a burst of static over the audio channel. When the image righted itself, things had changed on the other ship.

Charon was at Red Alert now, with emergency warnings screaming and flashing all around and her entire bridge suffused with the same scarlet glow.

"Tuvok," said Riker. "What the hell just happened?"

"Unknown, sir," said the Vulcan. "*Charon* is close to the center of the flux effect. It is likely these conditions are more pronounced there."

Captain Fortis, unaware that she was still broadcasting, gave precise unemotional commands to her officers, commands Riker found distressingly familiar.

"We'll have to eject the core manually," she said to someone unseen. *"And send casualties to the auxiliary medical bay on deck five. Those systems are still up."*

"Brace for another wave," said the big Orion, and before anyone could react, it hit. As the bridge crew held on for dear life, several of the visible control stations exploded or went dark.

Captain Fortis was knocked to the floor by the body of one of her officers who had been too slow to anchor herself. Casualty and damage reports flooded in, and Fortis fielded each one with an almost Vulcanesque resolve as she climbed to her feet.

Riker felt his respect for her increase exponentially as he watched her calmly but firmly prod her people to keep focused, to do the necessary work to get the ship to safety.

"I don't care if you have to blow a hole in the bulkhead and shove it through, Matis," she said to her very distressed chief engineer. *"Get that warp core off my ship before—"*

She was cut off by another flickering of the screen, another cycling through the color spectrum. Riker wasn't sure, but he thought he could hear someone screaming under the static.

It was horrible enough not being able to let *Charon* know her sister vessel was close and could see her predicament if nothing else. Being forced to impotently sit and watch their distress was intolerable to Will Riker. His mind raced. There had to be something they could do to help.

"Forget about talking to them," he said, nearly coming out of his seat. "Narrow-cast *Titan*'s shield and code modifications directly to their main memory core."

"Attempting to comply, Captain," said Tuvok. "Local flux conditions prevent—"

"Deep water!" Lavena's gasp cut off the rest of Tuvok's complaint, and as the image on the screen resolved itself, the rest of the bridge crew knew why.

Charon's bridge was in a shambles, a destroyed mirror image of *Titan*'s own. The only illumination came from three monitor screens at the science and tactical stations behind the captain's chair. The screens themselves displayed only fields of static. The dark silhouettes of the dead or comatose members of the bridge crew lay draped over consoles, slumped unnaturally in the turbolift entrance, or pinned beneath a piece of exploded equipment.

For a moment nothing moved, and Riker began to suspect that the emergency broadcast had only been triggered by some barely active section of the ship's dying computer system.

Then, with an ugly, gurgling moan, *Charon*'s captain lurched into view, hauling herself back into her chair and fixing the viewer with her frosty blue gaze.

"This is Captain Bellatora Fortis, of—" she stopped, the breath seemingly obstructed by something broken in her chest. *"Of the Federation Starship Charon. We have encountered a—we don't know what it is—a region of extreme temporal flux and randomized—"* She coughed

into her fist, and there was blood on her hand when she moved it away again. *"My crew are mostly dead. Evacuation protocols were ineffective.* Charon *is being consumed, torn apart, by the conditions in this region. My science officer—"*

Fortis glanced off to her left at something not visible from this angle. For a moment her mask of perfect calm shattered and her terrible grief showed through.

"Me paenitet," she said softly. *"Formidolose me paenitet."*

In addition to everything else, the translation matrixes were obviously malfunctioning. No one on *Titan* needed the help. *Charon* was done. Fortis knew it and so did they.

The image spasmed as *Charon* was hit by another powerful jolt. Fortis winced, grimacing as she was forced to grip the arms of her chair to maintain her upright position.

When the shaking subsided and she turned back to the viewer, her mask had returned. If one could ignore the blood on her face and the carnage all around her, it was easy to see the slender patrician woman taking her ease in some lecture hall or at the symphony instead of captaining the graveyard her ship had become.

"I am using the time we have to broadcast the required warning messages to prevent this happening to another ship," she said. *"Our nearest sister vessel is* Titan, *captained by William Riker. I ask that any sentients who receive and understand this message communicate* Charon*'s fate to him. We believe this dangerous phenomenon to be expanding. If so, the consequences for any life-forms in its path are . . ."* She faltered again and recovered. *"This*

was not the result of an attack or any hostile action by any species known or unknown. It is simply our fate. I am Bellatora Fortis, daughter of Atheus and Cerisan. Parata mori sum. Fortunam meam complexo."

There was another rainbow flash, accompanied by a short burst of static, and then the screen went black. It seemed an eternity of silence followed, during which time on *Titan* stood still.

"Catastrophic shield failure in one hour, fifty minutes," said *Titan*'s computer.

"*Charon* is gone, sir," said Tuvok. "I cannot establish a sensor lock."

"What was that we just saw?" Bohn asked, trying to come back to the situation at hand rather than dwell on all those deaths. "Some sort of time-delay glitch in the broadcast?"

"I don't think so," said Lavena slowly. "I think it was live."

"It was, Ensign," said Tuvok.

"But how can that be, sir?" said Bohn. "We came here looking for *Charon,* didn't we? She only just got here."

"The space-time distortions have damaged normal causality in this region," said Tuvok. "The message Captain Fortis just broadcast is the one that *Titan* received four days ago."

Four days, thought Riker. *Have we only been at this for four days?* It didn't seem possible. Staring at the flat black panel of the main viewer, feeling his own vessel buffeted both by the ongoing chaos outside and the slowly contracting Orishan grappling field, all he could hold in his mind was that what had happened to *Charon* had also happened to the *Ellington*. That and the people who were responsible.

"Captain Fortis was correct, however," said Tuvok. "This flux effect is expanding. It will grow past the boundaries of this system within three standard days."

"Tuvok," said Riker after taking time to digest the full meaning of the Vulcan's words. The particular timbre his voice had acquired mandated silence in the bridge personnel. "I want to talk to the Orishan captain."

"Channel open," said Tuvok.

"This is the captain of the *Starship Titan,*" said Riker, standing and facing the flickering image of the Orishan vessel that had appeared on the main screen. "We didn't come here to fight you, but if you don't stop your attack on my ship I will be forced to respond in kind."

He waited precisely ten seconds for the response he knew wouldn't come.

"Catastrophic shield failure in one hour, forty-five minutes," said the computer.

"Right," he said. "Your choice." He signaled for Tuvok to kill the broadcast and contacted the sensor pod.

"Roakn here. Go ahead, sir."

"Tell Cadet Dakal he can launch when he's ready."

"Yes, Captain," said Roakn.

Riker swiveled to face Tuvok. "I'll want to see this," he said.

The Vulcan, recognizing the expression on his captain's face and its promise of a bleak future for their assailant, tapped the appropriate keys to display the probe telemetry on the main viewer.

"If this works," said Riker in a glacial tone that none of

them had ever heard or hoped to hear again, "that thing is either going to be shunted fully into whatever dimension it's straddling or it's going to become solid and be subject to the same effects that have been hitting *Titan*. Either way, we're finishing this."

"Your hypothesis is sound, Captain," said Tuvok. "As is your attack strategy. However, it is my duty to remind you that disrupting the systems of a vessel utilizing so much unknown technology may have unforeseen consequences."

If the captain heard Tuvok's warning, he gave no indication of it. "I want a boarding party ready to beam over to that ship the second it's in phase," he said in that same iron voice. "Then we'll show them some consequences."

"I presume the captain will be leading this team?" said Tuvok.

"You're damned right he is," said Riker, and in his mind, the image of his wife as she died screaming played over and over.

Chapter Fourteen

In the centermost eave, nestled safe in webbing that linked her body with that of the great vessel around her, A'churak'zen watched the approach of the tiny metal object through the lens of her despair.

Even as she marshaled the waves of the vessel, closing the fist she had formed around those who had caused Erykon's wrath to fly howling and burning down on her people, she sent other waves out into the void to search for a sign that any of them might have survived.

It was the eleventh time she had done so since Orisha had been consumed, and with each failure to find even a single breeder male or larva sac floating in the aether, her despair darkened and grew.

She was only two things now: rage and sorrow. At first the rage had driven her and she was happy to do as it commanded. She had seen the wave, one bigger than anything anyone had ever conceived, explode out from Erykon's Eye, consuming everything in its path.

Its first meal was the little metal box that had served as a home for those newcomers whose blasphemous work had woken the eye from its ten-thousand-cycle slumber. It and the creatures inside had been sucked up into the vortex of wrath in less time than it took to imagine.

That was Good and she had rejoiced in its Goodness. Erykon's judgment was final and Just in all ways. This thought pleased her briefly and so she flexed the bit of her mind that controlled the wave around the thing called *Titan,* increasing the pressure on the spindly sheet of protection it had managed to erect.

Why Erykon had spared them the worst of the destruction was a mystery, but it was not her place to question the ways of her god. Erykon's will, Erykon's wish, Erykon's judgment, Erykon's wrath all were the same and all were equally perfect and immutable.

Though she had questioned in the past, hadn't she? She had questioned everything early on and had been punished whenever those questions ranged too far. She had spent too much time with the Dreaming caste before being taken by the Guardians and the center of the Dreaming was the questions.

How does this chemical reaction progress? When was that hukka *vine first fertilized? Where is the heart of creation?*

So many questions, and often, even more answers, but when the question was *Why?* The answer was always the same.

Why does the Daystar shine? Erykon's will.

Why do the Children thrive? Erykon's will.

Why did the lightning strike my Mater's nest, incinerating her and all my sisters? That too was Erykon's will, they told her. Rejoice.

She couldn't at first. After her family had died, she couldn't even believe, though she knew enough to pretend. All she really had left were her questions and the punishment for asking.

Then the Guardians took her, telling her that her mind was right for a working they had made, a great woven working that was as much alive as it was mechanical and as large as any of the Spires that the Guardians made home.

"It needs a mind to move it, A'churak'zen," the Guardian Mater had said. "Yours may be the one. Will you try?"

She asked questions then, many, about the nature of their working, about their intention for it, about the particulars of mind that would be necessary to be chosen to be its mistress.

The Guardians didn't punish her for those, only kept silent and told her to proceed with her work. They would inform her if she was or was not the one.

She did as she was told, running their mazes, taking their tests, eating the strange lichens they had grown exclusively for this purpose.

They never showed her the working though. The sight of it was only for the one who would one day bond with it and bend it to its unknown purpose. But she knew where it was kept, all the Guardians did, just as they knew to stay well clear unless their Mater told them otherwise.

But the question burned in her, *What was it they had made? Why had they kept knowledge of it from the rest of the Children? How did this new working serve Erykon's will?*

The need to know burned so hot in her she was sure its fire could be seen and smelled for hectares in every direction. She was a beacon of desire, and yet none of them, not even the Mater, could see.

She was just a Hunter to them, a Hunter who had been raised by Dreamers, a Hunter who had enough evolutionary variance from the rank and file to warrant inclusion in their secret plan. Yet they knew nothing of her thoughts and less of the questions to which she must have answers. And, even more significant than the ignorance of her fellow Guardians, was that of Erykon.

Why was she still alive? She didn't believe in Erykon's divinity anymore, and yet she had not been punished for this, the worst of all transgressions.

All through her testing she had thought, today they would catch her. Today Erykon would know her heart and she would be punished, perhaps even killed. Every day, she won through, defeating the other test subjects, solving all the logic puzzles, passing all physical exams. Nothing ever happened.

The Daystar rose and fell. The Children lived and ate and bred and died. She went on thinking her blasphemous thoughts absolutely unmolested.

One day there were no other test subjects and there were no more tests. A'churak'zen had outlasted and survived them all and now stood alone in the testing chamber waiting for the Mater to speak.

"You are the one," she was told. "Now come and see our working."

• • •

They had no name for it as they had none for any mechanical working beyond a description of its function. This they only called "the vessel." To A'churak'zen it looked like the triple-pronged head of a spear.

It was huge, massive, its topmost portions easily approaching the roof of the cavern the Guardians had cleared for its construction. It was a little bit alive and a little bit mechanical, and even while dormant, it both radiated and absorbed waves of energy from its surroundings.

It was made to use the waves, made to eat them and convert them into waves that could be directed, modified, used for many purposes. It would slide sideways out of the chamber, passing through the earth and crystal above, going up and up away from Orisha until it floated free in the space beyond.

Before she could stop herself, still marveling at the thing before her, A'churak'zen asked the Mater why the vessel had been built.

"To approach the Eye," was the response. "We must know Erykon's nature. We must know Erykon's will. The Eye has slept for so long and we have built too much for it to open again and destroy us."

There had been pain in the bonding of her body to that of the vessel. There had been pain that she could never have imagined in a thousand cycles.

When the pain was over, when every bit of her was somehow bonded to or wired to some bit of the vessel, when it responded to her wishes as quickly as her own now-useless limbs, when she could see with its eyes, feel with its sensing mechanisms, when all that was done, they told her to go.

"Go to the Eye and wait," said the Mater. "Wait for some sign."

"How will I know?" she said.

"You will know."

How stupid they all were, she thought.

As the vessel moved like a ghost through Orisha's soil and then like a beam of light up through the clouds, A'churak'zen rejoiced.

She would certainly approach the Eye. She would certainly wait for the Mater's sign. She would certainly make contact with Erykon. But she wouldn't ask the Mater's questions. She wouldn't work to preserve the Orishan civilization or even its people. She had her own questions for Erykon and her own response should the answers to those questions prove unsatisfactory.

The vessel had weapons, terrible destructive wave-folding weapons that she had been given in order to shatter anything that might threaten either itself or the Eye.

She would ask Erykon the question she had been asking since she had lost her family. If she didn't like the answer, Erykon would feel the wrath of A'churak'zen.

Only there was no sign. There was never an inkling that the Eye was even aware of her presence. She hung in her vessel, her new body really, circling the Eye like a flesh mite waiting, waiting, waiting.

One cycle became four, four became ten, ten became a hundred, and one day she realized nearly five hundred cycles had gone by.

There had been no word from Orisha in as many as forty. She had been forgotten as she danced in the Void with the Eye. She no longer needed food; the vessel sustained her. She no longer slept; the vessel turned off the bits of her that needed periodic rest and kept perpetually alive those that did not.

She fell eventually into a sort of half dream in which only she and the sleeping Eye existed at all. She began to feel it was speaking to her and only to her. She began to feel that she had been wrong all those cycles ago. She began to feel that she was not a Guardian, not a Hunter, not even one of the Children anymore.

She was something new.

She had been sent to probe the Eye, to learn something of its wishes for her former people. She had meant to take revenge on it for allowing her family to die. She had meant, at the very least, to confront it and demand to know why Erykon had made life so cruel and unyielding.

She had meant to do all those things, but now, after dreaming and gazing at the Eye for so long, she knew that she was meant to be its servant. Why else had Erykon stripped from her everything that could tie her to Orisha? She was to be remade, to serve and protect the Eye.

So it had gone for cycle after cycle. Orisha thrived below and above, intangible and invisible, A'churak'zen danced before her god.

And then the soulless beings came with their ugly little wave projectors and their hideous jabbering speech.

She had failed to destroy them, failed to protect the Eye, which had rewarded her failure with an explosion of waves that had looked to consume everything—the soulless ones in their little metal box, the planet Orisha, and, she hoped, herself as well.

Yet, the wave did not destroy her. It didn't even touch her. It ripped through everything else, rolling out into the larger Void, seeking other creations on which to spill its wrath, but it had left A'churak'zen alone and filled with that same familiar question.

Why?

Why hadn't she been killed with the rest? Why had the Eye not closed again? Why, why, why, why, why?

She had almost opened her poison sacs then, seeking to follow her people into oblivion. Then the vessel informed her of another group of soulless beings, farther out toward the rim of this creation, living in another of the metal boxes.

She had decided that this was some test, that if she could destroy this second nest of soulless intruders, Erykon might take pity on her and let her sisters and their lovely little world return. Even her Mater, dead and eaten all these long cycles ago, could come to her again.

Only these creatures, like the first, stubbornly refused to be killed. They chattered on about names she didn't know and concepts and places she didn't understand, but they continued to thwart her efforts.

Via the many inorganic senses the ship fed her mind, she was able to watch the little orb they had fired putter its way toward her.

The soulless creatures were clearly both stubborn and stupid. She was a ghost. Whatever this thing was, she could tell it was solid matter and would pass through her body as harmlessly as any meteor.

And then, very soon, their resistance would end. They would be crushed, and Erykon would give her her reward.

"Probe is in position, sir," said Dakal's voice, still cracking a bit despite the flawless performance he'd just given.

The modified probe now sat in the heart of the ethereal Orishan vessel, which seemed as impervious as ever.

"Begin quantum broadcast," said Riker.

Pain lanced through every part of A'churak'zen as the strange little orb began to scream inside her vessel, inside *her*.

The scream cut through her, searing the phantom parts of her body, of the vessel's body, like the hot focused light the Weavers sometimes used to bind metal to metal. It was like nothing she had ever experienced.

She thought she was being torn to bits. Parts of the vessel seemed to rip and tear at one moment, only to be pristine and working in the next. The vessel's voice, her constant companion since their bonding, spoke nonsense in her mind. She felt she was going mad, that Erykon was finally meting out her punishment for not destroying the soulless beings quickly enough.

She thought she heard her Mater's voice and her siblings playing hop-skip nearby, but it was only a fantasy. The burning inside her became a series of soul-rending pains, each more excruciating than the last.

Suddenly the vessel spoke to her again, telling her that they were being somehow forced out of the ghost state by the scream of the alien orb.

Even as she processed that news, she and the vessel

were solid again. This time when the vessel screamed, she screamed along with it.

The storm of destructive waves that had been unleashed when the Eye had awakened, the chaos from which the ghost state had protected her, now ripped through A'churak'zen as it had everything else in this creation.

It was worse, far worse, than the shrieking of the alien orb. Worse even than the pain of being bonded to her vessel. This was agony beyond understanding, beyond thought, beyond questions.

This, she thought as her torment shredded her rationality. *Can this be death?*

But it wasn't death. It was only pain and therefore something she understood. They had forced her back into Erykon's creation, which, of course, made her subject to Erykon's wrath.

She was pounded as they had been, buffeted as they had been, the contours of her vessel scored and battered as theirs had been. She had watched them suffer and had found pleasure in it. She had made them suffer a little herself and had found it just. But, if that was justice, what was this? Was Erykon's punishment so indiscriminate, so random and impersonal?

She wondered, before the pain overwhelmed her senses, how they had done this to her, how they had thwarted Erykon's will and wrath. She couldn't. She couldn't escape or thwart or do anything but suffer and fear her god's next inscrutable whim.

"The Orishan vessel is in phase with normal space," said Tuvok's voice in Riker's ear. Not knowing what sort of

conditions to expect on the alien ship, he and his team had been outfitted with tactical EV suits. *"They are experiencing catastrophic failures to many key systems. Stand by."*

The team stood beside him on the transporter pad—Rriarr, Denken, Pava, and Hriss—while a somber-faced Lieutenant Radowski looked over his controls as he waited for the go order.

Titan lurched suddenly, and before he could be asked, Tuvok said, *"The Orishan grappler has disengaged. Shield strength is returning to previous levels. All internal systems nominal."*

"Put us as close to their bridge as possible, Lieutenant," said the captain. "I don't want to lose anyone fighting our way in."

Radowski nodded and began tapping in commands. Presently a look of puzzlement crossed his face.

"Sir," he said. "I don't read anything like a bridge over there. It may be distortion from the quantum flux, but the whole place seems to be tunnels and crawl spaces. No decks or specialized areas at all."

"What does that mean?" said Pava without too much obvious trepidation. "It's like a Borg ship?"

"Inconclusive," said Radowski still trying to make sense of what he was seeing. "Frankly, Captain, with all this distortion, it's lucky we're able to get a solid lock in there at all."

"Lieutenant Radowski is correct," said Tuvok's voice. *"Sensors indicate a network of thin interlocking tunnels radiating from a single aft chamber."*

"How many aboard?"

"One, sir. Sensors read one living being aboard the Orishan vessel."

The Orishan ship was nothing like a Borg cube. It was brightly lit, its tunnels easily large enough to accommodate the members of the team walking two abreast. It was, aside from them, empty.

Everywhere there was light. Some came from obvious sources like the faceted blue crystals embedded at intervals in every wall. The rest seemed to be an effect of some sort of esoteric energy exchange between various systems.

Every aperture was hexagonal, giving many of the visible surfaces a honeycomb appearance. Delicate webs of microfilaments crisscrossed half of them, some seeming to emerge from the walls and disappear again into the deck.

"Oh!" said Pava, running one graceful hand along the wall nearest to her. "There's a pulse."

Indeed there was. They could all feel it now; a steady staccato beat thrumming through every surface that was very much like the pulse of a living thing.

The whole place smacked as much of organism as machine, Riker thought, but in a perfectly synergistic way. Whatever else they might have done, the Orishans had apparently created a unique technology that melded organic and inorganic materials in a manner that somehow seemed more, well, natural than anything the Borg had achieved.

Telling the others to form on him, Riker moved ahead. His phaser, like all of theirs, was already in hand. He hadn't known what sort of resistance to expect, but he had expected some. Perhaps a few attack 'bots or automated traps. He'd been on enough hostile alien vessels to be ready for anything.

But there was nothing, only the sound of their footfalls on the deck and the hum of the alien machines.

They found the probe, or half of it, still sparking on the deck. The rematerialization of one of the walls had cut the thing neatly in two as they had tried and failed to occupy the same space.

What Tuvok had called the anterior chamber was just ahead. Pava and Rriarr flanked their captain as he surged forward, while the other two brought up the rear.

As predicted, their little corridor opened up a few paces on into a much larger chamber whose every surface was covered in crimson and gold hexagons.

There were no computers visible, no workstations or control panels. The chamber was just that, an empty room, but for the one odd, vaguely oval shaped object that hung from the ceiling, supported by thousands of glowing microfilaments.

It was mildly translucent, obviously containing something suspended in what appeared to be fluid of some kind. It was very large, more than two meters from end to end and half as wide.

At first they supposed that it was just some damaged bit of the ship that had been shocked free of its normal position by the vessel's wrenching return to normal space. On close inspection it turned out to be the farthest thing from that that was possible.

Tiny sparks of light traveled along the translucent

filaments, disappearing into the strange, vaguely plasticine oval. It was soft to the touch, almost leathery in fact, which Rriarr found out when he prodded it gently with his finger.

Whatever was inside shuddered when he sustained the contact longer than a few seconds.

"Relax," said Riker, feeling Pava tense beside him. "Everyone, relax."

As they watched, a seam opened wide along the bottom of the oval container, allowing the thing's viscous internal fluid to spill out on the floor below. When the thing was empty, the skin rapidly dried to the point of brittleness and simply flaked off in large clumps before their eyes. When it was gone, Pava stifled a gasp.

Inside what everyone present now realized had been a cocoon, suspended by and intertwined with the thousands of microfilaments, was an Orishan. Or rather, most of one.

All six of its limbs had been removed at the second joint and replaced with caps composed of some organic resin into which tightly bound clusters of the filaments disappeared.

There were similar, albeit smaller, versions of the caps attached to the creature's head and corresponding to where its eyes and antennae had been. Three thick cables, also translucent and also carrying streams of unknown glowing particles into the Orishan's body, were connected to its spine, with a similar one running into a plate on its abdomen.

It shuddered again, though none of them touched it, its mouth and lower mandibles flexing uselessly.

"It's alive," said Rriarr, holding up his tricorder for a quick scan. "Higher brain functions are active."

"It's trying to speak, sir," said Pava.

Ignoring the warnings of his subordinates, Riker moved close to the shuddering alien. He had come here full of rage, not knowing until this instant what he might do to the person he held responsible for all this, for Deanna.

His thoughts had frightened him, so he had put them in a box. He knew he would do something and that he might regret it and he hadn't cared. Of all the fears he'd ever had to master, the loss of Deanna, the real permanent loss of her touch and smile, of her presence inside him, was the worst he could imagine. So he didn't. He put it in the box as well and sealed it tight. It was the only way he could live this life and live with her at the same time.

After all their escapes and adventures he even began to think that maybe, just maybe, they had the sort of luck that would always allow them to cheat the reaper.

Then they decided on making a child and the boxes opened their lids, spewing all that fear inside him again like an uncapped geyser. Some days it was so awful he couldn't look at her.

He knew it was irrational and he knew he couldn't ever let her feel the brunt of it. So he had used techniques he knew to keep her out, techniques she had taught him.

It had opened a chasm between, and if he relaxed for one moment, he knew he would fall in. The idea of losing her or, worse, losing any child they had made, hung over him like a headsman's blade, and nothing he did could make it dissipate.

Now it had happened. She was gone. These Orishans

and their dangerous tinkering had done to her what they had done to *Charon,* and someone would answer for it.

Only, looking at this mutilated creature writhing gently in its web of cables, all he could feel was pity.

What sort of mind could have conceived something like this and then made it acceptable, even desirable? What sort of fear had these Orishans felt to do this to one of their own?

He lowered his phaser and reached out a hand to gently caress the Orishan's cheek. It shuddered again dramatically, perhaps unused to physical contact, but then grew still.

"You are just flesh," it said in its low clicking voice. "Only flesh." It seemed surprised. What had it expected?

He bent close to it then, stroking it gently as he would an injured child. He tried to speak to it, to make it understand that all this could have been avoided, that there was still the danger of the expanding wave to thwart and the rest of his crew to save. Could it, would it, help them?

"Titan *to away team,"* came Tuvok's voice in his ear.

"Go ahead, Commander," said Riker.

"We are receiving a signal from the Orishan vessel, sir," said the Vulcan. *"I believe they are logs. Sensor data, schematics—the vessel is uploading its entire datastore to* Titan.*"*

"Thank you," said Riker, smiling down into the Orishan's destroyed face.

"Fear," it said. "Why is there always so much fear?"

The Orishan convulsed, a bone-wrenching tremor that set its body shaking as if caught in a storm, and then went still. Rriarr scanned it and confirmed that it was dead.

• • •

There was no mistaking the cheers that rippled through *Titan* as her systems, most significantly her warp core, returned to nearly fully operational status.

The Orishan database was full of information that was either totally alien or, if not alien, impossible to implement with *Titan*'s technology, but what they could use, they did, and to amazing effect.

The condition of quantum flux that existed in this system that so confounded Starfleet technology was simply the norm for Orisha. Almost all their science was based on manipulating or drawing power from the flux in some way, and many of the tricks they learned served *Titan* as well.

The consensus from his officers was to evacuate as soon as possible, to get *Titan* well clear of this system and its effects. Then they could contact Starfleet and any local spacefaring races about how to check or reverse the expansion of the wave of quantum flux.

The Orishan database had given them some ideas on the subject of collapsing the wave in on itself with a series of counterpulses directed at what some were now calling the Eye of the storm.

Leaving was the right thing to do. Orisha was gone. *Charon* was gone. The *Ellington* was gone. Once the flux wave reached its sun, the rest of the system would go too. In fact, *Titan* would be cutting its escape close to the bone if they left within a few hours.

Riker knew the prudent course, what the manuals required him to do, but as he and Doctor Ree examined the body of the dead Orishan pilot, he wasn't sure the prudent course was the one he wanted.

"Suicide, sir," said Ree, looking up from his autopsy. "This female released poison into her body from her own stores of venom."

"She killed herself," said Riker. Ree only cocked his head and watched his captain mull. "Why? The fight was over."

"May I suggest, sir, that this may be precisely why she did it?"

"What do you mean, Doctor?"

"From your account of her logs, this poor creature allowed her people to modify her this way in order to make contact with their deity," said Ree, sealing the corpse again and sliding it into a cooling bay for quick freeze. "She made contact. Perhaps it proved unsatisfactory."

"That thing isn't a god," said Riker.

"I was under the impression that we don't know what it is," said Ree. Riker snorted.

"You don't think it's really a god, do you?" he said.

"My beliefs are immaterial," said Ree. "Pahkwa-thanh do not see ourselves as separate from nature, Captain. We have many deities, hundreds, and all of them are equally enmeshed."

"I'm surprised by that," said Riker. "Your species isn't noted for its esoteric lifeview."

"We do not promote our beliefs," said Ree as he sealed up the samples of the Orishan poison and secured them for later study. "They are *our* beliefs. They inform us. Do you see?"

Riker wasn't sure he did. As he watched the doctor run his long slender digits through the sterilization field, he wondered about his home planet and the raptorlike carnivores who were its dominant species.

He had seen Ree eat—live animals if he could, raw flesh when he couldn't—and it indicated a homeworld of extreme violence, at least by human standards. But Ree was, with the possible exception of an android Riker had known for many years, the most gentle, even serene being he'd ever met. Was that the result of Ree's nature, or was he implying that the nature of the apparently aggressively pantheistic Pahkwa-thanh faith was somehow responsible?

"We do not separate in this way," said Ree when the question was put to him. "Instead let us consider: What is the function of belief in any deity? It is an attempt to better understand the universe, to see the order and structure that defines it. It is, in essence, the beginning of scientific inquiry. In my experience, deities bind societies; sometimes they define them. So, we must ask ourselves, what definition did this Eye of theirs inspire in the Orishans? How did its presence inform them?"

Why? Why is there always so much fear? came the wisps of her voice in his memory.

Riker thought about it. He thought about the Klingons, who had supposedly killed their troublesome gods only to elevate their murderer to a nearly divine focus of worship.

He thought about the Bajorans, whose deities were certainly real and present but so obscure and alien that it was a wonder that either group could interact with or understand the other. Yet they seemed to.

He thought about the Q Continuum, whose members were possessed of seeming omnipotence, omniscience, and, in at least one case, functional omnipresence. Even they didn't claim to be gods, but if the Q weren't, who was?

Then he thought about Orisha and what he knew of its people. Whatever the Eye actually was, its presence had tortured an entire civilization for millennia. Either with actual cataclysmic violence or with the perpetual threat that such violence might be visited upon them at any moment, the Eye of Erykon had taught its people only one lesson.

Fear.

He pictured the flux wave now expanding out from the Eye, sweeping over entire systems, destroying them, yes, but before that destruction, infecting them with the very same fear that had ultimately killed Orisha.

He suddenly found the idea of that intolerable. This thing had to be stopped, and it had to be stopped here and now.

He'd argued with Deanna about the Prime Directive, about the consequences of abandoning the rule book on a whim.

"Sure, jazz is improvisational," he would say when she would inevitably toss up his love for the form as an example of the beauty of stepping outside. "But there are still rules."

"No one is telling you to abandon them," she would say. "Only that you're always at your best when you are interpreting them in your own way."

She was right. He loved her and she was right.

"Captain?" said Ree as the other turned and moved to exit the autopsy area. "Are we finished here?"

"Not quite yet, Doctor," said Riker. "But thank you for the talk."

• • •

"It is an extremely powerful, extremely delicate network of space fold devices," said Ra-Havreii as he and Modan continued to struggle with the alien controls.

"Not a warp field?" said Vale, deciding that the seated position might be best for riding out these damned quakes.

"Not exactly, no," said Ra-Havreii. "I presume you know the difference?"

Vale did, and it didn't bode well. Space folding was monumentally dangerous under the best conditions.

"What does it mean, Xin?" said Troi.

There was a pause as Ra-Havreii asked Modan to move to an adjacent console and translate the pictograms there. She rattled off something that Ra-Havreii apparently understood but which was just so much babble to Vale and Troi.

"What it means, Counselor, Commander," he said, picking up where he'd left off, "is that the Orishans have been aggressively folding the space around this planet."

"Define aggressively," said Vale, not at all sure she wanted to hear it.

"The Spire generates a folding field large enough to englobe the planet," said Ra-Havreii. "There are eighteen identical Spires dispersed around Orisha, each generating folds of the same dimensions."

"You mean simultaneously?" asked Vale, scarcely believing it. Ra-Havreii took the time to look back at her and nod before joining Modan at the second console. "That's insane."

"What is it meant to accomplish?" Troi asked.

"They call it the Veil, yes?" said the engineer. Modan was back at the first console again, translating the new symbols that flickered on the viewing screens. "This implies they are trying to cover something. Since the fields encompass the planet . . ."

He didn't have to finish. The Orishans had wrapped their planet in multiple, fantastically large space folds in an effort to—what? Space folds were for travel. These were stationary, centered around a single set of points in space-time. And why eighteen of them?

Then it hit her. This had never been an attempt to create interstellar travel. It was an attempt at a cloak, one big enough to hide an entire world.

"There's more, Commander," said Modan.

"Spit it out, Ensign," said Vale. She was doing her best not to hate Modan, but it wasn't easy. Every time she looked at the golden metallic flesh, all she could think about was Jaza.

"The folds are reacting with each other," said the Selenean. "The interaction has caused the fields to link into a single four-dimensional object."

"A tesseract," said Troi in a small voice. "We're inside a tesseract."

"I'm guessing that's worse than the space folds," said Vale.

"Monumentally," said Ra-Havreii.

All at once the tremors stopped. Modan and Ra-Havreii stepped back from their respective consoles with identical masks of relief on their faces.

"Tell me that's it," said Vale, getting to her feet and brushing the dust out of her hair. "We're done, the Veil is offline, and we can concentrate on getting the hell off this planet. Tell me that."

"We're not finished, Commander," said Ra-Havreii.

Of course we're not, she thought. *Things can always get worse.*

"Tesseracts are objects that exist both inside and outside of normal space-time," he said. "Their contours can, with precise mapping, be used to navigate temporal jumps."

"Which is what happened to us when we passed through the field, Chris," said Modan, sounding too much like Jaza again. "When the computer beamed us out, the tesseract split the transport beams like light going through a prism. You materialized here, a few days before *Titan* arrived. Najem and I ended up in the distant past."

But you're here now, aren't you? thought Vale. *And he's still stuck back there.*

"All right," said Troi, her face showing tiny creases as she turned it all over in her mind. "The Spires make the space folds and the folds have collapsed into each other to form this tesseract."

"Correct," said Ra-Havreii.

"And we're inside the tesseract," she said.

"Also correct," said the engineer.

"And that is causing these ground quakes and the eruptions from the sky?"

"Ah," he said. "Not exactly."

Modan and Ra-Havreii gave each other a pregnant look, and Troi felt something like resignation wafting off them. They asked the two senior officers to join them at a breach in the wall where the sky showed through.

Things had calmed somewhat now that the Spire network was stable, but there was still that unnatural tint and occasional clusters of what Modan claimed were tachyons flickering in and out of sight.

"You see that?" said Ra-Havreii, gesturing toward the barely visible Eye of Erykon still floating, seemingly dozing now, just beyond the Veil field. "That is the planet Orisha."

"This is the planet Orisha," said Vale.

"Yes," said Ra-Havreii. "And so is that. The tesseract effect is shunting the planet in and out of regular space-time at random intervals. When the network is stable, there is relative calm, as there is now. When the network destabilizes, Orisha tries to reenter regular space."

"Tries?" said Troi. "Tries and fails, you mean."

"Yes," said Modan. "Whenever the planet Orisha tries to reenter normal space-time at a point in the past, something is there to block it."

"What?" said Vale.

"The planet Orisha," said Ra-Havreii. "You may not understand all of the math or physics, Commander, but you must know what happens when two objects attempt to occupy the same space at the same moment in time."

Indeed she did. Vale had seen a transporter malfunction once while attempting to beam down some machinery from a spacedock above Izar. Due to the fault in the reintegration matrix, a crate of microprocessors and another of copper filaments that had dematerialized on two separate pads, had tried to reintegrate on a single pad at the end of their trip.

The result had been an explosion of shrapnel and energy that had left Vale hospitalized for two weeks while her pockmarks and burns were repaired. Now these two were saying Orisha was trying to do the same thing?

Yes, she thought. *Things can always get worse.*

"There's more, Commander," said Ra-Havreii. Of course there was. "While time moves as we expect inside the tesseract, outside it is completely random. It is my suspicion that each time the network destabilizes, we appear in the Orishan sky of the past and inspire the same effects or worse on the planet up there just as its proximity creates the same effects here. When the Veil fails completely, when the planet reenters normal space, both versions of Orisha will be destroyed."

"I'm sorry," said Troi. "You said *when* it fails."

"Yes," said Ra-Havreii.

"Not 'if.'"

"Correct," said the engineer. "The network will fail eventually. That is guaranteed. It's over a century old, and it's been taking too much punishment from overuse."

"We can keep it stable for a little while," said Modan. "But the Veil will fail. Soon."

"So we're back to where we started," said Vale. "Turn the damned thing off."

"There may be a way to implement a controlled step-down of the individual Spires," said Ra-Havreii, suddenly thoughtful.

"Yes!" said Modan, jumping on. It was odd watching her light up the way Jaza would have over concepts she wouldn't have understood only days ago. "We remove the components and the tesserect just fades away. We should reenter normal space-time in Orisha's present."

"With no previous version of itself blocking reentry, everything should be fine," said Ra-Havreii.

"*Should* be isn't *will* be," said Vale. "Tampering with this could make things worse, couldn't it?"

"It's the best we can do, I'm afraid, Commander," he said. "It's your decision, of course, but you had better make it quickly."

As if to punctuate Ra-Havreii's words, the ground beneath them seized ever so slightly and there was a spark of the rainbow lightning in the distance.

"All right," said Vale. "What do you need to get this done?"

Keru was up and looking like his old self when the three women returned to the shuttle. He had stripped off his torn garments and replaced them with the same gray and white undermesh that Modan wore.

As the ensign rummaged for the tools Ra-Havreii had requested, Vale brought Keru up to speed.

"So," he said when she was done. "We're in it. Again."

"Looks that way," she said.

"All right," he said, sucking it up. "What are your orders, Commander?"

"Just keep an eye on her for now," said Vale, indicating A'yujae'Tak, still trapped in her corner of the hold. The Orishan was also up again, lucid and watching their every move. She had, apparently, only tested the force field once before settling back on her haunches to watch and wait.

"No worries," said the big Trill. "She's been quiet the whole time."

"Good," said Vale, moving toward their prisoner. "Maybe she's calm enough to listen."

A'yujae'Tak shifted her position slightly when Vale drew near. Two of her arms extended to the floor while the higher ones flexed outward like some raptor bird testing its wings. It was easy to see that she meant to pounce on her captor the instant the shield went down. Ignoring the threatening pose, Vale dropped down to one knee to meet the alien's gaze face-to-face.

"Listen," she said. "I'm sorry about all this. I can let you out of there if you promise not to attack any of us."

"You should have killed me," said A'yujae'Tak.

"We don't do that," said Vale. "Not unless it's absolutely necessary."

"I will kill you," said the prisoner. "For what you have done to us, I will murder you all."

"We're trying to help you," said Vale. "This Veil network of yours is the thing you want to kill."

"Do not touch the Veil!" yelled A'yujae'Tak, lunging at Vale so quickly she barely had time to register the movement. "You will leave us naked before Erykon! Do you mean to kill us all?"

"As I said," said Vale, rising. "We're trying to help."

"I'm ready, Chris," said Modan, emerging from one of the lockers with a small satchel full of the necessary tools.

"*Commander,*" said Vale, sharply enough for Keru to raise an eyebrow. Troi looked about to intervene, but a look from Vale told her to save it for later. "Commander Vale, Ensign. Not Chris. My friends call me that. Understand?"

"Yes, Commander," said Modan stiffly. "I understand."

Just as Modan transported back to the surface, another quake rippled through the ground. From their vantage they could actually see the soil liquefying, spewing giant shards of the blue crystals into the air like missiles while conversely sucking vast tracts of the jungle down to oblivion.

"It's one of their cities," Troi said to Vale. "The quake is causing a cave-in. They're dying, Christine. Thousands of them."

"Murderers," screamed A'yujae'Tak, lunging at the force field again and again. "This is your doing! Erykon will destroy us all!"

"Not if I can bloody help it," said Vale. "Shuttle to Ra-Havreii."

"Hands full right now, Commander," said the engineer's voice. *"What is it?"*

"Are you still all right there?" she said.

"We're fine," he said, clearly through his obviously clenched teeth. *"Stop talking to me and let us work."*

She switched off and told Keru to join her on the flight deck. She had been feeling useless with all the technical mumbo jumbo. The destruction of the Orishan city was something she might actually be able to handle on her own.

They would have found it even without the scanners. A great canyon was in the process of ripping itself open in the ground some fifty kilometers from the Spire. The noise alone was excruciatingly loud. Each time the earth split, it was as if an impossibly large fist were being smashed into an infinite number of cymbals and drums.

Great jets of combustible gas shot up from smaller cracks that opened near the new canyon, some igniting when they were struck by one of the bolts of multicolored lightning. There was smoke everywhere, and above them, the sky, once again, seemed to burn.

Vale could only imagine what the primitive Orishans had thought the first time their god had appeared in the sky. Without a framework for understanding what was killing them, it was small wonder that they learned quickly to fear Erykon's wrath.

As Keru deftly avoided a sudden burst of flaming gas, Vale told him to get lower. The clouds of dust rising up from the upheaval below, coupled with the smoke from the burning jungle, made targeting whatever survivors there might be impossible. If she was going to salvage any of this, she needed a closer look.

"It's going to be bumpy," he told her as he set the *Ellington* in a wide, downward-looping arc. "You'd better strap in." She did as he asked quickly, hollering for Troi to do the same below.

There was one harrowing moment when the black plume of smoke from one of the burning geysers enveloped them, completely stealing their view of the world outside. To his credit, Keru only grunted and altered the descent trajectory by a few points.

They emerged from the black fog almost instantly and much closer to the trouble below. When her eyes were able to focus on the dying Orishan city, Vale almost wished she'd stayed behind with Ra-Havreii.

From the air it bore a horrible resemblance to the maw of the creature that had tried to make a meal of Vale two days before. Instead of row after row of teeth, however, this opening was ringed with giant structures, buildings of some sort, most of which now either tottered at hellishly odd angles or, worse, had already slid down into the sinkhole at the center of the growing abyss.

There were people down there. She could see them now. Some, those with wings, were attempting to fly their fellows out of danger in ones and twos, but the added drag on the gossamer-thin appendages mostly resulted in both rescuer and rescuee being sucked back down. They were the lucky ones. The mass of the Orishans were wingless and were thus forced to scramble and cling to anything that offered even a moment's purchase. A few, too few to inspire hope, had managed to climb or fly up to the lip, but the majority of them were stuck screaming below.

Troi was right. If they weren't helped somehow, soon, all these people were going to die.

"What's the plan?" Keru asked her, wrestling to maintain control of the shuttle as another chunk of the crystal whizzed past them.

"Closer," said Vale, trying to think. "Get closer. We're no good up here." She activated the shields and, in doing so, gave herself an idea.

"That's only a field patch, Commander," said Keru as the shields came up. "This thing wasn't designed for maneuverability. Whatever you want done we'd better get to it."

"Easy," she said, looking for the right candidate. Then, seeing it, "There! Ten o'clock! Go!"

As he guided the shuttle that way, Keru tried to see what it was she planned to do. They were headed to the far edge of the canyon, where a row of the strangely curved structures was teetering like a ship sinking at sea.

Hundreds of the Orishans had made it to the top side of the nearest edge and then realized to their obvious horror that there was no way to cross from that position to the relative safety of the solid ground. What was worse was the sight of so many of those still on the lower levels simply cowering in fear and not even attempting to save themselves.

It was clear that was where Vale wanted him to go so Keru threaded a path between the flying rocks and crystals and the jets of exploding gas to bring the shuttle within a few meters of the target.

"What are you doing?" he said as he noticed her hands inputting codes into the computer.

"Changing our shield configuration," she said. "There!"

She told the computer to extend the new shield configuration to encompass the area ahead of them. Nothing happened in the visual spectrum but, via instruments, Keru could see that the shuttle was now at the apex of a giant, egg-shaped force field, the *Ellington*'s shield.

He was about to protest that the shield would cut through the structure, that moving now would send the whole thing into the abyss when he realized that was precisely what she wanted.

"Take us up," she said.

The shuttle rose and, as he had predicted, only took with it the part of the structure enveloped by the shield/tractor combo. The rest, after straining to maintain coherence, broke off and fell tumbling away into the darkness below.

The extra drag made navigation even more difficult, but Keru managed somehow, carrying the massive section of building and its many occupants to the relative safety of a wide flat area of veldt that, thus far, had not been touched by the tremors.

With surprising delicacy he set the whole thing down there and, once Vale released the shields, watched as several hundred Orishans streamed gratefully out onto solid ground.

"Nice work, Commander," he said. "That was inspired."

"Nice work, yourself," she said, grinning.

"Now what?" he said.

"Now we do it again, Ranul," she said. "That was only a couple hundred. There are thousands of them down there and we don't have much time."

They performed their strange ballet seven more times, scooping up nearly three thousand very surprised, very grateful Orishans in total. It wasn't perfect or even close; as they raised their meager few to safety, they were forced to watch thousands more plummet to their ugly doom in the depths.

On the eighth and probably final attempt they ran into trouble.

"I can't get closer," said Keru, trying to do it in spite of what he said. "These damned gas jets are too powerful."

The last of the surviving structures, a sort of corkscrew tower now bent perpendicular to its normal position by the shifting ground, was only seconds away from falling in.

A large cluster of Orishans, maybe six or seven hundred of them, stood and knelt at the farthest edge and wouldn't budge. Either they hadn't seen the previous rescues or they were all simply too petrified with fear to help save their lives.

The shuttle's modified shields could only extend so far and that limit was just shy of the area in which the Orishans now stood. They had to move forward, toward the danger if they were to be saved. Thus far none of them had, and Keru was antsy to get the shuttle clear as their luck at avoiding the flying debris couldn't possibly hold out forever.

"Ra-Havreii to Vale," said the engineer's voice.

"Can it wait, Doctor?" she said. "We have our hands full now."

"Maybe," said the Efrosian, clearly struggling with something of his own. *"A very few minutes, Commander. No more."*

"We have to leave them," said Keru, meaning the Orishans. "There's no time."

"We're not leaving them," she said, unhooking herself and heading for the access ladder. "Open the rear access hatch."

"Are you insane?" he said. "Commander, we have to go!"

"Now, Lieutenant," she said, and disappeared below.

She found Deanna safely strapped to one of the emergency jump seats and flung herself into the other. Even as she closed the last buckle, the rear hatch opened, exposing the entire hold to the outside. A gust of hot air rushed in along with the cacophonous sounds of destruction that had been muffled before by the shuttle's thick hull.

Behind the opening, tens of meters away, they could make out the crowd of Orishans cowering on the far edge of the doomed structure.

"A'yujae'Tak!" Vale screamed to be heard over the blow. "Listen to me. We are trying to save your people. Do you understand? We are trying to save as many as we can!" The big insectoid moved forward in her makeshift cell, perhaps trying to get a better look at the scene outside the shuttle, but she didn't speak. Vale pressed her. "If they don't come this way, right now, they are all going to die! Do you understand? They have to move toward this ship, right now!"

There was the smallest of pauses and then, "I understand you," said A'yujae'Tak.

Vale ordered the computer to drop the force field that held A'yujae'Tak and watched as the Orishan moved slowly but steadily toward the open hatchway.

She stopped at the lip and let out a loud piercing burst of chatter that the translator could not decode. As a mass the endangered Orishans began to surge forward. When the last of them was in position, without a word, A'yujae'Tak jumped down to join them.

Vale hit the manual hatch control, closing the door behind her. A'yujae'Tak would live with her people or die with them.

"Keru," she called up to him when the noise had subsided enough. "GO!"

"We've got them, Commander," he called down as the ship and its cargo rose away from the destruction. "We're on our way."

"Vale to Ra-Havreii," she said as soon as she was sure they were clear. "Tell me you have good news."

He didn't. In fact, his news was about as bad as it could get. He and Modan had managed to stabilize the network again and were in the process of implementing the timed stepdown of the Spires when the entire network was hit by a powerful energetic pulse.

"What do you mean, 'hit by'?" said Vale.

"A second field, one outside the network, is interfering with the Orishan Veil," said Ra-Havreii. *"I believe it is trying to collapse it."*

"Is it something you didn't account for?" said Vale. "Is the tesseract somehow reacting to what you're doing there?"

"No, Commander," said the engineer. *"In lay terms the frequency of the counterpulse is too precise to be a natural phenomenon. It has clearly been specifically configured to collapse the Veil."*

"You think someone is doing this intentionally?"

"I think it's Titan," said Ra-Havreii. *"I believe they have survived and are trying to collapse the tesseract."*

"Why would they do that?"

"It's possible the effects of the eruption that brought us here are expanding," he said. *"In fact, now that I think of it, it's likely."*

"What happens if they succeed?"

"I've already told you, Commander," said Ra-Havreii. *"Tiny chunks of planet where Orisha used to be."*

"Solution, Xin," said Vale. "Tell me you've got one."

"Possibly," he said. *"You'll need Modan."*

"Not you?"

"No, Commander," he said. *"I have to stay with the network. Modan doesn't have the skill to do what's necessary here. There is an improvisational aspect that—"*

"Fine," said Vale, cutting him off. "Beaming her out now. What's Modan going to do for us that we can't do on our own?"

"She's going to get you back to Titan *and get them to stop what they're doing."*

"Oh," said Vale, a bit taken back. "All right then."

"Good-bye, Commander," he said. *"If I never see you again, thank you for calling me Xin."*

Chapter Fifteen

Something was wrong.

Dakal knew it. He felt it, a strange acidic churning in the bottom of his stomach, as he sat at his station in the sensor pod. He could feel something had gone horribly wrong with the captain's plan. He had no evidence of any failure, certainly nothing on which he could put a finger. Still the feeling persisted.

Titan had learned to protect herself from the worst of the quantum flux. Its systems and crew were back to full capacity or very nearly so. They had come back so far from the edge that the captain was now attempting to remove the author of all their recent troubles rather than prudently cut his losses and run for help.

It was not a very Cardassian way of handling things, and though he was loath to admit it, the whole business of staying here to attempt to collapse the bizarre knot in space-time made him a little nervous.

There was good luck, after all, and there was tempting fate.

He wished Jaza were here. The big Bajoran scientist had a way of putting things in the right perspective even when it wasn't immediately clear how he was doing so.

Of course Jaza was dead, along with the rest of his away team. He wouldn't be there again, ever. It had never occurred to Dakal that he could miss anyone so much before the Dominion war. Afterward he never thought he'd stop missing the people he had lost. His time at the refugee camp on Lejonis and his stint at the Academy had led him to *Titan* and, strangely, a kind of peace he never thought he would have again.

There were so many kinds of people here, so many ways of interacting with, well, everything, that he had withdrawn a bit from what he had perceived as chaos.

Jaza had drawn him back in again.

I don't believe in dunsels, Cadet. Never have, never will.

Jaza with his serenity, his good humor, and his understated manner had somehow managed to put Dakal in the thick of things socially and with people he would never have dared to approach on his own. He had begun breathing again in the old familiar way, had become more of his old self than since well before the war.

Jaza had been his good friend, though neither of them had ever referred to their relationship that way. After everything their people had been to each other. Friends. Amazing.

And now he was gone.

Dakal eyed the TOV rig, sitting dark and dormant in its corner, and wondered if his sometime mentor had enjoyed its use as much as he had.

"Please don't dwell, Dakal," said Hsuuri softly. When the others had gone off shift, she had stayed behind to complete some personal project. Their shipmates had all drifted off to their beds or their poker games or their holodeck adventures as soon as their allotted time had passed. There wasn't much left for them to do just now, no exotic bodies for them to scan. The bridge was handling everything right now, and the bridge was focused on the Eye of the storm.

Roakn had actually invited Dakal to join him at poker, which had so surprised the young cadet that he almost forgot to make his refusal polite.

Now that things were essentially back to normal on *Titan,* things were essentially back to normal. At least they seemed to be for everyone but Dakal.

"My apologies, Lieutenant," he said. "What did you say?"

"It's Hsuuri, please," she said, leaning heavily into one shoulder as her large green eyes watched him. "And I think Mr. Jaza wouldn't want you grieving like this."

"I'm not grieving yet," said Dakal. "We need a body for that, and we haven't seen one."

She put a soft fur-covered hand on his shoulder and said, "We may never find their bodies, Dakal. It's likely whatever destroyed *Charon* destroyed them the same way."

"Then I won't be grieving, I guess," he said sharply, pulling away from her. He regretted it immediately but couldn't bring himself to go back over. He didn't want tenderness right now, not even from her.

Instead he busied himself with a check of the recent sensor data they'd got back from their scans of the Eye. He'd already checked it, of course, twice, but he needed something to do and it was hours before the new shift assignments would be posted.

It was funny. During their troubles with the flux and the attack by the Orishan ship, Dakal hadn't thought of Jaza once, only of his own duties and, maybe, how they might all survive this latest incident.

Now, no matter how he tried to focus on other things, his mind kept looping back to Jaza.

"When a hunter dies on Cait," said Hsuuri, remaining where she stood, letting him move if that's what he needed or not move if not. "Even if her body is never recovered, her entire pride gathers to sing and tell stories of her great deeds. Some of them are even true."

"Sounds lively." *But not very dignified,* he thought bitterly.

"It can be," she said. "Which I guess is sort of the point."

"That's not how we do it on Prime," he said. "Our way begins with the body."

He thought of Jaza Najem, pumped full of preservative chemicals or inside a stasis field, laid out on a death couch, undergoing the four days of testimonials, readings of personal anecdotes, and listing of the members of the family tree that comprised the bulk of a traditional funeral rite on Prime, and he smiled.

Dakal had no idea yet how Bajorans marked the end of

a life, but he was pretty sure it didn't involve family insignias or tithing to the central authority.

"It's good to see a smile on you," said Hsuuri, completely mistaking its meaning. "Mr. Jaza liked smiles."

"That's true," he said, and then fell silent for several long minutes as he appeared to busy himself with the sensor logs.

We'll make a scientist of you yet, Zurin.

The minutes dragged between them then to the point where he became uncomfortable with her eyes on him. He enjoyed that look very much under normal circumstance and the occasional touch of her hand or whisk of her tail, but just now he felt too exposed somehow to be seen by her.

"I'm sorry," they said in unison, causing him to go silent again while she managed a little silken laugh.

"It's all right, Dakal," she said. "Everyone grieves, or doesn't grieve, differently. If you would like to learn another way Caitians have to honor Mr. Jaza's life, or all life, please let me know."

She left him there with his thoughts and his sensor logs, and it was a long time before he realized what she had said or that she had gone.

Dammit, thought Riker, looking at the readings again. *There's something wrong.*

There shouldn't have been, but there was. The information they'd gotten from the Orishan vessel's upload had been more than enough to generate the algorithms necessary to recalibrate *Titan*'s main deflector.

The instant the modifications were complete, Riker had

ordered the ship to begin projecting the counterpulse that would inspire the Eye to collapse.

Everything had gone according to plan until it suddenly hadn't. The Eye was not collapsing. The effect of its last expulsion of force and energy continued to spread. Something was definitely wrong, and so far, they had no idea what that something was.

"It's as if the Eye is compensating for the counterpulse," said Tuvok. "Each time it shifts its vibrational frequency, we compensate. Each time we compensate, it shifts again."

"You make it sound like there's somebody in there, Mr. Tuvok," said Lavena, holding *Titan* steady in the face of the Eye's continuing undulations of force.

"I am currently at a loss to explain it," said the Vulcan. "But the Eye is behaving as if driven by some intelligence."

Even as he said it, the Eye's frequency shifted again though not by very much. It was as if it knew that a minor change in its field density would be enough to block *Titan*'s counterpulse but that a large shift might cause it to collapse without prodding.

There was no possibility that this cat-and-mouse game was the result of random phenomena, and yet Tuvok could not allow himself to accept that the Eye was, in fact, in some way sentient after all. There had to be another rational explanation.

"Talk to me, Mr. Tuvok," said Riker, watching as the Eye continued not to collapse under *Titan*'s onslaught. "What did we do wrong here?"

"One moment, Captain," said Tuvok as he reset the

main sensor array. His face never betrayed it, but internally he was extremely concerned.

This stalemate couldn't last forever. Eventually the constant shifts in force and frequency might inadvertently cause the Eye to collapse, but it was just as likely that this tug of war would inspire another of the massive eruptions. *Titan*'s shields had held so far, especially after adding Orishan-inspired modifications to Torvig's, but there was no guarantee they could withstand another of the explosions.

The chances of survival were lower in fact, now that Captain Riker, deeming the close-range attack to be best, had ordered them nearer to the Eye.

"Bridge to sensor pod," said Tuvok.

"Cadet Dakal here, sir. Go ahead."

"Are you monitoring the wave fluctuations of the Eye?"

"No, sir," said Dakal. *"I can have Lieutenant Roakn up here in just a—"*

"There's no time for that now, Cadet," Riker chimed in. "You're elected. Give Mr. Tuvok whatever he requires."

"I'll do my best, sir."

In short emotionless bursts, Tuvok rattled off a series of calibrations and coordinates for Dakal to input into the pod's ultrasensitive scanning array.

He was sure he had missed something, some apparently minor characteristic of the Eye that allowed this bizarre stalemate to occur, but the main sensors had come up empty.

"Sensors aligned, sir," said Dakal. *"Initiating first sweep."*

There was silence on the bridge as the young cadet trained the array on the Eye. They had less than an hour before the distortion wave reached the sun. Once it did, the star would either supernova several billion years before its time, flash-frying everything within light-years, or it would instantly implode, crunching itself down to a dwarf of some kind with the sort of extreme gravimetric pull that would crush the ship and everything else in the system just as quickly.

"Dakal," said Riker. "What have you got?"

"I'm not sure, sir," said the Cadet's voice. *"There seems to be a very small point of distortion in the Eye's lower anterior hemisphere."*

"Can you pinpoint it?" said Tuvok.

"Adjusting," said Dakal. *"Please stand by."*

"I don't see how this can work," said Vale, peering out at the multihued aurora currently enveloping them. They had passed through the layer of apparent fire that still surrounded Orisha and were now zipping back and forth a few meters from the tesseract's event horizon looking for an exit.

They had to be extremely careful not to try to pass through the thing at the wrong junction of angles or they would be shunted along its vertex to some point either forward or backward in time.

"It's simple," said Modan, fretting over the science station. "If you think of the tesseract like a gem with solid facets and permeable flaws, you just have to understand that we're looking for a flaw."

"And the shield modulation?"

"That's to help us punch through when we find it, Chris," Modan said, and winced when she realized her mistake. "I'm sorry. *Commander.*"

All at once the shuttle suffered a massive jolt and Keru had to fight to regain control. It was the fifth such event, and everyone was sick of them.

"That just never becomes fun," said Keru as he leveled off again.

"*Titan*'s counterpulse is affecting the field's coherence," said Modan. "As long as Commander Ra-Havreii can compensate quickly enough, we should be all right."

"Can't we just open a channel to *Titan* and tell them to hold off for a few seconds?"

"Absolutely," said Modan cheerily. "From our current position the message should reach them in about forty-seven years."

Keru grumbled something about Jaza's sense of humor but stayed focused on not letting the shuttle drift into the tesseract's field.

Having nothing to contribute for the moment and hating every turn of phrase uttered by Modan that reminded her of Jaza, Vale slid out of the navigator's cradle and moved back toward the jump seats and Troi.

"Well," she said, sliding in beside her. "Looks like you were right. *Titan* survived after all."

Troi looked up then, and Vale could see she had been crying.

"Yes," she said. "I was right all along. Now, if only I had really believed it."

They shared a bittersweet laugh at the events of the last few days. There had been so much tragedy and so much loss that there was little else to do but laugh. All that tension had to go somewhere.

Jaza was gone. *Titan* had survived, but the hundreds

aboard whichever of her sisters had crashed into Orisha had not. Three-hundred-fifty-plus lives had been snuffed out by the Eye of Erykon. It didn't matter that most, perhaps all of them, were strangers. And now, with *Titan* so close they could almost see her, there was still no real certainty that any of them would come out of this alive. Modan would lose access to the knowledge she'd borrowed from Jaza soon. If it happened before they returned to *Titan,* well, that would be bad.

You really had to laugh.

So they did.

"But the worst thing is," said Vale, between chuckles, "I still have this awful color in my hair."

"I would have mentioned it," said Troi, also giggling too hard now to keep still. "But I couldn't tell whether or not you were playing a joke of some kind."

"It's not funny," said Vale as she erupted into a string of apparently uncontrollable giggles.

"It's a little bit funny," said Troi, following suit.

Soon the barely controlled laughter developed into full-throated guffaws, loud enough to draw the attention of the other two in the shuttle.

"What's the joke?" said Keru. Modan only looked puzzled.

Before either Vale or Troi could answer, an enormous fluctuation in the tesseract's field density rocked the shuttle hard to its port side.

"There," said Modan, scrambling back into her chair. "It's right there." She passed the coordinates on to Keru who, in spite of his better judgment, pointed the shuttle's nose at the invisible breach and plunged through.

• • •

"There, Mr. Tuvok," said Dakal excitedly. *"It's right there again! Do you see it?"*

Tuvok informed the cadet that he did indeed see the strange pattern of fluctuation and that there was no need to shout.

Taking control of the sensor pod's primary array and synching it with the main sensor grid, Tuvok trained all of *Titan*'s attention on that one small spot of distortion. It didn't make sense that the tiny shiver in the Eye's field would have anything to do with their current difficulty, but as no other culprits had presented themselves, he owed it as close a look as possible.

Sure enough, on deep inspection, Dakal's area of distortion did exist. Moreover, it had contours that were too regular to have been produced in nature. Whatever else it was, this thing was artificial, probably mechanical.

Was it responsible in some way for the Eye or for its ability to offset whatever version of the counterpulse was thrown its way? Further examination was required.

Narrowing the scan to exclude everything outside the point of distortion gave Tuvok and, tangentially, Dakal a much clearer view of its contours.

It was shaped like a cube that had had the sharp points of its corners sanded down. There were protrusions of some kind on two of its wider planes: a small oval-shaped bubble on what he arbitrarily designated as the top and, along the bottom, two long slender cylinders running the object's length.

"It's the Ellington,*"* exclaimed Dakal. *"Sir, don't you see, it has to be them."*

Ignoring Dakal's excited outburst, Tuvok altered the scan to ferret out signs of a warp core that had been configured according to Starfleet specifications.

"We're not going to make it," said Keru, still wrestling with the controls. He wasn't able to do much with them just now beyond keeping the shudder to a minimum, and he was quickly coming to the end of that rope as well. "Modan, you're supposed to be on point. What now?"

No one aboard the shuttle was laughing anymore. They had plunged into the supposed flaw in the tesseract's four-dimensional body, and though they had not apparently been forced forward or backward away from their proper time period, they could not push through into normal space.

"It's the damned counterpulse," said Modan. "Every time Ra-Havreii shifts the Veil configuration I have to re-modulate the shuttle's shields. I can't do it fast enough to push through to the other side."

"Not good enough, Modan," said Vale. "This is why Ra-Havreii sent you, to get us through this."

"I'm trying, dammit," she said. "Just—just let me think for a second."

She's losing it, thought Vale. *Jaza would have solved this already. Whatever she got from him is fading fast.*

"Ranul," she said. "Hail *Titan*. See if you can let them know we're here."

"That won't work, Commander," said Modan. "The signal won't penetrate the tesseract field."

"Mr. Keru," said Vale, ignoring Modan. "Hail *Titan*."

As he tried and failed to get a signal through the tesseract, Modan fought to hold on to the skills she'd borrowed from Jaza. Normally she could have counted on days of additional talent, but having to help Ra-Havreii not only solve the dilemma of how to shut down the Veil network but to keep it from failing before they could do it had pushed her to her limit.

She wasn't a telepath. Her species had simply learned to link their nervous systems with those of other organisms in order to borrow some of their chemical or genetic information. She'd used this talent to copy those of Jaza's memories that could have been useful. It was as if she had made an electrochemical model of his scientific knowledge and skills inside her brain. Like any chemical modification, the faster she worked her metabolism, the faster she burned out the changes.

Orisha had kept her burning nonstop for hours. She had only a little longer before she lost it all, and they hadn't even gotten back to *Titan* yet.

Think, she told herself. *You have to hold on to this. Calm down and think!*

It was no use. She could feel the bits of him, his memories, his past, his knowledge of how to save them, all slipping away. All this excitement was burning him out of her too fast, too fast to do what he had sent her to do.

She cast around the shuttle's cockpit, as if hoping to find a solution written on one of the displays or magically burned into the air by the power of his Prophets. There was nothing, only the increasing sensation of loss as his memory patterns dissolved into their base peptides.

She fought it as best she could, trying to use her own memory to reconstruct or approximate his.

A tesseract, she knew the thought was his but she forced it to be hers. If she could only keep remembering . . . *A tesseract is a four-dimensional object with vertices in both subspace and conventional space with the ratios of the angles corresponding to . . . to . . .*

"Modan," said Vale from somewhere far away. She sounded angry, still obviously furious with the younger woman for leaving Jaza to his fate. But Jaza had told her to do it, had *ordered* her to—

Tachyons move backward in space-time, no slower than the rate of C. The Vulcan physicist Stang has postulated five potential means of harnessing them for practical use.

What were they? What help could those five theories be now? Was it something to do with the space fold or just some random bit of errata that meant absolutely nothing? She couldn't think. She had to think. She couldn't.

"Ensign," said Troi's voice, also from somewhere far outside the chaos inside her. "Ensign are you all right?"

No, dammit, she thought. *I'm losing it. I'm losing everything Jaza gave me and we're all going to—*

Suddenly she felt hands on her, pulling her back from the control console. Keru was yelling something about turbulence, Vale was shoving past her to get into the other pilot's cradle and Troi was—

Troi was—

"I'm here, Ensign," said the Betazoid, guiding her down to the cockpit floor. "Be calm."

"It's fading away," said Modan, her distress making her voice tremble along with her body. "I can't hold on to it."

Causality is an illusion supported by a limited ability to perceive. That wasn't from Jaza, was it?

"Be calm," said Troi and, suddenly, she was. Her mind stilled itself, her respiration slowed, her body ceased its tremors. "Good."

"My body is metabolizing Najem's memories," said Modan weakly. Vale cursed but couldn't do anything to assist Troi. She had her hands full helping Keru keep the ship from being smashed in the tesseract's event horizon.

"What can you do to stop it?" said Troi, her wide dark eyes showing nothing but assurance and calm.

"Nothing," said Modan. "I could pass them to another Selenean, perhaps, but there aren't any—"

"Pass them to me," said Troi.

"You don't understand," said Modan. "It's not telepathy. It's chemical. I will be changing the chemistry of your brain."

"You did this already, Ensign," said Troi. "You showed us Jaza's past."

"Images," said Modan bitterly. "Emotions. Simple things. Minor changes. This is information, complex theories, equations. It could damage you."

"We're all about to get damaged to death," said Keru. "Give her the damned memories."

The *Ellington* took another violent jolt as the tesseract shifted in space-time around them. A few more and Keru's pronouncement would become a fact.

"Do it, Modan," said Vale. "That's an order."

Terrified, the Selenean did as she was told, striking Troi's temples hard with her linking spines. The counselor cried out softly, more in surprise than pain. Her eyes rolled backward in her head as she pitched forward across Modan's prone body.

"We're losing it," warned Keru as the ship shook and rattled around them.

All at once, Troi sat up, apparently reenergized and alert. She hefted Modan's body up into one of the jump seats and quickly strapped her in.

"Well?" said Vale through clenched teeth. "Can you get us out of this?"

Wordlessly, Troi ran aft and disappeared into the engineering compartment.

The ship lurched again, eliciting a curse from Keru. Warning lights activated all across the navigation console.

"Troi," yelled Vale. "What the hell are you doing? Leave the core alone."

"Wait," said Keru. "Wait, I think—I think we're getting through. Whatever she did is working."

Sure enough, the multicolored light show was slowly fading, giving way to the familiar twinkling blackness of normal space. They were almost home.

"Nice work, Counselor," said Keru as Troi returned and flopped into the jump seat opposite Modan. "What did you do?

Troi seemed not to hear him.

"Deanna," said Vale. "What did you do to the core?"

"What?" she said, distracted, her attention still focused inward. "Oh, nothing. We needed extra power to push through to normal space, so I removed the plasma buffers and disabled the safeties."

"Oh," said Keru. "That explains it."

"What?"

"Why the engine's building to overload," he said.

"Well," said Captain Riker, the tension in his voice telegraphing the growing concern in his mind. If it was the shuttle, why couldn't he feel Deanna's presence reasserting, reconnecting? Where was she? "Is it the shuttle or not?"

Tuvok would not be hurried or prodded by the increasing tension and excitement in the non-Vulcans who surrounded him. He was methodical. He was precise. He would be absolutely sure before making any pronouncements.

"Yes," he said, after a silence that generated thoughts of his homicide in the minds of nearly everyone present. "It is the *Ellington*. Somehow it has survived inside the Eye and is attempting to return to normal space."

Will? Troi's mental fingers reached out to him from what seemed a great distance. *Will, I'm here.*

He tried to project his relief and pleasure back at her but was unsure if his feelings could make it through whatever was impeding her communication.

"I am reading four life signs," said Tuvok. "One human, one Selenean, one Trill, and one Betazoid. Mr. Jaza and Dr. Ra-Havreii are not aboard."

It was difficult not to be elated at the shuttle's return, but they managed. They had no idea what could have happened to the missing away team members, but there was little hope that the news on that score would be good.

"Give me a visual," said Riker. Immediately the main viewer zoomed closer to the Eye, where what had been a small grayish dot now resolved itself into the familiar shape of the shuttle.

"Sir," said Lavena. "I'm getting an anomalous reading off the shuttle. The warp core—"

"Bridge to transporter room A," said Tuvok.

"Radowski here, sir," came the instant reply.

"I believe the *Ellington*'s warp core is about to breach," said the Vulcan. "Target all organics aboard for transport on my mark."

"Aye, sir."

"Tuvok," said the captain.

"One moment, Captain," said Tuvok. "Mr. Radowski, do you have a lock on all personnel?"

"Yes, sir," said the transporter chief. *"Solid lock on all four."*

"Energize now," said Tuvok. "Now, Mr. Radowski."

At that moment there was a tremendous flash of white light that filled the main viewer, obliterating any other image. When the light cleared, the shuttle was gone.

Deanna? He could feel her, he thought, but he didn't want to trust the feeling until—

"We got them, sir," said Radowski's voice. *"Mr. Keru and the rest are back aboard."*

"Cutting it a bit close there, Mr. Tuvok," said the captain, beaming. "Dramatic license?"

"No, sir," said Tuvok, seemingly as appalled as a Vulcan could be at such a suggestion. "The shuttle was not fully integrated into normal space. Had we attempted to transport them too soon—"

Before he could finish, *Titan* suffered a powerful and

unexpected jolt that set the lights flickering and put several of the surprised officers on the deck.

"What the hell?" said Riker, helping Ensign Bohn back into the navigator's chair. There was no need for anyone to answer. The Eye appeared in the visible spectrum for the first time, and it was not an appealing sight.

Still not quite all there, the Eye had manifested itself as a violently undulating orb of bubbling energies that seemed unwilling to decide if it was bloodred or a sinister indigo blue at any given moment.

Around its edges, framing it like the halo of a black hole, a jagged rainbow aurora sparked and shot lances of what looked like solar flares in every direction.

"Brace for second wave," said Tuvok. Even as he finished, the wave hit, just as powerful as the previous.

"What's happening?" said Lavena. "I thought this part was over!"

"The shuttle explosion seems to have destabilized the Eye," said Tuvok as the third shock wave hit the ship. "The established counterpulse is not effective. I am attempting to compensate."

The fourth jolt hit just as the turbolift doors opened and sent Troi and Vale stumbling onto the bridge.

Imzadi! Deanna sent to him along with a flood of deep emotion nearly as powerful as the waves of force currently emanating from the Eye. There was another presence there though, an unfamiliar, incredibly orderly set of thoughts and emotions that hit him like a fist.

Deanna? he sent, but she brushed his thoughts aside.

No time, she sent back. *Explanations later.*

He watched, puzzled, as she moved right to Tuvok's tactical station and began conversing with the Vulcan in low tones. The conversation was entirely technical with Deanna evidencing knowledge of *Titan*'s systems that Riker hadn't known she possessed.

Vale threw herself into the chair on his right. She, like Deanna, looked like hell, but, also like his wife, she was very much alive.

"Welcome back, Commander," said Riker, glancing back at Deanna, still in deep earnest conversation with Tuvok.

"Thank you, sir," said Vale. "Sorry we're late."

"Just in time, actually," said Riker, still distracted by his wife's odd behavior.

"It won't work, Counselor," Tuvok's voice said over the chatter. "The shuttle's warp core explosion—"

"I can compensate," she said, obviously desperate. "I can key the right corrections, but you have to let me do it now."

Without waiting for an answer, Troi elbowed Tuvok aside and began recalibrating *Titan*'s counterpulse.

At first the Vulcan meant to continue his objections, but when he saw what she was doing, he fell in with her, adding supplementary code to her modifications.

"I need phaser control," said Troi absently. Her hands moved like lightning across the console, and Tuvok was pressed to keep her pace.

"Here and here," said Tuvok, gesturing. "Counselor, how are you accomplishing this?"

"It's not me," she said. "It's Jaza. And I'm losing him. We're only going to get one try at this."

"At what?" asked Riker.

In response, Tuvok and Troi simultaneously activated

both the phasers and the newly recalibrated counterpulse. The pulse wasn't visible, of course, but the twin beams of phased energy were. They lashed out across the intervening darkness, striking the Eye at its core.

Where they hit, a soft golden glow began to spread outward across the surface of the Eye until the glow had replaced the red and blue oscillations completely.

"Not yet, Najem," said Troi softly. "Stay with me."

The glow grew as they watched, becoming brighter and brighter until it was difficult to look directly at the viewer. Troi entered second-by-second modifications to the counterpulse while Tuvok modulated the phaser frequencies, muttering corrections to each other as they went.

"Almost," said Troi. "Almost . . ."

The glow from the screen became oppressive. The light was everywhere now, nearly bright enough to overload the viewer.

"Aili," said Riker, shielding his eyes. "I think it's time to go."

"Yes, sir," said Lavena, already punching in escape vectors.

Then, before she could finish, Troi said, "Now!"

Tuvok input the final modulations to the phaser frequency, and the whole world went white. *Titan* shook as violently as a paper sailboat in a hurricane.

Alarms went off all over the ship as wave after wave of unknown energy again tore through it and its crew.

The main viewer, finally overtasked from projecting such a powerful image, shut down, plunging the room into relative darkness.

"Get that viewer back online," said Riker when the shaking stopped. Presently the main screen lit up again, and instead of the Eye or the storm it had created, there sat the planet Orisha, a study in lilac, white, and powder blue.

The Eye of Erykon was gone.

"Local quantum conditions are returning to normal, Captain," said Tuvok as the sensor data came in. "The flux wave has dissipated. May we stand down from Red Alert, sir?"

Riker nodded but said nothing. What was there to say? They had finally won through, but at such a terrible cost it was difficult in that moment, for him, for any of them, to want to raise a glass or cheer.

Troi let out a low moan and collapsed, exhausted, into Tuvok's waiting arms.

Chapter Sixteen

It took only a few days for the Orishans to pull down the Spires and demolish their fold devices. Without the Eye hanging over their heads they had no need to conceal themselves or the civilization they had built.

Titan hung in orbit over the planet, helping to coordinate rescue and relief as the survivors of the apocalypse made their several ways to the surface they had avoided all their lives.

There were fewer of them now, hundreds of thousands fewer, but there were enough to begin again and more to continue this time what they had started with fear.

"It is something we can never repay," said A'yujae'Tak. "You are truly the servants of Erykon."

"I thought you were done with all that," said Vale. She wasn't challenging the insectoid, only concerned for their future well-being. You didn't need the orb in the sky to instill fear, especially in those for whom fear came as naturally as breathing.

A'yujae'Tak made an untranslatable noise that Vale took to denote amusement. "You do not imagine, because we know the Eye was not truly from Erykon that we have given up following Erykon's ways," she said. "Erykon is. We are the Children of Erykon."

They offered to leave some people behind—an engineer or two, some social planners, just to help kickstart them on their long ascent. It would be difficult to rebuild everything, impossible in some cases for generations.

The Orishan refusal was polite but firm.

"It is our fate," seemed to be the consensus. "We will make it ourselves."

Well. You have to admire their grit.

While the gathering of stragglers and refugees continued, A'yujae'Tak gave them the run of the planet should any of them wish to take a stroll. It was a beautiful world for all its strangeness, and many of the crew took the opportunity to put their feet on some honest to goodness soil.

She found him in the wreckage quietly scanning and occasionally digging. He hadn't seen her since that night in the sensor pod when she'd offered him comfort.

She asked what he was up to and he made some noises about getting clean scans of *Charon*'s bones to provide Starfleet HQ with the most accurate record of the event. It was a Cardassian thing, and he didn't really expect her to understand.

She told him she did understand, that news of Mr. Jaza's strange but beautiful sacrifice had already been distributed via the rumor mill. If he didn't mind the company, she said, she would be pleased to help him search for some remnant of their friend's presence here.

He didn't mind the company.

He found her loitering around the skeleton of the central Spire, intentionally keeping well clear of the others who had come down for some time in the sun.

"You did well," he told her. "Exceedingly so."

She, of course, disagreed. She had lost Jaza to time and his Prophets. She had nearly destroyed the *Ellington* and almost taken herself, Troi, Vale, and Keru with it.

Had she not been able to count on his ability to understand and improvise, none of them would be here now.

"I have much to tell the Mother," she said, but expressed doubt at how much of it would please.

They walked together for a while, mostly in silence, listening, as if for the first time, to the myriad happy and mysterious noises that every jungle makes.

He told her that he knew a bit about carrying regret around like a stone, and if she would agree to remind him not to do it overmuch, he would certainly remind her.

She smiled at that and accepted.

Later he offered to play her some music and she accepted that as well.

She found him in a dense cluster of the thick vines, decidedly out of uniform and romping wildly with several creatures that reminded her of frogs and of bats and maybe a bit of turtles.

He roared at one of them for attempting to steal a nut

of some kind on which he had been sharpening his teeth and sent it scurrying away into the bush. It returned presently with a small army of its fellows and pelted him into oblivion with an assault of the very same nuts. The scene brought a smile to her face.

"You should have guessed that would happen," she said. "You're supposed to be a counselor."

"My counsel is sound," he said, biting into one of the sweet juicy leaves he'd also recently discovered and getting covered in its sap. "It's my patients that are sometimes lacking."

She laughed again and called him silly. He agreed and said she would do well to occasionally strip down and run naked through a jungle or two.

She asked him if that was his professional opinion. It was. She was a smart woman, he told her. Therefore her need to play, to just play, was greater than most.

"You're awfully free with advice," she said, "considering your track record."

"If you mean Trois," he said. "I stand on my success. Happy together at last viewing."

"What success?" she said. "They fixed the problem themselves."

"Time apart reminds the heart," he said, and clawed his way up the vine to discover the real true nature of the very attractive piece of hanging fruit.

She laughed at that too and kept her clothes on. But she stayed and watched him for a while.

He found them together, sitting in happy silence in the shade of several of the low-hanging lilac fronds. They graciously invited him to join them, he graciously accepted, and for some hours the three of them discussed gods and fears and the restorative aspects of going through, sometimes, rather than around.

Then the sun dipped low and they all had the same other place to be.

Before they parted, he finally told them with cautious optimism the news he had come to share, clicking his foreclaws as he delivered it.

They thanked him, watched him go, and after a few tears, they celebrated.

He found him at dusk, hiking, taking him very much by surprise. Neither of them said a word, only stood there looking.

Both of them smiled.

After that they walked along together for a bit. And then the sun dipped even lower and they had the same other place to be.

They gathered in the place where they discovered his secret home. They never found his bones or any sign of how it had ended for him.

They never mentioned to the locals who their Oracle had really been, but they knew they couldn't leave him sleeping there without saying their good-byes.

Their leader spoke, telling stories of his quick mind and easy ways and the times he played and fell for practical jokes.

His protégé attempted to speak, failed to find the words, tried again, failed again, and ended with a promise to live up to expectations.

His former lover said a few official things about bravery and commitment. She said a few things about faith and what she did and didn't understand about that. She said one bawdy thing about the placement of ridges and one quiet thing about love. Then she said good-bye.

Then, one by one, in all their secret ways, his friends said it too.

They left Orisha the best way that anything can be left: better than they'd found it, freer than its people had allowed themselves to dream, and a little sad to see them go.

Prologue

"We must move on. Now. Before hearts cool and hands grow tired with waiting. We must move on, downstream, on the great river, which is Life. We have fought the battles and made our peace and all that's left us is our time and how we fill it."

—Excerpted from the *Ascension of Makkus,*
First Sovereign of Ligon II

The sky was lovely. The Daystar was at its apex, shining its bright benign light down on everything. The other great orb, Erykon's Eye, continued its slumber and the people below rejoiced. It had been a short war as they went here, lasting only those few days that their god had spewed wrathful fire from above and deadly tremors from below.

The thousand clans, each with their own notions of how best to serve Erykon and remove any offense from the world beneath the Eye, had done their best to slaughter one another on a nearly unimaginable scale.

Now all that was done and the survivors had crawled back to their warrens and hives to lick their wounds and learn if enough of their breeder males had endured to rebuild the ranks of their clans.

It would be some time before any of them tested another clan's territorial border or tried to raid their food stores or steal their breeders.

Time was what he needed, and he had it. He knew the Eye wouldn't wake again for a thousand years, tens of thousands of what the locals called cycles.

He might live a tenth of that if he took care. Not long, but perhaps long enough to ensure their future.

His first convert, Tik'ik, was loyal and resolute as she had been from the first day, but, of course, she had the benefit of seeing his magic firsthand.

She came and went at the times he dictated, bringing news of the clans and of their relations with one another. She never questioned his need for this information or asked why Erykon's representative never showed himself. She didn't question. She was devout.

New apostles would be harder to come by. It was both a help and a hindrance that he could only ever be a disembodied voice to them, a collection of unusual scents, but he had known that going in. One glimpse of his true form and they would tear him to shreds, eat what was tasty, and immediately fall back on their self-destructive and violent ways.

They would wipe themselves out in a generation if left to their own devices, and, as he had seen that that was not in fact their fate, he would never allow himself to do anything to compromise his ability to save them from the abyss.

His people had polluted Orisha's destiny by slamming this graveyard of technology into its surface. It hadn't been their desire to do this, but it had happened, and now, to ensure that Orisha's future proceeded as it should, indeed that Orisha even had a future, he would stay and play shepherd.

He made his home in one of the more intact parts of the crashed remains of the starship, the area they called the Shattered Place. Already the myth of the strange goings-on there had grown. He would do what he could to cultivate that. They needed to fear this place just a little if he was to survive long enough to do them good.

If nothing else, the insectoids had already proven they had a talent for fear.

The first steps would be the toughest and the most important. They had to be kept from ever thinking of this place as anything but holy and taboo. They were too smart and inventive a species even to be allowed near this wreck for too long. Anything they built or discovered had to be done without the benefit of the "magical" items they might find here.

He'd already found a few himself to make his stay slightly more pleasant—random power carts, medical supplies, some interactive novels, bits of undamaged circuitry he would need in case the tricorder ever died. The most significant find was the tool kit, and he considered it a gift from the Prophets.

He'd left the one in the shuttle for Modan, not knowing what she might find on the other side of her journey back to their own era.

Her own era.

This was his home now, this time and this place.

His little room was in what was left of the ship's former holodeck, still mostly intact. He liked it for its size and hidden ventilation ducts, but mostly for the fact that its entrance had been so fused with wreckage and the ground that it couldn't now be navigated by any but the smallest of the big insectoids.

He needed that privacy in order to give his stealth apparatus a rest or to repair it if need be. And he needed it to remind himself that he was not, in fact, an Oracle or a seer, but a man, the student of his Prophets, servant of these Children of the wrathful god Erykon.

After some months, when the first of his acts as their shepherd began to bear fruit, he woke up in a cold sweat with images of unfulfilled paradoxes in his mind.

Through Tik'ik, whom he had taken to calling Yujae, the word in her language that meant "vessel," he had brokered the first merger of two formerly rival clans into what he hoped would one day become the Guardian caste. She called him Spirit Guide and never wavered in her devotion to him and his requests.

He could never truly remove the Orishan adherence to hierarchy, certainly not with the limited time available to him, but he could shape it. He could bend it into a configuration that didn't lead to constant bloodshed and useless destruction.

He had sent Tik'ik back to them to celebrate and to iron out some of the finer details—how many female fighters to breed with how many Weaver males, how many larvae the new superclan could support and remain healthy. How much territory they could use before infringing on their nearest neighbor. What to do when they inevitably did.

She had been happy to go, though still clearly puzzled at his ultimate goals. He hadn't cured her of prostrating herself before him yet either, but he would eventually. He had been happy to see the back of her if only for a few days so that he could relax and update his star charts and logs.

Then the thought crept in. Just after his evening supper of what the locals called heart beetles, just before he actually dropped off to sleep, he thought—

If, as he had tried to do, Modan had been sent back to the proper era with the necessary tools and information to prevent *Titan*'s coming here, shouldn't the wreckage have vanished? In fact, he himself should not be here, as he would never have had a reason to enter the shuttle.

He'd never enjoyed paradoxes, and this one was no exception. The only way he could resolve it was to assume she had failed and that everything would play out as it had before, despite his effort to save his friends.

The thought depressed him deeply, and for a time, when Tik'ik came to call, he couldn't be bothered to see her except to send her away again. What good was his plan, his sacrifice, if his friends could not be saved?

He took to wandering through the wreckage in the early mornings, the time when the Orishans were mostly sluggish or asleep, identifying bits of the wreckage and remembering moments or people that were somehow linked with them in his mind.

There was the broken and scorched galley table where he and his friends had debated ethics and science and everything that lay between.

There was the charred remains of a computer console from one of the research labs in which he'd spent so many happy hours.

There was a section of the wall of the bridge that had contained the turbolift, still nearly pristine somehow though mostly buried in the dirt. He could see the edge of the dedication plaque.

Suddenly he had to have it. He needed something from his time that wasn't tarnished or burnt or somehow cannibalized to serve his mission.

Unmindful of the potential danger, he began to claw at the earth around the plaque. The soil of Orisha was more coarse than on other worlds, less apt to come apart with only the use of fingers, and this was no exception.

It quickly became clear that if he wanted that plaque, he was going to have to get a tool and dig it out.

His hidden room and the tool kit were on the far side of the crash site, nearly a kilometer away. If he went back now he couldn't return until the following morning for fear that some passing scout would hear or smell him and come to investigate.

He'd had a close call already when he'd set up his lavatory and bathing facility in the remains of one of the large cargo drums. He had spent two hours pressed into the interior of the small bubble at the top of the drum while the intruder wandered around the crash site attempting to isolate the new and unusual scent. He did not want a repeat performance.

He cast around for something with an edge that was sharp enough for digging and yet would not be so jagged that he would slice up his hands using it.

He settled on a nearby bit of plasteel that had once been part of a chair or perhaps a section of cable tubing. He looked it over quickly to ensure it wouldn't splinter and then, literally, dug in.

When he finally pulled it free, he was amazed at what he found inscribed on the plaque. A broad smile spread across his face as he reread it for the fourth time, and presently he began to laugh.

The Prophets had a wonderful sense of humor: it was robust and subtle and full of lessons. Later, when he thought about the other meaning of the words on the plaque and the deaths of the hundreds who had sailed under its banner, he wept as well.

He hung it the next evening, just beside the innermost entrance to his little garret where he would see it every day, coming or going.

He needed to see it, he realized. It gave him strength somehow, even though the authorship of the inscription was unknown to him.

The words were simple and powerful and they gave him hope.

U.S.S. CHARON

LUNA CLASS

STARFLEET REGISTRY NCC-80111

UTOPIA PLANITIA FLEET YARDS, MARS

LAUNCHED STARDATE 56980.2

UNITED FEDERATION OF PLANETS

And then, below the names of the beings behind the creation of the ship, the ship's motto:

ONLY SEEK, AND YOU SHALL FIND.

He would never know for sure how Modan's journey had ended. He would never have proof that she had returned, safe and sound, and used what he'd given her to help save *Titan*. He would never have that confirmation, nor any knowledge whatsoever of the events transpiring in what was now, for him, the distant future.

Maybe Modan would not succeed. He chose to believe she would. Maybe *Titan* had not survived this ordeal as it had its many others. He chose to think it had. Maybe Orisha would finally be consumed by the forces unleashed by the thing they thought was god. He chose to believe they wouldn't.

He chose these things because they were the only choice. The Prophets had guided him this far, and they would guide her and them too, whether or not any of them believed it.

He had no tangible evidence of this, no empirical finding to hold up in front of a peer review, but he didn't need it.

He had faith.

About the Author

Geoffrey Thorne is the prize-winning author of the short story "The Soft Room" in *Star Trek: Strange New Worlds VI* and the equally prize-winning "Concurrence" from *Strange New Worlds 8.* His other *Star Trek* tales, "Chiaroscuro" and "Or the Tiger," appeared in *Star Trek: Deep Space Nine—Prophecy and Change* and *Star Trek: Voyager—Distant Shores,* respectively.

He has contributed installments of *Reality Cops: The Adventures of Vale and Mist,* a web serial from Phobos Entertainment, as well as being the creator and executive producer of the critically acclaimed original web series *The Dark* (thedarklines.blogspot.com), and he's a contributor too.

He still lives, inextricably, in Los Angeles with his lovely and supernaturally patient wife, Susan, and he still very much enjoys *Star Trek.*